# Waxed and Feathered

## A novel by Char Luerlock

Book Cover and POV Dividers by Angel Windowpane.

ISBN: 979-8-9915474-1-3 (paperback)
ISBN: 979-8-9915474-0-6 (e-book)

Published by Syrette Press.
www.charluerlock.net

"There is a time in every man's education when he arrives at the conviction that envy is ignorance; that imitation is suicide; that he must take himself for better, for worse, as his portion; that though the wide universe is full of good, no kernel of nourishing corn can come to him but through his toil bestowed on that plot of ground which is given to him to till.

The power which resides in him is new in nature, and none but he knows what that is which he can do,

nor does he know until he has tried."

*Ralph Waldo Emerson, "Self-Reliance."*

# ACT I

*Lilac* sheets caressed bare skin. Flowering gardens embroidered with golden thread sprang up from silk, a sea of floral rising and falling over naked legs and stomachs. Dim lamp light reflected off the soft material, casting shadows into crevices and illuminating the glossy surface, creating soft purple waves that rippled out over the bodies as they rose and fell with quiet breaths.

Giovanni was currently working over a bright red lollipop, shaped like a heart and semi-transparent, giving the impression of a thin ruby gemstone. He licked at it lazily. Its flavor was of the sweetest, most sugary of candies; syrupy cherry, tangy and tart in its highest notes, very strong and very artificial, stickying his saliva and turning his tongue deep red. It was the sort of obnoxious sweetness that certainly would have caused an aching ring in the roots of his teeth, had he not had them replaced with stronger ones that could better withstand the sugar years prior. He lay flat, staring up at the ceiling, blankly watching the golden patterns swim before his bleary eyes. Each lick brought another burst of sharp sweetness to his taste buds and he was struck with a little spark of elation in the core of his chest, a whimsy and an airiness that spread across his limbs and clouded his thoughts with warmth much more fulfilling than the light silk that covered him.

To Giovanni's left was a girl, asleep, as naked as he and with considerably less of the sheets covering her, only sparsely draped over her legs and sprawling upwards like ivy to her pelvis. She had been attractive enough, he supposed, but he conceded within himself now that he had cared less about her looks and more about her availability. She was a new cook in the house, a younger woman with long yellow hair held in a high ponytail and big, dark brown eyes like his father. She had been excited to work and eager to please, and he had received no complaints at all upon inviting her up to his room, save for the question of if she could lose her job for this. They always asked that. Her nerves had been eased with breathy reassurances between wet kisses, sticky with

Giovanni's lipstick and her own. His was darker and thicker, plum, and quickly overpowered the drab pink gloss she wore, leaving hers forgotten and his smeared across her face, her mouth, her jaw, her neck and shoulders and even lower still.

It felt now a waste of lipstick. In his defense, his nerves had been running high the past week, Giovanni rationalized, as his father's show loomed nearer and nearer. He was desperate for a distraction in any form that he could find, and she had been an easily accessible and very willing distraction.

But with that thought, the awareness of the upcoming television spot, a source of ceaseless anxiety which had plagued the back of his mind since he had first landed the gig, began to weigh on him once more. Giovanni sucked more aggressively at the candy in his mouth, greedily trying to draw out all that was captured within the heart-shaped sugar gem. It was a leftover from the Valentine's Day batch from a few months prior. His father gave him free access to leftovers, the older candies that were not bought in time. The chemicals in them worked as a preservative and kept them safely edible for months after their recommended sell-by date. If he failed to eat the rest from this batch, which, despite his appetite for the candies, was most certainly in the realm of possibility on account of the massive quantity in which they were produced, there was a good chance they would simply be repackaged to be sold the following year.

Giovanni attempted to focus on the candy, allowing himself to feel its effects seep through his veins and muscles and slow every organ from his lungs to his brain. His head turned drowsily to the bedside table beside him. Discarded candy wrappers and lollipops that had been sucked down to the stick lay scattered. There was nothing consumable left, which meant that once the one he was working over was finished he would have to either get up and fetch more or else face sobriety, and neither option sounded appealing with this woman still in the room with him, curled up and asleep, in his lipstick, in his bed.

He sat up a little, causing the blanket to fall to his lap. Quickly, he pulled the rest of the sheets off of the girl, leaving her naked body fully exposed, and drew it up to his neck to cover himself. He looked across the room, to the restroom with the big mirror and the cabinets of countless cosmetics. His makeup felt smeared and sticky on his face and he itched to fix it, to properly make himself up again, especially before the girl woke up. The memory of the sensation of her fingertips against his face, the knowledge that his foundation had been rubbing off on her clingy hands, made him shiver.

With a little huff he stood up, lollipop clenched tightly between porcelain teeth, still holding the silk blanket so as to protectively drape it over his body. Then, only very briefly, he glanced once more at the girl as she slept peacefully, eyeing her, her hair sprawled about her and her eyelashes shut against her lipstick-stained cheek, and Giovanni thought, *You're not that pretty.*

It was early in the afternoon, when the heat was at its most intense and the sun at its brightest, but no light could creep through the black curtains that draped Vittoria's bedroom windows. That had been a very specific interior design request: The ability to create the illusion of night, to suggest that one could have total control over the sun itself, had been crucial to her. Dark walls, dark furniture, dark velvet sheets that covered her bed and herself, currently bundled within, with her dark hair and her dark pajamas. The room was one of shadows and midnight, where the rays of the late morning sun could not reach no matter how hard they tried.

Although the first half of the day was already complete and the hours had trudged steadily onward without cease, Vittoria's day had only just begun. Hiding away within her fortress of shadow she lay, having awoken only a short while before. Just as the black of her room drowned out daylight, from the record player on her bedside table echoed the loudest of music, drowning out all sound and any suggestion of life beyond the bedroom walls. Echoing from her bedroom was a cacophony of the most abrasive music she could get her hands on, shrieks of agony and the crashing of drums and otherworldly noises that most certainly had been sampled from the deepest pits of Hell. Vittoria allowed herself to drown in it, eyes shut, a meditation on the layers of sound presented to her, the harsh thrashing and guttural cries and the electric punch of noise. Nowadays, it was as much for research as it was enjoyment. She was working, really.

So loud was the music and so entranced by it she was that Vittoria did not hear the first knock at her bedroom door. Or the second, or the third. It was only when a meek voice cried out her name that she became aware of the fact that a new sound was attempting to penetrate her dark fortress. She sat up with an irritated grunt, a mess of raven hair emerging from raven blankets. She brushed some to the side, out of her eyes, to turn to the door and glare at the thing that had dared disrupt her ever-so-laborious affairs.

"What is it?" she asked, audibly irritated, and in the hazy, barely awake stupor that she was in, the words came out with the barest hint of an Italian accent, which she heard and she hated. She cleared her throat, and when she spoke again her accent was strictly new age American. "What is it?"

"Mistress Marcello?" the timid voice on the other side of the door called out, just barely audible over the music. "Your- Your mail."

With a groan Vittoria reached, slowly, to the record player and turned the music down, so that only a dull throb of noise could still be heard, permeating through the room like burning incense. She reluctantly stood up and stretched, taking her sweet time as she forced her body to life, joint by joint, and then slowly walked to the door to open it. A young servant girl stood on the other side, clutching a single envelope. Vittoria grabbed it, tugging the letter free of the girl's hands, a task made easier by the girl immediately jumping back and letting go of it. Dumbfounded, the servant girl stood there with her hands still raised as they had been when holding the envelope, as if too nervous to remember how to move. Vittoria wrinkled her nose at that. "Are you afraid of me?" she chastised. The girl opened her mouth as if to stammer out a response, but Vittoria cut her off before she had to hear more of her feeble chattering. "Fuck off and grow up." With that, she shut the door.

With that Vittoria walked back to her record player and turned the noise back up, once more transforming her room into a cave of horrors as the distorted, electronic wails echoed around her. She walked back to her bed, sat down cross legged, and skimmed over the return address printed on the envelope. "Embalmed Records" was scrawled in the corner in red ink, the penmanship a very careful display of tall, ornate cursive. A flicker of intrigue passed Vittoria's face and she ripped the envelope open unceremoniously, barely avoiding a papercut or damaging the letter within. At the top of the letter was yesterday's date: June 11, 2089.

*Dearest Vittoria*, the message started, and Vittoria's brow furrowed a little, her interest piqued further by the brazen display of intimacy—Who could possibly consider themselves to be on a first name basis with her was beyond her. The letter, she noted, was written in the same careful, calligraphic cursive.

*It is my understanding that you have recently delved into the Underworld we here like to refer to as the music industry. Wait, did I mix that up? Hahaha! Anyways, I send you my sincerest best wishes; it is a big world out there for a little pup, and I understand that finding your footing when everything is so foreign can be quite the struggle. I first immigrated to this country with a dream of music and art and a heart full of inspiration and passion for creation. I empathize deeply with you from one artist to another, and I have an offer to make. But first, I should formally introduce myself. I am Anubis.*

Vittoria stopped reading and tensed, eyes locked on the name. Of course she knew Anubis. Everyone did. Being in the front row of an Anubis concert would make one the center of attention in milieus of all sorts, as artists across an unfathomably wide spectrum of genre, medium, and subculture waited with bated breath to hear the first-person account, to inquire eagerly upon if the view gave any insider information into the many tricks he had up his sleeve, what was illusion, what was flesh and blood. She recollected vivid memory of the red chaos that splattered the stage as ears were pounded with screams and all senses were blasted tirelessly, assaulted and tortured to the brink of exhaustion with heavy guitar and bass and drums and noise, noise, noise. There was something entrancing and fascinating and so very alluring about it all, the aggressive power of his performances, the unhindered and untamed ferociousness of it, not to mention the stunts that he was famous for pulling on stage... Her heart quivered and her mind raced, thrilled by the thought of Anubis and all he was, hardly able to believe that it was truly he who had written to her.

The letter went on to extend an invitation to Anubis' upcoming concert, an event only a few days away. Of course, Vittoria already had tickets. She had made sure to get them the moment they had gone on sale, with the help of her father's servants, making them wait in the early hours of the morning at the Pharaoh's Tomb concert hall so that they could be the first in the long, winding lines to acquire them. But he promised her something even better: An assurance that she would be on the guest list, as he desired an in-person meeting with her, promising that the plans he had in store for her were much, much larger than what could be captured within the confines of the written word. Vittoria felt her heart flutter in her chest, sending reverberations downwards and making her feel vaguely sick to her stomach. She had been holding onto the show as a symbol for her to get through the arduous week ahead of her, and now her anticipation was only heightened.

Still, there was a thought that nagged at the back of her mind, stabbing through her fantasies not unlike the knives Anubis was so keen on using in his stage shows. She bit her lip and set the letter down, staring instead at the wall ahead of her as she tried to think. Tomorrow she had the live interview that her father had set up for her, where she would be announcing her newest project formally to the public. She was not quite over the bee-sting sensation that seemed to jab at her when she remembered that it was through her father only that she had been able to land the television spot to begin with. Her hand had already been held much too tight throughout the thick of her plans thus far, and she found herself between the thrill of the letter in her lap and the awareness that she did not want to jump so immediately at the first offer handed to her, as tantalizing of a golden platter that it was. She should, she told herself as she drew in a breath and tried to summon a sense of professionalism, at least wait until after the interview to make any brash decisions.

Vittoria let her eyes travel over the dark walls of her room as her mind jumped from conflicting thought to conflicting thought, burying concerns as quickly as new ones sprouted up. Dozens of paintings adorned the wall—little dazzling jewels of color amongst her otherwise black world. Each one was a portrait of her, all from different artists, painted in their own unique, individual style, and with the same muse in each—herself—it only further highlighted the striking differences of each distinct vision. Each a unique interpretation of her, of who she was, what she embodied in the eyes of each artist. Her eyes lingered admiringly from one to the next, traveling slowly and taking each one in with acute intentionality. Dozens of silver eyes, one almost always hidden behind her jet-black hair, stared back at her.

Vittoria picked up Anubis' letter and looked at it again. She had not contacted him; how he knew of her endeavors was beyond her, but it did not surprise her that he would have endless and immediate knowledge of what went on in the music world. He was otherworldly like that, all-powerful and all-seeing, she was certain of it. She skimmed the rest of the letter, forcing herself to ignore the disappointment bubbling at the edges of her decision to refrain from thinking too much about Anubis' offer quite yet, not allowing herself to give into the fantasy of whatever it was he was offering (allegedly, it was some sort of project that would, in his own words, *most certainly propel you to an unfathomable and unparalleled level of fame*) before she had even managed to prove herself worthy of the funds her father had put into the primetime television spot he had landed her.

As Vittoria reached the end of the letter, she noticed that at the very bottom, attached to the back, was a sleek, black card with golden lettering, simple but elegant. On it was printed only the word *ANUBIS*, beneath that a line of hieroglyphic symbols that she could not make sense of, and beneath that a phone number and a small portrait of an ankh with an eye in the center, all in the same shimmering gold.

*You have been in the public eye for quite some time; I have watched your interviews and advertisements, kept up on the various projects you have headed, and I will humbly admit I have indeed perused the tabloids as well. You are interested in music, but I believe that with my decade-spanning career as a performance artist, I can make you much more than a musician. You are a canvas, Vittoria Marcello, and I am eager and hopeful to have the opportunity to make you my art.*

*Attached is my business card. Do call if you have any questions at all. And trust thyself: every heart vibrates to that iron string.*

*Warm thoughts to You and the entire Marcello Family.*
*Signed,*
*Anubis, the Rock God of Death.*

In the mornings, Giovanni made sure that his makeup was done up before he dared step foot outside his bedroom door. To sleep in it was much too uncomfortable, devastated his skin, and would ruin his fine silk pillows, which meant that he reluctantly had to remove it at night, but the moment he was up (which was often quite early) he was willing to spend as long as needed to rectify this tragedy.

And it was not on an empty stomach, of course; he kept plenty of candies in his room. Although in his daily life he often preferred chocolate, it risked melting off on his fingers or sticking under his long acrylic nails during this delicate application, which could stain and smudge and ruin everything. Instead, while applying makeup he preferred small, hard candies that he could tuck under his tongue when he had to concentrate.

Giovanni had learned from experience to always have a candy in his mouth before facing the mirror, so that he had something with which to distract himself when forcing himself through the hardest part of the morning routine. Still, each morning he could not help but wince at the sight of it: Wrinkles cracked his flesh, more and more each year, his nose stood out too large, his cheeks too round. Echoes of old scars sliced through baby fat that should have dissipated long ago but had continued to cling to him like a needy child, his brow plucked ever since it had begun to turn gray, his lips cracked and dry. The shadow of stubble that made his skin too rough, the faint off-color of a mark or blemish. Every detail, for a moment, sent a surge of dread through him that could only be partially stifled by the saccharine sweet distraction.

And then, after taking a moment to process the horrors before him, he got to work. For Giovanni, aided by the stickiness of sweet candy in his mouth and years of practice, could fix these horrible flaws of genetics and age. It took only that moment, that acceptance, that swallowing of sugary saliva, to distance himself from the face he had seen and instead view it as a bare and ready canvas, his tools moisturizers and creams, brushes, razors, his little pink sponge that helped even and spread the layers he applied, and, most crucial of all, his makeup. Pale foundation replaced skin and any possible imperfection. Shadows were created where there were none, eyebrows and cheekbones delicately painted on. He reshaped the horrid features like magic springing from his fingertips, turning his canvas into the most beautiful of artistic masterpieces with careful, delicate work around his eyes, colorful dust sprinkled beneath lovingly. Every color imaginable was available at the tip of his brush; sparkles and glitter and ashy black and pastel skies of any time of day; sunrises and sunsets and dusks and dawns and overcast noons and vibrant middays, all at his disposal; thick lipstick that made his lips feel sticky and moist, deep red and plum purples, blended into new, exciting color combinations, an entire prismatic gradient accentuating his candy-coated tongue and his perfect teeth. A final brush of highlighter and powder and the jolting cold of setting spray signified the end of a long process, and then, finally, Giovanni could step back and admire his work.

What stood before him now was art, a daily magnum opus. Although Giovanni could not love his face bare, he had learned through passion and skill to love it as a vehicle for something so much greater, a tool for his creation. He gazed upon himself, upon the makeup that blanketed him, for a bit longer, and then, sighing with a sort of smitten pride, he went about the rest of his morning routine. He slicked back his hair, tying it into a loose ponytail and checking for any visible silver that may need to be dyed over. Years of experience made this procedure a breeze.

There was still much to be done before he would be ready for what the day had in store for him, such as finding proper cologne to match the mood of the day and picking out a suit and accessories that would adequately accentuate this morning's cosmetic masterpiece, but this was all less of a concern than his face, and he did not want to keep his father waiting for too long. By now he most certainly was up and about, and Giovanni liked having the chance to see him off before he left for work.

Especially on a day as important as this.

Giovanni, face fully done up but otherwise still in his nightwear, made his way to the home kitchen, a bright and cheery room with yellow walls, creamy floor tiles, and beige cabinets. It was small and quaint for a family as rich as the Marcellos. There was another kitchen in the house, one that could easily rival a five-star restaurant in terms of size, equipment, and staff, where cooks were paid to prepare great meals for events, but the home kitchen served the secondary purpose of personal meals for individuals of the household and snacks. It contained only the necessities of a cooking space, and a little table with a foxglove bouquet in the center. Sitting at the table was Vittorio Marcello. Tall and robust, face cracked with age, Vittorio had always had a great air of power to him, and Giovanni was humbled by the appearance of his father, as even now, sitting at the kitchen table with a newspaper in his hand, existing as anyone else would in the early hours of a workday, he was imposing, a figure of regality and authority. His hair was slicked back, the same as Giovanni's, although his was a shining silver rather than Giovanni's meticulously dyed black, and it was shorter than the shoulder-length ponytail Giovanni kept his in, a more modest, tight cut.

On the front cover of the morning's paper was an article titled *TRUST HIM, HE'S A DOCTOR!*, with the subheading: *Dr. Marcello to be promoted to chairman of Himmel's new 'Experimental Cosmetics' sector.*

"Papa!" Giovanni called, hearing his voice waiver as he entered the room. He cleared his throat and a smile lit up his plum lips. His tongue instinctively twitched in search of candy that was not there. "*Buongiorno!*"

Vittorio looked up, slowly, from his paper. His eyes were dark, a striking contrast to Giovanni's pale blue, and he looked at Giovanni in silence before speaking. "Giovanni," he began, voice soft, "You're late; the tea in the kettle has turned cold. Where have you been?" His voice was deeper than his son's, slower, each word spoken with pride and intention, his Italian accent thicker on his tongue than Giovanni's, who had grown up speaking a blend of English and Italian and was much more fluent in the former.

Vittorio set his paper down, and Giovanni's eyes followed his hands, as he was growing nervous staring at his father's face. There was always too much to try to understand in his visage. The expressions, the slightest twitch of his lips or raise of his eyebrows, every crease and crack that formed and shifted with each subtle new change in emotion—Giovanni felt he could too easily suffocate beneath it all. Still, he willed a smile to remain firmly on his lips. "A- Ah, I was just getting ready for the day, Papa. I can make my own tea!" He walked to the cabinet where the cups and glasses were kept and rummaged carefully until he found his favorite, a pastel purple mug with little sparkles embedded within the ceramic that made it glitter in the sunlight. He stared at it as he added, "I know how important today is to you. I wanted to look my best."

"Can I trust you using the stove on your own?"

The question, the tone, was sharp but slow; a father talking to an audacious child. Giovanni paused, back turned to Vittorio, holding the handle of his mug in one hand as the fingers of the other hand rubbed against the side of it, feeling the smooth, cool pottery against his fingers. "*Sì, sì,*" he reassured, giving a nod that Vittorio would not be able to see, willing the sides of his painted lips to remain turned up in a smile visible to nothing but the wall. "I have done it before. Remember?"

"Very well," Vittorio said. Giovanni hoped it was all he had to say on the matter, but with an instinctive knowledge of his father's speaking habits he waited still before making another move, and sure enough, Vittorio added then, "Do not light anything on fire, Giovanni."

"I will not, Papa." Giovani promised. He set his mug on the counter and reached for the tea kettle, which still sat on the stove. It was a pristine white with golden poppies painted along it, and he picked it up from the base rather than the handle, feeling it slosh with the dregs of room temperature water. As he went about adding more water to the kettle and setting it to boil, he heard the crinkling of newspaper behind him and knew that his father had returned to his paper. There was silence between them now. Giovanni said nothing, focusing on preparing the tea, and focusing even more on making sure that he followed every step as carefully as possible so as not to disappoint his father. Vittorio remained silent as well, seemingly fully absorbed in the paper.

Giovanni set the kettle back down to boil on the stovetop, his eyes transfixed on the flicker of blue flame that engulfed the bottom of it. He was very aware of his own heartbeat, aware of the way that his fingers had trembled slightly as he turned the flame on, aware of the sweat trapped beneath his foundation, the exposed, empty holes in his ears where jewelry should have been, his lack of cologne, and he swallowed and said suddenly, "I have been preparing all week for the show today, Papa. I know exactly what to say, what to wear. I will be fantastic. The people will just love me." *You will love me.* "I promise it will please you, Papa."

"I expect nothing less," Vittorio said, tone unchanging, distracted and hollow. Giovanni heard him slowly flip the newspaper to another page. "You understand the importance of his interview, yes?"

Giovanni turned around to face his father finally, staring at him with wide, earnest eyes, nodding eagerly. "Yes, yes, of course I do! The public needs to know who I am!"

"Your brother's reputation is tied to this family. That means that we are all responsible for making sure that he can succeed in the public sphere as he furthers his career by upholding our good name. You must help him to help our entire family and everything that we have worked for."

Giovanni nodded vigorously again. "Of course, Papa, of course!" he chirped, bouncing on his heels. "You know how happy I am for Giorgio." He twitched in surprise as the kettle began to whistle, but he did not turn around, instead keeping his eyes fixated on his father, who had not so much as looked up at Giovanni, still flipping through the paper idly. "I am loyal first and foremost and always to my family."

Vittorio still did not look up, but he gave a small nod. "The world is cruel even to those of us who have striven our entire lives for perfection. And it is especially unforgiving to those who are imperfect."

"I will be perfect, Papa." Giovanni promised.

Vittorio's dark eyes scanned with furrowed brow down the newspaper page. Giovanni was still bouncing. He wished he had brought something sweet to suck on. The tea kettle was still whistling, although by now the initial piercing shriek had subsided into a weak whine that sounded something like a dying animal.

"I will be heading off to work soon. A limousine will be here to pick you up in just a bit. Be ready and waiting out front within the hour. And shut up that damn stove."

"I will, Papa!" Giovanni promised. He turned back around to face the kettle. Mind racing and heart pounding, the impending interview fresh on his mind and blanketing over all other thoughts including the most basic rationale, he reached to grab the boiling kettle as he had before. With a sharp, pained gasp he withdrew, jumping back and looking down instantly at his fingertips to find them red and burning. He glanced to his father, eyes wide and fingers throbbing, but found as he blinked away the tears threatening to form in the corner of his eyes and ruin the eyeliner that he had so delicately applied that Vittorio had gone once more to listlessly reading the paper, paying no mind to what Giovanni was doing now. Giovanni walked quickly and quietly to the sink to run his fingers beneath cool water.

Vittoria was awoken by a knocking from outside her bedroom door. In an instant she was up, running fingers through long, unkempt hair in a hurried attempt to make herself look more awake. She knew what day it was and did not want to appear as if she had been sleeping so late into the morning, even if that was exactly what she had been doing. She blinked back sleep and fought back a yawn as she called out, "What the fuck is it?"

"Manners, Vittoria," Her father's voice came loud yet reserved from the other side of the door, and Vittoria froze, heart clenching in her chest. "Come to the door, please. I must speak with you before I go."

Vittoria stood and hurried quick to the door. She blinked furiously a few more times, rubbed her eyes, rolled her shoulders in a circular motion to rid them of the tenseness of sleep, doing her best to force herself into full alertness. Then she opened the door, wincing as the bright light from the hallway poured into her shadowy chamber of a bedroom. "Sorry, Dad, I was just... getting ready." Her American accent was exaggeratedly harsh, it stood out in her words as she forced the sounds to conform away from what she had grown up with. And yet, in contrast, as Vittorio looked down at her she shrunk back again, meeker than her voice and her dark hair let on, submerging herself into the shadows of her room. "Wh- What's up, Dad?"

Unlike her, in her silky black nightgown, Vittorio was already dressed for the day, wearing one of his expensive suits, and he watched her with a hint of judgment in his dark eyes that made her conscience shatter into shards of icy glass in her stomach. "Vittoria," he said her name again, tone restrained but still harboring a frustration that her keen ears picked up on in an instant, "How do you expect to ever leave this house when you sleep in late on the most crucial of days? Does nothing matter to you?"

Any attempt at a defense was caught and trapped in Vittoria's throat. She hesitated as she held the door open, unsure of if she should open it fully to confront her father more face-on or if she should close it entirely right then and there, shutting him out. She knew she would not be able to bring herself to do the latter. "I- I know, Dad. I know. I'm excited about the interview." Her tone betrayed her words, coming out quiet and devoid of any earnest emotion but discomfort.

"Then you must hurry, Vittoria, you do not have much time. A limousine will be here to pick you up within the hour. I recommend waiting outside as soon as you are ready." Vittorio turned away from Vittoria and was silent, appearing almost as if he was going to walk away, but Vittoria watched, knowing that his refusal to move yet from the spot he occupied before her meant that there was something else, something he was turning over in his mind, deliberating how best to express it. Something was not right. There was something that he was not saying, and she certainly could not find words within herself to bring him out of his silence. Her palm was moistened with sweat as she gripped the doorknob tight.

Finally, Vittorio spoke again. "Make sure that you do not leave without your brother. I fear that he may take too long getting ready and will be at risk of missing your ride."

Every muscle in Vittoria's body, heart included, came to an immediate halt.

She froze, staring at her father with wide eyes, jaw agape and fingers going slack against the doorknob. Her tongue felt heavy as she tried to move it. "Giovanni? Giovanni isn't coming-"

"Giovanni will be attending the interview with you, yes." Vittorio said plainly, not so much as turning to look at Vittoria as he spoke.

"He can't!" Vittoria shoved the door open, taking a step out into the hallway, to her father, her voice a desperate plea as she added, "You can't- I've been preparing for weeks, I- I need this interview." So much hinged on it.

"So does Giovanni." Vittorio said. He turned to face Vittoria, and his expression, the obvious anger in his eyes, made her wince and back down. But then, the coldness dissipated from him, and a glimpse of something else entered his disposition, the wrinkles of his eyes and lips, the tenseness of his brows, softening. "But you can help him to help yourself, daughter. There have been whispers about Giovanni. The public does not know him and they would like to. I cannot keep one of my sons hidden from the world. People talk, they ask questions, and

Giovanni making himself known is crucial not just to him but to our whole family. Our whole *business*."

Vittoria watched her father, silent. Protests whirled around in her brain like a storm but she kept them down.

Vittorio reached out to place a hand on her chin. His fingertips brushed her neck and Vittoria sucked in a breath to stifle a shiver as he lifted her head up, forcing her pale eyes to meet his dark ones. When he spoke, his voice was softer than ever, a whisper, or perhaps a hiss, under his breath. Urgent, direct, and piercing deep into Vittoria's cold heart. "You want out of here, do you not, Vittoria? This is how you prove yourself. You know as well as I do that Giovanni is not capable of this on his own. You have been given the opportunity to prove yourself as the woman you want to be. Do not disappoint me."

Vittorio let go of Vittoria and stepped back, watching and waiting for her to respond. She stared, her head still tilted up at him as he had left her, and she took a moment to snap from the trance she had fallen into and regain her composure. She blinked a few more times before she finally responded, a vague quiver in her voice: "I understand, Dad."

"Good," Vittorio's tone had returned to its usual regal, commandeering demeanor. "As I said, a limousine will arrive within the hour." He turned away once again, and Vittoria watched as he walked down the hall and left her, alone, standing out in the hallway with her heart pounding. Even after he was gone she remained frozen, her eyes stuck on the spot where he had stood, goosebumps still springing from where his hand had rested on her chin. She reached to touch the spot gingerly, as if she had just been burned.

Then she sighed, straightened herself up, and willed the discomfort away. She had to get ready.

Typically, Vittoria avoided the family kitchen, because it was just too easy to run into her brother or father or, God forbid, other siblings when they visited. She did not care for breakfast, or food at all, really, but she still knew well enough that she needed some source of energy to be able to function through the morning, so as she headed back into her room she picked up her house phone. The house phone ran on a line unique to the mansion and could contact any other room in the house with just the touch of a few buttons. With practiced ease she tapped the numbers that corresponded to the grand kitchen, fully staffed with professionals who were paid to cook elaborate, gourmet meals. Within seconds the voice of an American man on the other end greeted, "You've reached the Marcello Kitchen. What can I do for you?"

"This is Mistress Marcello," Vittoria said, her eyes running over the various portraits of herself as she spoke, landing on the bright blue eyes of one of the paintings. "I'll be down in twenty to grab some coffee. You know how I like it."

She hung up then and tore her eyes away from her paintings to walk to the bookshelf in the corner. Instead of books adorning the shelves, there were stacks of vinyl records, all part of her private collection. Lazily half-alphabetized, Vittoria skimmed through the *A* section until she found one labeled *ANUBIS.* His most recent album, "Surface and Dream." She may have had her father pull a few strings to make sure that she had a copy of the record the very same day it was released, without having to worry about waiting in line at a record shop. The album cover was adorned with a striking, grotesque painting of a very fleshy tree, with branches that curled like fingers, a base that was soft and pink and squishy, veins running up where bark should have been, leaves protruding like pimples. A knife was stuck in its side and blood trickled down to the sickly yellow chaparral of the local wilderness. It was a striking image, something that she remembered spending a great deal of time staring at with fascination and pride the day she had first gotten her hands on it, and she felt that she related to it in a way, although she had never thought to explain the connection in words.

Vittoria wondered what Anubis looked like—What he *really* looked like, beneath the jackal head he wore on the stage, away from the lights and the blood and the theatrics. He did not make public appearances, or any appearances at all, without a mask, his iconic Anubis mask, and even appearances off of the stage *with* the mask were far and few between. A rare interview here and there, an occasional photo shoot for a magazine, an elusive appearance in a documentary on the modern resurgence of industrial rock, all with his face hidden beneath the gold and obsidian canine—modeled after his namesake, no doubt. She glanced up from the album art she clutched tight to the portraits on the walls all around her.

At least she had the concert to look forward to after all of this was over, Vittoria thought to herself, thoughts tugged back to her present reality and the dread latched to it. She walked to the record player on her bedside table and put the record on, turning it up loud enough that she could hear it clearly through every inch of her room. As the album opened with the sound of shuttering, coarse breathing and frantic percussion of increasing volume, she stepped to her closet to begin getting ready.

Vittoria's wardrobe, like her room, consisted primarily of blacks; Vittoria liked leather and lace and occasionally velvet, stockings and collars and clothing that looked torn and faded before it was even out of the packaging. There was a pang of guilty awareness that her clothes betrayed the DIY look that they embodied with the price that she had paid for them—These were designer pieces, items that had been crafted to fit her like a glove, to accentuate her and give the impression of an aesthetic that she was well aware she had little claim to. Sometimes she dreamt of finding the time and energy to put the effort into actually crafting a wardrobe from the depths of old thrift stores and garbage bins, like a real and true good-for-nothing punk with no fear of making a "statement," but whenever such fanciful ideas crossed her mind she was quickly and vividly reminded of the expectations she had to live up to, and, perhaps more importantly, how very, very busy she always was with much more pressing matters.

In her private bathroom (the music loud enough that even there she could hear the guttural, machinal shrieks of Anubis' vocoder and the throbbing, reverberating bass that backed it, only the angry guitar and organ synth muffled by the walls between her and her beloved record player) she set to work on her daily above-the-shoulders routine, which for a voyeur would seemingly depict a stunning inner battle between laziness, desire for aesthetic, and crippling fear of failure. She would draw dark black rings around her eyes, sloppily at first, before steadying her hand to go around a second time, and after a moment of hesitation she would add a careful wing that momentarily revealed genuine artistic prowess which she would then awkwardly scribble over, thickening it and once again making her whole face look like an amateur's first attempt at makeup. She was certainly capable with makeup and had been applying it for nearly all of her life, but she still was unsure of what direction she wanted to go with it all, how she really felt about what each little change connotated when viewed by another. Although she had a mirror in her bathroom, when doing her makeup she spent at least half the time glancing back out to the bedroom walls, to the paintings of herself, trying to gauge how exactly she was viewed from the outside, what the makeup would do to change that. There was something nerve wracking in the control she had, she thought as she painted her pale pink lips a deep, dark red. Pale foundation and a dab of white powder over skin that was already pale due to an astounding lack of Vitamin D turned her into a porcelain doll, or perhaps a corpse.

With her makeup and clothing finished and not much else left to do (her hair, for example, would need to be combed through, but she could do that quickly in a little bit, and she was currently barefoot save for stockings encasing her feet and legs, as she had chosen a pair of heavy boots to wear today, which she thought looked fantastic but would most certainly be a pain to lace up and gave her a foot ache to wear, something she would save for when she was actually leaving the house), she turned now to leave the bathroom and reentered her bedroom proper. She found her eyes running over her portraits yet again, looking at each one, one by one, until she stopped at the large painting that hung over her bed, making it impossible to see during the many hours she spent laying beneath it, but the doorway to the bathroom made a perfect line from her vision to the piercing silver eyes. It stood out against the black of her walls, stark as a Caravaggio painting, and she paused to admire it. Or, really, study it. She tried to mentally put herself in the position of the many painters who had sat and depicted her likeness, knowing fully that depicting Vittorio's daughter accurately was a high stakes commission indeed. How did the many painters who had used her as their muse interpret her? Dark lips protruding from pale skin, dark eyeliner from pale eyes. She hoped it was striking. Mature, strong enough to handle herself and the world around her.

She evened out her short leather skirt, clenched her hands into fists at her side, and nodded to herself. Giovanni would not ruin things today. If anything, Giovanni's presence could help her, she reasoned. Giovanni would make a fool of himself and leave her as the one in control. She would be the level-headed one, wise beyond her years and more mature than her elder brother. Giovanni was a fool, while she, on the other hand, was capable of taking care of herself. That was what mattered.

Vittoria, resigned to her fate, turned off her music and exited her bedroom. She walked down the hallway, down a long flight of stairs, to the grand banquet hall, which was on the bottom floor of the house so that guests did not have to travel too far through winding hallways and staircases to find the main event. The hall was currently empty, though even as it sat unused it was grand and inviting, done up in warm colors, wooden surfaces, and gold trim that decorated the chairs and tablecloth, the bright-colored posters on the wall that depicted vintage advertisements from the Marcello Candy Company when it was still new as well as newspaper and magazine cutouts, headlines and cover pages that showed the company's rise to fame and fortune.

Through the banquet hall she walked until she reached the back doors that led to the kitchen. It was rather empty at the moment, as there were no major events planned tonight, but a skeleton crew of staff still remained, performing only the duties that needed to be done each day to keep the place in top condition, as well as putting together dinner for the family tonight.

The kitchen was sleek, stocked with the best equipment that money could buy, white and shiny like an operating room. Vittoria walked through it, ignoring the cooks and staff who greeted her with pleasant calls of "Morning, Mistress Marcello!" Her step had something of a stomp to it as she attempted to remain firmly on the ground even as her feet, bare save for her stockings, slipped against the smooth, white tile floor. In the back of the kitchen she reached the head chef, a taller, broad-shouldered man, Italian just like her own family as per her father's request—A full-time employee who probably knew her father better than her.

"Mistress Marcello! *Buongiorno!*" He greeted, his own accent very thick. "Is there anything that I can do for you?"

Vittoria looked around, not saying a word for a moment, eyes scanning over the kitchen, the other cooks scattered about like ants that had been separated from their trail. After a moment, she said, "I called down and ordered coffee a little while ago."

"Ah... What?" asked the chef.

Vittoria turned to stare at him, brow furrowed. "Just, like, ten, twenty minutes ago. I ordered coffee over the phone. Is there some kind of problem?"

The chef shook his head furiously at that. "No! No, no, just, ah... I was not informed of your order. I assume another one of the cooks must have taken it-" He turned now to the kitchen and the many chefs working within it, and clapped loudly once, twice, three times, before shouting out, "Alright! Alright! Who here took Mistress Marcello's order over the phone earlier, eh?"

There was silence for a moment, in which Vittoria watched, expressionless save for a slight, irritated purse to her lips and crease in her brow, as the cooks paused their own work to listen in on the head chef's request. Then, a younger cook, who Vittoria knew in an instant was newer for she did not recognize him at all, stepped forward. He was a handsome man, with tousled blonde hair and bright eyes. She eyed him up and down and he gave a strange, awkward wave to her, which she did not return, and spoke out in an incriminatingly American accent: "That was me over the phone, Mistress Marcello. Sorry, it's right over here." He sounded good-natured, a tone of voice that strove to make peace. He beckoned to her and she followed him, and they walked to a small counter where, as promised, her cup sat, still hot enough that steam rose and swirled like misty tendrils over it. Vittoria accepted the mug and the man raised a hand. "Careful, Mistress. It's still hot."

Vittoria nodded and took a cautious sip. But the expected bitterness of black coffee did not come. Instead, her senses were bombarded immediately with a tangy sweetness, and without hesitation she immediately spat the drink out.

"I warned you it was hot," the cook said, tone pleasant as ever. Vittoria looked at him, eyes wide, aghast. The man had the indecency to flash a cocky little smile, as if bemused by the situation.

"It's not that it's *hot*, retard." She spat the words out with the same violent distaste as she had the coffee. "You added *sugar*. You fucking sweetened the fucking thing."

The man's expression changed in an instant. "I just- I thought-"

The head chef came running over, having heard Vittoria's voice begin to rise. "You added sugar to the Mistress' coffee?" he cried. "Fool! Mistress Vittoria never sweetens her coffee!"

"She's a Marcello!" the cook argued, voice wavering. "I just thought- I thought-"

"-That I'm a drugged-out junkie addicted to granulated poison like the rest of my fucking family?" Vittoria interrupted. Her hands had curled into fists at her sides. She knew in her heart that it was only placebo, that she had not had even a fraction of enough of her father's sugar for it to have any adverse effect, but she could not shake the sense of disorientation that had begun to seep through her sugar-stained mouth and upwards into her brain. She breathed a ragged sigh. "I'll see to it that you are not invited to continue working in my father's home any longer."

The cook did not speak. His mouth was agape and he looked at her as if he was certain that she must be joking, or he must be dreaming, that if he just waited this one out a perfectly reasonable explanation would be presented to him that would undo the wrongs he had just committed against Vittorio Marcello's youngest daughter. He was taller than she was, physically stronger, as she was of average height herself and her body lean and lithe, but still, in this moment, both of them knew that she held absolute power over him.

Vittoria knew this and she reveled in it as her anger made the blood in her veins pump red-hot, the thrill of the dominance she imbued only driving her further. The adrenaline of the power high satisfied the anger, gave it a space to thrive, as she watched every mannerism on his face—the hesitance of each blink as he clearly feared their eye contact breaking for even a second, the way his tongue trembled visibly behind his teeth as it sought for words it could not find.

"Coffee, Mistress," A voice punctured the tenseness of the air and Vittoria turned to find the head chef offering her a freshly brewed mug. She unclenched her hands, not realizing until she had freed her nails from the flesh of her palm how very tight her fists had been. She grabbed the mug, ripping it from his hands, and then turned back to snarl at the young cook once more:

"I suggest you grow the fuck up before you apply for your next job."

Vittoria turned back towards the entrance of the kitchen, and the head chef called out, "Oh, Mistress Vittoria, do be careful, the coffee is very hot!"

Vittoria huffed, shaking her head a bit to clear her vision of the hair she had styled over her eye as she made her way to the exit, heart beating rapidly with the fury that the exchange with the young cook and the complete display of disrespect shown to her had incited, not to mention at the thought that he had been able to present himself up until now as responsible enough, somehow, to work in a place as upscale and significant as her father's grand kitchen in the first place. Her breathing heavier and her vision red from the pure incredulity and disdain at the thought of her authority, her autonomy, being disregarded, her mind wandered quickly from the painstaking task of walking carefully in tights on the smooth, hard floor, and as she stomped angrily towards the door her foot slid out from under her, causing her to lose her balance and fall hard to the ground, where she landed with an uncomfortable grunt that quickly rose in pitch and volume to a cry of pain as the coffee she had been clutching spilled over her, scalding hot liquid splashing her bare arms.

"Mistress!" a voice, multiple voices, called at once, and Vittoria, dazed by the fall and trying to recollect herself, was aware of the sound of commotion and footsteps and many words being said at once as multiple cooks scrambled to her before she even looked up to see them. Her face was red beneath the pale foundation and she hurriedly stood, ignoring the men that surrounded her with wide eyes and punctured her with endless questions about her physical state, if she was alright, if she needed anything. Her shirt, soaked and heavy with hot coffee, clung to her body. Fragments of the shattered mug surrounded her and a few shards fell from her clothing to the ground as she stood; she had not even noticed it crashing, as the pain of the fall and the burning coffee had distracted her.

"Get away!" Vittoria snapped as one of the cooks reached to try to help her. She threw a hand out threateningly, but no one was in reach to strike. "Get away from me!" she snapped again. "Anyone who speaks a word of this will be fired, do you understand? Fuck you." Face still burning with embarrassment long after the burning of the coffee had subsided on her arms, she turned and walked quickly out of the kitchen, sans coffee, and back towards her room to change.

With his father off to work, Giovanni's breakfast consisted of a Danish pastry, a Marcello partnership with a local bakery, half a box of chocolate to help put his nerves at ease, and the tea he had made earlier (with milk and a generous heaping of Marcello sugar). Once his heart had stopped pounding and the knot in his stomach had loosened, no doubt in part from having something in his stomach as well as the increasing distance from his father, he returned to his room to complete his morning routine.

The mansion was big, and Giovanni had to traverse many twists and turns through the extensive hallways in order to get back to his room, but he had long ago memorized the steps that it took to travel from each room of the house to another, having lived here for the entirety of his thirty-four years of life. Long halls with doors leading to rooms of all kinds passed him as he walked, servant quarters and storage closets and the now-empty bedrooms his older siblings had once resided within. He passed by each door with little thought given to it, perfectly content to focus entirely on his destination. Soon he came to the hallway where his own door, bright white with a pretty golden doorknob that he made sure the servants frequently polished, waited for him invitingly.

Like the doorknob, the entire room was adorned in gold, and looked much like a luxurious white chocolate bar wrapped in golden foil. Gold furniture sat against walls that were painted with intricate gold swirls spiraling against snow white backgrounds. The bed frame was gold, as was the floral pattern sewn delicately into silky, deep purple bed sheets. With the help of the finest designer that his father could find, he had very carefully selected the colors and patterns. Mirrors were hung on the walls and sat up on stands across the room like a sea of glittering portals, showing off the gold patterns on the walls from every angle; that way Giovanni could always check in on himself, could make sure that he could catch within seconds, at any moment, the slightest hint of imperfection threatening to show itself underneath his makeup.

Giovanni hummed to himself as he entered the room, shutting the door behind him, making himself safely alone and cut off from the labyrinth of doors and hallways on the other side. He let go of a breath he had hardly realized he was holding. Here everything was in order and his only audience was his own reflection in the numerous mirrors. He walked up to one mirror, hung up like a portrait with a golden frame on the wall across from the door, and gazed at himself, studying the lilac he had dusted his eyes with and checking to make sure that his lipstick was still as bright and thick as when he had first applied it.

The Mirror was a funny thing to Giovanni; it was an object that he both detested and adored. It felt as necessary to life as breathing, or eating, and yet it had been, throughout his life, such an agent of pain as well, reflecting back at him every insecurity and imperfection, every ugly transgression upon his features. He feared it and he adored it, for without it, his art would only be half complete. After all, without a reflection, how else could he admire his craftsmanship, the perfection he had worked to achieve through practice and dedication and thick layers of paint and powder?

After taking a proper moment to make sure that nothing had become soiled across his face, Giovanni forced his eyes away. He had something to prepare for, and the clock raced much too fast, as did his heartbeat. Distractions were only able to stave off the anxiety of the coming day for so long. He looked around, trying to organize a plan, but the nerves had already surmounted in the pit of his stomach. He needed a distraction before he could go any further. Instinctively, he stepped to a cabinet in the corner—white, trimmed with swirling gold designs, like the rest of the room—where he kept wine, candies, and other necessities. He selected from it an unopened bottle of a white dessert wine. Giovanni liked sweet wine that burned his tongue with sugar as much as it did alcohol, and although his preference for achieving an altered state of consciousness would always be candies, he was open to mixing it up on occasion.

Foregoing the grace of pouring the drink into a glass, Giovanni took a swig directly from the bottle. When that failed to immediately alleviate his nerves he took another, then one more still, and after blinking a few times, willing the sweet intoxication into his veins, he could confidently feel the onset of a light buzz. Giovanni drew in another breath as he glanced up to his clock, calculating how much longer he had to get ready before he would be expected to appear at his father's interview. He did not want to move, did not want to take any step towards the inevitable, but he knew what it was that his father wanted, *needed*, him to do. With the bottle still in his hand he moved now from the cabinet to his closet, where he began to search for something to wear.

Although he rarely left the house these days, Giovanni's closet consisted of only the finest of clothing: Designer suits made of sleek silk and soft furs and smooth leather of any color that he could possibly desire. He picked a purple suit, which matched the long, soft, silky purple scarf that he pulled out next; one of his favorite items. Giovanni always wore purple for good luck on especially momentous or otherwise stressful occasions. It was royal, it felt luxurious and protective in the glamor and beauty that it displayed. He took another swig of his bottle—his longest yet—and began, very quickly, to unbutton his pajamas. As he reached the bottom few buttons he began to see the exposed soft pink of his chest peeking through the opened shirt and he paused, flinched a bit, and walked without another thought to his cabinet again, this time plucking from the top shelf a little, wrapped hard candy that resembled a golden gemstone—Marcello brand butterscotch. It was not until after he had the candy securely in his mouth that he was able to even attempt finishing the job, undressing the rest of the way as quickly as possible, fingers fumbling due to the alcohol in his system and the rush at which he moved, deftly ignoring the endless hall of mirrors that peered down at him from his walls, trying with all his might to focus on the soft, exquisite, lilac material beneath his fingers and not the flesh that bulged and protruded with each breath beneath. He tugged up his pants and buttoned up his shirt with fingers even faster and did not dare to even look up again until he was fully and entirely dressed.

Alcohol and candy mixed well, Giovanni thought, as long as he was careful not to swallow the candy like a pill and waste its flavor. He kept both nearby as he completed his morning routine, with much more leisure now that the second most difficult part was over (the top contender, of course, being the initial confrontation with his bare face in the early morning). He had an affinity for dangling earrings that hung low from his ears; he could toy with them and twirl them and tap them, making them sway with his long, fake nails. He liked sweet colognes that smelled like a pastry shop, scents like vanilla extract and cupcake batter and creamy frosting. Every so often he would pause his work to stop at a mirror, drag nails through his hair in search of anything lighter than stark black, and check again that his makeup had not been smudged or smeared.

Giovanni was not sure how long it was until he felt confidently perfect. His makeup was beautiful and elegant and crafted with tireless passion and attention to detail, his hair dark and long and slicked back and tied up just as he desired, kept in place with a plum-colored bow that matched his makeup; his outfit was sharp, luxurious, bright, stood out in both color and price; he smelled sweet and fresh and his earrings twinkled as they fluttered in the light and his scarf was warm and caressed his neck and brushed against his chin like the trace of a lover's fingertips. A sigh of relief: The job was finished.

Loud pounding suddenly came from the bedroom door, causing Giovanni to nearly choke on the candy in his mouth. He whipped towards it just in time to hear a voice cry out:

"Get a fucking move on, Giovanni!"

"Vittoria?" he called back, recognizing the voice even as the shock of the interruption still left him somewhat breathless. There was a sound of impatient, fruitless tugging at the doorknob, and as Giovanni relaxed he found his surprise melting into annoyance. Who did she think she was, trying to intrude on such an intimate, personal moment? As if he would *ever* allow the door to be unlocked during his sacred morning routine, as if he would ever risk being walked in on while he transformed himself by the likes of *her*. This was the most private of times; he would be more likely to carelessly leave his door unlocked while seeing a woman than now. The mere implication, the utter lack of respect, that resounded from his sister's hands as they scrambled for entrance and banged on the doorway to the sanctuary he had so lovingly crafted for himself, that demand he rush his process or, even worse, allow her to partake in it, left him bitter and resentful. His lips pursed and his brow furrowed and he sucked at the candy in his mouth aggressively for a moment before he finally spoke again: "What do you want, sister?"

"We gotta get going, idiot. You better be fucking ready 'cause I'm not gonna be late for you," Vittoria's voice came back harsh and frustrated on the other side of the door.

Giovanni did not move from where he stood, did not unlock the door for her or even think to move closer out of even the vaguest of consideration that he should. She was not going to come inside. "Why would you worry about being late? This is *my* interview, Vittoria."

"Shut the fuck up, asshole. I've been planning this for weeks. I need this for my music." Vittoria answered. Giovanni flinched again as an especially loud thump caused the door to shake, as if Vittoria had attempted to kick it down, or perhaps had thrown herself against it. "Besides! Did you really think Dad would trust you to do this alone?"

Giovanni paused at those words, his expression softening from the bitter scowl on his face. He let his tongue rub against the candy in his mouth, lapping at it for flavor as he thought of a response. He looked away from the many mirrors that adorned his walls to focus instead on his own feet. "Papa said that this interview was for me. To prove myself."

"Well, it's time you learn to share," was Vittoria's reply, and although her expression was concealed by the door between them, Giovanni could easily envision the look on her face, the annoyance and disregard that he expected of his younger sister. She continued: "...For once in that pathetic waste of time you call a life. Open the fucking door, Giovanni, I swear to fucking God."

"I'll be out shortly, sister. I am not finished getting ready just yet." Giovanni said, trying to sound stubborn despite the deflatedness of his tone, as the realization that his sister's accompaniment was unavoidable had finally begun to dawn on him. He walked to his bed and sat down on it, crossing his legs and keeping his eyes on his long, sparkly nails, hoping to recollect himself, as well as position himself even further from the attempted intruder. *At least I actually take the time to make myself look good*, he thought bitterly.

"You have *maybe* fifteen minutes. Dad is sending a limo and he said to be ready by the time it got here. It'll be live on air, so we can't be late. You don't wanna make Dad look bad, do you, Giovanni?"

Giovanni stiffened a little, eyes leaving his nails as his fingers curled, closing his hand. He rolled the candy around on his tongue. "I won't," he said.

"You better not. And you better not make *me* look bad, either, because I'll be there with you whether you like it or not." Vittoria snapped, and this time Giovanni knew for certain that she had attempted to kick the door down, for the loud, echoing bang, unmistakably Vittoria's heavy boots colliding forcefully into the pristine white wood, which followed these words made his heart skip a beat as he jumped in surprise. He sucked in a quick breath, and with it the butterscotch he had been working on went down his throat and he gagged. Coughing breathily, he reached briefly to instinctively cover his mouth, but, remembering the lipstick he had so carefully applied, he hesitated just as his nails brushed against his lips. As he huffed and attempted to regain control of his breath, over his rasping he heard Vittoria walk away from the door. "God, I'm so fucking sick of you always ruining shit for me," she muttered, voice growing softer as she walked away.

Giovanni, finally given a reprieve, was grateful to be left alone to cough up the butterscotch, which he immediately swallowed once he had managed to force it out of his windpipe, not eager to take the chance at choking on it again but certainly not wanting to waste the rest of the sugar, either. He stood up and took a few deep breaths, lungs still weak from the saccharine battering they had just received. He walked to his cabinet once more as his breaths continued to tremble, rummaging through it, searching for candy that was less of a choking hazard; chocolates and other chewables, preferably. Vittoria's attempted intrusion had left a considerable dent in the demeanor he had been carefully ironing out over the course of the morning, and now he had little time to repair the damage she had done before he would be off to his father's interview. He drew in a breath, the first full and even one he had managed to take since his coughing fit, and stuffed a handful of chocolates into his coat pocket.

As he turned to leave, Giovanni paused at one of the mirrors hanging in his room for a final time, eyeing his reflection haloed by the intricate golden frame. His judgment day was fast approaching. The thought of the impending interview left a lump in his throat much more intrusive than the butterscotch and it took Giovanni everything in him not to choke on his own nerves. His eyes darted from detail to detail: Lips painted, carefully, fully; eyeshadow, eyeliner, delicately traced around pretty blue eyes; clear face, crafted jawline, sprinkles of blush up his cheeks. He combed his long nails through his hair once, brushed his fingertips against the bow that kept his ponytail in place, and then reached into his pocket, already pulling out one of the chocolates. Clutching it in his hand, fiddling with the wrapper, he nodded to himself and walked to the door, finally ready to unlock it.

When Vittoria was young, she had tried to run away.

Now she stood entirely still in front of the mansion, gazing at the great driveway and the golden gate surrounded by tall green hedges that kept her father's home secluded from the rest of the world unless they knew the passkey for entry. It was already unpleasantly warm out, although the summer was still fresh and young and the California heat not overbearing quite yet—but it was certainly only a matter of time. Vittoria pushed up her dark sunglasses and rolled up the sleeves of the black blouse she had changed into as she glanced around, waiting for the limousine, and waiting for her brother.

"Vitta! Vittoria! I am ready now, sister!"

Vittoria turned to face Giovanni as he pushed through the grand doors of the mansion and stepped carefully down the front stairs. She watched him, lips pursed, looking him up and down and disliking the bright purple of his suit, the shiny silk of his scarf, horribly out of season, the burst of colorful makeup around his eyes and lips. It objectively clashed with her, and she found another heavy drop of dread fall into the accumulating pool of nerves in her stomach as she imagined how very clownish the visual of their shared stage presence would be. As he came to stand beside her on the curb, she drew in a breath and found her senses assaulted by the cologne he wore, the breath in her lungs replaced by the heavy, alcoholic vanilla scent that he had put on, and she loathed imagining having to sit beside him in a car. She hated sweets.

"Listen to me, Giovanni. If I had my way, this would have been *my* interview. Alone." Vittoria hissed. "I'm not letting you fuck this up for me."

"I assure you, the feeling is mutual," Giovanni answered plainly. "Papa has been saying for weeks that this would be my interview. For me." Vittoria felt her face redden with frustration beneath her pale makeup. She hoped that his being wildly overdressed for the weather would give him heatstroke and he would drop dead before the limousine even arrived. "He says that this will make us all look better, the whole family. Not to mention the company. And especially with Giorgio's new promotion—He said that the people want to know me! Papa says they want to know who the marvelous Giovanni Marcello is, and who am *I* to deny them-"

"I don't give a single fuck about Dad's company, Giovanni, and I don't give a fuck about what Dad says. I need this for *myself.*" Vittoria felt her fists tighten at her sides, her nails scratching at her palms, already raw from the stress of this morning alone. She drew in a long breath and loosened her grip, willing herself to stay calm. "Giovanni, I can't have you fucking this up for me. I need this."

"Then I have a question for you, sister."

"What's that?" Vittoria rolled her eyes as she turned away from her brother, conveying as blatantly as she could that even so much as responding to his request for inquisition was something she had as little disregard for as possible, and certain that if she had to look at his gaudy purple self any longer she would snap. She kept her eyes above the tall hedge; she could see the skyscrapers in the distance, huge silver buildings that jutted into the sky and littered the horizon from the view in her bedroom, and she wondered how many of the countless people within those buildings would be tuning in to watch her today.

Giovanni took in a breath, as if he were really planning to say something profound: "If you are so-"

"Wait." Vittoria cut him off, for in that instant the gate opened with creaky wailing as the metal bars parted for the limousine that their father had promised, long and jet black, windows tinted to hide the identity of those within, and yet still promising to all who looked upon it that it held those only of extreme wealth and importance. "Our ride is here—save it." Vittoria said. She hoped that Giovanni would forget the question, and, best case scenario, just stop trying to talk to her altogether. She had detected the hint of a challenge, the way that the question had begun with an air of confrontation in his voice, and she was certain that anything that left her brother's mouth now would surely push her past the limit of how much bullshit she could handle in a single day.

Thankfully, Giovanni did indeed remain quiet, and the two siblings waited in silence as the limousine pulled up to the front of the house and parked. The driver stepped out, a suited man with nice skin and hair with too much mousse. Vittoria's nose scrunched at the cologne he wore, almost as intrusive as whatever nauseating scent Giovanni had coated himself in.

"Mistress Marcello, Mister Marcello," he greeted with a little nod, very proper and polite, a demeanor that reaffirmed to Vittoria the officiality of the event that was about to transpire. The man opened the door of the limousine and offered her a white-gloved hand which she did not accept.

"I'm fine," she said, and she climbed into the limousine herself.

Giovanni, whom the limousine driver did not offer a hand to, crawled in next and sat across from her. Just as she had feared, his perfume permeated through the entire limousine, and Vittoria was certain that by the time they got out that she, too, would be drenched in her brother's sugary stench. She felt sick just thinking about it, and she watched with narrowed eyes as he got comfortable and looked around the inside of the limousine like a child, his eyes wide, a sort of curious excitement glowing in them. As if he had never been in a fucking limousine before. She noticed one of his hands at his ear, fiddling with the dangling earring that he wore, swaying it back and forth in a way that would surely make her nausea even worse if she stared for too long, while his other hand fidgeted inside of his coat pocket.

"Don't touch anything," Vittoria hissed.

Giovanni flinched and turned to look at her, a sort of stupid bewilderment on his face. He huffed. "I didn't touch a thing,"

Vittoria snorted and looked away, ignoring the fact that Giovanni was, for once in his life, right. She looked out the tinted window to stare at the tall hedges that walled the mansion, eyes not focusing on any particular detail but rather resting aimlessly on green nothingness as her mind wandered. She wanted to open the window, to take a breath of air free of Giovanni's cologne, but decided against it as the driver stepped back into the limousine and pulled out of the driveway towards the gate. The limo drove beyond the hedges that walled them in and out into the open, down the hill that their home rested upon and into what were the wealthy, upper class suburbs of the city, just outside the heart of it, where giant towers shot up into the sky and crowds bustled and cars honked without cease. The houses on either side of the road as they reached the bottom of the hill were tall and grand and expensive, but not nearly as large as their father's mansion. The Marcello Estate was something else entirely, a whole other species of regality and wealth that quite literally shadowed the entirety of even the wealthiest block of homes in the city. Vittoria looked down at her own hands, which clasped each other in her lap, and rubbed one thumb against the other in an attempt to distract herself from her nerves.

"Oh! I forgot to check on my birds this morning!" Giovanni said.

Vittoria let out a little breath and looked up at her brother, who was staring at her, but when her eyes met his he looked away. His hand was still in his pocket. Irritably, she spat, "What?"

"I don't think I checked on them last night before bed, either. Do you think that anybody checked in on them?"

"Why the fuck would someone else check on your birds for you? They're your- Why the fuck would I even *know* that?" Vittoria scoffed, rolled her eyes, and looked away, the most blatant display of annoyance that she could possibly muster. Then, keeping her eyes on the window and the rapidly approaching city before them, she asked, "What do you have in your pocket?"

"Ah..." Giovanni made a little sound, as if he had been about to answer and something had suddenly driven him to reconsider.

The hesitance was enough to force Vittoria's gaze back to him. "What do you have in your pocket, Giovanni?" she asked again.

Giovanni's eyes quickly darted away, averting her stare. "I'm sure you understand the stress of this interview, Vitta. I simply... did what must be done in order to assure that things go as planned." He spoke in a winding little singsong tone that Vittoria recognized immediately as one born of guilt or avoidance and her eyes narrowed. His hand finally left his pocket in a fist, and when he opened that fist he revealed a little handful of candies, shimmering in their colorful foil wrappers, each adorned by the printed image of a golden M, shaded like metal in sunlight. His eyes did not meet his sister's, but the corner of his lips twitched in a strange half-repressed smile.

"You fucking idiot!" Vittoria spat as her narrowed eyes turned wide, disbelief on her face and coursing through every vein in her body.

Giovanni twitched in the vaguest of winces. "You can't fucking bring candy to the interview, my fucking *God.*" She reached suddenly to grab the candies, to throw them out the window or smash them or stomp them into sugary pulp, but Giovanni quickly pulled them back towards him, towards his breast, holding them close as if he was protecting a baby animal. "What the fuck, Giovanni," Vittoria continued, "You bitched about wanting to make a good impression for Dad and you planned to get strung out before the show, is that it? How many have you had this morning?" With his tolerance, she thought, she wasn't sure she wanted to know.

"That is not any of your business, Vitta," Giovanni replied, loosening his grip on his candies just enough to look down and admire them, gazing at the shiny confections lovingly. "I can take care of myself."

"Couldn't take care of your own fucking birds, though. When was the last time you had to beg Dad to buy you more because the last batch dropped dead... Last week?"

"I could say the same about your business ventures,"

Reaching a breaking point, Vittoria lunged at Giovanni's fist again, trying to grab at his candies, willing to rip Giovanni's whole wrist from his arm if that was what it took to get them out of his hand and the smugness out of his voice. But Giovanni's reflexes were just as fast as her own, and he quickly moved away, jumping aside, a motion that he had plenty of room for in the wonderfully spacious limousine, and retracting his arm, leaving Vittoria to fall to the floor of the car and land on her hands and knees.

"Vittoria!" Giovanni scoffed, and when she glanced to his face she could see genuine surprise in his expression, as if even he had not expected her to stoop to this sort of level. Her face burned, a scowl on her dark lips.

Vittoria quickly got up. Determined to stick to her initial plan and keep her eyes off of Giovanni entirely, she glanced to him only long enough to see him shove his candies away, before she dusted off her knees, ran a hand through her hair, and looked to the front of the limousine as if to make sure that the driver had not happened to see what had transpired. Then she sat back down and breathed a long sigh. She straightened out her skirt, fidgeting with it in frustration. Failing to distract herself, she let her eyes return to the window. They had made it onto the freeway that would carry them into the depths of the city. Around them the skyscrapers were growing dense. They were entering the heart of a forest of metal that sprung up from the concrete and loomed over them amidst the colorful neon signs, logos, advertisements, traffic lights, and screens that adorned the streets, but Vittoria could hardly focus her attention on any of it now. Her mind raced and her heart pounded in her chest; her breath felt restricted despite the looseness of her blouse. Her moment on those screens was rapidly approaching, as was the limousine to its destination.

Giovanni rubbed at the candies in his pocket, comforted by their presence, gliding his fingertips across the smooth wrappers. Meanwhile, he watched Vittoria furtively, glancing to her and wondering what it was she was thinking, and then looking back around at the interior of the limo, eyes traveling aimlessly yet anxiously around the tinted windows and sleek metallic trim and the luxurious, scarlet cushioned seats. He wished he had a mirror so that he could check on himself and make sure that his makeup and hair were fine. Although he was used to feeling the layers of makeup on his face, and although every day he was concerned about the perfection of his workmanship, he felt especially aware of it all today.

There was a noticeable decrease in speed as the limousine took an exit and left the freeway, driving up a ramp into the depths of the city, onto streets that bustled with people walking beside them on the pavement and before them on the crosswalks, and a steady flow of cars going in all directions on the traffic-ridden roads. Giovanni felt his heart plummet and he drew both a candy from his pocket and a great, deep, trembling breath of air. He looked to his sister again: She was staring out the window on the other side of the limousine, and with her attention on the passing cars and tall buildings, Giovanni quickly unwrapped the candy.

Shoving the wrapper back into his pocket, Giovanni stuffed the little orb into his mouth, doing his best to be as silent as possible, keeping it from clacking against his teeth and careful not to let it rub against his lips and potentially smear his lipstick. Still, even his best efforts were not good enough to avoid generating suspicion, for at the tail end of this process Vittoria turned to look at him.

"What the fuck are you doing now?" she asked, and the irritated boredom that dripped from her tone was a relief to Giovanni's ears, for it meant she was not aware enough of what he had just done to be truly angry. Yet.

Giovanni rolled the candy under his tongue with ease. Deftly capable of hiding things in his mouth at this point, he spoke with only the faintest trace of a struggle when he replied, "Nothing, sister, nothing."

With his sister's eyes still on him, unflinching as if trying to intimidate, Giovanni looked to his hands, not liking the way that her eyes, cold and piercing as his own, bore down on him. She did not believe him; he knew that perfectly well. But what she wanted was of no concern to him. The moment he saw her turn her head away once more from the corner of his eye he let the candy leave its hiding spot under his tongue to suck at it. Being a chocolate, it dissolved in his mouth quickly, which was useful when he was doing this under Vittoria's surveillance. The candy melted effortlessly against his tongue, soft enough that it need not be chewed, coating his mouth as it released its flavor as well as the patented Marcello brand sugar with which it was infused. It was a milder candy, a product that could be bought at a gas station register. Giovanni was not stupid; he knew better than to get completely inebriated on a day as important as this. And besides, although its impact was not as intense as other products that his family sold, it was able to do its job, and it took effect just as fast.

In just a few short moments, Giovanni's muscles, previously tightened with anxiety, returned to a gentler, resting position, and his racing thoughts turned sluggish. Like a weight lifting, his whole demeanor turned lighter with each breath in, and he closed his eyes for a moment, feeling the knot in his chest uncurl even as the brief wave of nausea that came with the initial high crawled down his neck and into his stomach, leaving a thickness in the back of his throat and goosebumps down his back—easily manageable side effects. Then he opened his eyes, vision just ever so slightly hazier, a soft glow to the world now present, and looked out the window.

They were driving into the upper region of the city, where businesses flourished, office buildings thrived, and the entertainment industry held domain. Tall skyscrapers jutted from the ground like an invasive species over the dry California landscape. The limousine, halted frequently by traffic and pedestrians, was moving slow enough that Giovanni could take everything in, despite the delayed reaction from his eyes to his brain as the candy worked its way through his system. Great big screens hung over them, peering down at the cars and passersby, displaying images larger than life. Currently, there were shots of a medical car on its side, smoking as it lay lifeless as a corpse. The car had clearly seen better days; it was missing its back doors and its tires were badly damaged. A man with silver hair stood before the wreckage, talking into a microphone. From within the limousine it was impossible to hear a word, but on the screen subtitles flashed: ANOTHER PRESCRIPTION CAR WAS ATTACKED IN WHAT IS REPORTED TO BE THE DEADLIEST RAID THIS MONTH. FALCONS AND HAWKS ARRIVED ONLY MINUTES AFTER RECEIVING THE CALL, BUT BY THEN THE DRIVER HAD BEEN TERMINATED, AND IT IS ESTIMATED THAT AROUND FORTY PERCENT OF THE-

Giovanni found it hard to concentrate on the little white and black words as they scrolled across the screen and let his eyes wander away, to the street and the people walking on it. In the heart of the city, the people here had the riches to adorn themselves in the nicest clothing, attend the best salons, and afford the most high-end and innovative of cosmetic surgeries offered by only the greatest of medical companies: Himmel Medicine. Giovanni watched each person walk by, looking at each woman's legs, each man's broad shoulders, each elevated cheekbone or chiseled jaw or perfect hairline or full, thick lips, breasts that bounced within the most expensive of blouses, studying and admiring features of the wealthy strangers that spent their time in this part of the city. He then noticed pigeons fluttering about and stopped people-watching to look at them instead, watching as they hopped about and scurried between the city-dwellers.

Soon enough, the limousine came upon a tall, silver, metallic building covered in screens of its own, each with something different to look at: News reports, sports, interviews, but mostly advertisements. An endless barrage of information and color and ideas that could be purchased, that would better the life of the buyer in some way or another. Giovanni could hardly even begin to process it all. The view of the building caused a spike in the well-stifled anxiety residing in the pit of his stomach, doing its damndest to break free of the cage he had temporarily coaxed it into via the chocolate. He let his eyes wander to the front of the building. Over it, in huge, white, strikingly clean and shining letters that were almost blinding beneath the bright heat of the day and his hazy, sugarcoated vision, were the words DOWNTOWN FRESNO BROADCASTING STUDIO.

The limousine had safe, secluded, VIP parking around the back. When it came to a halt, signifying to its passengers that it had finally reached its destination, Giovanni's hand wandered to his pocket once more to fidget with the remaining candies again. He looked at Vittoria, who was still looking out the window, but as if able to feel his eyes on her she turned and furrowed her brow at him.

"You better not fuck this up for me, Giovanni," she said.

Giovanni snorted and rolled his eyes but said nothing. A moment later the limousine door opened and the driver stood waiting. Giovanni, closer to the door, got out first and took a look around. The parking lot was clean and much too large for the number of cars parked in it. The cars that were given the privilege to park here were clearly luxurious, clearly the newest models at the highest prices, although he admittedly had never followed car trends as he could not drive, so it was not a world that he was familiar with. In front of them was the back of the broadcasting studio. Giovanni looked up at it, his eyes following it to the very top, upwards into the sky until it hurt his eyes to look at.

Vittoria stepped out after and kept herself at a distance from Giovanni. A moment later, a man walked out from the studio. He wore casual clothing, black dress pants and a gray button-up with the letters FBS printed on it in red letters.

"Vittorio Marcello's kids, right? Are ya ready?" the man asked as he approached, tone chipper but very artificial in the way only present in the voices of polite businessmen. The man glanced down to his clipboard, then looked back up at the pair of siblings. When neither had replied, he asked, "Ya nervous?"

Giovanni swallowed and shook his head. "No, no, I can assure you, I have been preparing for weeks on end for thi-"

"We're fine." Vittoria interrupted briskly.

Giovanni's nose wrinkled, bristling at the interjection. Glaring across at her, he repeated stubbornly: "-I have been preparing for this interview for weeks. Though I do not know if I can say the same for my little sister, here. I have not been involved in her preparation, and I know she can be a bit disorganized." He smiled then, mimicking the forced pleasantness of the man before him.

"I know it's hard for my *brother* to realize this, because he stays cooped up inside his bedroom all day and forgets that the world doesn't revolve around *him*, but I actually have been prepping for this for weeks too, and I have all sorts of exciting news to share." Vittoria said now. Her voice was cheery as well, more upbeat than Giovanni swore he had ever heard from her before. She walked over to him now and grabbed his wrist before he had a chance to say anything else.

Giovanni was not sure if this was meant to be taken as a threat or if she was simply trying to puzzle him, but either way, he would not back down. After all, he knew that Vittoria could do very little to him, especially in public, especially at an event as momentous as this, so he chose to pay no mind to her hand on his arm as he said, "I do not need to come up with 'news' of plans doomed to fail from the start to be interesting; I am not in the business of theatrics. Just my presence should captivate the audience enough!"

Sharp nails dug into the underside of Giovanni's wrist and he tensed, stifling a surprised squeak and tugging his arm away forcefully, glaring at his sister. "At least I'm *in* business. Any business. At all." Vittoria snapped, her regular demeanor beginning to barrage its way through the sprightly attitude she had been attempting. She then turned away from him altogether, leaving Giovanni to rub gingerly at where she had scratched him. "Are we ready to go in?" he heard her ask, presumably to the man with the clipboard, as the tone was much too polite to possibly be directed towards him.

"I was just about to ask you two the same question!" said the man, perky as ever, clearly intending it to be a joke, though neither Giovanni nor Vittoria laughed.

The man led the siblings into the studio. The siblings followed him down a dimly lit hallway lined with various doorways to restrooms, dressing rooms, offices, and whatever else could possibly be needed within the depths of the broadcasting station. Adorning the walls were photos, many signed, of local celebrities who had attended various events or shows in the station, or headshots of staff members. As they continued walking through the long corridors, the man spoke again, but this time his tone had changed to one slightly more professional, more direct: "Your dad called ahead and gave us some details," he explained, which made Giovanni's heart stop in his chest. The chocolate's effects were still mildly polluting his bloodstream but had most certainly weakened quite a bit at this point, the most intense of the high long gone before they had even entered the building. "So we already have everything ready for you. If you need to piss or anything else do it now because we aren't stopping anything once the cameras are on, got it? Once you're out on the stage give us about five minutes to get things rolling. You're gonna be interviewed by Will Baer. You know him."

He sure did. Giovanni froze completely at this news, his body seemingly needing to pause to give his brain the power that it needed to begin to process this. "William Baer?"

The man nodded without so much turning back to look at him, without even lifting his eyes off of his clipboard. "You betcha, the one and only. Everybody loves that guy. Though I'm sure it isn't much of a surprise to you, a child of Vittorio's could probably get anyone in the damn city to bend over backwards for 'em." A hearty little laugh.

It was not a surprise, but not for the reasons that the man appeared to presume. As he continued walking Giovanni reached into his pocket to toy with his candies again, and he weighed the pros and cons of running to the men's room to scarf down one or two more before the show. He knew William Baer, alright. Alongside being the charming host of Fresno's evening show, he also happened to be the husband of his older sister, Francesca, one of Fresno's most beloved debutantes. Because she had never lived with them, Giovanni did not know Francesca or William on any intimate level, but he remembered the first time that they met—he remembered how intimidated he had been by William, who held his own with a demeanor not unlike his father's, strong and confident but so very impossible to read, everything so easily suppressed and hidden beneath the plasticine skin, molded with years of cosmetic surgeries and so picturesque in its perfect lack of blemish. He looked like a wax figure, or a Roman statue. Giovanni remembered stumbling over his words as he tried to speak with him that day, and, later, he remembered the anger he had felt towards his sister upon learning that they were engaged.

The man escorted Giovanni and Vittoria into a brightly lit stage with three comfortable red chairs in front of a backdrop of a nighttime cityscape, with blurry, distant images of neon signs, glowing apartments, and the large television screens that were a staple of the modern city lighting up the dark sky. Giovanni, very aware of how incredibly soon the interview was to occur and feeling increasingly sick to his stomach, had to give up his hope of sneaking more candies beforehand. There was no escape now. Instead, he walked to one of the chairs and sat down, getting comfortable and taking a few deep breaths, shutting his eyes for a moment and trying to block out the brightness of the lights that shone down on the stage from above and the ceaseless gaze of the cameras before them.

"There's no live audience." Vittoria's voice echoed around the stage and into the empty studio. Her words piqued Giovanni's interest enough that he opened his eyes to look out, noticing that, indeed, the space before them was entirely barren, save for the scurry of studio attendants that rushed back and forth occasionally, carrying equipment or speaking in a mumble into earpieces. "Isn't this supposed to be a live interview?"

"Oh, yes, this is going to be *broadcast* live, don't worry. But live *audiences* can be a hassle. We don't want to have any interruption." The man explained. Giovanni watched Vittoria walk over to sit down in the big red chair furthest from where he sat. Immediately, the man spoke again: "Why don't you sit next to each other? That way Will'll be able to face ya both at once. Makes for better composition on the stage." Giovanni could see the glare of pure vitriol cross Vittoria's features and she stood, sighed loudly, and threw herself down onto the chair beside Giovanni, not saying a word. "Great! We'll have Baer out in five. Get ready, okay? Good luck, kids." Giovanni watched as the man gave a good-natured thumbs up and walked backstage, leaving the two of them alone.

For a brief period of time, Vittoria and Giovanni sat in silence, neither addressing, let alone acknowledging, the other. If there was anybody else in the room they were doing a fantastic job of staying quiet, for the only sound Giovanni could hear was the faint hum of various electronics and the murmur of voices backstage. He fidgeted with his earrings, carefully brushed his hair from his face, gently rubbed his lips together to feel the smooth glide of the lipstick he had applied. William Baer was arguably one of the most popular and, by extension, most influential entertainers in Fresno. It was her relationship with him that convinced their father that Francesca, deemed a bastard child at birth due to the nature of Vittorio's relationship with her mother, was worthy of the Marcello name. Giovanni looked over to his sister—Did she have any qualms, had she bristled at the name as much as he? He had not been paying attention, and a small part of him wanted to ask her for her thoughts, see what she made of the situation, but he held off, deciding that he would rather not speak with her, especially out here, before the empty auditorium.

Despite the many layers of makeup he had applied, even with the extravagance of the costly suit that he wore, Giovanni felt very naked up on the stage, very exposed and very vulnerable. And as the candy high had been on a downwards descent since they exited the limousine, Giovanni felt helpless to control his thoughts as they spun at increasingly faster speeds, downwards into a pit of dread.

In a bout of desperation, he reached into his pocket and took out one of his shiny chocolates.

Vittoria turned in a heartbeat. "Don't you fucking dare, Giovanni."

Giovanni decided in that moment that he was not going to listen, that he did not quite care what Vittoria said he should or should not do, and in the next moment he had taken a brief glance around the studio, made sure that there was no one but him and Vittoria around, and quickly unwrapped the chocolate and shoved it into his mouth before she had the chance to stop him.

"I can't fucking believe you!" Vittoria's voice was shrill and high and Giovanni winced at it, recoiling to preserve his eardrums. She lunged at him, grabbing him by the glittery scarf around his neck and tugging him towards her. "You fucking idiot," she snarled, face inches away from his, "You stupid fucking retard. What if they're recording you right now?

What kind of fucking impression is that supposed to make on you? On us?"

Giovanni looked away uncomfortably as he sucked at the chocolate in his mouth. "Papa's candies are not illegal, Vitta. I would try to worry less about matters that do not concern you," He tugged himself free of Vittoria's grasp.

This response did nothing to satiate Vittoria's anger. If anything, it seemed to make it worse. "Doesn't concern me?!" she repeated, the indignation in her voice loud and clear, "We're in this show together, you fucking idiot. You're going to ruin everything for us—for *me*. Oh my God." Giovanni refused to turn to look at her, doing the best he could to not acknowledge her, but saw from the corner of his eye as she grabbed her hair and tugged at it in frustration, groaning loudly, her nails digging into her own scalp with uncontainable fury. " *You're going to fucking ruin this*," she hissed, voice strained with the pure rage coursing through her. "You're going to ruin everything, like you always-"

"Giiii-ooooo-vannnnn-eeeeeee! Viiiiiii-ttoriaaaaaaaaa!"

Giovanni tensed in surprise and swallowed the half-melted chocolate whole. From the corner of his eye he saw Vittoria's chest rise and fall in a deep breath, presumably just as startled as him. A man came walking out from the wing of the stage. He was dressed in the most modern and cutting edge of casual, laidback fashion. Exorbitant but relatable to those watching, a look of perfect approachability while still retaining a sort of dignity that only money could buy. Perfectly tailored jeans that clung tight to his legs, sculpting them, highlighting exactly what needed to be emphasized. Giovanni swore he saw the most subtle trace of motion between his legs as he walked, accentuated by the cut of the denim to only just barely hint at the suggestion of impressive masculinity. A simple black t-shirt made of a soft silky material, with some sort of effect on the fabric that made it flicker with iridescent rainbow light as it fluttered with each footstep. His hair was brown and tousled, intentionally messy, and he had traces of stubble on his perfectly structured jaw. His cheekbones were high, his lips soft, his eyes bright and, Giovanni swore, also possessing just the softest, slightest echoes of those rainbow flecks that sparkled across his shirt. He was smiling wide, and his teeth were very white and very fake and perfectly sculpted, just like the rest of his clothing, body, and personality. Giovanni's eyes were wide and he was star struck to silence as he gave him his hand, which the man shook vigorously. William Baer had finally made his much-anticipated appearance on the set.

"Giovanni! Great to see you, boy. It's great that you two could make it. FBS is so excited to have ya both."

"Will..." Vittoria greeted, causing both Giovanni and William to turn to look at her. "It's, ah, been awhile."

William, still smiling big, held out his hand to her. "Vittoria," he greeted, "Just lovely to have you, really." Vittoria accepted his hand, expressionless for all that Giovanni could tell, and he watched as, instead of shaking her hand like he had his, William took it gently to his mouth and kissed the back of it. Vittoria's expression did not change, but Giovanni felt a tenseness drop in the pit of his stomach, bristling, the chocolate not working its magic nearly fast enough.

Will walked to the empty third seat on the stage and angled it in such a way that it was positioned a small distance from the other two, facing them enough that it looked as if they were having a conversation while still fully visible to the camera. He plopped down on the chair, sighed as he got comfortable and settled in, and then looked down at his watch, a shiny gold piece that Giovanni could tell from experience was incredibly expensive. Then, he spoke once more, "Listen, when the show starts up, I'm gonna give you guys a little introduction. Just wait until it's your turn to speak, and answer questions nice and simple. Make yourself sound nice for the public and smile wide for the camera, got it?"

Giovanni flinched as Vittoria tapped his leg with her boot, as if to silently reinforce that order. He turned to her and glared, then looked back at William.

"Take turns. The audience will want to hear both of you speak equally."

Giovanni took the opportunity to turn and kick Vittoria in return, possibly a bit too hard, for when his shoe hit her leg, bare save for leggings, she sucked in a surprise breath through her nose and kicked him again, significantly harder than the first time. Giovanni stifled a whine of pain and was planning to return the favor when the lights in the studio dimmed and somewhere from within the wings a voice shouted, "One minute!"

William sat up almost mechanically; immediately his posture changed until he was broad shouldered, alert, but relaxed, legs crossed and leaning in a way that made him look calm but assertive, holding the highest position of authority in the room but still easygoing and personable to all who gazed upon him. Giovanni stared, impressed. William took a few deep breaths, then turned to Giovanni and Vittoria. "You two ready?"

Giovanni looked down to his hands, his fingers fidgeting with each other. He felt the lingering euphoria of the chocolates clouding his anxiety, but they were unable to fully push it down, leaving him feeling lightheaded and detached but still antsy, very distant from the world even as his nerves remained, from his sister (who said something in return to Will's question, but he did not catch it), from the activity in front of the stage: Crew members setting up various equipment and getting the show ready for live broadcast, the crackle and hum of electricity as the cameras and lights and other electronics powered on. It felt like a nightmare. He shook his head as if hoping it would clear the saccharine mist, although he knew that sobriety would not feel any better.

Before Giovanni had the chance to muster a verbal response, the voice from the wing of the stage was calling out again.

Live in three...

...two...

...one.

Giovanni wondered if his father was going to be watching the show.

"Welllllll-cooooooome back, Fresno City! Folks, we're here with some very *sweet* guests today, and that is the two youngest children of the great Vittorio Marcello, CEO of none other than the great Marcello Candy Company, so stay tuned for that, because in *just* a second we'll be getting to know them, but as I'm sure all of the parents out there know, no matter how sweet the treat you've gotta have dinner before dessert, so FIRST on the menu today is a brief update on this morning's medical raid."

Vittoria listened to Will speak, his words spilling out in an endless torrent of quick, attention-grabbing jargon, hitting each syllable with the emphasis needed to draw in the viewers and keep them there. She could hardly follow it. Not when she knew that the cameras were on her, her time rapidly nearing. Still, she did her best to keep her eyes on him, refusing to look at Giovanni, not wanting to think about him and all of the many, many horrible things that he could say or do to ruin this for her. The knot in her stomach was worse than she had expected; she was no stranger to interviews and public appearances, but the whole of the situation did not sit right with her. Not just the presence of her brother, although that certainly was not helping, but the presence of her brother *in-law* as well.

Vittoria had known Will as a public figure before he had been an in-law: It was every young entrepreneur's dream to land an interview with him, to be publicly broadcast on Fresno TV with his name and face attached. She remembered the bad taste in her mouth when the news first broke that her sister would be marrying him; another of many reasons to dislike her. She remembered avoiding the engagement party and the wedding. She had never met the man until now, despite their strangely close relation, and she could not make sense of why he had agreed to do this interview. It felt surreal, incomprehensible. Here was William Baer, brother in-law and local celebrity, in all of his charismatic glory, hosting the interview that very well could make or break her future dreams, her career, her father's legacy, her father's opinions of... Her mind raced with the various possibilities and she tried her best to ignore them and stay focused.

"I'm sure you all saw my buddy Wolff on the news earlier, reporting the raid in real time. As of now Himmel's Birds of Prey have released a statement with more details on the situation. It'll be playing in its entirety on the overhead screens down on all major city streets over the course of the day, so tonight is a great night to go out shopping, check it out while you're crossing the street! The good news is that the car was headed *back* to the hospital to reload after making its morning rounds, so the loss isn't too extreme. The bad news is that the driver was killed, but lucky for us, the Birds made it over fast enough that most of the raiders, save for a few runners, were executed at the scene of the crime. So Good still has the upper hand in the end!

"No pun intended, but a little birdie told me that the folks down at Himmel Medicine have plans to issue out their own statement addressing the situation and ensuring us in detail that they are making big plans to put a stop to prescription car raids once and for all." Will continued to speak, and Vittoria had long since given up attempting to follow along, too focused on using all of her functional brain power, most of it drowning much too deep in a pool of anxiety to work at its fullest capacity, to run through the various things she intended to say once given the chance to speak. Right then, however, William's tone changed, and he sat up from his lounging position so suddenly that Vittoria flinched, her attention snapping back to him in an instant. "Buuuuuut enough on that! On the topic of Himmel Medicine, as you all know, the company recently announced an expansion into a whole new branch of medical procedures, the 'Experimental Cosmetics' department. Heading this branch of the company will be Dr. Giorgio Marcello, second oldest son of the great Vittorio Marcello, who himself is the esteemed CEO of Marcello Candies. This family is a gift that keeps on giving, aren't they? Well, my friends, I'm here with you today with a few more presents to unwrap." Vittoria's heart dropped. She swallowed as if trying to push it down further, if for no other reason than to try to find reprieve from the endless pounding in her chest.

William turned to the two siblings. "As I mentioned before, I'm here today with two *very* special guests, the two youngest kids of the man himself! That is, Giovanni Marcello and Vittoria Marcello, is that right?"

The moment seemed to come so suddenly that Vittoria was left in shock, her brain failing to move fast enough to supply words to her mouth. She parted her lips to speak, but before being given the chance, Giovanni interjected.

"*Ciao! Sì*, yes, that's right! I am Giovanni Marcello."

After a moment of silence in which neither William nor Giovanni said anything, Vittoria took her chance to add, "And I'm Vittoria." She brushed some hair from her face, clearing her vision of the darkness that she typically covered an eye with. "It's a pleasure, Baer."

"Great! Fantastic!" William marched on with his smooth voice and professional rambling, "Now, Giovanni, Vittoria, your father doesn't work *directly* in the medical industry, but he certainly has been a major competitor for a while now. With Dr. Marcello rising in ranks to a head of his own department, there are whispers that your family is looking to monopolize, or that one company will be subsidized into the other. So before we get off into the personal questions about the two of you, do either of you have any commentary on the state of the two companies? That you're allowed to share, of course. I'm sure the people out there are dying to hear from inside sources about the happenings within the Marcello household." He gave a good-natured, comically large wink, much more for the camera than for them.

"Ah-" Again, Giovanni made a noise to respond before Vittoria had the chance to. In fact, he spoke so quickly that Vittoria knew in an instant that he was not prepared to give a response. Her theory was proven correct by the way in which he stuttered, mouth hanging open like an imbecile, wordless for a moment. "I- I am, ah-" He glanced to Vittoria, rubbing his hands together. Amateur. She let out an exasperated breath. Why did Will even bother asking him anything? Why was he bothering to even try to answer? She shifted, wanting to interject but grudgingly allowing him a second chance to redeem himself when he finally opened his mouth to speak again. "I am... of course happy for Giorgio. I am sure he will do very- very well in his new role!"

Will raised an eyebrow with animated, intentional exaggeration, a caricature of an actual expression a human might make. "Is that all, Giovanni?" he asked. Vittoria was not sure if she should feel infuriated or relieved by the non-answer, but she was unsurprised nonetheless. Giovanni hardly *knew* Giorgio. She was certain of that, because *she* hardly knew him, either. He was their older sibling, but she could count on one hand the number of times he had actually interacted with her in her adult life, and Giovanni was not exactly getting out of the house more often than she. In fact, it seemed that beneath the rapidly cracking exterior he was attempting to form for the camera, he was unable to contain beneath the surface the fact that he spent nearly every day of his life cooped up in his bedroom. Whether this boded well for her remained to be seen.

Giovanni was still fumbling for a response. "I don't... I suppose I do not follow the news as closely as one may... assume. I do not even keep a television in my room." Vittoria wanted to roll her eyes, and it was only the thought of the cameras projecting her image onto the huge screens above Fresno City that kept her eyes fixed in place.

"I suppose you get all of the news you need directly from the man himself, being Vittorio Marcello's son," Will replied, clearly goading him on once more.

Giovanni looked clueless as ever. "Er- Well, the way I figure, I simply do not need to focus my energy on screens or words on a page to remind me of the ugliness and the horrors of the world. I would much rather spend my free time focusing on the beauty of the world's great pleasures."

"And where can these pleasures be found, Giovanni?" Will asked.

"Ah... My... my bed... sheets...?"

Vittoria could not tell if her face was hot with anger or humiliation.

"...Right." was Will Baer's response, with a tone that Vittoria could not entirely decipher, although it sounded one less of disgust and more of disappointment. Still, there was a light here, she thought, as she straightened herself up and drew in a breath. Her brother had done a fantastic job setting the stage for her, making himself so dim in comparison to her that she was guaranteed to shine. As if on cue, Will turned to her. "Well, what about you, Vittoria?"

Now was her chance to redeem the conversation after Giovanni had done his best to defile it. Vittoria cleared her throat, and when she spoke, her tone was clear and sophisticated, bubblier than usual, a voice she had developed from years of public appearances and advertising: "To be honest, William, although I am a Marcello, I don't tend to associate myself directly with my father and his business. Instead, I prioritize my own projects. I'm trying to make a name for myself as my *own* self, you know? Which is actually what I'm here to talk about today." That was a much better answer, she thought. It looked like she had her priorities straight: Priorities that were not distracted by the petty squabblings of her family's industry and instead put a spotlight on herself and her own, personal accomplishments.

But when William spoke again, instead of acknowledging her directly, he turned straight to the cameras and spoke to them. His tone remained unchanged from his reaction to Giovanni's response. "Well, I guess the youngest Marcello kids don't consider themselves too 'plugged in' to current events, eh?" He crossed his arms and looked back at Vittoria, whose lungs were starting to feel like punctured balloons. "So, Vittoria. You aren't interested in your father's business or the happenings in the medical industry, and the last time you made headlines it was announcing that you were selling your makeup line. So I'm sure all of the people at home are dying to know: Where does your heart really lie?"

Vittoria glanced to Giovanni and drew in another long, deep breath. Now was her chance. Clasping her hands together, she forced a wide smile, prying the sides of her dark lips upwards as she said, "Well, William, that's *exactly* what I was hoping to talk about today. As the public knows by now, I have always had a fascination with the arts, hence my dive into makeup, and fashion before that. I do not consider these projects failures, but simply experimentations, and my newest experimentation is one that leaves me the most thrilled I have ever been to finally be able to announce. One thousand ways not to build a lightbulb, right?" She paused for emphasis, wanting to make sure that the countless number of people watching across the city were given the time to process and prepare for her imminent proclamation. "I am dipping my toes into a brand-new pool of opportunity and looking to get involved in the music industry! I've contacted multiple record companies and am in the process of determining which contract best suits my goals." For just a moment between breaths, she thought back to the single, red-inked letter that sat on her nightstand. "It's been an exciting process. Music is very close to my heart; the raw emotion of it, the intimate connection one can establish with the singer, all of that. It hit me not too long ago that I'm pushing thirty, and I didn't want to live any longer without having fulfilled my real dreams. So I came here today because I wanted to make the public aware: Keep an ear out on the radio for Vittoria Marcello in the upcoming months!"

As her monologue came to its end, Vittoria breathed out a huff of air that had been trapped in tight, quivering lungs. *That* was what she had been practicing, night after night, as this interview drew nearer and nearer. That was what she needed to say. The word was out, now she just needed to commit to the rest. Having the chance to speak, she felt her muscles relax slightly, felt her breathing ease as a pressure left her chest. She had done this before; she knew what interviews and talk shows were like and this was no different... But then she glanced to Giovanni. His hand was in his pocket, and Vittoria remembered the candy he had scarfed down like an animal only moments before the show had gone live, and she struggled not to make a face as she felt the relief begin to dissipate like steam from boiling water. She swallowed, forced her smile to remain as it was, and looked to Will expectedly. Giovanni would not ruin this for her.

To her frustration, William replied to her words with nothing but a chuckle and a brief, dismissive, "Very nice, very nice," slicing through her relief and utterly decimating the sense of significance in her announcement in just a few short syllables. Then he turned to Giovanni. "Vittoria, we've seen you plenty of times between all of the various projects you've worked on in the past few years, but no one knows Giovanni beyond a few scattered appearances in advertisements for your dad's company. Can I ask you a few questions, Mister Marcello?"

"Oh! Of course!" Giovanni sounded as surprised as Vittoria. "Do ask away." Vittoria liked to imagine that maybe she had been *too* good. Maybe Will, slimy entertainer that he was, had been unable to make her out to be a fool, was unable to extract any sort of clever response and was thus forced to return to Giovanni, who was so very capable of making himself look like an idiot.

"So you're here with your sister today, and we've established that she's a relatively big name," William began, making Vittoria tense. She crossed her legs and gave what she hoped was a mature nod of agreement that masked that fact that every molecule in her body begged her to beg him to change the subject right here on live television. "Are you two close?"

Vittoria's heart stopped. Giovanni, clearly unable to help it, threw his head back and cackled. She probably would have done the same. "Little Vitta and me? No, no, not at all. I am seven years her senior; we hardly grew up in the same vicinity."

"But you both are the product of Vittorio's second marriage, is that right?"

"Vittoria must be proof that blood is not as thick as people enjoy to claim," Giovanni insisted, "While it is true that she is the only one of our siblings to which I share a mother, that has done little to improve our own closeness through the years. We are simply on separate paths, she and I, and there has not been a moment in which I have felt the need to rectify that." Vittoria instinctively found herself glancing to the camera, eyes darting to it only briefly, begging the audience to disregard whatever Giovanni may say. Not that she could deny his claims, but she certainly, perhaps more than anything else in the entire world, did not want Giovanni speaking for her. And yet he persisted: "And besides, if I want the presence of a woman in my life, there are *plenty* who serve a much more enjoyable purpose than anything dear Vitta could supply to me."

The panic levels had risen to Vittoria's throat, not only blocking her ability to breathe properly but making her feel utterly nauseous as well. She wanted to kill him. She wanted the audience to watch her brother get brutalized on live television and she wanted them to cheer for her as she did the deed.

William made the authoritative choice not to continue on with that conversation, and instead jump back to the previous comment, as he said, "I had a hunch you two might've grown up in pretty different worlds, considering you've got an accent and she doesn't. Did your father stop speaking Italian after your mother died?"

Vittoria watched, burning behind eyes that icily betrayed the heat of her anger, as Giovanni blinked, shook his head, then paused for a second long and suddenly gave a nod. The series of gestures made Vittoria roll her eyes and try, feebly, to remain calm, trying to accept the fact that whatever Giovanni had to say would be stupid, irrational, uninteresting and meaningless at best, harmlessly yet embarrassingly foolish at worst.

"Oh, well... not exactly," Giovanni began, looking at Vittoria briefly. Their eyes met and Vittoria looked away. "Vitta and I both, we grew up speaking both. Although I am more comfortable with English, I certainly have no trouble speaking in my family's native tongue. It's very romantic, I think." Giovanni had the gall to smile slightly at that and he pulled the long black hair he kept in a ponytail over his shoulder to run his fingers through it. "Since she was a teenager, however, Vitta has chosen to speak in a very boring accent, for reasons I do not know. You would have to ask her."

Giovanni made a sound that almost sounded like a giggle, or perhaps a hum. Was he getting comfortable with this? Did he enjoy this environment, now that he had been given the chance to humiliate her? she wondered, bewildered, blood running cold. She thought back to the tall buildings that pierced the sky outside, lined with dozens of windows;

how many of those windows led to rooms with televisions, tuned in to this right now? She remembered the screens that gazed down at the city streets for everyone and anyone to see.

Determined to fix this before it went any further, she sat up again and opened her mouth to defend herself. "I-"

But William was focusing on Giovanni, not her, and he only laughed at Giovanni's response as he replied, "Well, we do value authenticity here. But it sounds like Vittoria may have a rebuttal-"

"Enough about my little sister, William. I would much rather discuss myself," Giovanni interrupted. Vittoria could not even take this as a good sign, although she should have been happy that he was at least bored of insulting her. She had worked so hard and planned so long for this. Why did Giovanni have to be here? Even if all he spoke of from here on out was contrived, narcissistic bullshit, it was her career rapidly deteriorating with each passing moment, while his was nonexistent, and thus impervious to harm. She remained sitting up, on guard and alert, listening carefully to every word that was spoken.

She would not let him ruin this.

"Alright, sure, enough about Vittoria, we can get back to her in a minute. Giovanni, why choose *now* to come onto our show and introduce yourself to the people? What are you up to right now?"

"He already answered that," Vittoria said, ignoring Giovanni, who had clearly been opening his mouth in preparation to give an answer. "He said he's lying in his bed and having sex or whatever."

William and Giovanni both turned to her in surprise, but Vittoria was pleased with the silence that followed, feeling a sense of relief that it had at least shut her brother up for a moment. She did not notice that her nails were digging into the flesh of her palms again, too distracted by the adrenaline of the cameras pointed at her and her desperation to salvage the situation to care about or even process the pain.

It was Giovanni who finally broke the silence. "Okay, Vittoria," he began, a new tone in his voice. He looked at her, staring out from his colorful clown makeup, expression masked by layer upon layer of glittery paint but eyes burning with an intensity that she knew well from her own. "I meant to ask you before, but I supposed that if you are so eager to answer questions, then I will ask now." He crossed his arms. "If you are so keen on refusing anything to do with Papa and his company, why are you using his money and name to be on this show right now?"

The question hit a nerve in Vittoria like a truck slamming into a glass window and she felt all at once like her world had shattered in front of her. The panic that had been slowly building within her, piling up on top of itself and stuffing her throat and lungs and threatening to burst from every orifice, immediately shrank down, shrinking itself and turning itself inside-out until a massive, empty hole filled her and she felt numb as she tried to comprehend the question, numb to the burning of her cheeks beneath her makeup and the tremble of her hands as her nails cut through her own raw skin, numb to the nausea caused by Giovanni's cologne. Numb even to the cameras that gazed at her, that presented the question, taunting on Giovanni's pretty, plump, painted lips to however many thousands of people across the city were watching right now.

"Shut the fuck up, Giovanni." Vittoria's voice was cold. "Shut your stupid mouth for five goddamn seconds and try for once in your fucking life to be something other than a stupid junkie bitch who gets in people's fucking way."

"Vitta-"

"Stop calling me by a stupid pet name like I'm a fucking child. I have a full goddamn name and you can spend an extra fucking second to say it. Or is your tongue too fucking fat from your candies?"

"Shut up about the candies!" Giovanni hissed, grabbing her arm, which she quickly tugged away and scowled at him.

"Couldn't go a goddamn hour without shoving it down your throat like a pig-"

"Shut *up*, Vitta-"

"I fucking told you, it's-"

"VITTORIA."

A voice cut through Giovanni and Vittoria's squabbling, deep and loud and imposing, echoing and reverberating through the recording studio. Both siblings went still, frozen solid, recognizing the speaker in an instant. In less than an instant. The studio went silent. William Baer did not say a word. Vittoria could not so much as hear Giovanni breathe, and she, too, caught herself holding her breath, eyes wide, her mind in a state of such disbelief that it could not function enough to work together with her body to move even a single muscle.

Vittorio Marcello, CEO of the beloved Marcello Candy Company, tall and stately, face devoid of expression, walked from the wing of the stage out to face his two youngest children.

"Cut." Vittorio said calmly, but the anger in his voice was apparent. "I do not think we need to go any further." Every light turned on, the hum of machinery died down, and at once they were all just people on a stage in a grand, empty room. He turned to William. "Thank you, Will, for taking the time out of your busy schedule to waste it on this. You of course will be paid generously."

"Hope I didn't haze 'em too hard, Papa V." William gave one of his good-natured smiles and charismatic laughs.

Vittoria stared at her father in shock, half certain she was dreaming. What little ability to form coherent thought she still had was not enough for her to wrap her mind around the situation. Endless questions churned through her brain but were beaten to a bloody pulp by the slamming of her heart in her chest and ears before they could leave her mouth.

Giovanni, however, seemed to find his voice quicker, for he cried, "Papa! Vittoria, she-"

"Enough, Giovanni. You have not done any more to make me proud than your sister." Vittorio said in an instant, raising a hand to Giovanni. "I do not want to hear excuses."

Before she knew what she was saying, Vittoria spoke out suddenly: "How do you call cut on a live interview?"

As surprised as she was by her own ability to speak out at a time like this, Vittoria was even more surprised by how instantly she recoiled, shrinking back when Vittorio turned to look at her, dark eyes locking onto her face and staying there. "That was a lie," he said plainly. "We were recording the footage in hopes of broadcasting it later, chalk it up to a networking error and claim there was a slight delay. Did you really believe that I would trust either of you to handle this? To handle the way the public views my name? Your family name? Times are changing, and I have a business to run. And I will not let your siblings' careers or the future of my company be tarnished by inconsiderate brats."

"I- I've done interviews before, Dad. I've been- I've never caused trouble. I've been out in the world. I've been successful. I'm not like Giovanni." As Vittoria's words left her mouth they felt finalizing; a final, despairing plea, her first and last words to God Himself on Judgment Day.

"Successful? What have you to show for these interviews, Vittoria? What have you done of any worth, for me or for yourself?" Vittorio's voice was raising, louder and angrier, his eyes wide with fury between the cracks of age in his flesh. "Tell me. Give me a reason that you deserve my pride. Selfish, greedy, stupid children. What have you done—what have either of you done—to make you worthy of my name? Of my fatherhood?"

Vittoria was silent. The numbness from before had returned, but with it came a different emotion, a sort of empty despair with which there was nothing she could say or do, from which there was no point in even attempting to escape. There was no point in trying to do anything. Nothing was left. From the corner of her eye she saw Giovanni, and she could tell that he, too, was rigid, unmoving, but she could not bring herself to turn, could not look at his face to know his expression. Just the thought of his face disgusted her.

"I prayed to God that my lack of faith in the both of you could be proven wrong," Vittorio said, when neither Giovanni nor Vittoria found it within themselves to reply to him. "Do you think I asked for children who could not so much as try to put forth the most minimal of efforts? Who could not be bothered to even attempt to display any care, any thought at all? Do you think I wanted children who bring me nothing but shame and failure, again and again *and again*? I prayed to God that you would prove today that you were capable of being something, but it seems that even God cannot save you."

# ACT II

## A Note on Fresno Fashion: Accents

First impressions are everything! Secondary only to the clothing one wears, there are few stronger ways to promise intrigue, a guarantee of secret, an elusive background that differs from the homogeneity of Fresno daily life, than to wear an accent on one's tongue. In the past decade, it has become an increasingly popular trend across all economic groups to adopt an accent, if unlucky enough to have not been born into a family already possessing one. They add a hint of spice to the monotony of one's daily life across all classes of society, from sparking interest at business parties to bringing out an exotic, seductive allure in escorts.

Those with the privilege of possessing an accent naturally, such as the romantic Italian found on the tongue of the Marcello family, have taken to retaining as much of their family's accent as possible. Reportedly, some parents have begun raising children with accents they themselves do not naturally possess, in hopes of influencing a natural accent to occur down the line of future generations, inserted like rogue DNA into the bloodline. Speech therapists have become an increasingly sought after commodity, and an anonymous source from within Himmel's walls has stated that there is talk in the neurology department of finding a way to directly interact with, modify, and rewire the speaking and language center of the brain, inserting accents of choice retroactively into those wealthy enough to afford it, although this is certainly something of a distant goal still lacking a significant portion of the technological progress needed to make a reality, for the time being.

Of course, like all fashion trends, there are caveats. To be worth anything, an accent must flow but not hinder; should English be unintelligible, the accent is rendered useless. European accents and dialects certainly tend to fare better in upper class settings, and even then, not all accents will be perceived as equal. Dialects in general, very different from a true *accent*, are risky business. The wrong dialect will come across as nothing but dirtied English, something much more low class. And speech impediments may fare even worse. It is heavily recommended that in these latter cases, a speech therapist be called upon... Until Himmel finds a better solution.

When Vittoria was young, she had tried to run away.

With her father so very busy and no mother to speak of, with her being the youngest of eight siblings, with an age gap of seven years between her and the sibling whose age was closest to her own, it was not difficult to sneak away when nobody was looking. Few people ever looked. What began as daring escapades to the great big garden out back, where she would wander for eternity amongst the flowers, feeling very small in comparison to the ocean of flora around her, soon, by the time she was barely five, turned into the much more dangerous undertaking of sneaking out to the front of the house, down the steps, across the pavement until she had reached the tall hedges that loomed over her, unfathomably tall to a child, fencing her in.

Or so they tried. There was a button, high above Vittoria's small head, that could be pressed for exit, to make the big metal bars that kept her gated in open up and allow her freedom. But the button was too tall for a child her size to reach.

Still, Vittoria was young and determined, and, after much shoving and wriggling, managed to squeeze her little body through the bars of the gate, and then she was, all at once and surprisingly easily, no longer confined to her father's estate. Button be damned.

Aimless and too young to be aware of the many dangers that the outside world presented to a child, Vittoria wandered down the hill on which her father's mansion sat atop and into the rich suburbia below. But to her, the houses were strikingly small; two or three stories seemed like nothing to her eyes, so adjusted to the grandeur of her father's wealth, and she wandered down the street paying little heed to the neighborhood.

Too young for time to mean much to her, and with the absurd amount of energy bestowed upon ambitious children, Vittoria spent a great deal of time wandering at her own pace through the streets, exploring without direction or fear, wandering through the pristine and colorful lawns of distant neighbors. It was at some point that she came upon a park that she finally stopped, as if she had reached a destination that she had not known she was seeking.

Fresno was not a particularly green city; the dryness of the air and what was left of the natural nutrients in the soil caused the ground and the wildlife that sprung from it to remain a dull tan for most of the year, and it took a great deal of water to keep any sort of brightness. The majority of the local flora that had any green in it at all was a sickly pale color, or a dark color that was nearly black. Bright, vibrant green was rarely a sight to behold within the plant life of the city aside from on wealthy lawns, and even then often sparingly. The little water that did exist naturally had long since been privatized, and as she stood facing the vibrant green sprawled out before her, Vittoria was too young to recognize the sign of man's interference with nature—but even she could sense how striking the sight of the luscious, bright landscape was against the dry Fresno background. Dark, rich green grass spread out like a regal carpet, tall trees loomed over her and cast great shadows on the shrubs and bushes and the little sparrows and pigeons that hopped around, shading the ground from the overbearing sun. She followed the pigeons, chasing after them and watching as they flew away, and then grew bored of that and wandered some more, eyes upwards on the branches and leaves that blanketed over the bright blue sky. Although still in the heart of the suburbs, here she felt freer than she ever had before.

But this could not last, for soon the outside world punctured through the bubble of peace she had found. It was as she was exploring the edges of a small, muddy pond that many men, tall, in dark uniforms, came running to her. They spoke into handheld devices, out of which emitted voices that sounded distorted and inhuman. Vittoria was grabbed by large, gloved hands and held tight, tight enough that it hurt her ribs and chest and she yelped in surprise and pushed back against her captor, but they were much stronger than she, and all she received in return, far from the dignity her little self was demanding, was a hand covering her mouth.

"We found her," a voice said, and another chimed in with, "Are you sure that's her?" and another still, "*Shit,* that's a long walk for a kid." The conversations continued on, voices made of radio static buzzing through the devices and the voices of the men, deep and aggressive and rough, back and forth, saying things she could hardly understand as they trapped her in overpowering arms.

The one that held her tight said, "Your father has been looking for you."

And indeed he had. Vittoria was driven home in a small, dark car. She remained silent, even when questioned, and she kept her eyes on the park as they drove away, watching as the greenery shrunk into the background and the tall hedges of her father's mansion at the top of the hill grew taller as they approached, shooting upwards into the skyline. She was dropped off at the door, and the pleasant smile and earnest thank yous that her father gave the dark men quickly dissipated as they left. Vittoria was scolded and punished, was not fed dinner that evening, told that she could not leave her room for the following week unless accompanied by an adult, and warned that the consequences for running off would be much more severe in the future, should she dare try again.

Soon enough Vittoria found a second taste of freedom in the form of school. Like most of her siblings, she attended an elite private school, and her peers were the children of only the wealthiest upper-class citizens. Still, as she matured and developed the first inklings of self-awareness, the urge to run returned to her twofold, too strong to ignore, and she found herself keen on skipping classes, sneaking out and spending the day in the city, wandering the streets as a dark, ghostly presence, too young to be recognized yet for the status behind her family name and thus avoided by most. But it took little time for her father to be made aware of her truancy, and her father kept true to his word: She was taken out of school for the remainder of the year, a horrific time that she dare not recall, watched over by her older brothers and punished swiftly and harshly for failing to stay focused on her schoolwork, barred from leaving the house. When the new school year began, she was given a second chance, told that she could return to private school and prove herself responsible, or else wind up permanently homeschooled like her brother, an idea so deeply horrifying that she was eager to swear on her life that she would stay put and not wander too far from school grounds.

And this time Vittoria kept her word. Without physical escape she turned to music, and to art, and to the freedom of the thrill of creation that could not be taken from her. And her curiosity of the world outside of the tall hedges around her father's house was satiated, just barely, by her time spent at school, where she flourished. And in the back of her mind, even as she aged and matured and became increasingly aware of the fact that in Fresno it was only the most extravagantly wealthy and elite of places, controlled carefully by sprinklers and pesticides, artificial entirely in its nurturing, guarded heavily to keep the lower classes out, that could ever possibly be so very green and alive, and that her conception of it as a place of freedom and solitude was a myth, she remembered vividly the lush green park she had reached the day she had, if only briefly, escaped.

Vittoria dragged heavy feet in heavy boots up the stairs to her bedroom. She had not said a word to her father or brother on the drive back from the recording studio, and remained silent as she left them in the entryway, and neither had spoken up to stop her departure. Now her throat felt thick, as if not speaking for all that time had left a buildup of plaque. This did nothing to prevent the feeling of emptiness within her, however, body and mind exhausted to the point that she felt incapable of producing so much as a proper emotional reaction to the events that had just transpired. And the emptiness did nothing to hamper the sensation of lead weights in her feet, and the hallway to her bedroom felt very, very long.

The darkness of her room, with its black walls and drawn curtains and sleek, dark furniture, helped ease a headache she had hardly even noticed, but the eyes of the many portraits, a sea of colors that ranged from icy silver to electric blue, stared down at her from all around the room, and, dizzy as she was, she felt infinitesimally small, with only her two eyes against the dozens that littered the walls of the bedroom. Although she did not even bother to take off her shoes as she climbed into bed, she did stop by the drawer with her records and grab one, any one, whatever first reached her fingertips. She put it on and turned it up to full volume before it even began, not caring what the music was so long as it drowned out everything as effectively as the black curtains covered the overbearing afternoon sunshine.

She pulled her blanket up past her eyes, craving more darkness than even the black wallpaper could provide, desperate to escape the gaze of her portraits. If they were meant to be a depiction of her at her best, brought to life with the intentionality and soul of an artist, they must have looked at her now with such bitter disappointment.

As Vittoria pressed her face against her pillow she could feel the foundation rub uncomfortably, could feel the way her eyeshadow smudged and stained and her eyeliner smeared, but she could not bring herself to care. Worn makeup and heavy shoes that constricted and weighed on her feet could hardly rival the discomfort that ran much deeper, straight into the hollow pit of her stomach.

Although it was only midday, with the curtains drawn it was as good as night, and soon Vittoria had fallen into a dreamless, vacuous sleep.

Giovanni watched as his birds fluttered about in their little golden cage, snow white feathers glowing in the sunlight. He was entranced by them, by the way their feathers ruffled and fluffed up and the way they blinked their big, black eyes that sparkled with life in spite of their darkness. The way they interacted with one another, pecking at each other and chirping back and forth, and the way they hopped from perch to perch, into little trays of water where they splashed about in the sparkling artificial spring, all enthralled him so.

He adored them, and he was so fixated on them that he was unbothered, briefly, by the heat of the outdoors that had only grown heavier over the city as the day wore on. So transfixed on the birds was he that even his candies sat idle in his pocket, untouched, his tongue at rest in his mouth for once rather than instinctively seeking the sweets that he so often indulged in.

Giovanni still remembered very clearly his first encounter with birds. Or, rather, perhaps he had *seen* them earlier, pigeons on rooftops or flocks of geese flying through the sky at dusk, but it was not until he was about four or five that he could vividly remember truly acknowledging their existence. Back in those days his mother had taken him out frequently. His father's presence was nothing but the traces of a shadow, dark and foreboding, looming over the house for the majority of his early life, but his mother took him with her on expeditions out of the house as frequently as she could. One frequent destination was the park a few neighborhoods away, and that was where Giovanni had first become acquainted with birds.

Giovanni was not particularly fond of the outdoors. He disliked the unpredictability of the weather, the way that days could begin at sixty degrees and quickly rocket to eighty, he disliked the dirt and the bugs and the messiness of it all, and even as he watched his birds, it was with a vague sense of awareness that he was without control of the heat, that there were no air conditioners around to cool him and in this warmth he would eventually begin sweating, causing his makeup to grow oily and smear down his face. Flowers he enjoyed, but he much preferred them in vases, kept bright and beautiful in ornate containers, than stuck up in the mud, where they wilted fast and were eaten alive by insects.

But that had not always been the case. The first time his mother had taken him to the park, Giovanni, through the eyes of a child who had very little experience outside the walls of his home, found it strange and foreign. Threatening, even. He clung to her hand, unwilling to explore as she had insisted.

She had sat down then, right on the grass. Giovanni still shuddered to imagine it; the thought of staining his pants with mud and grass was utterly abhorrent. The park, kept green and pristine in spite of the dryness and the heat that loomed so heavily over the city, was in a state of constant dampness. Sprinklers lay scattered about, hidden near trees and in bushes, a vague attempt at hiding the artificiality of the foliage's lusciousness.

So he sat on her lap. Giovanni did not remember the details, it had been so long ago and he had struggled, still, with understanding words, but she had spoken to him, and he remembered the tone of her voice, and he remembered the way she had pointed out various birds as she spotted them: A crow perched in a tree, a duck waddling by the bank of the pond, a pigeon pecking at the grass. Giovanni watched each one, studying them as he sat against his mother, admiring their pretty feathers, and finally letting out a soft gasp of awe as they took off into the air. His joy at the birds had encouraged his mother to return to the park with him on numerous occasions, eventually bringing crumbs and seeds for the birds so that Giovanni, braver as he had grown more comfortable, could run to them and toss food at them with tiny hands and watch as ducks and pigeons flocked to it.

The park became a magical place for Giovanni, full of wonder, safe and secluded from his home and his father, where just he and his mother existed with the birds. And when he received his first pair of birds, two little zebra finches with round, orange cheeks that flitted around in their cage like dainty fairies, it had been as if he had managed to capture that magic in a way, and brought the marvelous essence of the park into his father's cold, lonely house.

Of course, Giovanni had learned quickly there was much more to pet ownership than the magic of watching the wild city birds strut and fly about. The inhabitants of the golden cage had been replaced numerous times over the years, and, most recently, it had become home to a trio of white doves—Originally four, but Giovanni had had to end the life of one early on. A mercy killing, of course. It had been sick from day one of its adoption, and the amount of scars and calluses that had begun to form along Giovanni's fingers from its incessant pecks and scratches when he had tried to nurse it to health had been indication enough that it was far too miserable... Giovanni was unphased by it all now. He remembered in the early days, when his father had first agreed to allow him to take up bird ownership, when one began to show signs of illness or injury, when feathers grew sparser, patches of pale skin revealed, wings began to jut uncomfortably from where they typically rested, when it became harder for it to walk, fly, or feed itself, he had struggled a great deal with the grief, the guilt, and what he was meant to do about it.

"The owning of animals is a lesson in taking responsibility," his father had told him, when he had come to him, distraught, eyes welled up in tears for the pretty thing flapping about helplessly at the bottom of the cage, fallen feathers scattered around it, too weak to even flit up to its water bowl. And so Giovanni had learned to do just so—snapping the necks of the miserable creatures to free them of their suffering.

Giovanni did not go to the park anymore. After his mother's death he did not leave the house very much at all, and the park of all places was the last location he could imagine wanting to spend any time. Not when the grass was wet and the mud beneath even wetter, a serious threat to his fine clothing, and worms and bugs crawled and writhed, and the heat bore down through the trees until his makeup seeped into his baking pores.

In fact, it was getting warm now, and Giovanni could feel his makeup becoming moist and heavy on his face. And so he stood, calculating what his chances were of getting through the mansion to his bedroom without running into his father, and walked through the garden, past the bright, colorful blossoms that beamed up at him, leaving the birds behind to flit about in the heat, and as he made it to the door he reached into his pocket to find the remainder of his candy.

On the way up to his room, Giovanni bumped into a young woman clutching a handful of letters. She was simple looking but pretty, a servant girl with plain clothing and long brown hair, her skin tan and freckled. Plain indeed, but she had a skittishness to her and she all but trembled when she looked up to Giovanni's face, tensing as the realization seemed to dawn on her that it was one of the Marcellos whom she had run into so carelessly. A flurry of apologies began to rush from her lips.

"I'm- I'm just delivering mail to Mistress Marcello, sir-" she explained, her tone a plea for forgiveness.

Giovanni rolled the candy under his tongue so as not to inhibit his speaking, and his painted lips curled into a smile. "I had wondered why you were so nervous, dear little one, but if you work for my cruel little sister then I suppose that that is the answer to my question, mm?" He reached out to her. His nails, long and glittery, traced gently down her jawline to rest on her chin. The girl's face turned pink and Giovanni snorted in amusement. "I can only imagine how miserable of a job that must be. I would surely go mad from it myself."

"Ah, no, no, Mister Marcello. I'm fine, really." She took a step back now and shook her head, holding the letters tighter to her chest. "I'm just doing my job."

"Papa has plenty of other servants willing to answer to my sister's every whim, dear," Giovanni cooed. He reached out again and took hold of the letters in the girl's hands. "I think you will find what I need of you to be much more satisfying of a job to complete, anyhow." Vittoria could wait.

The girl's grip on the letters weakened; she was not going to play tug of war with her boss' son. Giovanni took the mail and set it down on the floor, against the wall. Someone would find them and deliver them in due time. There truly were plenty of other servants who would undoubtedly stumble upon them.

"And I won't get in trouble?" the girl asked.

Giovanni smiled again. They always asked that. "No, no, lovely," he reassured her, taking hold of her now-freed hand. He brought it to his mouth and kissed the back of it, staining it in bright, sticky lipstick. "Come now, follow me." He turned down the hallway and tugged her along with him, and she followed silently, willingly dragged along, her eyes wide and her lips parted, towards his bedroom.

Just as the sun was beginning to set on the city, Vittoria was woken by a knock at her door. She had not eaten anything today, a fact she was only aware of due to the dull, empty ache in her stomach. For a moment the sensation of her brain slowly rebooting after her long nap made her disoriented and fuzzied her memories, leaving her unable to recollect the events that had transpired earlier but still vaguely aware of the nauseous dread thick in her stomach and coursing through her veins like sludge.

"What is it?" she called out, stifling a yawn, reaching to turn off her record player, as it was still blaring music on repeat through the room. Most dwellers of the Marcello estate knew at this point to knock nice and loud if they hoped to be heard from within.

"Uhm, mail for you, Mistress," a man's voice came calling back. "It was out in the Western corridor, just... on the floor. I wanted to make sure it had been delivered to you."

Vittoria's brow furrowed. "It hadn't," she said. She stood, reluctantly, knowing she was a sight to behold, with worn makeup that had rubbed and smeared against her pillow, hair a mess from sleeping on it, her nice interview-ready outfit still on, now unkempt and slept in, heavy boots still compressing her aching feet. She combed her nails through her hair and reached to flip the light switch and bring some brightness to her dark chambers. Then she opened the door to find a man standing with a small pile of mail in his hands. "You found this in the hallway?" She took the stack of envelopes from him and skimmed over them; they were indeed addressed to her.

"Yes, Mistress. I suppose whoever was assigned to deliver them got caught up in something else," he said, and he took a step back, as if hoping to sneak away.

Vittoria, noticing this movement, glanced up to him. "Fantastic," she drawled, "Find whoever was responsible for delivering my mail and see if you can have them fired." She shut the door without another word and walked back to her bed. The mail of the day was all, unsurprisingly, entirely useless to her, information about various projects of hers that she had begun and given up long ago but continued to be periodically updated on, either from those who had bought the projects from her or from the company employees that her father had hired to continue them on in her name until they were worth enough to sell properly.

Briefly, as she stared between the various letters, each one as meaningless to her as the next, she envisioned a future for her music career that careened down a similar path, and her stomach grew tight. Her brother's absolutely nuclear obliteration of the interview still weighed heavy on her mind; she had not even had the chance to get her name out yet. Would she, in a year, be gathering her mail to find measly checks of the royalties she was owed for one EP that never charted? Would she be planning her next career move by scripting her apologies and excuses for why this, too, had not been seen to the end? How much more money would she have to take from her father, how much more would he be willing to give? Vittoria crumpled up one of the letters and tossed it to the bed, feeling a lump in her throat which she could not differentiate between nausea and the faint urge to cry, a compulsion to which she absolutely would not give in.

Symbols of failure scattered across her bed, she walked over to the drawer at her bedside table and pulled it open. There sat Anubis' letter, kept safely tucked away in its envelope. She picked it up, pulling it out and skimming over it once more, swallowing thickly to keep emotions down.

Vittoria had hardly had the chance to make it halfway down the page, rereading the alluring writing, eloquent and so delicately worded, words she could sink into and drown in were she not careful, especially after a day such as today when drowning seemed like a much more appealing fate than whatever it was the future held for her, when the phone rang— A servant calling to ask her some stupid question, she figured. Perhaps they had caught the bitch who had thrown her letters on the ground.

"What do you want?"

"Vittoria."

"Dad?" Vittoria nearly had a heart attack. She sucked in a breath and held it there, frozen, hands clutching tight around the letter.

Vittorio's voice was appropriately cold on the other end of the line. "Vittoria, come downstairs to the banquet hall. I must speak with you and your brother immediately."

Vittoria remained still. She had not spoken with her father since the disaster earlier and she had a dreadful sense in the pit of her stomach that this would be a follow-up, perhaps some sort of consequence he had decided upon.

"Vittoria, did you hear me?"

Vittoria jumped, the phone nearly slipping from her grasp. "Sorry, sorry, I- I'll be right down."

She hung up at that, instinctive and panic-driven, not wanting to allow her father to get another word in. She glanced down to Anubis' letter still in her hand. Dread mounting in her with each passing moment and seemingly fogging her thoughts even more, she lingered in her room a bit longer, delaying going downstairs for as long as she possibly could. Her eyes scanned over her paintings, one by one. *You are a canvas.*

Vittoria went to set the letter down on the table, and as she did so her fingertips brushed against the hard backing of the business card, still attached by adhesive to the back side. She pulled it off now, and stuck it into her pocket. She then walked to the door.

She took one last glance around the room, eyes making contact with the striking electric silver eye that one particular artist had depicted her with. She was fond of the colors of this portrait; there was a reason she had placed it carefully so that it was easily visible the moment she entered her bedroom. The paint was thick, layered on in heavy strokes that stood out in three dimensions on the canvas. Her hair swept down over her face in textured waves of black paint. She left the room.

Down the hallway and staircases Vittoria descended until she had made it to the first floor. She hated the weight that had formed in her stomach; it grew heavier and heavier with each step she took, weighing down in the very pit of her core, begging her to remain still rather than trudge onward, forcing unwilling limbs towards their destination; she felt like a child, and there was a part of her that begged to run away. But she knew that she had nowhere to run. Her father was waiting.

"Vitta is coming!" Vittoria heard her brother call from the banquet hall as she approached. She could see the glittering purple of his scarf. He was standing right by the door.

As Vittoria entered, she was immediately assaulted by the sickening stench of her brother's cologne. He was watching her with an anxious look on his face, and as she walked up to him he did not say a word. This was peculiar and immediately amplified the uneasiness in Vittoria's stomach, as Giovanni was not typically reserved. For a brief moment she was so distracted by her brother's rare reticence and his strangely wide, expressionless eyes that she failed to notice her father's presence at all.

The banquet hall was a grand room, a striking contrast to the quaint family kitchen with the little dining room table. This room was connected to the main kitchen, and, should the occasion require it, could fit at least fifty people. Comfortable but elegant like a hunting lodge, the room was dark and warm in its tone, implicitly suggesting a fireplace that did not exist, with wooden walls. A long table stretched from one end of the room to the other, and above hung a chandelier, a complex-looking, intricately patterned golden item that bathed the room in the light of faux candles. Vittorio sat, silently, in one of the chairs, and that was part of what had made Vittoria miss that he was there: He was not at the head of the table, or the very center à la Christ in Da Vinci's Last Supper, both places that he would sit depending on the evening and which guests he was currently entertaining. Rather, he sat off to the side, in a lone seat that was neither in the center or at the head, inconspicuous among dozens of empty seats. His head was down, he stared at the empty placemat before him as if he had just been served something rotten.

"What's going on?" Vittoria asked, and in the silence of the great room her voice echoed much larger than herself.

Giovanni winced. "Papa said he would not speak until you had arrived."

He was still much more subdued than usual. Vittoria looked to her father again. He was still silent and unmoving, save for the subtle rise and fall of his shoulders with his breathing, which was slow and calm.

Not liking any of this, Vittoria mumbled, attempting to keep her voice quieter so as not to make the same disturbance as before, "Well, clearly he talked to you, if you know that."

"That's all he said!" Giovanni insisted, voice rising a little.

Vittoria was beginning to feel very helpless, but she did not dare say a word to her father. Instead, she continued to desperately attempt to rely on her brother, although she was keenly aware that this had never worked in her favor before. "What's happening, Giovanni?" she asked, tone sharper, hissing out the words through her teeth in an attempt not to snap.

"I don't *know*, Vittoria!" Giovanni broke before she did. No longer able to stifle his emotions, his voice came out loud but weak, cracking between syllables, on the verge of shattering completely. The pathetic wail of a response echoed horribly around the room and Vittoria grimaced and fought the urge to cover her ears. The only thing that stopped was her father, who, without warning, stood and turned to face his children.

Giovanni took a step back as Vittorio walked over to him and his sister. He felt very, very small before his father—He imagined he felt not unlike the way a cockroach must feel when it scattered in a hurried panic before a human, fearing that it would be crushed beneath a foot more massive than its insect brain could even comprehend.

"This world... is a terrible place," Vittorio stated, and despite the deep regality always present in his voice, the powerful, overwhelming confidence in which he said every word, his tone was very plain, as if he were doing nothing but recounting the morning news. "Human beings are a greedy, selfish species, far too stupid to care for themselves, much less each other. There is little hope for any of us, I believe."

The silence that followed these words was deafening. Giovanni reached up to fidget with a dangling earring, tapping long, stiletto nails against it and letting it quiver where it hung, a distraction from the awareness of his inability to form a response as his father gazed at him.

"You both represent the lowest form of humanity," Vittorio continued on, tone unchanging. Giovanni saw Vittoria move in the corner of his eye, but he did not look at her. His eyes traveled down to his shoes. Vittorio continued to speak. "Right now, the economic state of this city is changing rapidly. Small businesses are crumbling, even great ones that have stood firm as strongholds in the fight for survival have succumbed to the power that companies such as Himmel exert onto them. Marcello Candies has thrived, but it cannot continue to do so on its own for much longer. I fear the shifting tide does not promise change for the better should this family not jump into the sea of progress and learn to swim alongside its strong currents." He let out a sigh and wrung his hands, and the first change of expression since he had begun speaking crossed his face now. Giovanni thought he looked like he was mourning a loved one, although he had never seen his father do such a thing before for comparison.

However, when Vittorio spoke again, his tone was entirely different than the somber quietude he had displayed a moment prior. It was cold, angry, and Giovanni flinched instinctively at it, already aware through years of experience that it was a tone of accusation and punishment. "I have fought long and hard to be where I am now. I have worked my entire life to build from the rubble left behind by my parents in order to provide a home for the two of you and your siblings, who are far more deserving, I must say. Even your bastard sister has risen into power and made herself a worthy heir with her connections within the media. And now your brother Giorgio has made a name for himself with one of the strongest players in Fresno's economy. With the power he alone holds our family could continue to thrive. And yet you two... You have done nothing but prove yourselves, time after time after time, to be nothing but disappointments, not only to me but to your blood. *Our* blood. The blood of the Marcello family which so undeservedly runs in your veins." He turned to Giovanni then, looking directly at him. Giovanni could feel his lungs tremble as he struggled to take in a breath. "I did everything that I possibly could for you. I was a single father with a company and seven other mouths to feed and I paid more than your stupid brain could even comprehend to get you the help that you needed and it all went to waste. You're a useless embarrassment, and you have served no purpose to me in your decades of life than taking space in the home I have built around your fat body. And *you*."

He turned to Vittoria. Giovanni said nothing.

"At the very least your brother has the excuse of being a hopeless halfwit. Despite the fact that you came into this world with a trail of death behind you, you showed potential success. You were a clever girl and you had ambition, but alas, again and again you prove incapable."

Vittoria was frozen where she stood, fully stunned to silence for once. Giovanni tried to feel some sort of relief or comfort in the fact that his sister was being chewed out alongside him, that he was not facing the brunt of his father's wrath alone (especially considering the fact that so much of the disastrous occurrence that morning had so blatantly been her fault). Still, it was hard to fight back the mounting sense of dread building in his chest, an agonizing, panicked tightness that he could hardly keep down. He had been berated by his father before, but this felt different, more severe, more final...

Stammering, eyes wide and mouth half open as her tongue seemed to struggle to find words, Vittoria finally said, "In- Incapable of what, Dad?"

"*EVERYTHING*, Vittoria. Name something you have done. Something you have to show for your twenty-seven years on this Earth. *Anything*. I paid out of pocket for your education and you could not even last a year. I helped you with each new startup, believed each assurance that this new project would work, that you would succeed at makeup, at fashion, at jewelry, at perfume, at *anything*. I waited, praying that you would show that spark that Marcellos hide behind their eyes. But I see now that both you and your brother are too dim, to your cores."

Vittorio looked between his two children with his lips tight, the cracks of age on his face more prominent than before. Neither sibling said a thing. Giovanni could not find it in himself to take any amusement from the berating of his sister, something that may have been very funny indeed in a different scenario. But not now. Not with his father towering before him, exerting the full force of his sheerest disappointment onto the both of them. "I refuse to waste money and resources on pathetic, useless children. If the city crumbles, I will make sure that my company, my family, and my name, is standing proud and tall in the ruins. Your brother promises that. You two do not, and that is, to be succinct, a very big problem." Vittorio sighed. "I will be blunt. I no longer want either of you in my home. Effective immediately."

"What?"

Vittoria spoke first, before Giovanni was even able to process what Vittorio meant, and the loud, indignant, panic-stricken cry of her tone made him turn to look at her. The fear that had broken through her cold facade was apparent.

"Everything you own is rightfully mine. The money I have spent on you far outweighs anything you have contributed financially to your own life or this household. And besides, I have seen your rooms, they hold nothing but junk. You have thirty minutes to exit my estate, and what you do not bring on your person will be promptly discarded. If you are on my property for any longer than that, I will call the Falconiformes and see to it that they deal with you as they would any other trespasser."

Giovanni was finding it difficult to make sense of his father's words, and he looked to Vittoria as if hoping she could translate for him, although he knew by now better than to rely on her for anything. She clearly had comprehended what he was unable, for the look on her face was one he had never seen before. She looked terrified, and yet her features were not exaggerated; there were no raised brows or wide eyes, no jaw dropped in horror, but something more subtle on the tense lines of her face told Giovanni that something was very, very wrong.

"Dad, you- you can't-" Vittoria shook her head so violently that her hair whipped about her head and caught on Giovanni's shoulder. He took a step away from her. "You can't do this to me, not this... not this fast. Give me a month- a- a *week*, even. Give me time."

"I have given you twenty-seven years worth of time, Vittoria," Vittorio said, looking between his son and daughter again. "But take a deep breath, please. I am not an unfair man, and I do not wish for you to die out there, nor do I care to see either of you attempt to ruin my good name with petty accusations. You are no longer welcome within my home, but I will treat you as I do your bastard siblings, and you shall receive a small sum of money from me each month. This way I can sleep easy knowing that my stupid children will not kill themselves through starvation or lack of shelter."

Vittoria took a step forward suddenly. "You know any journalist would take this story. You claim to care about family but you kick your youngest out of your home? I- We could go to any journalist in the city and they would pick this up in a heartbeat. Then we wouldn't even need your fucking money."

Vittorio blinked calmly. "If you say a word to anybody, I think it should be easy enough to spin the tale around, daughter. *Vittorio's youngest children, after failing to achieve success for decades, decide to venture out on their own to find their passions and make names for themselves. While doing so, they turn on their loving father, still supporting them financially behind the scenes, and make a dramatic public tantrum in which they try to garner fame and media attention by tarnishing their good father's name with cruel lies like rebellious teenagers.*" He chuckled quietly. "Do you really believe that anything you claim would hold a candle to my word, Vittoria? Sofia has tried plenty and look at how successful she has been."

Sofia was one of their half siblings, born out of wedlock, who had tried—and failed—to start some sort of revolution against the Marcello Candy Company, or so Giovanni understood. He had not, admittedly, followed the situation very closely, and it had been something of a taboo topic at the dinner table. Her words had been shoved out of the paper quickly enough when Vittorio had claimed it was all a publicity stunt from tabloids trying to exploit his family name for a quick buck, and she a sick and manipulative daughter who was slandering her loving father out of desire for media attention, or perhaps some sort of psychological duress, undoubtedly inherited from her mother's side of the family.

Vittorio reached into his pocket and pulled out two envelopes. "I have set up bank accounts for the both of you. Presently, your pin numbers are your birthdays, and your passwords your middle names. Feel free to change them to your liking." Vittorio handed both of them the envelopes, and Giovanni had not noticed how much his hands were trembling until he tried and failed three times to take it. "Have I made myself clear? Is there anything else with which you must waste my time before you get a move on?"

Giovanni's voice was soft when he spoke. He wished he had something to suck on, but he opted for swallowing his spit, squeezing the envelope in his hands and saying, "Why are you... Why are you doing this, Papa?"

Before Vittorio could answer, Giovanni's attention was caught by Vittoria, who snorted aloud. Giovanni could see her shake her head from the corner of his eye.

"God, you're such a fucking dumbass." she snapped, her voice shrill. Giovanni could still see that strange, bland fear on her face that he had never seen before, the panic in the whites of her eyes like an animal. "You're so fucking stupid. You're going to fucking die out there." Her accent was slipping, Giovanni could hear the stress of Italian on her syllables and she almost sounded like she was going to cry, although perhaps his ears were deceiving him, for he certainly had never seen Vittoria cry before. "You've gotten us fucking kicked out."

Giovanni was frustrated to find that he did not have the words to describe the emotional response he experienced to Vittoria's words, and he hardly knew what he was saying as his tongue moved faster than his brain could manage: "But she started it."

"God, you're so fucking retarded," Vittoria snapped.

Vittorio broke the silence with a scornful scoff in the back of his throat. "Even now, you two cannot even pretend to possess any care, let alone tact. Broken, damaged beyond hope or prayer, the both of you." He walked, slowly, back to the chair he had been sitting at before, and collapsed back down into it. "Neither of you have anything of value in your rooms. Your lives are shallow, there is nothing to be missed aside from the squandered time and resources. I have already deposited a sum into your accounts; you can afford basic necessities. Take only what you must and get out of my home."

If Vittoria were asked about the events that followed directly after the confrontation with her father, she would not have been able to recount them in clarity, but rather with a strange, vague incoherency typically present only in dreams (or, more apt a comparison in this case, nightmares). The frantic rush to her room, panic only half set in, thoughts empty as she scoured her bedroom for anything she might need and threw them into the biggest purse she could find, glancing around at the plethora of silver eyes looking down at her that she refused to process she would likely never see again. The trek from the bedroom to the front door felt like the most grueling walk she had ever taken in her life. Centuries passed as she dragged heavy feet one step at a time towards the entryway to her demise, and yet it was within only the blink of an eye, a single, strangled breath inward, that she found herself outside. She could have forgotten her brother even existed, she very well may have liked to, until they encountered each other outside of the mansion, just as they had that very morning.

And now they stood, past the tall gate, on suburban pavement in the dim light of late sunset. The dense, smog-beaten air of Fresno city night was entangled with the vile aroma of Giovanni's cologne.

Vittoria stood very still, and the world moved around her very fast, and nothing happened for a long time. No one was out; the grand, expensive houses that lined the street sat pristinely behind their well-watered lawns as the color drained from the sky. The distance between them and the greater part of the city gave it an illusion of quiet calmness, although she knew that it was very much alive, and that thousands upon thousands of people were existing within the busy streets, blissfully unaware of her misfortune. Giovanni was being oddly quiet again. Then he shifted a bit; from the corner of her eye Vittoria could not tell what he did, but there was a distinct presence of movement that woke her from the nightmare that she was trapped in only to plunge her into a reality much worse.

Coming to her senses as she turned to her brother, the first thing Vittoria managed out was, "So. What the fuck."

Giovanni blinked stupidly at her and then looked up at the sky as it darkened. "I... I didn't bring any candy with me."

The brainlessness of the statement began to revitalize Vittoria. The deep, unfathomable terror within her was charred to nothing by a burst of white-hot anger. She began to pace, and the boots she wore thudded rhythmically with each step, loud and heavy on the pavement. "This is all your fucking fault, Giovanni," she hissed without looking at him, "I was *fine*, I was fucking... I was going to do something with my life. I had... I had plans, and dreams, and- and I was going somewhere. You fucked me over. God, you fucked me over so fucking bad, you fucking idiot, you dumbass, fucking, stupid-" She paused, the flow of pejoratives running dry as she glanced back to the gate and the tall hedge that had kept them locked from the outside for so many years.

"I am not going to die on the streets." Vittoria said firmly, and she was not sure who she was speaking to, but her eyes remained on the hedge that loomed high above her, trying to force down the sickness that bubbled in her throat when she thought of the paintings she had spent nearly half her life accumulating, now gazing down into a forever-empty bed.

"V... Vitta?"

She turned to her brother and looked at him, and he was staring at her with wide eyes that were dimmed to an ugly, puddle-gray in the dark. "What do you fucking want, Giovanni?"

Vittoria watched as Giovanni breathed in, looked around a little as if hoping someone else would answer the question for him, and then swallowed and said, "I... I do not know. I don't know. But I know that I do not want to stand out here all night, and I- I know that I would like to find candy, and some new makeup, and a comfortable bed to sleep on before it gets too dark."

Vittoria grunted and rolled her eyes. "There are drug stores all over the place. You can buy the shit you need there." She walked past Giovanni, a few paces down the street, and then turned back to look at him. "And I'm sure you can find some shitty motel that'll let you live from month to month on Daddy's allowance."

Giovanni stiffened and even in the darkness, even with the thick layer of makeup masking his face, Vittoria could have sworn she saw him pale a bit. "Absolutely not!" he cried, shaking his head so that his ponytail whipped back and forth behind him. "I refuse to step foot in a place like that, I will not take up residence in a- a dirty, roach-infested, glory hole pit of filth!"

"Really? Because all of those things sound very up your alley," Vittoria spat back. "And, coincidentally, you'll be sleeping in an alley tonight, unless you get over yourself."

"Well, what are *you* going to do, sister?" Giovanni asked, walking up to meet her where she stood ahead of him on the pavement.

"I haven't spent my entire life lounging around like a useless slob." Vittoria took a few more steps forward, distancing herself from Giovanni again. "I have connections. I have places I can go. I'm sure-"

"Now? This late? With no warning?" Giovanni insisted, running to meet her again. He grabbed her by the arm and she immediately pulled away, but his grip was tighter than her reflex and she did nothing but scowl helplessly as he clung to her. "Look around, Vittoria. The sky has gone dark, and we are alone with nothing but the clothing on our backs. You may have what you claim, but tonight you have nothing but me."

Vittoria responded to this with a vicious slap that struck Giovanni across the face and echoed like a gunshot down the quiet street. "What are you trying to do, Giovanni, seduce me?"

Giovanni, stunned by both the slap and these words, recoiled and rubbed his cheek. "Vitta!" he whined, and he became even more upset still upon looking down at his hand and seeing how much makeup had been smeared in the process. "I- No! Never, I- ew, no, no, I- I just... I was only attempting to suggest that we work together, is all."

Vittoria rolled her eyes. "You've got a lot of fucking nerve for someone who needs to be babysat at age thirty-fucking-four." Giovanni whimpered and returned to rubbing his cheek.

He was pathetic, and he disgusted her, but Giovanni was right, she thought, hating this realization but unable to deny the truth of it as the sky turned dark over her, over the both of them. Vittoria clenched her hand into a fist and let her nails dig deep into the flesh of her palm. She hated him—she really, truly hated him—but out here, with nothing but a purse of necessities and helplessly dependent on the small pension her father reserved only for bastard children, she realized that she must have looked just as pathetic as him, and she hated that truth even more than she hated Giovanni.

And she, too, did not want to sleep in the cheapest motel that money could buy.

"Come on, then."

Giovanni turned to her, visibly surprised. "What?"

Vittoria, not wanting to look at even the silhouette of Giovanni's face anymore in the darkness, not even able to find amusement in the clownish reddening of his cheek after being struck, turned and began to walk down the street. She could hear hurried footsteps echo behind her as he rushed to keep up after a moment of confused delay, no doubt having to process the sudden, grudging change in her tune.

"If we split the cost of a hotel room we can afford something nicer than your roach-infested glory-hole-whatever." Vittoria said. "We can find somewhere livable and figure out what to do next from there." She did not pose it as a question or offer an alternative. If he was so keen on not being alone then he could have his wish, but it would be on her terms. Her own survival would continue to be her primary goal: Giovanni was an asset, a means to an end.

"What about my makeup? Or candy? Or-"

"You'll have to figure out your shit on your own. I'm offering to split the cost of a room. Be grateful." Vittoria said, still keeping her distance from Giovanni as they walked.

All of a sudden light erupted above them, casting long shadows on the pavement, and for a moment Vittoria paused in surprise, looking up to see that the streetlamps overhead had come on, signifying with finality that nighttime had fallen.

Giovanni felt terribly out of place within the interior of the hotel lobby, which was dressed up in faux gold and scenic paintings of distant places where fields were green and bright. There were men sitting in business suits by a fireplace, reading books and magazines. The room smelled like cigarette smoke, a scent that he generally disliked due to the way it interfered with his cologne and clung to his fancy clothes. He was still dressed nicely himself, and save for what had been rubbed off on his cheek his makeup was still in acceptable enough condition, but there was an internal dread that something within him had broken, and he was half certain that even the most minor of provocations would lead him to puking up shattered fragments of whatever that something was.

The hotel was just outside the major center of the city, just as the skyscrapers began to jut out of the earth and the traffic began to grow denser, just close enough to the major streets that the ambiance of city night could be heard from outside. Here, people who could not afford to stay directly in the city would opt to stay instead as a second-best option.

That was their life now, Giovanni thought, nauseated: Second best options.

Vittoria took Giovanni's envelope from him and he watched as she walked to the counter to speak with the man at the front desk. He listened to her speak in her silly American accent and watched the transaction take place, but his mind drifted before the words could even make their way from his ears to his brain and he looked around the hotel lobby distractedly. One of the paintings was of a bright meadow, within it a pond, and on the pond a swan, sitting atop the water with its neck long and elegant and its eyes shut delicately. Giovanni stared at her, at the way the artist had drawn tips of golden sunlight on her otherwise pure white body, certainly whiter than anything in nature would ever truly be amidst the dirt and mud, and he wondered at that moment what would become of his birds. His tongue sought candy that was not there and he tried to push the thought from his mind, but not before his nausea, and the deep-rooted dread, had worsened considerably. He turned back to his sister as he heard her approach.

"Come on, I have a room." She handed him his envelope, which was now open. Giovanni peered inside and noticed that there was a bank card within. When he looked back up at his sister, she said, "I split the bill."

"How can I trust you?"

Vittoria rolled her eyes and gave a loud groan; a comically exaggerated movement to truly convey her annoyance. She pulled out her own opened envelope from her pocket and shoved it into his face. "Check the balances in a fucking ATM if you have to, smartass."

Giovanni decided it was not worth the time, her permission enough for him to believe she was not being dishonest, and followed her to the room, which was down a hallway to the left of them. Although the hallway gave off the initial impression of fanciness, Giovanni could tell that it was not nearly as elegant or ornate as the long and winding halls he had grown up in, cleaned every day by servants and covered in decorations and trim and artworks commissioned exclusively by and for the Marcello family, lit up with shimmering lights adorned in real gold and silver and gemstone. These walls had an artificiality to them that was much more apparent; the light did not glow as bright and was a pale, sickly yellow from bulbs that seemed far weaker than they had been in their prime, and hints of wear and uncleanliness, chipping gold paint on chandeliers and torn edges of wallpaper, gave away the fact that it was not nearly as immaculate as it dressed itself up to be.

The room was at the end of the hallway, and Vittoria unlocked it with the room key she had received from the front desk, and did not hold the door open for her brother, but rather made him have to grab at the handle before it shut as she walked in and left him out in the hall. The interior of the room was quite similar to the hallway; it was pretty enough, and sported a color theme of wine red and a pale off-white that looked acceptably nice, but there was something markedly unpleasant about the atmosphere of it. The room smelled like dust, and the dull, grey glow of the hotel light made Giovanni feel dizzy.

"Well. Here we are." Vittoria said, and she walked to the couch and sat down, unceremoniously putting her heavy boots up onto the coffee table with a thud and causing the cheap structure to tremble slightly beneath their weight.

Giovanni winced. "Don't be so disgusting. The least you could do is take your shoes off before you make yourself comfortable," he insisted, doing just that, using the toe of one shoe to pull down the heel of the other in order to force it off without bothering with untying it, and then repeating the motion with his now-shoeless toe for the other. Vittoria did not look at him. "If we are going to be calling this place home, it would be smart to-"

"What the fuck do you know about 'smart,' Giovanni?" Vittoria snapped. She pulled her feet up to the couch now, letting the bottom of her boots rest heavy on the couch cushion as her knees pressed against her torso. Giovanni could not tell if she was trying to give him an aneurysm on purpose or if she was truly just trying to get comfortable in the most slobbish way imaginable.

"I know that you called me a smartass not ten minutes ago."

"Shut the fuck up." Vittoria let out a long, strained, frustrated breath, sounding like she was on the brink of losing it just as much as he was.

"And I am not calling this shithole 'home.' I'm calling it a place to sleep while I figure out what the fuck happens next."

"You have not been in the wild for even half a day and you are already regressing to a wild animal." Giovanni muttered back, his eyes still stuck on the sight of Vittoria's shoes sinking into the couch. He had to get out of here. "Well, I saw a store in the lobby. I am going to see what they have. I must have some candy or I will surely go as mad as you."

Vittoria turned around to look at him. "So if they do have Dad's candies, you're just gonna go give him money the same fucking night he kicked your ass out the door, huh? From his pocket to your shiny allowance card and back into his pocket?"

Giovanni did not answer that. He had already left, shutting the door behind him and finding himself alone, barefoot, out in the strange, uncanny hallway. Long hallways such as this were meant for the opportunity of stumbling upon beautiful servant girls to speak to and delight and charm, he thought, but instead this one was starkly empty, and there was an uncomfortable sense of awareness that behind each closed door to either side of him were total strangers, existing in the strange transient state brought about only by quiet hotel rooms at night. The mounting anxiety as one attempted to sleep on a bed that was not their own, the uncertainty of what the future would hold, found in each quiet murmur or footstep or sound of rummaging suitcases that reverberated through the walls. Giovanni stood, uncomfortable, looking down towards the front lobby.

He decided quickly that he didn't much like being alone, although arguably being trapped with his sister was far from a more pleasant alternative, but the strange unfamiliarity with these surroundings, coupled with the awareness that he was trying to stave off of the fact that his life was rapidly changing in ways he could not even begin to predict, left him with a keen sense of growing, inescapable dread. His thoughts raced. He needed candy.

Giovanni walked in a daze as he reached the lobby, where the businessmen still sat in their suits. The man at the front desk turned to him.

"Can I help with anything?" the man asked. Giovanni did not respond, but rather turned to where he had noticed the small store before, a crevice of a shop in the back of the lobby where the shelves were lined with travel necessities and other basic needs. He walked into it and looked around. The mahogany wooden shelves darkened the place a bit compared to the bright golden trim of the lobby. His eyes scanned for only a moment before they settled on a brilliant golden insignia that he recognized immediately, would recognize anywhere: The shining M that adorned a candy wrapper. They could be bought separately, or in baggies of twelve or twenty-four, and Giovanni picked the latter option, knowing that this particular type of Marcello brand candy was a chocolate that melted rather quickly in one's mouth with effects that lasted for shorter bursts of time than the lollipops and other hard candies that he often preferred for their longevity, or the slightly more expensive chocolate options that packed a greater punch even if they dissolved nearly as fast.

Lingering a little while longer in the store, Giovanni managed to find a sorry excuse for a makeup section nestled in the back, comprised only of vital travel necessities: miniature bottles of only the cheapest products, brands he could hardly imagine willingly letting near his face, moisturizers and lotions and cleansing towelettes that he knew without even a second glance were lying through their teeth about their effectiveness. But he would not dare sleep in his makeup, which would ruin his skin, and he would rather die than be caught out without a fresh coat painted on in the morning, so he settled sadly on what he hoped would be the least terrible options. A toothbrush, a razor, deodorant, and some soap came next, and Giovanni was having trouble keeping everything in his hands, and without a cart or bag he settled on keeping the candy satchel dangling between his teeth. Figuring that he had enough to last him at least the rest of the evening, he walked out of the small store and back to the front of the lobby.

Caught off guard by the brightness in comparison to the dim store lighting, he walked, slightly disoriented, to the man at the front desk.

It was the first time Giovanni had given the man's appearance any thought. In the queer synthetic brightness of the lobby he looked like an angel. He was older, probably at least twenty years older, than Giovanni, and although there were wrinkles in his cheeks as he smiled pleasantly at him, his skin practically glowed as it reflected the pale golden light like rays of morning sunshine. He was tall, and although he was thin he did not appear frail. His voice was deep but gentle when he asked, "Did you find everything okay?"

Giovanni was silenced by the bag of candy he held tight between his teeth. Trembling hands clumsily spilled the rest of his items onto the counter before letting the bag free from his teeth and setting that down too. "Ah... *Sì.*" he said quietly. He wet his lips and tasted lipstick and watched as the man reached beneath the counter to pull from it a plastic bag. He took each item from the counter with large, strong hands; long fingers, delicate in spite of their size, curled around and gently lifted one after the next: The razor, the makeup, the candies, each thing checked and bagged with skillful ease. Giovanni watched in silence, and he felt dizzy, and he wished that the candy placed in the bag was in his mouth instead. With the man's head down, Giovanni could see his hair, which was a light brown that had been paled and thinned and pushed back slightly by age, strands of silvery white intermingled with strawberry brunette, and while Giovanni's hair was slicked back tight, this man's, while combed back, was left loose and soft on his head.

The man looked back up at Giovanni when he was done with this job (which likely had only taken a few moments, but to Giovanni it had felt like a very endless affair). He spoke again to give Giovanni his price, which was higher than Giovanni cared to think about when aware that he was on a budget, and asked, "Are you on a trip?"

"Er... Yes," Giovanni gave a nod. The man was smiling, and the long crow's feet that sprung up made his eyes smile too. They were painted gray, not unlike Giovanni's own, and shone royal silver in the hotel light, and despite the coolness of the color they were warm and friendly. Perhaps it was the smoke from the cigarettes, or the heat of the fireplace in the corner, or the anticipation of the candies that would soon be in his possession after a frightfully long period of sobriety, but Giovanni was beginning to feel very warm and his makeup sticky on his face. What was worse still, and Giovanni liked to believe it was caused by a sort of deliriousness evoked by the chaos of the evening, the same warmth in his face was springing up from elsewhere in his body, as well... He fumbled with sweaty hands as he handed the man his card.

"Stay safe out there, kiddo."

The moment the card was back in his hands and the bag of necessities paid off, Giovanni took off down the hallway, horrified of the man being made aware of the growing embarrassment between his legs. He felt hot all over, uncomfortable in his own clothing and skin.

Giovanni walked uncomfortably, stiffer than usual, back to the door to his current reluctant living space. Disoriented still, he tried to pull on it only to remember that he was presently in a hotel, and to get in he needed a room key, and it was his sister in possession of such a tool, and not him. He knocked. "Vittoria!"

"What?" a voice came back from inside, muffled by the door but audibly disgruntled by the interruption.

"Let me in?" Giovanni requested, knocking again. He listened as his sister let out a long groan, and a moment later there was a click and the door unlocked. It opened only partially, just enough that Giovanni could see his sister's face, which was free of the makeup she had been wearing earlier. She looked down at the bag in his hands.

"Got your bullshit?" she asked.

Giovanni nodded. "Yes, and I would like to come in. I paid for half of the hotel room, you know. You cannot just-"

Vittoria rolled her eyes and opened the door a little wider, enough that he could enter, as she backed off to the side. "Relax. I'm not going to lock you out, idiot. I just don't want the door thrown open while I'm fucking naked." Giovanni stepped inside and looked at his sister. She was in her underclothes; her bra and underwear were the same solid black as the rest of her wardrobe. He walked to the small kitchen area and set the bag on the counter there. He pulled out the candies eagerly, mouth practically watering as he hastily unfasted the top of the bag in which they were held. Vittoria entered with a little huff.

"How much did that shit cost you, anyway?" she muttered.

Giovanni did not answer. He was much too preoccupied with pulling out one of the pretty candies, all wrapped up in its shiny gold foil. Long nails worked eagerly to unwrap the chocolate with practiced ease and in a second it was in his mouth, the milky sweetness hitting his tongue and melting into the warm wetness of it. He hummed, feeling almost like himself again.

"I'm going to take a shower," Giovanni said to Vittoria, after the chocolate had melted enough that his speech was not hindered by a full mouth. He picked up his bag, leaving the chocolate on the counter but making sure that the makeup and hygiene products he had bought would be with him.

"Whatever." Vittoria replied. She walked to the doorway of the bedroom. "I went exploring, by the way. There's a single bed in there and a foldout couch. You get the couch."

Giovanni was halfway across the room to the bathroom when he paused at his sister's words and turned to her. "What?" he shook his head. "Why should I-"

"Because as far as I'm concerned, this mess is your fault. *And* because while you were out supporting your father's business like a good bastard son, you missed the opportunity to claim it. I sleep in the bed: You dug your grave and now you get to fucking sleep in that." Vittoria shrugged and crossed her arms.

Giovanni glared at her. "I am *not* more at fault than you. It was you who could not control your temper enough to make the interview work. Had you even a moment of restraint perhaps we could have-"

"*Restraint?*! What, like, being able to restrain myself from blowing all of my money on candy after the entire goddamn reason the interview got fucked was because I had to get fucked up beforehand? Being able to restrain myself from making smartass comments on live television?" Vittoria snapped. "I planned for that thing for ages, asshole. I was trying to fucking do something with my life. If you hadn't been there none of this would have happened. Go take your fucking shower." Vittoria entered the bedroom and slammed the door loud enough that the walls shook in response, once more hinting at the craftily concealed cheapness of the interior. Giovanni stared at the closed door, considering saying something else, but his makeup stuck sweaty and wet to his face and he wanted it off before it ruined his complexion, so instead he made his way to the bathroom to take his much-needed shower.

It was late, and Giovanni was trying to sleep. The bed beneath him felt like it was stuffed with some kind of taloned beast bent on scratching and clawing at his back every time he shifted his weight on the mattress, and it creaked and wailed if he moved too much. His hair, free of its ponytail and falling in dark waves around his shoulders and over his face, smelled like hotel shampoo, a cheap herbal scent with too much tea tree oil. Intermingled with the baby lotion floral of hotel lobby skin care products, he was overwhelmed with tacky, unfamiliar smells that truly drove the foreignness of the situation home in an escapable way. He was in his underclothes, which he hated. He had a preference for soft pajamas that covered him in warm security. He did not have that now. Everything felt wrong, and unlike the typical quiet of his bedroom, outside of the hotel he could hear the ambiance of the city, and the occasional honk of a car would make him jump out of his uncomfortably dry skin.

Sleep was not coming easily, and Giovanni would occasionally shift to stare enviously at the shut door to his sister's room, wondering if her bed was any nicer than his and having a sneaking suspicion that it absolutely was. She had not come out again after shutting her door earlier. With the total radio silence from her for the rest of the night for all he knew she could have died in there, and an increasingly frustrated part of him thought that he would not mind finding her corpse the next morning. After all, corpses could not insult you, or scream at you, or claim beds.

At some point in the night Giovanni found himself growing horribly hungry, and it occurred to him that he had not eaten anything for dinner. He used that as an excuse to scarf down a few more of the candies he had bought earlier. It hardly helped with his hunger, but they gave his taste buds and stomach something to be distracted by, masking the churning discomfort in his stomach with an airier feeling through his entire body, not to mention the way it lifted his mood and gave him a reignited sense of security and the vaguest flickers of optimism, providing a fraction of replacement for his lack of pajamas. He went back to bed feeling a little lighter than he had before, his thoughts spaced a bit further apart. He was certainly more relaxed, but still he struggled with getting fully comfortable, and the smell of cheap soap permeated through his thoughts, too powerful for the chocolates to fully suppress.

Unused to the city noise piercing the silence of nighttime, Giovanni flinched as somewhere in the distant streets of Fresno a car shrieked as it skidded across the road.

When Vittoria awoke, she noticed it was relatively late in the morning. The sun was high in the sky, pouring in over her through cheap curtains, a strikingly foreign sensation after having spent so long with thick, heavy curtains that shielded her from the sun at all hours. She had slept for a long time, and it took her a moment of disoriented confusion to comprehend the fact that she was in a bed, in nothing but her underwear, and the bed itself was not her own. She sat up, pushing her dark hair from her face and looking around, and as the bleariness left her eyes and the hotel room came into focus she found the memory of the previous evening materializing in her mind. She breathed out a long, slow sigh, wishing that it had all been a nightmare and not the uncomfortable new reality in which she was trapped.

As the events of the night sank in, Vittoria stood and stretched. Giovanni, she remembered. She had left him out in the living room. Not wanting to face him but also not trusting him to be left alone, and curious to see if he, too, had managed to survive the evening, she picked up her bra, clasped it quickly, and walked out of the bedroom to the front of their current living arrangement. Giovanni was nowhere to be seen.

"Giovanni?" Vittoria called out feebly, because she already knew that beside herself the hotel room was utterly empty, not nearly capable of hiding a fat pig such as her brother. Still, she walked to the bathroom and peered inside. "Giovanni? Where the hell are you?" On the bathroom counter an array of makeups had been opened and used and left by the sink. Clearly he had been here and gotten his face on for the day. But where had he gone?

Frustrated and somewhat antsy, Vittoria went back to the bedroom and put on the same clothing she had worn the night before, a black blouse and leather skirt, and grabbed her purse from the bedside table. She made a mental note that she would have to go shopping later; that had not even been on her mind last night, but she had absolutely nothing to her name but the contents of her purse and what she currently wore on her body, and the full extent of the implications of that was beginning to dawn on her. She shook her head and stubbornly attempted to push such thoughts from her mind for now. In wrinkled, day-old clothing and with the entirety of her earthly possessions, Vittoria left the hotel room.

"Giovanni?"

Down the hallway she wandered, into the hotel lobby, which she found was relatively deserted, save for a few strangers in the lounge, talking amongst themselves or reading, and a couple checking in at the front desk. Still, she scanned each one, as if checking to make sure that they were not somehow her brother in disguise.

Vittoria walked to the counter, shoving past the couple trying to check in. The man working there was different than the one the night before, and he looked at her with surprise at her forcing herself to the front of the line.

"Er, Miss-"

"Did you see a fat man with a black ponytail leave here this morning?" Vittoria demanded. "He looks like a clown, he's not easy to miss."

"Ma'am, we-" The man whom Vittoria had cut in front of began to speak, and Vittoria turned to glare at him. Both members of the party were visibly upset, but Vittoria decided that she could not care less, as she was currently on what she considered to be a much more important mission than checking into a shithole hotel for a romantic getaway.

"Shut up, alright? I'm just trying to ask-"

"Look, lady, you can't just expect-"

"Fuck *off* for just a second, I-"

"Excuse me?! Did-"

"Giovanni!"

Just as the situation was undoubtedly about to escalate, the man going red in the face and most likely trying to figure out how cruel he could get with a stranger before it made him look bad in front of his sweetheart, Vittoria figured (and he was doing such a good job, checking them into a place like this!), she saw her brother emerge from the doorway in the back of the lobby, chatting with a girl she had never seen before. She froze where she stood, and the strangeness of this behavior made the couple she had been arguing with freeze too, staring at her in confusion and then following her line of sight to her brother and his new friend. After her initial surprise Vittoria's senses returned to her and he shoved past the man who was trying to argue with her, storming towards her brother.

"Giovanni!" she cried again, voice loud and angry. As Giovanni saw her coming towards him he jumped. "Where the fuck were you?" The girl beside him, a petite blonde thing with greasy looking hair that was long and flat against her head and an orange floral outfit that suggested she enjoyed pretending to possess more money than she really had, flinched at the language like a child. Vittoria rolled her eyes.

"Continental breakfast, sister," Giovanni said. "You missed it."

Vittoria had not even thought about food since their disownment, and certainly did not care about missing breakfast. But the trouble that Giovanni had put her through had caused enough anger to bubble and boil inside of her that finding him now was not enough to dissipate it. Especially when it was he who was at fault for this whole mess in the first place. She turned to the greasy blonde. "He's sharing a room with his sister and he doesn't even have the bed. He's not going to fuck you."

The blonde, mortified by that, went redder than Giovanni's cheap lipstick and turned and stormed off in a huff. Giovanni watched her go, visibly disappointed, and then turned back to Vittoria. "Why did you do that?" he asked, somewhere between angry and genuinely confused.

"I was telling the truth." Vittoria snapped, grabbing Giovanni by the wrist now. The surprise on his face did not leave and he did not even pull away initially, just staring at her. "I can't believe you're out here dicking around with girls right now, idiot. You do realize the severity of the situation we're in, right? You realize we have fucking nothing right now?"

"Why do you care what I do or where I am, then?"

Vittoria felt her own face turn red with frustration at the question. "Why do you always ask stupid shit?" she hissed. "You're paying for half the room. What do I do if you just walk out on me?"

Giovanni thought about this for a moment, and Vittoria could not fathom for the life of her why such an answer had left him so baffled, before he gave a resigned sigh and his expression turned noticeably more serious. "Well, what do you suggest we do, then?"

Vittoria shook her head, the anger in her stomach still too intense to let her think clearly. "Let's just... let's just go back to the room," she said. "We can figure out what the fuck to do from there." She tugged at

Giovanni's wrist, and now he pulled away from her, frowning but not arguing as he followed her back through the lobby and down the hallway to their shared room.

Back inside, Giovanni sat down on the pulled-out couch and winced as he settled into the clearly unpleasant furniture before reaching for the candies he had set on the coffee table nearby. Vittoria shook her head, looking away as Giovanni began to unwrap a chocolate, too disgusted to want to watch his gluttonous display and instead focusing her eyes on the strange, dim hotel light above them, which cast a cheap and sickly glow around the room, especially in the brightness of daytime overpowering it so.

"I want to get out of here," she said, and she was not particularly addressing Giovanni.

Still, as he was the only person in the room besides herself, his was the only answer she received: "Well, what do you propose we do then, sister?" His mouth was full while he spoke, and Vittoria rolled her eyes and let out a grunt of disapproval.

"I don't give a shit what *you* do," she stated, "But I'm not going to be trapped in this place, and I'm not going to be stuck depending on a fucking allowance to live." She went silent, trying to figure out the next move she wanted to make. Had her father been right, that going to the press with his disownment would only result in their own reputations being destroyed? In the quiet of the hotel room she could hear Giovanni's chewing and it was slowly driving her up the wall, the disgusting, wet chomping seemingly crunching down on her brain just as greedily as the soft candies. Her brow creased; she could sense something was building, surmounting within her that was much more intense than a typical outburst. The stress of the past twelve hours was wearing her down, leaving her exposed and raw, and the more time that passed the more sensitive she felt, the more vulnerable and the more volatile. Giovanni was still chewing. She bit down on her lip, worried it between her teeth, and when that felt raw, too, she snapped, "Jesus fucking Christ, just shut the fuck up already."

Giovanni looked up at Vittoria from where he sat on the couch-bed. "What? I didn't even-"

"Quit stuffing your mouth like a slob. Don't you give a single shit about what's going on?" Vittoria's palms were sore and they stung from her constant stabbing at them, her fists clenched so tight they burned. "God, I can barely fucking take this."

"You have eaten nothing today, Vitta. Perhaps you should-"

"I don't want to fucking eat." Vittoria snapped, hating the way that Giovanni spoke to her like a child; if it were not for the goodness of her heart he would have slept in a bush outside of their father's home last night, she thought bitterly. He needed her significantly more than she needed him, pathetic and useless as he was, and yet he had the gall to speak to her like he had any position of authority! "I'm not hungry," she spat, "I just need to get the fuck away from this, from you, from- I- *God*, I'm gonna go insane." Giovanni had gone back to smacking on his chocolates. How many of them had he eaten in the last few minutes alone? How many had he bought? Vittoria stormed over and grabbed the bag from Giovanni's hands and threw it. It hit the wall and landed on the ground in a sad little heap. "Just shut the fuck up for five minutes, Giovanni!"

Giovanni stared at Vittoria with wide eyes, visible confusion etched onto his face, and Vittoria hated him for how stupid he was. "Stop shouting, sister. Why don't you go shower?" he suggested. Vittoria blinked. Was he mocking her?! "I will even let you borrow my makeup, just this once, if it will make you stop yelling. You will feel better when you can comfortably look in a mirror, I can assure you." He stood up and moved towards the candies, but was stopped by Vittoria, who grabbed him by the wrist for the second time that morning, although she was not sure what she had in mind to do next.

"Giovanni, just... God, just fucking shut up. Oh my God," Vittoria said. At this point she was out of things to even say, but her tongue burned with anger and she felt like she had to say something, anything, to make even a measly attempt at expressing the intensity of her rage. "Just- God, please, for once in your life, stop being so fucking annoying." She let go of Giovanni and groaned, and Giovanni just stared at her, visible confusion etched on his face, and she hated him even more for that. Why could he not just understand? She clenched her hands into fists and let out a strained breath as she tried to stay calm.

Without saying a word to her, Giovanni walked over to pick up the candies. As he opened the bag to look inside, as if to check and make sure that nothing had been damaged, as if chocolates could possibly be damaged by being tossed into a wall in the first place, the concern on his face for the safety of the sugary treats more apparent then than when they had first been kicked out the night before, he said, "You're so on edge I'm amazed you haven't fallen and died yet." He let out a sound reminiscent of a giggle at his little joke, and pulled out one of the little chocolates, staring at it as the gold foil glittered in the dingy hotel light, turning it over as if worried it had fucking bruised.

"I'm not *falling*, asshole. I'm perfectly fucking grounded. Unlike you, lounging on your ass all day like a lazy bastard!" she retorted.

"And yet *I* was not the one who slept through breakfast." Giovanni unwrapped his candy and placed it in his mouth.

"I didn't want fucking breakfast!" Vittoria turned away. Her palms stung, her head ached; she was having trouble thinking she was so angry, and the fact that she knew that nothing she could say would get through to Giovanni only made her anger more intense and more futile, as if it were a snake puffing up as large as possible upon realizing its enemy was much bigger—and, in this case, significantly stupider—than it, a last ditch effort to survive. "Why can't you just give a shit about something, Giovanni," she said now, and despite the phrasing it was not a question. She was past the point of asking questions. She did not even turn to look at him as she spoke, despite addressing him directly. "Why... Why can't you fucking... why don't you ever give a shit about- about *anything*." She bit down on her tongue, punishing it for stuttering.

"Don't be stupid. I care about plenty of things, Vitta."

He had some nerve calling *her* stupid, Vittoria thought. Although she had not turned back to look at him yet, she could hear him beginning to chew on his candies again, forced to be hyperaware of the wetness of his lips and the glide of his teeth against the soft chocolate. "What, like your birds? The ones that you fucking kill every other week? Your daddy's drugs, even after he fucking disowned you?"

She could hear him pause, the chewing and smacking and sucking at the awful candy ceasing and leaving the room in silence. Then, Giovanni said, "At least I don't have the blood of family on my hands."

"What?" Vittoria whipped back around at that, daring her brother to say that to her face.

Giovanni stood his ground, and even had the nerve to raise his head a bit higher. Although at first he gave off the impression that he was looking her in the eyes, Vittoria noticed that he was looking just below them, avoiding her direct gaze. "Perhaps Papa was right. All you do is bring pain with you everywhere you go. At least I can sleep at night knowing that in order to come into this world I did not have to trade my life for that of another."

Giovanni may as well have punched her directly in the gut, knocking the wind right out of her with his words. As much as Vittoria wanted to lash out, she found herself wholly incapacitated, in such a state of shock that she could not even form a coherent thought, let alone force her body to obey her. She felt very cold, and although she wanted to lunge at him, to grab him or slap him and demand he take back his words, or rip out his tongue so that he should never speak again, she could not move her body beyond a slight tremble. She felt frail, her head too light and her thoughts too fast to keep track of, and instead of doing or saying anything to her brother, in the end she found herself turning to the door, almost automatically, and walking past him without so much as looking at his face.

"Alright." she said, as she reached for the door handle.

"What are you doing?" Giovanni asked.

Vittoria could hardly believe he was still trying to speak to her. "If I bring pain everywhere I go, then you don't want to be around me anyway," she said plainly. She scanned quickly around the hotel room, making sure to the best of her ability that nothing was needed and all was accounted for, although her head still spun and she was too dizzy to fully remember the events that had transpired up until now to fully figure out what she needed or not from here. But no, she thought: She had been conservative with her money, she possessed nothing but her purse, which held the new credit card, and the clothing on her back. In that moment the thought made her feel light and free and limitless. "I can't do this. I only paid for one night, you can pay for tonight on your own or you can fuck off somewhere else. I don't give a shit. *Ciao*, Giovanni."

Giovanni did not flinch when Vittoria slammed the door, nor did he go after her as her footsteps grew quieter down the corridor to the hotel lobby. She would be back, he thought. For now, her absence was a welcome relief. He waited for a short while to see if her return would be quicker than predicted, sitting alone on the bed in the room that she had claimed, taking that time to see if the television had any adult films for rent.

When an hour had passed and there was still no sign of his sister, Giovanni left the room. If she was going to be out for a bit, then he, too, should get on with his day. Although in the back of his mind and in moments that were just ever too quiet he was still overwhelmed by a deep sense of panic and dread that he struggled to keep down, he knew that there were things that must be done to begin regaining some comfort in this new living arrangement. Most importantly, he thought, remembering how horrid sleeping had been the night before, he needed to buy pajamas. Perhaps he could find a way to claim the bed before Vittoria came back too—but, either way, he wanted something more comfortable to sleep in than his underwear, and he wanted to begin to slowly return his wardrobe to the marvel it had been before he had lost everything. All he had now was the clothing on his body, the finest item being the purple suit jacket he had brought before departing his father's mansion for the last time. At the very least it was imperative that he had more than one single outfit to wear and a decent supply of makeup.

And, most importantly, Giovanni realized that he was already beginning to run dangerously low on candy.

The nearest place with a telephone was a gas station about half a mile from the hotel, and by the time Vittoria arrived she felt filthy. She had done enough walking last night, through sprawling suburbia into the far edges of the city, to find that godawful hotel, and the day was warm enough and her sleeves long enough that by the time she had made it to the gas station she felt sweaty and disgusting, dizzy and lightheaded because she still had not eaten, had not even had any caffeine, and overall exceedingly uncomfortable in every way imaginable. She kept her head low and her eyes to the ground as she stepped into the small convenience store, where she found an ATM. She withdrew twenty dollars in cash, and then she broke the twenty with a cup of cheap coffee, which tasted like water from a bathroom sink and had a bitter, burnt aftertaste.

In the back of the store was a payphone that was even filthier than she was, grimy and sticky in her hands, and Vittoria hesitated to put the phone to her ear, not wanting it touching her face and instead opting to keep it at a short distance. She then procured from her pocket the glossy black card she had received only a day before the horrible interview (if it could even have truly been called such a thing). She had forgotten that she had put it in her pocket, much too distracted by the events that had ensued and the disastrous meeting with her father, until she had gotten undressed to sleep and found it then.

Vittoria dialed the number.

The wait felt endless. The phone hummed and buzzed, and although Vittoria had already had enough gas station coffee to last her a lifetime, she hesitantly took another sip of it to distract herself, letting her mind linger on the fact that it was much too watery, dwelling longer than she pleased on the sour, boiled chemical flavor that lingered on her tongue.

"Hello?"

"Anubis?!" Vittoria spoke immediately, almost interrupting the voice that came from the phone in a moment of panicked and desperate excitement. She winced then, cursing herself for speaking too loudly for fear that someone would overhear and embarrassed by the tone of voice she had momentarily taken, and looked around the store to make sure that there was no one else around.

"Speaking, yes." the voice replied, seemingly unphased by the outburst but with a hint of uncertainty lingering in the tone, as if subtly suggesting: *Get to the point.* "To whom do I owe the pleasure...?"

Vittoria drew in a breath and looked down at her coffee, watching the way it sloshed and rippled in the cup as her hand trembled. "V-Vittoria Marcello," she said. "I got your letter. I'm sorry I didn't respond right away, I-"

"Vittoria!" The voice on the other end interrupted her this time, but Vittoria was so relieved to no longer have to speak and to hear some semblance of warmth towards her from another human being that she did not care. "No worries, please, don't apologize. I understand that you are a very busy woman. What is it that I can do for you?"

Vittoria drew in another breath and shut her eyes for a moment, her mind working fast, trying to cull the rapidly spinning thoughts of flustered excitement and think practically. She needed help. Would Anubis help her? She hardly knew him, she *didn't* know him, beyond her familiarity with his music, and she knew that she was only one individual in a countless sea of adoring fans. She did not even know what he looked like; the only image that she could conjure of him in her mind was a mass of blood and shrieking, a hellish display on stage that was betrayed by the cool tone in which he spoke. Logically, she did not know enough about him to trust him—but what choice did she have? Where else was she to go? She looked down at the bitter coffee. "I'd like to meet with you soon. T- Today, if possible."

"Oh! Yes! Marvelous!" The voice on the other end of the phone sounded delighted, and Vittoria again found herself relieved to hear someone excited by the thought of her for once. "Would five o'clock work for you? We can discuss over dinner and wine, if that sounds suitable."

An invitation to his home? Vittoria quickly thought this offer over. That gave her enough time to run to the store and buy at least one other outfit, let her get dressed in something fresher; she would certainly need it for such an occasion. It gave her time to mentally prepare, or at least try to. In reality she knew that no amount of time could fully prepare her for meeting Anubis face to face. But it gave her time to try. "That... That sounds great, yeah," she said weakly, mind racing and the whole situation feeling very surreal. And then, remembering how much she needed this, she put on the voice she did in interviews, lifting her head, forcing her demeanor to change into something that the public tended to like, and added, "Thank you *so much*, Anubis. I know it's very short notice, but I'm just so-"

Again, Anubis interrupted her. "No, please, you have no reason to thank me, dear, nor should you feel it necessary to apologize. Believe me when I say that you are someone whom I have wanted to speak with for a very long time. I would miss a loved one's funeral if it meant the chance to meet you." Anubis laughed. Vittoria forced a chuckle along with him that sounded to her more like a whimper. She had not realized it, but at some point during the conversation she had forgotten about her attempt to keep her distance from the speaker, and it was now pressed eagerly against her ear.

Giovanni hated the heat. He hated the sensation of sticky sweat clinging to his skin; he could practically picture the slimy concoction of salt and melting makeup filling his pores and clogging them with all sorts of gunk and muck, infecting his perfect skin and causing it to break out in pus-filled sores as it fought back against the intruders. And with a budget and few resources to his name, he hated even more the fact that once he arrived back at the hotel he would have very little in the way of proper skin care tools to even begin to address this. But for now, he had no choice but to stay on foot and trudge through the mid-afternoon Fresno heat, seeking out a store that would cater to his needs.

This was no Downtown Fresno, Giovanni thought, eyes running over the layout of the street, quaint corner stores and humble apartment complexes lining both sides of the road. In the distance he could see the tall skyscrapers that jutted from the heart of the city, shining proudly as they reflected the afternoon sun in their glossy chrome exteriors and sleek windows into pristine offices, apartments, hotels, hospitals, and anything one could possibly fantasize about at their fingertip. Here, the neon storefronts flickered feebly, burnt out letters making the names illegible. The apartments, though he imagined still plenty expensive to be this close to the main hub of the city, were visibly less cared for, with unimpressive, underwatered flora wilted pitifully in the front, rusted front doors, and cluttered balconies.

How strange it was, Giovanni thought, that one could practically turn a corner from his father's neighborhood and end up in a place like this. The walk he and his sister had embarked on to find the hotel had felt horrendously long in the moment, full of unpleasant, stiff silence and a sort of numbness that made time feel distorted and the world around him feel faint and distant, trying to repress any wandering thoughts by staring at his surroundings but finding that the desperation for distraction only made the time drag on longer, and yet now it felt like his father's mansion, where within the walls were laid the framework for all his earliest, formative memories and most of his lived experiences, felt so close, just barely out of reach, just around a corner and up a hill and into another universe.

Giovanni found himself staring aimlessly at a palm tree, an odd foreigner quite literally sticking out amongst the yellowed chaparral and dried out patches of lawn that lined the streets, and then, after recollecting himself, moved on.

After another block he came to an intersection with a gas station sitting at the corner nearest to him. Although it was far from a desired location for what he needed, it occurred to him that within the small convenience store they probably were selling easily-accessible candies; he could vividly remember his father discussing the different locations they sold the best, and gas stations were an easy market, perfect for travelers to stop and get their fix as they passed through. Nothing like Marcello Candies to perk one up for the rest of a long car ride. Giovanni walked towards it. The exterior of the gas station was a foreign world to him—he had certainly never learned to drive. It was an odd, dirty place, as he approached he began to notice that the concrete was filthy with dark gum and oil spills and littered with bits of trash, paper straw sleeves or candy wrappers or cigarette butts or glass shards.

At the moment there were no cars present, the parking lot oddly barren amidst the great city, and the gas pumps sitting alone in anticipation for the next customer to drive up and use them before driving on, continuing their journey in or out of Fresno. The only sign of life in this wasteland was a group of men—boys, really, significantly younger than himself—lingering in the corner. Giovanni watched them for a moment, dumbfounded at the sight of complete strangers existing on their own out in the vastness of the city. There were five of them and they stood, talking amongst each other on the black, tarred road. A few held what appeared to be beer bottles. Eventually, one of them caught Giovanni's eye and he looked away quickly.

But it was too late. There was a murmur amongst the boys, and when Giovanni looked back up he saw a finger pointing in his direction from the group. He looked away again and continued towards the store, but he could already hear a number of much faster footsteps rapidly approaching. He tried to muster up some sort of quick reaction, an escape plan to swiftly and gracefully remove himself from the scene, but he was not nearly fast enough, and before he had come up with even an inkling of a tangible idea of what to do a voice directly in front of him said:

"Hey, you."

Giovanni froze, looking up. He really was only a boy, he very well may have been a teenager, but his youth was betrayed by a heavy darkness beneath his eyes.

"What are you doing out here?" the boy asked. He looked Giovanni up and down, and Giovanni glanced down at his own clothes too. He had left his father's mansion in the rich violet suit he had picked out for his interview the day prior. This boy, on the other hand, was dressed in cheap clothing, stained and unwashed. Plain jeans, an old, worn T-shirt. Giovanni could not imagine himself to ever be so filthy.

"I could ask you the same." Giovanni replied, speaking before fully considering the meaning of such a response, but the murmur that erupted from the boys indicated that it had, perhaps, not been the correct course of action.

The boy in front made a sound of half-sarcastic shock, his eyebrows raising in a sort of amused disbelief. "Could you? What the fuck are you, some kind of rental clown for rich weirdo parties?" He laughed, causing Giovanni to flinch in surprise. "Look, I dunno who the hell you are or where you came from, but I'm pretty sure it's you who's in the wrong place." The boy stepped closer. Giovanni took a step back.

"Certainly," Giovanni agreed. "I would never dream of claiming a place such as this as my own."

"You wouldn't?"

"Never," asserted Giovanni, with a hopeful, naive confidence. "Do you know who I am, little boys? I am Giovanni Marcello. I come from a world far away from this yucky, nasty place."

The reaction was not what Giovanni had been expecting. The boys all went completely quiet. For a moment there was no sound at all from the group, as if they had all collectively stopped even breathing. Someone mumbled something quietly that nobody responded to. Somebody else let out a strange laugh that sounded almost forced. Giovanni had the vaguest sense that now would be a good time to turn and run.

"A Marcello? Bullshit." the boy spat.

Giovanni was unsure of how to proceed. Luckily, he did not have to say anything, for another one of the boys in the group spoke up first:

"I think he's telling the truth; I've seen him up on the screens downtown."

Another said, "Who the fuck else would dress like that out here?" and began to laugh. Giovanni gave a small nod of agreement, relieved to have somebody on his side, although unsure of what any of this meant.

Suddenly, the lead boy lunged forward and grabbed hold of the front of Giovanni's shirt. Giovanni, shocked, tensed and stared with wide eyes. It was beginning to dawn on him how much trouble he was potentially in, and he paled, his heart speeding up and his body going into a sort of frozen panic. The boy tugged at his shirt and Giovanni stumbled forward. "Who the fuck are you, clown?"

Giovanni gasped and tripped over himself in an attempt to pull away. "I told you! Giovanni Marcello! I am simply here to-" To what? What was he even doing here? The chaos of the past twenty-four hours seemed to catch up to him and his tongue flailed in his mouth helplessly. "I-"

Before Giovanni could come up with a coherent sentence, he saw the boy's fist fly towards his nose at a speed much faster than he could process or react to. Immediately, white hot pain shot through him as if he had just been electrocuted, so sudden and so overwhelming that he hardly felt the secondary blow, which was his body collapsing as the boy let go of him and he fell to the hard asphalt ground with a painful thud. He was momentarily stunned to complete immobility, seeing nothing but red and white and finding it immensely hard to catch a breath, for each time he tried to breathe through his nose his senses were overwhelmed by liquid, suffocating him, smelling like rotten metal. His vision blurred, he sat up, barely able to process where he was as a pain more horrible than anything he had ever felt in his life continued to rush through his whole body. It gradually became concentrated in the front of his face, which throbbed with white-hot, burning heat. He reached up to grab his nose and felt his hands quickly grow moist.

Panicking and gargling on the blood filling his nostrils, Giovanni hardly even heard the laughter from the boys around him. He could, however, feel when one of the boys gave him a hard kick in the side, which sent him tumbling down to the ground. Giovanni could see droplets of blood hit the black road as his nose continued to bleed freely and he stumbled, grasping at the asphalt as it scratched his hands, dizzy and disoriented, and he wondered if he was dying. He was in too much pain and too disoriented to even feel fully and properly afraid for his life, but he was dully aware that he most certainly should have been.

A foot pressed down on Giovanni's back, pushing him down, causing him to whimper with fear. "Spread the word back to your family that the Marcellos are over," The boy said above him. "Beg for your life and crawl back to them and give them the good news." He pushed his foot down harder, knocking the air from Giovanni's chest.

Giovanni blearily blinked tears from his eyes, his breathing still muffled by blood and saliva running from his nose and mouth. "P- Please, I don't- I don't-" *Don't know what you're talking about. Don't know what to say. Don't want to die.* Giovanni was at a loss. He scrambled pathetically, squirming beneath the weight of the shoe on his back as a powerful, throbbing pain reverberated through his nose. He sobbed. "Please," he said again.

The boy lifted his foot off, then crouched down and grabbed Giovanni's head. Giovanni choked and whimpered, half certain he was about to die but too disoriented to fully comprehend it, sniffling through blood, wondering if he would drown from the amount gathering in his nose if these boys did not kill him first. He felt hands fumbling with the sides of his head, and then through his disorientation he realized that the boy was pulling the glittery, dangling earrings out of each ear. Then he stood up and kicked him once more, with the same half-interest one might give when kicking a dead animal found on the side of the road in order to inspect it. "Get the fuck out of here." he said.

Giovanni did not have to be told twice. He scrambled, rushing as fast as he could possibly muster, limbs trembling weakly as he shoved the mass of his aching body up, pulled himself to his feet, stumbled dizzily. His vision spun. The ground below was red, his face felt hot and wet and it burned, the pain in his nose throbbing outwards to his brain and making his thoughts incoherent even as his heart thumped with panic. He could hear laughter around him, see the blur of faces staring at him; he was in a nightmare, he thought. He was surely dying. He began to run.

He was not very fast, and he knew he would be out of breath shortly, very much out of shape and lacking any practice with physical exertion beyond bedroom doors, but his terror, the pain coursing through his entire self, and his desperate drive for survival pushed his energy to the brink, forced him onwards down the streets. He could hear the whooping laughter of the boys behind him and he believed for a moment that they were following him, but as he continued through the city streets their voices grew quieter. Still, he kept on, turning corners semi-deliriously, with no rhyme or reason to his movements but escape, and to avoid being forced to choose between waiting at a crosswalk or running into oncoming traffic. He ran past people on the streets, brushing past his shoulder, even the lightest collision would make him feel like his entire world was thrown out of balance for a moment. He could hear the voices of passersby, concerned cries, angry yells, undoubtedly attracting attention considering the blood flow from his nose down his front.

How much longer could he last like this before he went completely out of his mind? Giovanni thought, delirious, the world around him a blur as his lungs felt like they had been stabbed by dozens of knives, his sides cramping just the same and the pounding of his heart rising to his ears alongside intense nausea. He knew he had not made it very far at all, despite his best efforts. He knew he was not fast, he was out of shape, and the city was very, very big. His throat felt as if it was on fire. Everything was hot, except for his feet, which had begun to feel like ice. He was dying, he thought. He gasped and heaved for dense, smoggy city air.

Giovanni turned another corner, into an alleyway wedged between two old buildings, tripped over an empty bottle lying beside a large dumpster, and collapsed.

Vittoria arrived at Anubis' house in stiff new clothing that smelled like a department store and did not quite fit, used to a more tailored feel (not to mention something that had been washed before wear, a luxury she had not had): A simple, black top with cut-out shoulders that hung off of her frame a little too loosely, a skirt that hung on her hips a little too low despite the faux leather belt that held it up—The best she could do on the limited budget and time she had been working with. She was not particularly comfortable, but she looked fine enough, and she had even had the chance to pick up some makeup on the way over and hurriedly throw it on, a pale imitation of the typical porcelain doll paint she most often wore, quickly blackened lips, a gooeyer, chunkier eyeliner than she was used to coating her eyes, an attempt to make herself look as much like *herself* as possible despite the excitement of the past twenty-four hours. The largest downside of it all was that, with nowhere to keep her things, she had been forced to leave her old clothing behind; the last of her possessions from a previous lifetime left forgotten in the wastebasket in a gas station bathroom.

Anubis' house was somewhat close to the wealthy suburbs that Vittoria herself had grown up in, but the surroundings were significantly more urban as it was a neighborhood that was much closer to the heart of the city proper; houses were shoved together here, all but stacked on top of each other, long vertically rather than horizontally. Vittoria found herself feeling very small against the tall, looming buildings, and she drew in deep breaths as she tipped her taxi driver and walked up the staircase to the front door and knocked, preparing herself for who—or what—ever she would find on the other side.

For a brief while she waited. There was no response from within. She could not hear anybody approaching, or anybody doing anything for that matter. She considered knocking again, or perhaps ringing the doorbell. It was just as she was reaching to do the latter that the door opened, the suddenness of which made her jump in surprise, betraying the calm demeanor she had been trying to hold onto.

"Vittoria Marcello!" a voice said from within, with the same coolness and politeness that she had heard over the phone. And now, as the door opened wider, she finally was able to get a look at the owner of the voice— the illusive physical manifestation of the man who had facelessly permeated countless hours of daydream and fantasy, whose music had penetrated the depths of her imagination and radiated like blacklight through her dark bedroom and heart.

He was very, very tall, and very, very thin, easily looming over her and yet the circumference of his waist rivaled her own, and she knew she was underweight. His hair was to his shoulders, a very carefully styled mass of brown-black curls that fell, fluid but wild, like waves down his head, with electric shocks of silver running throughout. His face was old; his eyes were sunken and surrounded by deep cracks on his face that extended down to his cheeks and mouth, but he gave off the air of accepting the aging process with elegance. Black eyeliner carefully outlined his eyes, delicately, with skill that showed the many decades in which his career had spanned, and above his strikingly dark brown eyes was a dash of glittering green eyeshadow.

He smiled, and more wrinkles formed around his lips, which had been painted a dark, wine-red, and he held out a hand to Vittoria.

"How do you do?"

Vittoria accepted the hand, and looked down to notice long, long nails jutting from even longer, bonier fingers. They did not look fake.

"I'm wonderful, ah..." Vittoria pursed her lips. "Do I call you-?"

"Anubis, please. And I hope that it should be alright if I simply address you as Vittoria. You see, I consider myself a forward thinker— That is, in the future I see us being good friends, so it would only make sense that I treat you as one now." He chuckled and stepped aside, holding the door open wider. "Do come inside, Vittoria."

Vittoria did as requested and stepped through the doorway. As Anubis shut the door, she was surprised by how very dim he kept the interior of his house; the lights were on, but only turned up halfway, forcing her eyes to adjust in order to fully take in all of the details. And there was *much* to take in. In just the front room alone, the walls were decorated in strange items, some paintings but many other memorabilia unlike anything she had ever seen before, despite her own growing up in a luxurious, stylish mansion, much larger and more outwardly, visibly expensive than this. Masks of all sorts: theatrical masks, operatic masks, tribal masks, the faces of animals and monsters and humans all adorning the walls, staring down at her in various exaggerated expressions and distorted, stylized features. Strange, foreign objects hung like ornaments, figures, many humanoid but some animalistic and some entirely abstract, made in all styles and from all materials, lined the tops of bookshelves completely bursting with books. Vittoria felt as if she had stepped into some sort of strange, exotic museum. And yet, still, there was a particular homely quality about the place that betrayed that line of thought, as comfortable, soft looking, old couches, worn from use, sat across from each other, a fireplace sat, unused currently but grand and clearly capable of procuring a bright and comforting warmth, and in front of her, a staircase to her right and a hallway before her reminded her that she was indeed within a living space.

"I hope you find the atmosphere suitable," Anubis said, and with Vittoria's attention on the many details of the room (presently she had been squinting at a strange doll on a table that looked as if it were made of metal or a polished black stone, trying to make out its expression), she had almost forgotten that he was there. She turned to him, looking at him in the dim light. "I am quite proud of my collections. In my many years of touring I have had the great pleasure to travel far and wide, and I enjoy picking up something that fascinates me in each place that I go. If you like, I could introduce you to some of them at some point."

Vittoria nodded, amazed by what surrounded her.

"But they can wait. If you would follow me, I have dinner prepared. I hope you like lamb?"

Vittoria had no preference either way for lamb, and in general was not someone who took a significant amount of pleasure in eating, but she resigned herself to enjoying the meal tonight. It would be the first thing she had eaten in a very long time; she could feel the dizziness in her head from the lack of food, the hunger stress that gurgled uncomfortably in her abdomen.

"That sounds lovely, A- Anubis," Vittoria said. She could still hardly comprehend where she was. It felt like a scene from a dream, standing here in his home now, in *Anubis'* home. Here he was, the voice, the figure, the very soul of the music that had awed her for so long, and after all she had endured through the past day, he was leading her to his dining room to serve her dinner. She took note of how lightly he walked; despite his towering over her he seemed to step on soft, gentle feet, barely making a sound across carpet, wood, and tile, all three of which comprised the flooring of his home. Vittoria felt very out of place in her big boots.

Should she have removed them at the door? She noted that he was barefoot and felt a slight twinge of self-consciousness.

They came to a room down the middle hallway that was lit up a bit brighter, with a dining room table that, while certainly very pretty and large enough around to host a small gathering, was nowhere near large enough for a dinner party, which surprised Vittoria somewhat. Surely someone as renowned as Anubis had people over quite often?

Already on the table were two plates, one across from the other, and a tall bottle of wine in the center between them. Anubis walked to one and motioned for Vittoria to walk across to the other side, so that they could be facing one another during their meal.

Vittoria sat. "Thank you again for having me," she said, but Anubis promptly shook his head.

"You have nothing to thank me for. It's a pleasure and an honor," Anubis responded, "And it is not altogether a wholly altruistic affair, as I've already made clear: There is much that I want to discuss with you. But first... let us eat. I am under the strict belief that there is no use discussing anything of importance on an empty stomach. We must first feed the needy animal within ourselves before the intellectual beast can thrive." He picked up the bottle of wine and an opener that sat beside it, and after puncturing the cork he poured some of the deep red liquid into the glass before Vittoria.

Vittoria waited in silence, save for the polite "thank you" that she murmured as she watched Anubis prepare, feeling almost delirious even as she sat quietly, as he, the Rock God of Death, tall and intimidating, carrying himself with all the charisma and cool of a rock star who had spent decades crafting himself into his own ideal, perfect image, drawing in the energies of countless crowds of people adoring him and his art, dashed in and out of the kitchen, pulling from it dishes that filled the air with sharp, foreign spices that Vittoria was not wholly familiar with, intermingling with the sweet, flowery incense that faintly permeated the air of the house, cutting meat and sprinkling the last dashes of flavor over vegetables.

When all was done, Anubis sat down and raised his glass. The red wine glistened like rubies in the light. "To creation and the self," he said. Vittoria picked up her own glass with fingers that struggled for a moment to wrap around it properly, raised it, and gave a little nod, unsure of if she should say anything. When Anubis lowered his glass she followed suit, and when she saw him pick up his utensils she did the same, imitating each of his motions with a moment's delay in order to make sure that she picked up on the etiquette expected of her.

The lamb was clearly cooked masterfully but Vittoria hated the metallic aftertaste that lingered in her mouth. Still, the rush of a day's worth of starvation hit her as the meat touched her tongue and she had to fight the urge to scarf the food down in an instant, instead taking small bites, forcing the flavor to linger on her tongue for longer than she pleased in order to remain polite. She sipped only briefly on the wine, never one for alcohol (or any substance aside from caffeine, for that matter), and she said nothing for a short while, focused only on her meal and waiting for Anubis to make the first move.

When enough time had passed that the silence was becoming awkward, however, and the sensation of her own chewing was becoming monotonous, Vittoria decided to take the initiative, and she looked up at Anubis and said, "Your letter." The moment she spoke Anubis looked up at her, but now that she had his complete attention she faltered, unsure of how to continue.

Anubis only smiled. "Yes. What about it, dear?"

Vittoria forced down butterflies. "You said you had some sort of... project in mind?"

Anubis' smile grew wider, more wrinkles erupted across his features, and his teeth came into view. Vittoria noticed them for the first time; they looked very strange, shaped very differently from any set of teeth that she had ever seen before, sharp and jagged, oddly spaced apart in his gums, unfamiliar in both shape and spacing. They were canine teeth, she realized after a moment.

As she stared, Anubis began to speak: "Yes, yes. That's right, I did say that, and it's very true. I have a very big proposition for you, Vittoria." He turned to his wine, and quickly downed the rest of the glass. "Death is the one great inevitability. It's the one thing that binds us together, all of humanity. *We look to it with satisfaction, saying 'there is the one reality which shall not dodge us.'*" Anubis mused, speaking in such a way that Vittoria presumed he was quoting something, although she was unsure of what. He poured himself more wine and held up his glass, peering at it in the light as he spoke, watching the way the deep red shimmered in crimson waves. "Not even the Rock God of Death can truly evade it, not forever." He turned to Vittoria, looking her in the eyes, and Vittoria did the best she could to hold his gaze. "I am very proud of the many years that my career has spanned, and I have decades upon decades of knowledge acquired in my many years traveling and performing and resurrecting myself beneath the stage lights. I hope you don't find me arrogant if I say that I have done things that no one else on the planet has done, and that I believe myself to be a person with a unique story that few truly know due to the secrecy in which I have preferred to live in my old age. And... old age it is indeed, Vittoria. I have come to a point where I admit I must confront the reality that I will not be around forever, and I would rather prefer it if my secrets were not buried with me when the day comes that I depart from this plane and travel to the next. Do you understand me?"

Vittoria was not sure if she did or not, but she gave a nod regardless, and Anubis smiled again.

"I want to give you a contract with Embalmed, Vittoria, but I also want to do much more than that. I would like to take you under my wing. Make you an apprentice of sorts. A protégé. I want to teach you all that I have learned over my many years so that when I begin my journey to the next realm of consciousness there will remain a fragment of my soul bound still to this Earth." Anubis stood suddenly. Vittoria flinched. "Are you finished? I am going to fetch some dessert from the kitchen."

Up until now Vittoria's mind had been frozen to a halt, enraptured by Anubis' words and overwhelmed by the entirety of the situation, but the moment Anubis stood it was as if a switch had flicked and her brain turned back on, whirring to life at a thousand miles per hour, attempting to decode Anubis' words. She hardly knew him, not personally. And yet she thought back to her records, the hours she had spent lying in bed and listening to his voice, the fascination and allure of his work and the strange, fleshy, bleeding tree on the cover of his album that she had felt drawn to in such a way that escaped words entirely. He was undeniably cool, collected and polite, intelligent, and... very wealthy and powerful. And her beloved record player and every record that she owned sat, abandoned, in a room that was no longer hers. If they had not already been thrown away.

It was an offer that she quite literally could not refuse... not that she wanted to.

"Do think it over, and we can discuss any questions you have over something sweet!" Anubis was saying now, and Vittoria frowned. She did not like eating in general, but she especially did not like sweets.

It was just as Anubis was making his way to the door that Vittoria said: "I accept."

"What?" Anubis turned to her immediately, whipping around to stare, thin and pointed eyebrows rising high on his forehead. She knew that he had heard her. He wanted to hear it again.

Vittoria swallowed and her hands clenched into fists at her side, but quickly they relaxed. She was not angry, but there was a swell of emotion in her that she was struggling to keep down. She breathed. "I accept your offer, Anubis."

Anubis' trajectory changed, instead of walking to the kitchen he walked across the room, around the table to stand before Vittoria, and held a hand out to her where she sat. "That's marvelous," he said, voice softer, and he eyed her up and down. His eyes were dark, so dark that she could not make out his pupils, and they wandered, carefully, up from her waist to her face to settle on her light blue eyes, and the expression on his face felt akin to that of a ravenous carnivore animal studying its next meal from afar, planning its attack. She bit the inside of her lip and reached out, accepting Anubis' hand. He pulled her up in an instant and tugged her into a kiss.

Vittoria's instincts worked fast, she had been half-expecting this, and relaxed in an instant into his arms, although her thoughts continued to race as she tried to process the situation and found that she was utterly unable, unable to even begin to comprehend that the man who held her to his chest now was the same as the one on her records, the same on the stage, covered in gore and shrieking madness through distorted vocoders. He ran his long, thin fingers through her hair, nails brushing through it like a bony comb, his dark red lipstick rubbed against her solid black.

Anubis pulled away to look at her, and Vittoria noticed that he was crouching to meet her eyes. She felt very small then, very aware of how large he was, both in terms of his physical size but also in terms of the power he had—a fact that she had been eager to take advantage of, but which now made her shrink in a sort of awestruck reverence.

"Why me?" she said suddenly. The words left her lips before she had fully processed them.

Anubis raised a brow quizzically. "Why not you, Vittoria?" It was not an answer, Vittoria thought, and unease settled in her stomach. Anubis was frowning now. "Do you believe me to have an ulterior motive, Vittoria?"

"What?" Vittoria felt a rush of nerves. "No, I... I just... Um." Her lips moved but no sound left her mouth, worried that she would say the wrong thing, that she had just sullied the good will that Anubis had been so eager to extend.

Anubis placed a finger over her mouth and smiled. "You have been given the offer of a lifetime, I understand that it may seem too good to be true, that the mists of doubt are swirling in your pretty head. I do not cast judgment. But there is no need for humility, Vittoria. I chose you because I believe in my ability to teach you, and I believe in your ability to learn." His hands traveled from her long, raven hair downwards, brushing light over the curve of her breast, stroking her sides and then coming to rest at her waist, long nails poking just above her tailbone at her lower back. His smile widened, and Vittoria stared at the long, sharp canine incisors that jutted from his gums.

Vittoria shivered at the touch, but she forced herself to remain composed, willing herself to make peace with the hesitation and uncertainty that caused her head to spin. She felt like she was going insane, like she was trapped in a game of chess with an endless array of moves she could make, and yet all choices led to one single answer: She needed, and... *wanted*, Anubis. She did not even have a bed to sleep in tonight, unless she wanted to return to that horrible hotel room. She had no one else to turn to, nowhere else to go, and Anubis was cool, enticing, older and wiser than she, and he held in his hands the key to a future that she had until now only dreamed of realizing. She was drawn to him, she needed him, she had admired him for so long, she was frightened by him and yet that fear only piqued her curiosity more. As she mentally stared over her chessboard, coming to terms with the reality that her multitude of choices had been only an illusion and feeling his fingers trace along the delicate skin at the side of her stomach, she realized now that he had had his checkmate the moment she had walked through his front door. "Is there... Do I need to *do* anything? Is there a contract I should sign? Any fine print?"

"The legalities will be taken care of tomorrow," Anubis said. "Tonight, we are bound by no legal contracts. Nothing but our own words, our trust in each other, and our... mutual desires."

It was nighttime. The sky above was a bleak black, starless in the city's smog and eternal radiating light. Neon adorned the front of buildings, OPEN signs flickered bright in shop windows, skyscraper windows lit up like glowing mosaics. Cars, unhindered by traffic as the night drew on and fewer souls could be found out and about, sped past at quicker speeds, briefly illuminating the darkness with bright headlights before disappearing down the street.

Giovanni sat on the concrete, wedged in between what appeared to be a residential building—a poor apartment complex of some sort—and a liquor store. It was quiet and empty here, darker than the main road due to a lack of streetlights. There was a putrid smell nearby, as if something had died and then sat out for days in the Fresno heat to rot. Giovanni imagined himself in a predicament not too different.

Comforted somewhat by the darkness cast upon him by the night sky and the shadows of the large trash cans to his side, Giovanni sighed and gripped his own legs tight. Deeper in the city, in the downtown districts, the great screens overhead would display the time periodically, but here he was entirely removed from the splendor of the main city streets, the fashion and the bright lights and commotion of wealthy people and endless prospects, and he had no idea what time it was, how long he had been out here. All he knew was that everything hurt and it was very dark and the day had felt very, very long, and it felt a miracle that he was conscious.

Giovanni could not remember feeling this much physical pain in his life, as the panic from earlier subsided it gave way to intense aching through his entire body, soreness where he had been kicked and a throbbing, sharp pain in his nose. It was surely broken, dislocated and permanently lopsided and bent on his face; he dreaded to ever look at his own reflection again. The physical discomfort extended down from his nose to his lungs and chest, which burned from the physical exertion from earlier, and his legs, which ached and burned. They had all but collapsed the moment he had found solace and now the muscles twitched weakly beneath skin that was drenched and sticky in sweat, causing his clothes to cling to his flesh uncomfortably. He knew that he was destroying the delicate fabric by sitting in filth as he was, and he could see, although he dared not look too close, the blood that had stained his front, but he could hardly even begin to think about it.

He could hardly begin to think about anything, really. Giovanni felt lost, unsure of what move he could possibly make from here. His head spun with a dizziness that had not dissipated since the initial punch to his face and he wondered if he had suffered brain trauma and would die in his sleep. Then again, it was not as if sleep was even a remote possibility in a place like this, wedged between garbage bins in a grimy back alley somewhere, lost, in the depths of the city. He looked across from where he sat to see trash and debris piled on the concrete; cardboard food containers, paper bags that even in the darkness had visible stains. He set his hand down to touch the cold concrete beneath him and immediately retracted it when it came to rest on shards of glass. His hand curled into a fist and he rested it back on his lap instead. His tongue twitched. If only he had even a single candy, perhaps he could find the strength to get back up, he thought.

He looked up. The buildings towered over him from his spot on the ground. Even the waste bins loomed over him, great masses of shadow and stench in the darkness. Giovanni closed his eyes, unable to bear any more of his surroundings. What time was it? he wondered again. He would have to spend some of his pitiful allowance on a watch at some point, he thought, although such a plan felt like a distant fantasy now; he could hardly imagine a world in which he stood up and was able to reintegrate himself back into society confidently enough that he could step foot inside a store and make a purchase

Giovanni rested his eyes and let his body relax. Or at least, he attempted to. But his clothing clung to moist skin and his own sweat felt cold and slimy. His body was still racked with pain and the ground beneath him and the wall against his back were stiff and hard. It seemed the more that he attempted to settle into the dark crevice the more aware he became of every discomfort. His mouth was dry, his throat burned, and his tongue felt restless as it sought candy that was not there. He swore he could feel the emptiness of his piercings. Each time he attempted to clear his mind enough to rest, perhaps even get some sort of sleep, he would immediately be snapped back to reality by the rigid concrete floor, or the hard brick wall, or the incessant chatter of city night, or the throbbing in his legs, his nose, his head, in every limb and muscle in his poor, beaten body.

He felt sick. Giovanni opened his eyes with a sigh of defeat. Nothing about his physical surroundings had changed. The night was still, even the silhouettes of napkins scattering the ground sitting without motion. He touched his throat lightly, disgusted by the way he could feel the muscles pushing upwards, the deep, vibrating ache of his throat that warned nausea. He swallowed hard, his mouth still too dry to conjure up any saliva and yet an unpleasant thickness rising in the back of his throat.

He stood, let out an audible cry as pain shot through his legs at the motion, and stumbled, half-limping to the garbage bin across from him. He lifted the lid, but the stench that emitted was so putrid that he slammed it back down, loud enough that it echoed through the alley. Gagging, he took a step back, nearly falling backwards, and doubled over, even more certain that he was going to throw up now. He heaved, coughed, and choked at the ground, his body wracked with shivers, aching still from being beaten earlier, his throat already torn and raw from his escape. He gagged again, the muscles of his mutilated throat pushing upwards in a desperate, panicked response to eject something, anything from his body, but he had nothing to throw up, save for a bit of burning bile that hit the concrete wall with a wet splat, alongside the sickeningly sweet taste of the candy he had eaten earlier that day lingering alongside the acid on his tongue.

Giovanni spat at the ground in disgust and coughed a few more times. His throat burned and he felt horrible, and the emptiness of his stomach left him feeling hollow and dizzy again. He had hardly eaten today, he realized, and although he felt no hunger he was certain it was only contributing to his deteriorating physical and mental state. His body was racked with trembles, worn down, as if he had used the remaining ounce of energy left in his muscles to vomit up nothing and it had reached a threshold for how much it could possibly bear. He shivered, his breathing ragged, stepped back on unsteady feet to where he had been sitting before, but as he turned back around he stopped, and although he was already pale he was certain that he went even paler, and his stomach, uneasy as it was, dropped even further, for he saw that there was a person standing in the back of the alley, facing him and watching silently.

"Hello?!" Giovanni tried to cry out, but all that he managed was a strained croak. He whimpered with pain.

"What's going on over there?" the figure said. From where they stood, surrounded entirely by the shadow of the alley, they were nothing but a humanoid silhouette, but they now began to approach him. Giovanni felt an uptick of fear in his chest as he remembered the altercation from earlier, but he could not bring himself to exert the energy to move.

As she came into view, the city lights helped illuminate her, although still she was mostly shrouded in darkness. She was a woman, and she was significantly shorter than Giovanni, bent slightly with age. She walked slowly, taking little steps forward, and she squinted at Giovanni in a way that made her flesh erupt in deep wrinkles.

"I heard a commotion and thought some sort of animal had gotten into the garbage," the old woman said, continuing to stare at Giovanni as if he were the most peculiar thing she had ever laid eyes on. "Then I heard choking, and I thought that somebody had been attacked and left to die, and I was really going to be upset then, because that would be a terrible mess to sort. But you're not an animal, and you're very much alive. Who are you?"

"I..." Giovanni found himself unsure of how to answer the question, and he stared at the woman. Although he was no longer afraid, the whole situation felt very surreal and very strange and left him at a loss for words. She was too old and too frail to be any sort of tangible physical threat, but there was something jarring about her appearance. She wore a yellow robe; he could tell even in the darkness, and it looked very soft, a striking contrast from the hard edges of the alley. She smelled like a kind of perfume that Giovanni imagined an older woman would wear, something floral. He tried to swallow, but this only made him wince in discomfort. His mouth felt like it was full of cotton and his saliva felt like sandpaper. "Giovanni Marcello," he finally said. "I am Giovanni Marcello."

"Giovanni." the woman repeated the name, still squinting at him. "You don't look like the kind who causes trouble in dark alleys at night, Giovanni."

Giovanni was relieved to hear that; perhaps he had not succumbed to being a complete lowlife just yet. "I am not!" he said, shaking his head. "I- I wasn't... I am just a bit lost, is all. Do you... What are *you* doing here?"

"I live here," the woman answered simply, pointing with a small, bony hand in the direction from which she had first appeared. Giovanni had not paid heed to the door in the back of the alley, he had been much too distracted by everything else to survey his surroundings with significant thought. It must have been an apartment complex or townhouse of some sort. "Would you like to come in? I imagine that with all of that retching you could do with a glass of water."

Giovanni nodded immediately. "Yes!" he said. "God, yes, please."

He followed the old woman to the back of the alley, to the door that he had missed in the shadows of the night. She pulled out a little golden key and unlocked it, and then walked through, holding it for Giovanni to enter behind her. Her home was warm, much warmer than the outside, and significantly more humid, to the point that there was almost an oppressiveness to the moisture that filled his torn lungs with each breath. When Giovanni saw a hanger on the wall he took advantage of the opportunity to remove his jacket, tragically dirtied by the events of the day, and hang it up, leaving him in a white button-up made of a loose, soft material, the front stained with his blood and dirt from the gravel; it had not been a good day to wear white, he thought.

The woman's house was filled with plants, and although they were not the same sort of extravagance that could be found in the vast garden with which he had grown up, with access to an endless water supply and blooming flowers of every color bursting from luscious green foliage, there was something uniquely impressive about her collection, if nothing else for the fact that Giovanni had never seen anything quite like any of it. The plants that she decorated with were homier, potted plants, and yet the abundance and the variation amongst them created an almost jungle-like, wild atmosphere. Some were oddly shaped succulent plants with lumpy swollen stems or thin needles leaves, or what appeared to be miniature palm trees with leaves that spread out like fans. A spider plant sat on a coffee table, a prickly aloe vera rested on the kitchen counter. A plant almost as tall as him with long, dark leaves sat by the doorway as if it were watching all who entered like a palace guard. The windowsill was overflowing with little plants lined up side by side like a row of ducklings, in colorful pots painted like easter eggs. So fascinated by all of them was he that Giovanni almost did not realize how small and worn the place was. Cracks and holes tore through the walls and ceiling, the ground, uncarpeted, was home to thousands of scratches and dents. Pipes and wiring hung visible overhead.

Giovanni's attention was finally pulled away from the interior of the place at the sound of running water. The old woman was at the sink, pouring water from the tap into a little mug. Giovanni's stomach churned at the thought of drinking tap water, but the bile on his tongue fought against that urge and reminded him that desperate times called for desperate measures. She walked to him where he stood, still frozen, just barely past the doorway, and handed him the mug with frail hands that trembled with age, murmuring a soft, "There you are," as he accepted it. In the light of the house Giovanni could see the woman's hair was kept in a ponytail, and it had been blonde, once (there were still wisps of blonde throughout it, its presence as frail as the rest of her), but what was left was mostly a pale, wiry gray.

Without saying a word Giovanni forced down the liquid in the cup, trying not to care about the unpleasant, metallic bitterness of the tap water. Like a sponge his tongue and mouth and throat seemed to come back to life, just a little, rejuvenated as they were moistened by the city water.

"My name is Beatrice," the old woman said. She was standing and watching Giovanni, looking up at his face. Giovanni wondered suddenly what shape his makeup was in, what impression he even gave off at this point, and he was not sure he wanted to know. Beatrice walked to the old couch that sat in the center of the small room. It was in a similar condition to the rest of her home, worn, lived in, decaying, and it creaked and heaved when she sat down on it as if it were gasping for air beneath her presumably very little weight. "You know, there are very few people out here who would invite a stranger into their home in good faith, and even fewer who would trust such an invitation in the first place. So I assume you are either very lost, very stupid, or you have nothing left to lose. Which is it, Giovanni?"

Giovanni walked and sat across from Beatrice in an old chair that was in no better shape than the couch. There was a little table with a lamp beside it that emitted a warm light, and a potted lamb's ear next to that. He reached out and let his fingertips brush over the soft leaves. Keeping his eyes on the plant, he said, "I... I just... I wound up here by mistake, I don't know-." He felt as if he were going to cry. He squeezed the lamb's ear between his fingers and swallowed saliva that was only now able to form after having something to drink. And now tears threatened to expel that precious liquid from his body once again. "I do not know the first thing about living out here."

"Clearly," said the woman, in a tone that was colder than Giovanni expected, making him look at her with a frown as she sat, stiffly, watching him. "I will answer your question for you: You are very stupid, Giovanni. Nobody in his right mind would announce himself a member of that family to a stranger out here."

These words were so bizarre that Giovanni could hardly process them. An inkling of concern caused his heart to skip a beat at the thought, suddenly, that he was perhaps in some sort of danger. Voice coming out meek, he said, "I do not understand why that makes everyone so angry." He looked down and realized that he was holding the leaf of the lamb's ear in his hand, torn away from the plant that had been giving it life. He rubbed the severed leaf between his fingers, fidgeting distractedly, eyes glancing from it to Beatrice.

"How old are you, Giovanni?" Beatrice asked. Giovanni could not for the life of him understand how this had anything to do with what he had just said.

"Thirty-four," he said quietly, helpless. "Are you going to hurt me?"

Beatrice let out a laugh, although it sounded almost like a cackle, loud yet frail, amused in a way that seemed almost belittling, although perhaps Giovanni was just paranoid at this point. He directed his attention to the leaf in his hand nervously. He tore at it a little, folded it, rolled it, did everything he could to keep himself occupied with it.

"No, Giovanni, I am not going to hurt you. You seem very lost, and I do not know how much I can do to help you, but I can tell you this much: You and your family are not seen kindly out here. They are a symbol of the powerful evil that permeates our world, and their reach stretches further across this city every day. And in the streets, too many people have lost everything to your candies."

"Papa has only... ever tried to do good for the people. They call him a hero." Despite Giovanni's words, his tone was not combative, but one of bewilderment, or perhaps a desperate plea, begging for better understanding like a child who had just been told that there was no Santa Claus or Easter Bunny. "They're cheaper than real medicine and they're easily accessible, every store sells them and people can afford them."

"They're certainly cheaper than medicine, yes." Beatrice gave a grim nod. "But that's hardly saying much when medicine has become impossible to access since the privatization. And rumor has it that your family is taking steps towards the medical industry too, now, and I can only imagine what will happen to those who are unable to afford the future of Marcello Candies henceforth. Withdrawal is a terrible thing, to watch and to experience." Giovanni did not know what she was talking about, and the blank expression on his face, jaw hanging open slightly, eyes on her, silent and waiting with nearly bated breath, clearly indicated that. "Your family treats us like animals in a circus, Giovanni. We eat lollipops and chocolate bars wrapped up in rainbow paper in hopes that the pain of inevitable death will be alleviated only slightly, while you... what, attend parties and spend frivolously on cosmetic surgery and high fashion?"

Giovanni shrunk back again, looking away. He did not know how to reply. Bubbling with a sort of defensiveness intermingled with a continued plea for understanding, he figured it would do no harm to tell her that he had been disowned, that he was all but a bastard child in his father's eyes, and he had nothing to his name, not even his own name, to cling to for identity any longer. He was lost and alone, and he was ashamed, and he held a hesitation within him at the thought of admitting to another soul that in barely a day he had fallen from the hilltop on which rested his father's mansion to the darkest depths of the city streets. He tore the leaf in half, rolled one half into a ball, and crushed it between his fingers, squeezing out the moisture within, and, very softly, he said, "I am afraid I've had quite the fall. My father... I am not welcome at my father's, I- I no longer have a home, and I have nowhere to go, and very, very little to my name."

"How much *do* you have to your name?" Beatrice asked.

Giovanni thought for a moment, having a hard time remembering clearly the events of the previous few days; it had all been so tumultuous. "The... The clothes I am wearing now. And a debit card with some money on it. I am not sure how much. It is a small sum that will be replenished by my father at the start of each month." That was it, he realized numbly. Even his earrings had been taken from him. "I suppose... I should lay low, and save until I have the funds to... to..." He choked back the urge to cry again as he realized how daunting any step forward from here truly was. "I would need a- a shower- to show my face out there again... Can I... Can I stay with you...?"

Beatrice sighed and said nothing for a moment. Giovanni stared at his hands. He wondered what his father was doing right now, what was happening within the confines of his mansion, what had become of his bedroom. The overbearing warmth of the room was making him feel dizzy and very out of place.

Beatrice finally spoke. "I'm afraid I can hardly be a source of good news or comfort for you, Giovanni," she said, "But, frankly, as you are right now, you don't have the privilege to lay low. You stick out like a sore thumb and any part of this city where saving money or building credit is a possibility will not welcome somebody like you." She pointed towards him, and Giovanni, still looking down, saw the movement only in the corner of his eye and flinched. "You're covered in blood. I can only imagine that that proves my point. I imagine the next time may be even worse."

Giovanni's heart had picked up in his chest. Feeling panic rise in him as what Beatrice was saying dawned on him, he said, "Then what am I supposed to do? I can't... I can't die out here!" The words felt like poison on his lips, he said them as if they had a vile flavor, quickly and uncomfortably, forcing them out of his mouth.

"You certainly can," Beatrice replied. "My advice for you would be to leave. Leave your belongings, your identity, and leave the city altogether. If you want a chance to live, it will have to be elsewhere, as somebody else."

"Fresno is all I know."

"Many would say the same," Beatrice agreed with a nod. "Especially when they have the luxury of having everything they could possibly need at their disposal, as I'm sure you have. But it's my understanding that you are not so lucky anymore."

"Have you ever left?"

"No. And I don't know what you'll find out there. Fresno used to be a centerpiece for numerous smaller counties, but I believe it's swallowed most of them up at this point. But I am certain that you won't find anything worse out there than what you would face penniless on Fresno City streets."

Giovanni furrowed his brow. "I am not penniless."

Beatrice nodded again. "Your debit card is not a concern of yours any longer. You need to rebrand, escape the Marcello name. In exchange for my kindness, hospitality, and advice, all I ask is that you leave that with me." Giovanni thought about this for a moment, silent, taken aback by the request. The old woman persisted, "I could just as easily leave you back on the street to rot, or, worse, call the Birds of Prey and tell them that a strange man has entered my home, tell them any story that I want. And why would your father believe you over me when, according to you, he has disowned you?"

Giovanni still said nothing. Despite the warmth of the house, he was beginning to feel very cold, and although the throbbing pain in his nose and the panicked, suffocating fear he had felt earlier was much more visceral, much more overtly threatening, there was a different type of uncomfortable nervousness beginning to creep on him as he stared at the old woman, avoiding her piercing gaze as it jutted from the sagging wrinkles around her eyes.

"I do not want to ruin your life, Giovanni. But everybody needs money. And you need my help."

Giovanni's mouth felt dry again. "Then help me."

Beatrice nodded. "There are buses that exit the city daily. My suggestion for you would be to stay here tonight, and then take the first bus out of the city tomorrow morning. Go as far as you can on it, no matter which direction it takes you. Leave your nice clothes with me and go in your undershirt; wearing fine material will only make you stand out anyway. I will give you the cash needed to pay the bus fare."

Giovanni had no way to argue with any of this, he realized. He had already locked himself into this situation, trusting this old woman and entering her home, sharing with her his name and his history. But what choice did he have? He did not know the city streets. He did not know how to survive out here. Only a day on his own had resulted in him getting into the state he was in now, bloodied, bruised, starving, and sick. Taking the risk of backing out now and choosing a different path meant risking his own life, and the thought of another night puking in a back alley, or being beaten half to death, terrified him. Surely she was right: Nothing outside of Fresno could be worse than what he had already seen.

Beatrice stood slowly. Giovanni looked up at her from where he sat, the torn lamb's ear leaf still resting in mutilated chunks in his hands.

"I'm going to bed now. You can sleep on the couch," she said. "You're welcome to some food, if you like. The pantry has plenty of snacks. Make yourself at home."

Giovanni watched silently as the old woman took a few slow steps towards a hallway that presumably led to her bedroom. It was only as she was about to turn into a doorway that Giovanni managed to find his voice and call out, "Are you... actually trying to help me, Beatrice?"

Beatrice turned back around and smiled at Giovanni, her expression barely visible in the shadows. "This city is dying, Giovanni. I have watched it become consumed by a sickness much too severe for even Himmel to cure, and now my own days are numbered by an illness that would have been treatable had I the access. And soon enough I—and perhaps yourself—will simply be a part of the growing statistics that young and optimistic children will use to fight an unbeatable battle. Plant food, should we be so lucky. I mean you no harm, nor am I trying to trick you. But understand that we all do what we must to survive."

Vittoria stayed awake long into the night, which was not an easy feat considering the inescapable exhaustion that weighed down upon her, and Anubis' bed, large and soft, luxurious, regal and pillowy and decorated with exotic furs and silks, felt like paradise on weary limbs and an overworked brain. But still, she remained awake, waiting until she was absolutely certain that Anubis had fallen asleep in order to carefully shift away from him, freeing herself of his touch, of his bony arm draped over her naked shoulder, hoping that the distance would free her mind as well of the thoughts that overwhelmed her brain. Still, sleep did not come easily. Anubis' presence was much too powerful for a mere few inches of distance to prevent her awareness of him, and her heart pounded with anticipation of what the future held until she finally, after much tossing, an eternity of lying awake with restless thoughts gripping her weary half-consciousness, fell asleep.

In spite of it all, the moment she allowed exhaustion to overtake her, Vittoria relaxed, freed from the stress of the day, into the first comfortable, restful, perhaps even pleasant sleep she had had in a very long time.

Giovanni was woken at dawn. Pale, thin light, muted by a layer of dust, dripped slowly into the room from an old window he had not noticed in the dark of night. He was dizzy and disoriented, and his body shivered violently as if he were freezing despite the ever-present humid heat of Beatrice's home. His back ached and he felt sick, his nose throbbed where it had been punched, and he had slept in his makeup, or whatever was left of it, which by now must have been horribly, clownishly smeared and seeping into all of his delicate, sensitive pores, alongside the unwashed blood that still stained his chin and clothing.

Beatrice gave him some fruit and toast, a small wad of cash, and directions to the closest bus stop. Giovanni, in return, gave her the debit card his father had given him barely a day prior, told her the card's pin, and left his fine purple jacket where he had hung it the night before. He took off his bloodstained white button-up as well, leaving him in nothing but a plain white undershirt that was stained with dried blood and clung uncomfortably to his body; at some point during the night he had broken into a cold sweat, which perhaps was the cause, too, of his constant shivering.

Within half an hour of waking, Giovanni was waiting at a bus stop. Although he had splashed water from the sink onto his face in order to wash off the blood, he had stubbornly avoided any mirrors as he could not bear to even begin to confront his own appearance. He could only imagine what he must have looked like: Stripped to a stained undershirt, hair a tangled mess, nose bruised and swollen, potentially even dislocated, any makeup left now smudged and worn, whole body weak and trembling with physical and mental exhaustion and a mystery sickness seemingly attempting to penetrate his already battered body. But, thankfully, there were very few around to notice him, and those who did walk past in the pale early hours did not pay him any heed. Just as Beatrice had promised, by leaving his old self and belongings behind he blended into his surroundings for the first time since his disownment.

The sun was higher and the sky had turned from a dreary gray with open wounds of red and orange into the light blue of morning by the time a bus arrived.

One bus transfer later, which took another hour out of Giovanni's morning and gave the sun ample time to rise and spread its rays across the landscape, drying the morning dew and promising an oppressively hot day, and he was on the first bus out of the city—entirely empty aside from himself and the bus driver, who said nothing to him, but eyed him with a vague distastefulness. They were heading South, and the map behind the driver did not have names for any of the stops beyond of the city limits, as if they did not even have an identity aside from being markedly "not Fresno."

But perhaps, Giovanni thought, that was a good thing.

# ACT III

A Note on Fresno History: Himmel Medicine

Himmel Medicine is renowned across Fresno and the globe for its cutting-edge technological strides, as well as its constant expansion into new territories, incessantly concocting new and inventive ways to save and improve lives. Alongside medical advancements, Himmel has worked to streamline the industry in other ways as well. For example, within the last decade, Himmel launched Prescription Vehicles, armored trucks to deliver medicine and medical devices on-the-go to clientele to eschew the need to pick it up from a pharmacy, be it due to poor health making travel difficult or simply out of convenience. On a related note, as a part of Himmel's ever-growing accessibility initiative, there are more and more Himmel satellite pharmacies popping up throughout even the poorest regions of the city, making supply distribution and accessibility to Himmel's resources easier than ever!

Himmel's origins begin as a humble plastic surgery company, focusing purely on cosmetic procedures, and later branching out to reconstructive surgeries, under the philosophy that through Himmel, anyone can become as beautiful as Heaven's angels. Quickly gaining traction due to their dedication to providing increasingly complex, experimental, yet always extremely successful surgeries at increasingly reduced costs and with always-accessible financial plans, Himmel grew rapidly in popularity, and soon spread its wings beyond plastic surgery. Himmel has since begun to buy out competing hospitals, merging with its competitors and branching out into more medical fields, monopolizing the Fresno medical industry—A move widely considered "for the best," given the great amount of lives that have been saved and the admirable work ethic shown in the company's push towards a healthier, happier, and more beautiful future.

Refusing to give up its spot at the very edge of progress, Himmel's has only continued to expand. Only recently, Himmel announced the opening of its newest branch, a highly secretive, research-based department known only as "Experimental Cosmetics," a simultaneous return to form harkening back to the company's origins in plastics, while still demonstrating the promise to the public that Himmel will continue to soar towards the future, ushering in a new age of medical procedures unlike that which could ever have been previously imaginable! This is hot on the heels of the controversial decision for Himmel to expand beyond the medical industry entirely by buying out a significant section of the Fresno Police Department, forming a new security team referred to as Himmel's Birds of Prey, followed swiftly by the partnership with the Fresno County Jail, which now functions, legally, as a branch of Himmel's hospital system. Whiffs of theories that this groundbreaking decision is in some way connected to the announcement of the "Experimental Cosmetics" branch have permeated tabloids, but Himmel refuses to comment at this time.

Matteo Marcello, former chief of police and a current Accipitriform, known colloquially as a "Hawk," of the Birds of Prey, tells us that under Himmel's control there has been a renewed vigor amongst former members of the police department, who have found a new life under Himmel's reign; paraphrasing Marcello's explanation (and be sure, folks, to pick up next month's edition of Himmel's *Guardian Angel* magazine for the full interview!), those who have been caught disturbing the peace of our great city will now be given the opportunity to shorten or even expunge their sentence entirely, creating a more just, incentive-based system where criminals are given more autonomy and the choice to be a part of projects that will improve the lives of countless civilians. Himmel giving criminals a chance at reformation under its care and guidance proves once again the lengths the company goes to always make sure that Fresno City is the best among the best.

At the last stop before the bus turned back towards Fresno, Giovanni got off.

Although he had been sitting in one place for well over an hour, he felt exhausted. His body was still racked with shivers that only worsened when he finally stood after such a long period of inaction, and so sore and weak was he that it was immensely difficult to extend his legs forward from one step to the next, down from the bus and onto the ground, shivering with each thump of his feet. The intense dizziness left him at least half certain that with each step he would trip over himself and fall, face first, into the dirt below, and it felt truly a miracle that he made it to the bottom in one piece.

The moment he was off the bus, the driver, without saying a word, shut the door and drove away. Giovanni blinked bleary, tired eyes and looked around, taking in his surroundings after he had spent the last hour staring at the bus' carpeted floor.

He was not in the city anymore.

That was Giovanni's first observation, and it felt like a very stupid one, given how obvious it was. Gone were the tall buildings, lights, cars, crowds. Giovanni looked first towards the direction he had come, the long stretch of road, the bus he had taken already growing smaller and smaller in the horizon as it knew damn well it had no imminent stops, and he could hardly believe that somewhere out there was the vast city that he had grown up in and the dark streets that he had been a victim of the night before. Now there was nothing but road, yellowed, withering grass, and a long field of dead nothingness for as far as he could see.

At least in the other direction there was some semblance of life. It appeared to be the crude outline of a town, something that had at one point been populated, with scattered buildings popping up from the dry, dusty road like graves.

Giovanni walked into the town on weak and exhausted legs, aching with each step he took, fighting back the incessant tremble in his body. He felt very sick. There were storefronts with signs that had long since faded, lights that had burned out, doors and windows boarded up. There were no people out, and Giovanni found a surmounting worry forming within him that this place was entirely deserted. Was this a dead end? Had he come this far only to find that there was nowhere else to turn but back around? Would the bus even return, and if so, how long would he be out here, alone in this heat, growing sicker by the hour? He was too weak and disoriented to feel anything but a deep sense of sluggish dread at these questions, so thick and heavy that it subdued any panic or urgency, and he found himself left with nothing but a vague thought that perhaps he was going to die out here, from starvation or dehydration or exhaustion or whatever it was that was making him feel so terribly sick at the moment, huddled for shade beneath one of the crumbling buildings until all that was left was a corpse as rotten and decayed as the rest of this ghost town.

It was hot; Giovanni had hardly even realized it on account of how viciously he was trembling. He felt out of control and out of touch with his own body, and the sweat running down his forehead and into his eyes came as a surprise to him. His clothing, the bare remains of it, clung to his skin, and the remainder of his makeup felt oily and greasy on his face, soaking into his pores alongside the sweat. He was nothing but remnants now, he thought, once more imagining himself as the rotting skeletal corpse on the side of the road. Eventually he would be found by some passerby, still wearing his bloodied undershirt, devoid of his jewelry, unrecognizable from any other poor soul left to die out here. Nobody would even begin to presume the journey he had traveled to get here, know who he was and his past. More sweat dripped past his brow, catching with it some old foundation and making his eyes sting. He scrunched them tight and rubbed them on the back of his hand, and when his vision had returned he noticed an open door a few buildings down, alongside a flickering red OPEN sign.

At best it was a sign of life, and if nothing else it was shelter from the heat. Either way, Giovanni was desperate, and he all but broke into a jog to reach it. When he stopped, although it had only been a few yards and he had hardly been moving particularly fast at all, he found himself winded and light headed, sicker than before, close to either puking or passing out, not sure which would happen first; his throat still felt raw from the previous night's dash through the city streets and there was a terrible burning in his lungs, but he willed himself to focus even as his vision swam and doubled.

Whatever faint flickers of hope remained in him reignited as he came to realize that was indeed life within the building before him. The door was open, the neon sign flickered, and there were windows on the outside; great, clear windows, the dust and grime cleaned off of them with obvious care, through which he could see a bar, with people inside, sitting at tables and barstools. The interior did not look much better than the town surrounding it, with old, decrepit, eroding wood of chair legs and tabletops, booths with torn and stained vinyl backing, and ancient looking, burned out bulbs that sat lifelessly in lamps, or were otherwise missing from the socket entirely, but it hardly mattered. He could find help here. He looked up to catch the name and found a sign, a large placard with text carved in wood, sporting the single word: UNDERCROFT. Giovanni stepped inside.

Upon his entry, everybody in the room looked up quietly, a sort of silent, yet obvious, awareness of his presence. Two men sat at a booth, talking over beers, while another sat at the bar alone, and another slouched over in the corner. A fifth man stood behind the bar, dressed nice enough, in a suit that Giovanni could tell was decent in quality and appearance but very worn and old fashioned compared to the modern suits that downtown Fresno boasted in storefronts. He could not speak nearly as highly of the men at the tables, however, who all looked to Giovanni as if they had spent the better portion of their lives just narrowly escaping death. Their clothes were torn and stained, their skin either tanned or burned by the sun, their hair unkempt, with dirt beneath their fingernails and clinging to the pores of their flesh, and he wondered what the lives of all of these sorry souls could possibly have been like, but with a pang of embarrassment Giovanni realized that in his present state he likely did not look much better for wear.

Giovanni felt half delirious as he stared from person to person, meeting faces that were blurred and distorted in his tired eyes, faces that furrowed and hardened with clear distaste at him. Then the man at the bar spoke up, causing him to whip around so quickly he nearly fell over. "Can I do anything for you, stranger?"

Giovanni stared, blinked heavy eyelids, and realized that, quite frankly, he probably could not. "I..." Giovanni wet his lips with the little spit remaining in his drying mouth. "I'm not sure." He felt very stupid, completely at a loss for words, incapable of explaining himself. His head was still spinning and he could not for the life of him remember why he had come out here to begin with. What was here for him? Was this the only sign of life in this dreary place? These filthy people in their rundown bar? "I'm afraid I'm... very lost."

"I'll say," the man at the bar said with what almost sounded like laughter in his voice.

Giovanni continued to stare, expressionless, mouth hanging open slightly. Then, slowly, his tongue found the ability to move again, and he mumbled out, "Do you have... any candy?"

One of the men in the booth dropped a glass, which caused it to fall to the ground and shatter with a sound so loud and so sudden that Giovanni leapt in fear, turning with urgency as if he had thought a bomb had just been dropped. The men began laughing, as did the man at the bar, as well. All eyes were on him again, and Giovanni felt like he must have been in a nightmare. He blinked, looking between the people.

"Just where do you *think* you are, stranger?" the bartender asked, with a tone of voice much more hostile than before.

Giovanni felt an intense embarrassment writhe in his stomach alongside the nausea that had been plaguing him throughout the morning. Tears welled in his eyes. His face burned beneath the sweat caked into his flesh and he cried: "I don't know!"

From behind him, a voice called out, "Oi, what's all the commotion about?"

The speaker sounded young, voice high and loud and accented, and Giovanni heard footsteps, light and dainty on what sounded like heels, and the swinging of a door. It slammed shut and Giovanni jumped again and looked up, across the room towards the source of the sound, with bleary, tear-filled eyes.

A person stood by the doorway on the far end of the bar—young, perhaps her mid-twenties. Her skin was warm and dark, a stunning contrast to the bright, sparkling silver-white of her dress and the long, matching silver curls that fell from her head to her waist. Her dress, despite the glitter that fell from it with each step that she took, was a rather modest cocktail dress, with long black gloves to match; she was quite glamorous upon first glance, Giovanni thought, but there was something markedly off in her presentation. The dress was visibly worn by age, subtly stained and torn, fraying at seams, and the sparkles that once had encased it now only remained in patches; it had probably at some point been a much purer white than the grayish color it was now. The only splash of color, and what appeared to be in the greatest condition, was a shiny, polished gold chain that ended in a heart-shaped locket, which hung low around her neck so that it rested in the center of her chest.

The other thing about this person that left Giovanni so very confused, alongside, well, everything else about her, was that he could not for the life of him detect with confidence her gender, at least not by her voice, the shape of her face, or the flatness of her chest against the dress she wore. He stared in shock, mouth still agape, tears all but drying just like the rest of his dehydrated self as he was too confused by this newcomer to even process what was happening anymore.

Looking at Giovanni with light brown eyes, so bright they were nearly orange, a second burst of color against the grays and silvers that she wore, the strange person said, "Well, who the hell do you think *you* are?" Giovanni was still staring, entirely perplexed. She rolled her eyes, then sat down on the bar stool nearest to where she stood. "Why don't'cha take a picture, it'll try to resist ejaculating all over your pretty face,"

"What?" Giovanni was knocked from his stupor.

"It'll last longer." Her words were deadpanned, but there was snickering amongst the other bargoers.

"O- Oh."

"Are you just going to stand there gaping like that, or are you actually going to explain what the hell you're doing out here?"

Giovanni opened his mouth to speak but found that his tongue and throat felt very dry again. He swallowed and stammered, trying to find words, and finally managed out, "I- I came here from Fresno this morning."

To his surprise, this made her hesitate, pursing her lips and staring for a split second at Giovanni's face before her eyes darted to each person in the room, scanning over them, taking a quick survey for reasons he could not imagine before quietly standing back up. As she stood Giovanni noticed her heels, which matched her black gloves but showed the same signs of wear as the rest of her outfit, with visible scuff marks and a desperate need for polish. She walked over to Giovanni and he watched nervously as she approached, reached out, and took his hand in her own, which was silky soft in its glove. An odd smile played on her lips. "You're here for me, then! Fantastic!"

"What? I-"

The stranger squeezed Giovanni's hand and let out a sharp "SH" through gritted teeth, her expression unchanging, and then tugged

Giovanni forward, towards the back door from which she had come. Giovanni noticed a sign on the door, neon like the OPEN sign out front, but this one was pink and simply read: "GIRLS!" Giovanni wondered if that answered his question regarding this person's sex as he followed her helplessly.

Once they reached the door she threw it open and all but shoved him inside before following him in and shutting it immediately. Giovanni stumbled, fell, and found himself on a soft, faded red mattress that took up a considerable portion of the little back room. He sank into it, and he was so exhausted physically and mentally that he nearly could have passed out on it right then and there were it not for a quiet clicking sound in front of him, and Giovanni looked up to see that the stranger had turned around, her back turned as she faced the door, and he realized that she had just locked them both inside. Having some idea of what this sort of place was, and what this sort of person was, he struggled to sit up, panicking, fumbling awkwardly and weakly on the mattress, and cried out, "W- Wait! I'm not a client!"

"Shut *up*, will you?" the person, who was most certainly a prostitute, said under a hushed breath. "I took ya here to talk to you, that's all. Rule number one of this place is not to trust anybody, ever. Although I s'ppose I could say the same for Fresno, so you should know that." She stepped away from the door and walked over to sit beside Giovanni on the bed, staring at him so intensely that he looked away, to the barren wooden walls of the little room, empty save for a small drawer beside the big mattress that took up most of the space. It almost looked like some sort of walk-in closet, renovated into... whatever this was. She spoke again, "Alright, then. Who are you and how did you end up here?"

Giovanni turned back around to this strange, glittery person, still utterly confused by the whole situation and not sure what to make of her presence. He had never been as scared of this question as he was now. Not after what had happened back in Fresno, with the group of men who had attacked him and what Beatrice had told him. He certainly could not tell this person that he was a Marcello. But then who was he? Why *was* he here? His mind raced to find a story, but it was unable to land on anything, so dizzy, so overwhelmed, so overexerted was he that nothing could form into a tangible, solid concept in his mind.

The stranger shoved his shoulder, making Giovanni jump. "Well? Spit it out, then."

"Giovanni!" Giovanni admitted, panicking and unable to come up with anything else. "My name is Giovanni."

The stranger peered at him for a moment, eyeing him up and down, and Giovanni all but held his breath in fear, wondering what could possibly happen if she discovered his identity as a Marcello. Then, after a moment of silence, she snorted quietly, the seriousness of her expression weakening and a little, amused smile fighting its way onto her painted lips. "Giovanni? What kind of a name is *that*?" she asked. "You show up in the outskirts looking like a walking corpse and you have a name like *Giovanni*." She said the name long and drawn out, enunciating each syllable in a posher accent than her typical speaking style, and then snickered.

Giovanni's face turned red, but his fears were not quelled by her mockery. "And who are you?!" he asked, wanting to draw attention away from his name, and trying feebly to defend himself.

"You've barely answered my question, *Giovanni*," the rude stranger said with another little snort, saying his name long and exaggerated again, turning it into a caricature of what it was. "Telling me your first name—if that's even your real name, mind you—won't do me any good. Who are you *really*?" She reached out suddenly and grabbed hold of his chin, forcing him to face her directly. Her eyes were bright and burning into his skin. Giovanni gasped and stood up, pulling away completely, only to find himself so dizzy that he lost his balance and fell back onto the bed again. The person crawled to him where he lay on his back and looked down at him.

Over him the stranger just looked like a mass of silver and brown; Giovanni's vision was blurry and he was too weak to even move. He felt utterly trapped, afraid of his own identity, at a complete loss for words and realizing once more how truly poorly planned this entire venture was, growing dizzier and more disoriented by the moment. He felt in some ways as if he were experiencing the conversation from a cage underwater, everything slow and muffled, vision blurred, removed from light or air or direction or a world that made any sense at all, trapped in a sea of disorientation and uncertainty and discomfort unlike anything he had ever imagined before. From his there was still a throbbing ache coming and going in, and his limbs felt sore, and he could feel his muscles tremble each time he exerted them. He could only imagine what he looked like, in his underclothes, lacking any jewelry, any makeup, his own blood staining his shirt, and his own name feeling like an expletive.

When Giovanni spoke again, his voice was soft, and he felt almost disconnected from the sound of it as the words left his mouth. "I'm... I'm afraid I am going to die out here," He was trembling, not just his words but his entire being, both from a deep, cold fear that was beginning to settle over him as well as the same involuntary shivering that he had been plagued with in the past twelve or so hours.

"Well, if it's any comfort, you wouldn't be the first and you won't be the last," the person over him said, and her tone had changed just a bit. "Sit back up," She grabbed his arm and gave it a pull. "Laying down will only make it happen faster." At that, Giovanni quickly allowed her to pull him back up into a sitting position. "What's going on with you? Are you sick?"

Giovanni could hardly even process the questions in his current state, heart racing from just the momentary exertion of forcing himself back up and the fear that had shot through him at her words. "Do you- Is there any way that I can... have something to drink? Just some water?"

She frowned and shook her head, making her silver curls bounce, a blur of glitter in Giovanni's bleary-eyed vision. "Ah, I'm sorry, love, but that'll come at a price at this place. Water isn't easy to get since the big companies drained it all up out here, so all the establishments charge a pretty penny for it." Her behavior had changed, Giovanni noticed, the hint of mocking distrust from before softening even as they spoke.

Giovanni was growing more and more hopeless by the moment, unable to understand any of what was going on. He felt that this strange woman was in on some joke that he was not, and he could not for the life of him process why he was even here. Why had she brought him here? Why was he in this strange place at all, so far from home? Where was his father?

"Withdrawal," she said suddenly. Giovanni blinked, eyelids feeling so heavy that he struggled to pull them back up, and when he did his vision was still blurry, the sparkly mass before him swimming in front of his eyes. "You're going through some sort of withdrawal, aren't'cha? That's what's wrong with you," she continued. Giovanni remained silent while he tried to comprehend this, the words spinning much like his vision through his brain. "What are you hooked on? Candy?"

Giovanni's body twitched almost instinctively at the word. Oh, it felt like so very long ago that he had last had any candy. He could still, only faintly, remember the last one, the little bag of golden candy he had bought at the motel, the sugary sweet taste on his tongue had been long since forgotten in favor of the metallic blood and acidic bile that had plagued his taste buds. If only he could feel the moist warmth of Marcello chocolate melting from the heat of his tongue and soaking into his mouth once again. His head spun. "Is there any candy out here at all?" he asked, desperate.

"Is that why you're in this mess, then?" the woman asked. She placed her hand on his arm again, resting the tips of her gloved fingers on him. "Listen, love, there's only so much I can do, honest. You need a bed and a drink, and I can't give you either here. But..." She looked around suddenly, and her hand tightened on his arm a little, and he stared at her, expressionless, salivating slightly, feeling like his brain was slowly withering away alongside his ability to comprehend the situation, drifting in and out of lucidity, still daydreaming half-consciously about the taste of artificial strawberry and milk chocolate. When she spoke again, there was a sort of resigned cautiousness in her voice, her tone hushed and uncertain: "If you can do me a favor, I think I can point you in the direction of somewhere you can get help. Or at the very least get a semi-fresh cup of water. Fair?"

"*Si*," Giovanni's voice came out weak in his own ears; everything felt weak, and he was not sure what he was agreeing to, and it felt like it took all of his strength to force his head to move in a slow and uncertain nod.

"Lovely," She clapped twice, making Giovanni flinch in surprise, and smiled. "I need you to deliver a message for me. I know a house out a ways from here. You'll have to walk there yourself, and if you get lost or can't stay conscious long enough to make it I don't have any advice for you, but if you can find it, tell the idiot living there that Cal sent you and said you were alright, and tell him not to forget that he owes me his bloody life, and-" She reached over to a drawer on the bedside table beside them and pulled from it a pair of pliers, which she tossed to Giovanni so abruptly that he failed to catch them and they hit his knee rather painfully, causing a dull ache to rattle through his bones, and bounced to the floor. As Giovanni slowly leaned over to pick them up, his limbs feeling almost too heavy to move, all of the blood in his body rushing straight to his head with his downwards movement, worried momentarily that he would not be able to sit back upright after the process was done, she continued, "-give him these. I nicked them off some sad farmer last night who had them in his jeans for some ungodly reason. He'll be back to question me, I'm sure, and it'll look good if I'm here with an alibi from the bossman that I never left. Capisce?"

Giovanni frowned and looked at the pliers. They were disgusting, caked in rust, dirtying his hands with sludgy grime. But he had no one else to turn to, nowhere else to find so much as a drink or a place to lay down, no other friendly face. He gave a nod and gripped the rusted metal tight. "Very well." And then, dully, he remembered the old woman he had spent the night with before, and asked, nervous that there was still yet a catch he was not privy to, "Why?

The woman shook her head, and when she spoke, the gentler demeanor than her initially brash exterior once more took charge: "If you've been arse-fucked by the Marcellos we have more in common than you think, and although *he* might not see it this way, I think the more we stand together the stronger we are. Just don't fuck me over too, got it?"

Giovanni did not understand what exactly this meant, but he nodded. "And you said your name is... Cal?"

"Hollywood California," the woman said. "At least, it's what you can call me." She smiled a little and gave a wink. "It's where the movie stars used to live. I think the whole world could learn a lot if they paid attention to history more, and not just the gritty war bullshit, not the politics and all, just what the fuck the actual human beings were doing. How they were living their lives."

Giovanni did not have the mental fortitude to ponder this comment. He looked back down at the pliers and felt his throat crack and burn as he swallowed what little spit he still had in his terribly parched mouth. The thought of walking more was daunting and he was not sure his limbs, weak and sore as they were, had it in them to carry him any further distance. But if he wanted to live, what choice did he have? Once more he was setting out on a journey to an uncertain destination, his only hope for survival in the hands of a person giving him directions to locations so far from home that they had never before even been in the realm of his imagination. He gave the pliers a squeeze that would surely leave a stain and looked back up. "Where is this house, Hollywood?"

Vittoria woke up alone in Anubis' bed, which was just as soft and comfortable as it had been the night prior, and for a brief while she felt no need to get up, no urge to move from the comfort of being sunken in the soft, pillowy mattress and silky sheets. Sunlight was dimmed by thin curtains and she shut her eyes and rested a while longer, calm and content. After taking a few deep breaths, the incense-scented air filling her lungs, she willed herself to slowly sit up and stretch. The only thing more tantalizing than the bed was the curious excitement piqued within her after the conversation—and the further interaction that had transpired even later into the evening—with Anubis the night before. She stood, found her clothing in the corner of the room, quickly pulled on her underwear and bra, and went to look for the Rock God of Death.

She did not find him in the upstairs bathroom, or anywhere upstairs, for that matter, so she traveled downstairs. The strange masks and dolls and figures peered down at her bare body from where they were hung up on walls or sat on Anubis' various shelves and tables. She glanced between them, still hardly able to believe that she was indeed in Anubis' home, that this was where she had spent the night and that the scratches that stung lightly on her arms and back were from his nails, but willed herself to walk past them and continue onwards. Finally, she found him in the kitchen, his back currently turned to her. He was washing dishes, an act that looked entirely bizarre to Vittoria. It was an action so very mundane, so domestic, and yet it was Anubis himself, tall, imposing, capable of holding his own on the stage, directing all attention onto him in shock and awe. And here he was washing the dishes. He was in a state of only semi-dress as well, shirtless but wearing dark gray skinny jeans, and he had taken the time to brush out his hair and return it to the state that it had been in the night before, a sea of carefully maintained black and silver curls.

"Morning," Vittoria called from the doorway.

Anubis turned, setting down the teacup in his hand with the utmost delicacy and revealing to her in the light what had only been visible in dim lamp light the night before, which were the plentiful scars that ran along his chest and abdomen, some fresher than others, of varying lengths, thicknesses, some pale and thin with age and others deep and dark, fresher. He looked as if he had been hacked apart and sloppily resewn, his skin contorted to fit an unnatural map across his bones and organs, a frankenstein of his own flesh. He was jarringly, uncannily thin, even more so than when clothed, as if he had no ribs or even internal organs to speak of. "Vittoria! Good morning indeed!" Anubis smiled brightly at her, revealing those sharp canines of his that she was significantly more acquainted with now. He walked to her and took her upper arms in his hands, squeezing them gently, and leaned in to kiss her forehead. "I've made some breakfast. It's a bit cold by now but I can reheat it easily."

"Er, um, no, that's alright," Vittoria said. "I... I'll just take a cup of coffee, please."

Anubis nodded. "Fabulous, I'll get right on it," He turned back to the kitchen. As he walked to the pantry, he said, "I have big plans for us today, Vittoria. I would like, if I may, to take you to the Embalmed recording studio and show you around. Then, tonight, I have my performance downtown at the Pharaoh's Tomb, and I would like you to attend the soundcheck before and see the goings-on behind the scenes. We do not have a moment to lose, Vittoria, time is of the essence and it waits for no man." He pressed a few buttons on his coffee maker.

Vittoria could hardly believe she had forgotten. Of course—The show tonight. A beacon of hope, the one thing she had clutched closest to her heart amidst the stress of the upcoming interview days prior. She could hardly believe now that she had forgotten that it was today, but then again, with the stress of absolutely everything that had happened to her within the past forty-eight hours, she supposed it had not necessarily been her first priority. Upon her initial disownment she had already begun attempting to mourn and then accept her losses: her beloved records, her paintings, and, of course, her concert ticket. And now, here she was, in Anubis' kitchen, confiscated concert ticket be damned.

"Of course, you will be attending the show tonight," Anubis continued, "You will be backstage, a privilege that many others have quite literally given up everything for." He chuckled as he watched the coffee brew. "Aside from that, is there anything on your own agenda today, Miss Vittoria?"

Vittoria nodded. "Ah, yes, actually. I..." She needed clothes. She needed *everything*. But now that she had a place to stay, she felt less concerned spending a bit of her frugal allowance on necessities. "I'm going to need to go home and pick up my things if I'm going to stay here,"

The lie came out naturally, before she had even given much thought to the decision to say it. She had not yet told Anubis of being removed from her father's home and name. She needed his help, and she knew her father's power, and she knew that Anubis knew, and she was not going to make it clear just yet that she was in such desperate need of him and his resources. Would he feel betrayed if he knew that she was in such a helpless position? Or perhaps he was using her, and she would no longer be a useful asset if he discovered the truth? The range of possibilities flashed through her mind and she resolved the decision to keep quiet on the situation. She would take a bus into a shopping center and pick up some new clothing, and Anubis would never know the difference. Still, there was a pang of guilt, lying to him, and, worse yet, there was a dull awareness that even now, in spite of it all, she was using her father to bolster herself forward.

She forced the thought from her mind and was thankful when Anubis spoke again to break the ceaselessness of her quickly-darkening thoughts. "Oh, of course," he said, "You may leave whenever, of course, but do try to be back by around one, and conserve some energy for our first lesson." He glanced back at her and smiled. "I predict that today will be very, very eventful."

He walked over to her now and handed her a cup of coffee and Vittoria, looking down at the cup, sighed in quiet frustration. Without asking, he had added cream and sugar.

The house that California directed Giovanni to was a ways out from Undercroft, beyond the main street and into the dystopian suburbs of scattered homes that sat, derelict, what may have once been a neighborhood reduced to piles of debris and the occasional skeletal frame of architecture. There was no sign of life out here at all, just yellowing plants, dead grass, patches of tan-brown dirt, but the long trail that he kept on, following the turns as California had directed, helped him at least keep his head up at the possibility of there being something out here that could help him.

It was a walk of about thirty long, slow, dry, painstakingly hot minutes. Giovanni thought it felt much hotter out here than it did in the city, and yet, despite the awareness of his flesh burning in the sun, the chill that ran through him worsened as he trudged forward, an underlying iciness beneath seared skin and sweat. He was dizzy, lightheaded, and struggling to walk straight, his feet trembling as they found footing on the dirt path, step by step. His brain pulsed in his skull, throbbing against his forehead and eyebrows. Waxy sweat dripped down his face in thick globs like a candle lit aflame for too long, the last remains of his makeup rolling down his face in smeared, oily droplets.

The numb awareness of mortality seeped in through sunburnt skin once more and Giovanni wondered vaguely if he truly would die out here, but with survival his only goal and only one single sliver of hope left to cling to he could not even conjure up the excess energy needed to feel any proper fear. As if the repression of this thought caused a physical reaction instead, at once his muscles took a spastic shove upwards, forcing him to stop and gag, dry heaving, sputtering, unable to even choke out any spit, his mouth and stomach long drained of any fluid. He sucked in dry, dusty air that burned his scarred throat, everything empty.

At some point, the spaces between the old houses became wider, signs of even the barest skeletons of former life becoming fewer and farther between, making way for more and more wide-open field of dead grass and dirt. The occasional tree, as lifeless as anything else out here, sat like a crucifix, jutting from the earth, dark and gnarled and dry as the rest of the world. It was out here, in this strange limbo past the abandoned suburbia and deeper into rural wasteland, a ten minute walk from any other structure, that Giovanni found the house he was looking for, if the sloppily painted string of numbers in fading white over the door was to be believed. Still, Giovanni could not find the strength within him to feel any sort of excitement, his thoughts far too subdued by exhaustion and pain that filled every crack and crevice of his being alongside a sudden pang of fear that this may truly have been some sort of cruel trick. The house appeared worn down, a state of disrepair not significantly better than the rest of the ghost town. Was this truly what he was looking for? A rundown shack in the middle of Hell? Had California lied to him, or had he made a mistake? He realized now that in spite of his exhaustion a small part of him had hoped that this house would provide him with the solace he sought, that within its very architecture the answer to his questions would be found, that his arrival would be glorious and resplendent. Every muscle in Giovanni's legs throbbed and trembled. The house sat before him, lifeless as a corpse.

He approached. It was a small, one-story building, a farmhouse that matched the landscape rather well in its earthy coloring. Regardless of what happened, Giovanni knew that he had to at the very least make it inside, find some sort of shade, perhaps even old, dusty furniture to sit in, before he collapsed.

And then, quite suddenly, Giovanni heard a cry from behind him and before he had any idea what had happened he landed face first on the ground. He groaned, his body so weak that despite the new burst of pain that coursed through him he was almost relieved to find himself horizontal. He was seeing double, his brain slow to reorient itself from the fall, when a voice above him cried, "Turn around and stay on your back!"

Giovanni was too dazed to respond, to which he felt himself promptly kicked in the leg. It was not a hard kick, and at this point Giovanni was convinced that any further pain would not even be felt as it was added to the heaping pile of preexisting pains already coursing through his body, but it was still enough to make him flinch and whimper. He slowly did as told, using what very well may have been the last of his strength to roll over, caking his sweat-drenched self in dirt, feeling the pliers in his back pocket press awkwardly into his skin. In an instant Giovanni felt a weight on his chest, pressing down on top of him. He groaned again and blinked heavy eyelids, his vision struggling to adjust to the bright sunlight boring down on his face.

He wondered for a brief moment if he was hallucinating, perhaps from exhaustion, or dehydration, or perhaps he had hit his head when he had fallen. Or perhaps he was truly dying.

Straddling him with legs on either side of his body, pinning him down hard against the dead, dry earth, was a young person—a girl, Giovanni thought—who could not have been older than her early twenties. Aside from the red tank top she wore, concealing breasts so small she was nearly flat beneath it, most of her appeared to blend with her surroundings: her skin was a dusty olive tone, her hair short and dark and tousled, her eyes a milk chocolate brown that were presently narrowed in anger. But it was hardly these features that Giovanni was concerned with. Rather, it was the pair of huge, white, feathered appendages that jutted from her shoulder blades and hung on either side of her body.

She had *wings*, Giovanni realized, staring with his dry mouth agape in as much shock as his body could possibly muster.

He was so shocked, in fact, that it was not until he felt the sensation of cold, sharp metal pressed to his throat that Giovanni realized that the winged girl straddling him currently held him at knifepoint.

"Who are you?" she snapped. Her voice was rough, deeper than Giovanni expected, although her tone was still shrill. "What are you doing out here?"

The first time Giovanni tried to speak no words came out. The second time, although he managed out "Hollywood-", after that his torn, dry throat gave out and he gagged and coughed for a moment. She waited patiently, but as he choked he could feel the cold metal of the knife press into his flesh just a bit, causing him to urgently recollect himself as quickly as he could. "Hollywood California sent me," he finally managed to gasp out.

The knife lowered, but her expression did not falter.

"California sent you? Are you a mechanic?" The wings twitched; it was a minor movement, but Giovanni could hardly keep his eyes off of them, the way the huge, feathered limbs, nothing like he had ever seen before, moved so organically with the rest of the stranger's small body. However, his eyes were brought back to her face when she suddenly shoved her hand against his throat. "Answer me!" she snarled. She had the look of a wild cat, inquisitive but threatening, piercing into him, studying with intent to attack, and the sunlight behind her made her silhouette almost blinding. Giovanni felt delirious, and even as it became harder to breathe with her hands to his throat he became increasingly aware of the awe he held towards her, staring up at her like she was a living deity before him or some desert mirage of divinity that his brain had conjured up in the throes of agonizing desperation he was in.

"M- Mechanic? No, but- but Hollywood California did... send me..." Giovanni insisted, staring up at her, lips parted and eyes wide in awe even as she kept him in the chokehold, but he breathed a sigh of relief when her hands left his neck. After a few rough coughs from deep in the back of his throat, he attempted to regain some composure, present himself better to this stranger (who, no doubt, was whom California had sent him to meet), or at the very least not be killed after making it so far, despite the incessant throbbing pain and perpetual, dizzying weakness. "Tell me," he began softly, because, he thought, in spite of it all, he knew how to talk to pretty young ladies, "What is a beautiful girl like yourself doing out here in a place like this?"

The girl froze. Her wings froze, too, stiffening and tensing. Her expression turned upwards, eyebrows raising, eyes widening, although her mouth remained firmly pursed, lips not twitching even the slightest bit up into anything resembling a smile. She seemed entirely caught off guard, unable to form a response for a moment. In the bright sunlight Giovanni saw a warm blush rise in her cheeks. He stared in a sort of wonder, intrigued by her even in his exhaustion.

Then she spoke: "Um, er, no. Um. I'm a guy."

As quickly as Giovanni's confidence had begun to ever so nervously peak its head out from the hot, dry cracks, it was violently stomped to nothing like a bug. He could not conceal the look of surprised embarrassment on his face, which rivaled the surprise he had exhibited upon first seeing the stranger's wings in the first place.

"Oh." Giovanni said. "Ah..."

The *boy* got off of Giovanni and sat on his knees beside him, watching with the knife still in his hand, but it was a more relaxed grip now. Giovanni sat up slowly, his back stiff and aching from the fall, and

146

brushed some of the dirt off of his clothing, although he knew this was futile. He could not begin to imagine what state he was in right now, what he must have looked like to this odd stranger. There was silence between the two of them; Giovanni did not know what to say. He had no idea whatsoever how to speak to this strange person, and he did not like that he still carried a weapon, although he was grateful to no longer have it pointed at his neck. And, on top of it all, Giovanni's head still throbbed painfully, he was still horribly dizzy, his torn throat still stung, his nose still ached, his thoughts swam only semi-coherently, and the adrenaline of the stranger's initial arrival was beginning to wane, leaving all of the various pains and discomforts to return in full force and allow fear to give way once more to pure exhaustion.

The boy spoke, directing Giovanni's attention back to him as his thoughts had begun to wander downwards into bleak, dark, empty despair. "So California sent you," he said again. "Who are you?"

Giovanni nodded slowly, his eyes moving from the boy's face to the wings on his back. They were huge, ethereal, they appeared almost uncanny as they hung so confidently from the otherwise recognizably human figure, but in the position he was sitting they rested on the ground, dirtying the tips of the stark white feathers. "Ah, yes, um..." He was having trouble focusing. "My... My name is Giovanni." No last name. No last name. "I just got here..." He continued to stare, his vision growing fuzzy. The two wings became four and then six and then back to four. He blinked bleary, blurry eyes and shook his head. "California, uh... I... I was told to..." He swallowed, which succeeded in getting absolutely nothing down his aching throat, his tongue, dry and caked in gritty dirt, twitching helplessly, and blinked again, staring at those bright white wings as they shifted and rose and fell gently as their owner breathed softly. "I..."

"Are you alright?" the boy asked, and he reached out and placed small, lithe fingers on Giovanni's upper arm. Giovanni jumped at the contact, a response so severe it was as if the boy had threatened to stab him with the knife again. He frowned. "You don't, er... You don't look too... You look like shit."

Giovanni didn't reply for a moment, struggling to even comprehend these words, their meanings blurring and becoming vague and uncertain in his head just like the rest of his fragmented thoughts, drowning in dizziness and dehydration. The image of his countless, bountiful makeup palettes and products, a dazzling, pristine collection of glitter and rainbow, flickered through his mind and felt like a lifetime away. "I'm not," he admitted quietly. "I need..." Candy, he thought in the back of his mind. "Water," he settled on. At the very least it would help the horrible burning in his throat.

The boy nodded and stood up, a motion that made Giovanni flinch again. "Can you stand?" he asked. "If you can get to the house I can... I can, um... I can fix you up a little, maybe, uh..." The boy stood there awkwardly, staring down at Giovanni.

It wouldn't be easy, but Giovanni knew that despite the pain, despite the dizziness, despite the fear, and despite the numb disorientation that blanketed over it all and left him hardly able to comprehend his own situation, he at the very least had the strength to make it into the house. He gave a very slow nod and began to force himself up onto aching limbs. It was close—so, *so* very close. And within it held shade, and water, and perhaps even the possibility that he would survive after all.

Embalmed Records owned a building near the very heart of the city, not far from the recording studio in which the catalyst which led to Vittoria's disownment had initially taken place only a few short days earlier. It was a tall, sleek, black building, with the words EMBALMED RECORDS hung in metallic golden lettering. There was a great screen on the front, high up above the city streets, visible for all who walked past to see. Currently, it bore a countdown, tracking the hour, minute, and second. Vittoria looked out the window of Anubis' car, watching the time decrease, second by second, as Anubis drove.

"It's counting down to the show," Vittoria noted.

"That's right," Anubis said, keeping his eyes on the road. They were stuck in a swamp of city traffic, although with the building in sight it would not be much longer now. "Truthfully, I need to test out the technology; I foresee public broadcasting to be a key to the success of a number of my future projects."

"Hm?" Vittoria turned to him curiously, and his eyes left the road for a brief second to glance to her and smile.

"I have big plans, my dear," he told her. "There is much to explain, much more than I can begin to get into right now, although I believe by tonight you will have received a decent portion of answers."

About five minutes later the car was parked in a small parking lot behind the building, clearly reserved only for Anubis himself and a very small selection of what Vittoria imagined must be other incredibly important individuals. He stepped out of the car first and walked to the passenger side, opened the door for Vittoria and held out a hand to her. She accepted it and allowed him to help her out, and then she stood and looked around, staring at the back of the Embalmed Records building and finding that, from here, it looked no different from any other of the big studio buildings that she had been in throughout the duration of her life, accompanying her father or to promote her own projects.

"Vittoria, tell me: How familiar are you with my performances?" Anubis asked, drawing her attention away from the building and back to him.

Vittoria panicked at the question. Not because she was unfamiliar, no. It was quite the opposite. An embarrassment settled over her that made her immediately hesitate to give an honest answer: She *adored* Anubis, and with a sense of melancholy like an open wound in her gut she thought back to her collection of records and the countless times she had played through his albums, allowing them to be the backing soundtrack of her life, the sounds that carried her through the long days where she felt exhausted and aimless. And yet, there was something that held her back now, from unloading to Anubis himself the amount of joy he had brought her, how enamored she had been with him, the fact that he was perhaps one of the biggest reasons she had begun pursuing music herself to begin with. It was too forward, she thought, too desperate. Instead, she stammered out, "Yeah, er, I first saw you when you toured for 'Ammit's Tooth.' It was... really cool." Even as she tried to hold back she could detect an almost breathlessness in her own voice.

"'Ammit's Tooth'... That album was a while back, so you've been a fan for some time. Marvelous."

"You pulled out your teeth on stage," Vittoria recounted. She was pretty sure they had still been human-shaped then, and not the razor sharp canine teeth he sported now.

"I was in need of a new set of transplants anyway," Anubis mused. "Anyhow, it delights me to know that you are not entering this world with a blank slate. You already know how things appear from the front of the house—It's time for you to see the goings on behind the veil. I think you are in for a treat, Vittoria." He reached out and took her hand in his own, squeezing it gently in his long, bony fingers and tugging her towards the building.

"I'm excited," Vittoria admitted in earnest.

She was surprised to see Anubis lead her around to the front of the building, out into the open, where dozens of cars waited aimlessly in traffic and people bustled past on the streets. She knew well enough that to say Anubis was an elusive figure was an understatement. He kept himself entirely anonymous and avoided the vast majority of public appearances, and in the rare moments in which he was seen he still kept his face fully covered. To see him out in the open now, walking down the busy Fresno street, face fully visible, felt almost dreamlike. Was this not his building, created for the singular purpose of distributing the music made under his record company, of which he was the CEO and founder? Was this not dangerously incriminating? Quietly, Vittoria began to say, "Nobody recognizes you-"

"Hush, Vittoria," Anubis said calmly, voice lowered as they walked past two men who hardly even looked up at the two of them, other than a quick glance to Vittoria that was likely nothing more than checking her out, perhaps vaguely recognizing her from television, but they did not so much as react to Anubis. "You will understand soon enough."

They entered through the front door of the building, which slid open with a dramatic, automatic whoosh, and Vittoria was instantly bombarded by the cool chill of no-doubt expensive air conditioner as well as the jarring interior of the place. The entrance was a long hallway, and the walls, ceiling, and floor were all a polished black. Intricate golden designs were etched into the walls, hieroglyphic-looking symbols: Snakes with barred fangs, jackals on the prowl, animal-headed beings and creatures that existed only in the imaginations of their creator all adorned the walls in stylized gold symbols. Surrounded only by shiny obsidian blackness and the glistening gold of the symbols on either side of her, she immediately felt at home.

She did not notice at first that Anubis had patiently stopped for her when she had stopped, and he was watching her now as she reacted to the portal-like entrance of the building. "Impressed?" he asked after a moment, turning her attention back to him. "When I initially bought the place, I was insistent on making it reflect my personal style. I had the money, the ambition, and the eye, and I was not going to let my City of Dis be stunted by the abysmal dullness that encompasses so much of the professional world."

Vittoria was still looking around in awe, but finally she turned to Anubis and said, "It's amazing,"

Anubis smiled brightly in the dark hallway. "I'm glad you think so," he said, and then he began to walk down the hall, towards a room that looked much brighter, an odd birthing that all entrants into the building had to undergo.

The main office was a bit tamer in its design choices, although it still struck Vittoria as odd and eccentric, with checkered black and white flooring and red velvet walls. Various posters and promotional photos advertising past tours, shows, and album release parties were hung up on the walls. Unsurprisingly, the art on these posters was as wild, exotic, and imaginative, if not dark and perverse, as the rest of Anubis' aesthetic, with severed heads, cut up limbs, stylized animals with vicious expressions and exaggerated carnivorous features, and often artwork or photos of Anubis himself in his concert-wear, looking much like his namesake, a deity among men, tall and menacing, poised to attack, face obscured by his dark jackal mask.

"Good afternoon, sir," a voice said politely, drawing Vittoria's attention away from the walls. A woman in a sleek black dress was sitting at the counter, and her bright red lips were smiling in the very blatantly fake way one does when interacting with a casual professional acquaintance, "You work up on Floor 14, right?"

Anubis smiled coolly and protruded his wallet from his pants pocket. "You'd be correct," he answered, his own voice a more stiltedly polite tone than Vittoria was used to hearing from him. From his wallet he drew a card,; from where she stood she could not see it, aside from seeing that it was black with golden lettering, similar to the building itself.

The woman nodded and made a gesture with her head to an elevator to their right. "Of course. Up you go!"

Anubis thanked the woman and gave Vittoria's hand a squeeze, and she followed him to the elevator. She said nothing, not wanting to ask Anubis any questions, while still in the room with the woman, after he had already told her off for asking anything while they had been out front. Still, as they waited for the elevator to arrive, she looked at him with uncertainty, trying to make sense of these interactions. Finally, the elevator doors opened up, and she stepped inside behind him.

The doors closed as Anubis hit the large "14" button. Before Vittoria could ask any questions, as the elevator ascended upwards, Anubis said, "You know, I was asked when designing the building why I chose to omit Floor 13, as I am not necessarily known for superstition, or avoidance of the taboo. As I see it, the number fourteen has significantly more cultural power than thirteen at this point. In humanity's attempt to run from a cursed number we replaced it with another... Fascinating, isn't it?"

Vittoria blinked, caught off guard by these comments, for a moment so lost in confusion that she nearly forgot what it was that she had been bothered by a moment ago. Then, just as the elevator came to a stop, she remembered. "Why didn't that woman know who you were?"

The elevator opened. A wide grin spread over Anubis' cracked features in time to the smooth glide of the doors. "Follow me," he directed, not answering the question, but with an excitement in his tone that gave her hope that he was certainly about to. The hallway was similar to the one downstairs, with shining black walls and the intricately designed golden creatures. There were doors, though, as black as the wall they sat within and only visible through their golden handles and the golden writing on each one, marking the room numbers. They walked down the long hallway to the door at the very end. Anubis stopped here, opened the door, and held it for Vittoria to enter first. As she did he turned on the light and illuminated where it was that their pilgrimage had finally led them.

The room was full of costumes and props. Elaborate decorations and specially made outfits, tailored for single performances and likely never worn again, except perhaps for photoshoots, hung up or sat carefully on shelves. Props of all kinds, but primarily weapons, sat scattered. Knives, guns, scythes, but also ankhs and crosses, crystal balls, candles, masks, skulls, and so much more that she could hardly comprehend it all at once. Gold and silver, jewel-encrusted, carefully crafted specially for his performances. Anubis walked past her to the box that sat on the table in the corner of the room, rather innocuous in its placement; she had not even noticed it among the other treasures that the room held. Anubis, however, opened the box as if it held his only child: carefully, lovingly, delicately. He pulled out an item wrapped in red linen, and when he unwrapped it, he revealed an intricately designed black mask, shining like polished obsidian, of a ferocious looking canine. It was almost a full head mask, in that it went over the head entirely and would cover the wearer's hair in a black, soft-looking fabric material, but it only covered half of the face; just beneath the nose it opened to allow the wearer to speak without obstacle. Beneath the eye holes were intricately carved and painted golden markings, and as Anubis picked up the mask, despite the fact that there was no natural light in the windowless prop room, it seemed to sparkle and glisten as if it was reflecting the sun. This, Vittoria realized, was the beastly mask he wore on stage, as featured in the many posters of him around the main office and lurking in the shadows of her own mind as she remembered the performances she had attended. As chaotic, bloody, and frenzied as the show had always been, it was unmistakable.

"I am known only while wearing this. Without it, I can glide in secret through even the hallways of my own palace, a ghostly presence to be left undisturbed. There is power in knowing what others do not." Anubis explained, staring at the mask affectionately, gingerly running long fingers over the cheek. "In all the years I have performed under the name I have used it, give or take a few modifications over the years to achieve perfection. I designed it myself, had it commissioned using only the finest material. It is the vessel through which I share the depths of my soul to the world."

"It's beautiful," Vittoria said, and she meant it. She could hardly take her eyes off of it.

"I'm aware," He smiled at her, and then carefully put the mask on, pulling it over his head and covering his great curls with the soft fabric sewn to the back, covering his face from his nose upwards with the solid, shining jackal face, adding even more height to his already tall figure with the long, pointed ears that jutted from the top. Immediately he was transformed, no longer the man that Vittoria had spent the past day with, no longer the cool and collected Anubis who had invited her into his eccentric home of exotic oddities and served her dinner; from the neck up he had become a beast, and even his deep, dark brown eyes seemed to become wild and untamed beneath his new costume.

"You look... incredible," Vittoria admitted, wanting to say more, unsure of how heavy to lay on the adoration she felt now, the absolute exhilaration of awe and inspiration churning within her.

Anubis' smile remained the same beneath the mask, and yet, when he spoke, Vittoria swore his fangs looked sharper, his teeth even more threatening as they flashed from the inside of his mouth with each word. "After I christened myself Anubis, I went through an extensive series of facial surgeries. I was reborn anew in both name and appearance. And that was only the beginning. I suppose you could say that I am not the man I used to be." He chuckled to himself, and walked to the hangers where costumes were kept. Then he turned back to her again. "Now, Vittoria, once we have collected what we need, we will head on over to the Pharaoh's Tomb, and the fun can really begin!"

Giovanni still did not have the winged boy's name even after dragging his aching body into the house and collapsing what felt like mere inches from death into the living room couch. The house's interior felt as small as it had looked on the outside, and not particularly any nicer, with peeling walls, a graying popcorn ceiling, cracks and rot along various surfaces—but it was furnished and surprisingly cool, and Giovanni was relieved simply to at least no longer be baking in the sun and inescapably caked in dirt. Now he lay, his consciousness drifting in and out as he felt dangerously close to passing out, fully uncertain of if he would wake up if he *were* to pass out, when he was returned to dull alertness by the boy saying quietly over him: "Hey,"

Giovanni opened heavy eyes. There was a glass of water in front of him.

Immediately he reached for it, and he did not even bother to sit up properly before desperately bringing it to his lips and letting the water spill over his cheeks and chin, running down his neck and over the front of his shirt as he drank greedily, finishing the cup in a matter of seconds. Once it was depleted, he looked up to see the boy was still staring, unmoving. Expressionless, the winged stranger said, "Are you dying?"

Giovanni felt a chill run down his spine. Refusing to entertain this question, he asked, "Do you... have more water?"

The boy nodded without saying anything else, took the cup from Giovanni's hands, and walked away swiftly. Even in the delirious state he was in Giovanni noted how quietly he walked, like a mouse, on the tips of his toes. Why sneak around in such a way? How was it even possible, with those appendages weighing on his back? Were they heavy? Giovanni had hardly even begun to try to make sense of them, had hardly been able to make sense of this stranger at all.

While he waited, Giovanni took a moment to look around the place, the water slowly bringing him to his senses, cooling his overheated flesh and giving his veins the ability to breathe, his heart the ability to pump with slightly more confidence, replacing the buckets of sweat he had lost. The house was not nice; it was worn and small, falling apart in places, and yet he was still surprised by the quality of it. It was entirely furnished, and the furniture was not the cheapest quality around. It had, unexpectedly, an uneasy comfort about it. It felt lived in, inhabited, brought to life in its worn out used-ness. Or perhaps he was just desperate, staring out at the yellowing walls in rose-tinted glasses after he had been so desperate to live, hopeless and trapped in the middle of an empty nowhere only a short while ago.

After a moment the stranger came back with another glass of water and handed it to Giovanni before returning to stand and stare awkwardly at him. Giovanni, trying not to feel watched, began to drink again, but, with less urgency this time, stopped after downing about half the glass and looked up at the boy, unable to ignore his gaze.

"I gave you my name, so it's only fair that you give me yours," Giovanni said.

The boy seemed surprised by this, although his expression changed only slightly, his eyebrows twitching upwards. He watched Giovanni in a way not unlike he had earlier, when they had been out in the dirt, like a wide-eyed cat studying its surroundings. "Isn't it 'even' enough that I let you in? I saved your life,"

"Well, I need *something* to refer to you by?"

The boy paused, his expression taut, then he blinked and mumbled, "You can call me Angel."

"Call you Angel?" Giovanni raised a skeptical brow. "That is really your name?"

"Is your name really Giovanni?"

Giovanni faltered. *Yes*, he thought, but it was not his full name, and he had long since learned that that was not smart to give out.

Angel nodded firmly. "Then, there. We're even."

Giovanni nodded in agreement and resumed drinking his water.

As Giovanni finished the cup, Angel sat down on the coffee table across from him, pulling one of his wings around to brush at the lower feathers, which were still dusty and off-color from the way they had been dragged through the dirt outside. Giovanni stopped drinking again to stare, watching his delicate fingers run through the feathers, and he struggled to comprehend that both limbs were attached to the same figure. After a moment Angel seemed to realize he was being watched, his eyes darting back up to meet Giovanni's, causing Giovanni to look away bashfully and a warmth to spread over Angel's cheeks.

"You... You have wings." Giovanni stated, realizing immediately that it was a rather stupid observation, but hoping in some way that perhaps even just saying it would make him more capable of comprehending the existence of the great feathered limbs protruding from the boy's back. This did not work, however, for as Angel furled his wing against his back again Giovanni was once more in awe of the motion, again pondering the possibility that he was dreaming, or if this was all some sort of strange desert mirage.

"Er, yeah," Angel nodded awkwardly and looked down at his knees. "They're, um- I don't... I can't fly with them, or anything. Don't get too excited. They're just... for show." Quickly, then, before Giovanni could ask anything further, Angel looked back up and said, "So California sent you?"

"Oh!" That was right. Giovanni, in his exhaustion, had stopped noticing the sensation of the pliers pressing into him from where they sat in his back pocket. He reached around and pulled them out. "Um... I was told to give them to you. And she said that I'm alright," he remembered, repeating the words with a fondness now. "And..."

"And what?"

"Er, and she said not to forget that you owe her your life,"

Angel let out a little scoff-like sound as he reached out to take the pliers from Giovanni and inspect them. "I owe Cal my life the same way a... a beekeeper owes a bee his life, or something. I mean... What I mean is, she's only even out here because of me. I haven't... I didn't even need... Er..." He went quiet at that, but not before making another little "hmph" noise and shaking his head. "It's a give and take relationship. She's being delusional." Giovanni furrowed his brow, but Angel quickly changed the subject, turning from the pliers up to Giovanni's face and, staring directly at him, saying, "So what's your deal, then? Why'd Cal trust you?"

Giovanni was not particularly sure what to say. Admittedly, he still barely understood that himself. He tried to remember more of his conversation with her, delirious as he had been in the moment, vision bleary and head pounding, everything hurting and new, helpless to the strange sparkling woman before him. "...the more we stand together the stronger we are," the words came out barely louder than a whisper as he remembered them.

"What?"

"The more we stand together the stronger we are," Giovanni repeated again. "That is what Hollywood said. I... are you familiar with the, ah, Marcello Candy Company?" It was a surreal question to ask, how disconnected now the name was becoming from his own.

Angel laughed a little at that. "I've only been out here for a few weeks. I haven't been living under a rock or something." He opened his mouth then, and looked like he wanted to say more, but closed it, instead giving a quiet nod as if to tell him to go on.

"Well, I... I, uh... I worked... for the company." Not entirely a lie, Giovanni thought. "I did some advertising for them, sometimes. Ph- Photos and commercials and stuff?" Still not untrue. One of the only things Giovanni had *ever* done in the professional world, certainly the closest had ever come to a paying job, was take part in various advertising campaigns for his father's candies. It was the only way the public had even known of his existence for quite some time. And he had not only done his own makeup, he remembered rather fondly, but the makeup of others as well; he had made sure that every girl on the set was properly, beautifully made up for the camera, and he had been quite good at it. It was a bittersweet memory now.

Angel nodded stoically. "I modeled for a company too," he said. "I..." He stopped speaking and pursed his lips. Giovanni was beginning to have the sneaking suspicion that Angel was hiding something, or at the very least that he frequently appeared to have thoughts come to mind that he would decide, sometimes at the last minute, that he did not want to share. Instead, he leaned in and, in a hushed voice that showed something akin to actual interest, asked, "So... what happened, then? What got you all the way out here, half alive in the middle of no man's land, huh?"

Giovanni hesitated again and thought, wondering how far he could take his lie, how dangerous it would be if he was caught in it. "Well... let's just say that I do not think that the Marcello Candy Company would write me a letter of recommendation," he settled on. Wanting quickly to change the subject, and once more reminded of the drying dregs of day-old makeup caked to his skin beneath a thick layer of sweat and dirt, a thought enough to make his heart ache for his pores, Giovanni asked, "Is there a... shower here?"

Angel shrugged his shoulders. The wings bounced along with them. "Yeah, but... there's no hot water."

Giovanni frowned and considered this. A cold shower sounded miserable; he had never taken one before, had never *dreamed* of taking one, but he felt truly dirty. His body was caked in every form of filth he could imagine, from blood to sweat to puke, to whatever remains may have stained California's bed. His hair, still kept in its signature ponytail, was messy and unruly, strands sticking out and clinging to his sweat-drenched face and neck. The remainder of his makeup as well as the dried blood, pale complexion, and dirt surely made him look like a clown that had been beaten half to death. And although the water had been refreshing enough to revitalize him for the time being, it was hardly enough to make up for the great amount of time that he had gone with nothing while physically exerting himself to such a degree. The idea of being surrounded by water, even cold water, was enticing indeed.

Giovanni sighed and nodded, looking at Angel, who still sat and watched him silently. "Can you show me to it?"

The Pharaoh's Tomb was not far from the primary Embalmed Records office building, still deep in the heart of downtown, a beautiful, old-fashioned music hall with a great Sphinx statue atop it, staring down at passersby with piercing golden eyes, a massive beast amongst otherwise lifeless metal and concrete, gazing down like a deity of the city. Beneath the Sphinx's paws was a billboard that announced all upcoming shows, with, of course, the show that would be taking place later that night receiving the main attention, centered in blocky, bold lettering: ANUBIS TONIGHT. Beneath that, already, a small crowd of concert attendees could be seen, dressed in their own eccentricities, with big hair, gold and silver jewelry, chains and leather and fishnet, hovering around the entrance of the theater in preparation for the rapidly approaching concert. Attached to the side of the building was a second, smaller, more modern venue with the text THE GOLDEN JACKAL NIGHTCLUB scrolled across the top in stylish gold lettering. As its name advertised, sitting over the doorway of this building was a golden statue, smaller than the Sphinx but still a striking display, laying with its paws outstretched before it like the Sphynx but with the head of a hungry canine: a jackal, no doubt.

Anubis parked around the back, in a VIP parking area, where Vittoria noticed a few other cars already sat. Still in the car, Anubis pulled out his beloved onyx jackal mask and put it on.

"When on the premises I prefer my true identity remain anonymous," he said. He then reached out to place a finger over Vittoria's mouth. "Hush hush for me, mm? You are the only person who knows of the corpse beneath the sarcophagus." He smiled at her. Vittoria struggled to even comprehend how high an honor she had been bequeathed.

They entered the venue from the back, traversing through dark hallways, dimly lit only by exit signs, closed doors sitting on either side of them. It felt almost like a maze to Vittoria, whisked along briskly by Anubis as she followed him left and right, down corridors and through what appeared to be backstage lounges, past restrooms, prop rooms, and dressing rooms, until, finally, they came upon an opening into the wing of the stage itself. Presently, the curtain was drawn, but the backstage alone was massive, with a ceiling so far above Vittoria's head she had to strain her neck to see it, lights, ropes, and wires, technology of all sorts, dangled and coiled about through the room, as if she was in some sort of artificial cave decorated by alien technology.

Near the other side of the stage two men stood, both dressed down in plain clothes, looking over some sheets of paper. At the sound of Anubis and Vittoria's entrance they looked up.

"Anubis!" one of them cried. Both walked over in a hurry and then came to a stop before the two of them, the behavior so automatic that they reminded Vittoria of soldiers reporting to a military sergeant.

"Petyr! Cosmo! You... made it." Anubis greeted, and there was a vague hint of something in his tone that Vittoria could not entirely discern, a fakeness, what almost sounded like sarcasm behind his mask. Vittoria was reminded of her "interview" voice, the practiced tone she used when trying to sound professional, personable, likable, but not too plasticine so as to become uncanny. He turned to Vittoria. "This is Petyr Vassili and Cosmo Halloway. They are my live ensemble," he explained.

She looked the two up and down. It occurred to her that she had indeed seen them before, or at least she thought she had. From the audience, she remembered, Anubis' backing band had been merely the ghostly presence of musicians. They were obfuscated by fog and shadow, with the lighting, blocking, everything focused on Anubis and Anubis alone. She had never given them much thought, although she supposed she could fit the men before her into her memories of the silhouetted figures on the stage. One of them was older, probably close to Anubis' age, balding, in a plain black T-shirt and denim, and may have looked more or less unremarkable were it not for the piercings which covered his face. Silver jewelry dangled from his ears at multiple points, jutted up from the cartilage at the top, a long silver cord ran from it to his nostril. A nose ring, studs along his eyebrows and lips, punctuating his dimples, on every surface of his flesh that was feasibly pierceable he seemed to have found a way to hook metal through it. The other was younger, probably even younger than Vittoria herself, with long, red dreadlocks.

He was so pale that he looked sickly, and he had a sort of sickliness to his demeanor as well, with dark bags beneath his eyes and a slight, weak tremble to his movement.

"This is the lovely Miss Marcello, my protégé. She will be witnessing the show from behind the scenes tonight for the first time. This is a very, very big day for her."

Vittoria nodded and extended a hand to each of them. The balding man's handshake was firm and confident. The dreadlocked man's was as feeble as the rest of him.

"Marcello? Of Marcello Candies?" asked the latter man.

"You are Vittorio's daughter, aren't you?" the other added. He spoke with a slight accent. Russian, Vittoria thought, or otherwise something similarly ambiguously Eastern European.

Before Vittoria could respond, thankfully, Anubis interjected, "We do not have time for questions right now, and Vittoria deals with enough nagging from the press, she doesn't need the both of you hounding her as well." Again, there was the softest hint of aggression in Anubis' tone, an artificiality to his usually polite demeanor, and something about such a tone behind his mask made him appear almost threatening to Vittoria, despite knowing it was not directed at her. She pictured a carnivorous animal, a predator staring down its prey, stoic, eyes certain, intention fixed and immovable even in stillness, and she wondered what the relationship was between him and these two men. But she did not have the time to think about it too much now, for he clapped his hands together, a sound that echoed around the empty theater and made her jolt with surprise, before saying in a voice noticeably more chipper than before, "Come now. We must prepare for the soundcheck!"

Giovanni had never taken a cold shower before, nor had he ever imagined such a terrible thing could possibly exist. Showers were so intrinsically connected to warmth that the very idea of willingly submitting to the assault of cold water over one's bare body seemed, to him, horrific beyond human comprehension.

But now he stood in the bathroom, a very small room that was lined with unpleasant, dull yellow tile, completely naked and watching with a great sense of impending doom as cold water poured from the shower head. The lack of steam rising from the faucet, the way there was no hug of moisture in the air as the water poured, felt uncanny and threatening. He reached out, letting it wash over his fingers, and recoiled immediately in horror. The idea of putting his entire body through it, all while he was still so weak to begin with, while he was already shivering and aching and nearly on the verge of collapse, was just utterly terrible. He looked around the room, as if trying to buy himself time before taking the inevitable plunge. Cobwebs lined ceiling corners, the inside of the tub had a grimy pinkish-yellow aura caked into it like some sort of skin infection, what was once white between the tiles had turned into a moldy brown.

But what choice did he have? Nothing would come from standing around. Giovanni had learned that well enough already; if he had stood still at any other point up until now he surely would be dead already. And besides, he could just imagine what a terrible state his pores must have been, filled to the brim with bacterias, sweat and dirt and blood and who could even know what else anymore, and with each passing second of inaction it was certainly only getting worse.

Giovanni forced himself into the cold water headfirst the way a baby might emerge from the womb, and his body reacted immediately to the cold with such an overwhelmingly visceral sensation of panic that he nearly jumped back out. The physical reaction was instinctive and almost too much to bear; he wanted to scream, or perhaps cry, his body tensing and shivers racking his limbs even worse than before. He let out a single, strangled gasp of a sob. He felt the need to explode in some way, to respond vocally to the intense discomfort, to voice the agony caused by the sharp knives of ice water slicing into his poor, worn down flesh.

And then, after a moment, the immediate panic had died down and Giovanni realized that, against the odds, his body was beginning to adjust to the cold, and the miserable, burning suffering that he had been trapped in melted away just a bit. Coherency returned to him and he drew in a trembling breath, his body still in a vague shock from the intensity of it all. He was okay, he thought, shocked by this revelation, and slowly moving further into the cold spray and rinsing his long, black hair. The cold was unpleasant against his scalp but no longer unbearable.

Growing more comfortable, he hummed softly, weakly, a small cling to normalcy, as he ran his fingers through his hair, feeling his body release the filth that had clung to him for so long, cleansed and rejuvenated against all odds.

Vittoria sat on a little stool behind the stage, waiting. Anubis was getting ready in the dressing room, and from the other side of the curtain she could hear people beginning to pour into the venue, the delight and anticipation in the air, footsteps, laughter, and the buzz of incessant chattering.

"Anubis must think very highly of you," a voice said, subtly accented, and Vittoria turned to see one of Anubis' bandmates, the balding man with the piercings adorning his face. Even now, with the show rapidly approaching, she was surprised to see how modestly he presented himself, in a plain black tank top and black jeans, no sign of Anubis' passion for aesthetics. It was clear in just how this man dressed that it was not he who was the focus of tonight's show. "He has always been reclusive. I didn't even know he saw any lady friends... he's certainly never brought one back here,"

Vittoria smiled at him, unsure of what to say, but thankful that the focus was on something other than her status as a Marcello. "It's an honor," she managed, "Your name was... Petyr?" she guessed between the two names she had been given, realizing Anubis had not indicated which belonged to which.

Petyr gave a nod. "If you need anything tonight, Miss Marcello, just let me know,"

"Vittoria is fine," Vittoria said.

A moment later the door to the dressing room swung open, and Anubis sauntered out in his full concert attire. The difference between what the two men wore was even more jarring than she had initially thought. Anubis was in a dark gray outfit, something like a robe, that was sewn and patched and stitched together; care and intention had clearly been interwoven into every stitch, every seam and patchwork, not unlike the chaotic cacophony of music that he created, or the scars that ran across his own flesh. Around his neck, arms, and tied around his stomach like a belt were silky red scarves that trailed behind him like endlessly flowing rivers of glistening, smooth blood. His long, sharp nails, freshly painted, alternated between a deep red and a shining black that evoked the way his obsidian jackal mask glimmered in the light. He wore long, black, heeled boots that went up to his knees, with a stylish sportiness that echoed perhaps the riding shoes of the Headless Horseman.

He approached Vittoria with a smile on lips that had been painted the same deep red as half of his nails, and said, "Excited, dear?"

He held out a hand to her, and as she accepted it she looked into his eyes to see nothing but black emptiness in the sockets—He was wearing contacts, she realized, but still felt a shiver run down her spine. "Yeah," she said breathlessly, overwhelmed and unable to take her eyes off of the empty black pools behind the mask.

Anubis, seemingly amused by her staring, tugged her closer to him. He nuzzled his mask into her cheek, which was an incredibly strange sensation to Vittoria. It was smooth, polished, and cool against her skin. Voice a low whisper, velvety and soft, vibrating as he spoke directly into her ear, he said to her, "When we meet again, I will have traversed Hell and returned triumphant." Then he let go of her, and walked to where the equipment was in the process of being set up, leaving her alone with Petyr.

Shortly after, the curtains began to rise. Vittoria sat in the corner, hidden from the crowd, but she could look out and see them. As the still-empty stage was revealed to the audience she could hear the roar, a collective scream made up of thousands of voices. From where she sat she could see a crowd the likes of which she could not even begin to measure; a sea of heads, thousands of faces, more people than perhaps she could ever remember seeing in one space in her life. She knew that she had been within that crowd before, but seeing it like this brought about a new perspective to the massiveness of Anubis' following, the inconceivable number of loyal followers, eager to witness his greatness, worship his feet, beg and grovel, like the god after which he had named himself.

The theater itself was inseparable from Anubis' essence as well; the size of the crowd aside, the building itself was larger than she could comprehend, a cavernous interior that seemed as if it could have fit within it a neighborhood of smaller homes. Vittoria would liken it to an Egyptian temple, perhaps the way that she envisioned the inside of the pyramids should look. Sphinxes sat above the stage, looming over the audience and performers; glowing, golden relic symbols adorned walls. It was a testament to Anubis' glory, fame, success, and vision. She almost wished she was in the crowd herself, able to feel the electric energy of the masses waiting eagerly for Anubis as they stood beneath his shrine, in the shadows of his greatness.

The screaming rose in volume again when the band finally came out. Or, at least, Cosmo and Petyr did. There was no sign of Anubis. And yet, even without his presence, the music began, a low growl of a sound as the instruments created the soundtrack of anticipation, of dread and longing and fear, and Vittoria looked around, wondering where Anubis was, just as enraptured by the suspense as the rest of the audience, feeling her heartbeat pick up in pace as the music increased in volume. Initially the sound was so quiet it was hard to hear over the audience's wailing, but it continued to build, a tense, ceaseless chord that slowly overtook the audience as the lights dimmed and the musicians became nothing but silhouettes on the stage, shadowy spirits conjuring noise. The sound continued to build still, the guitar slowly picking up tempo into a long, haunting cry, the drums accelerating like her own rapidly increasing heartbeat, louder and louder until the repetitive pounding echoed through the vast space. The music and the crowd, together in unison, escalated to an atomic crescendo when Anubis leaped from the shadows, and all at once the lights on the stage lit up in a jarring, blinding yellow light that poured in like the holy glow of Heaven's gates.

Bathed in gold, Anubis shrieked in an otherworldly voice, manipulated and mutilated by the tampering of his microphone, "Good evening, Fresno City, and join me on my journey through *Dual!*"

It was as if a trigger had been pulled. The music took off, firing from the stage in an explosion that echoed through Vittoria's bones and rattled her very guts where they rested in her rib cage. The lights turned red, darkening the stage and highlighting Anubis' features in scarlet. His first song was sung at a high shriek of a voice that occasionally broke into a breathy growl-like hiss that sounded like his lungs and throat had been ruptured, accompanied by the blinding flash of white light, flickering madly, only to then return once more to his animalistic screams bathed in the red glow.

On the stage, Anubis prowled like some horrible creature. He growled at the audience, reaching to them with his multicolored claws; he leapt and jumped and clawed like he was dying, like some crazed and desperate animal, grabbing and clinging to the air, collapsing onto his knees, onto all fours, onto the ground, pleading to an invisible force above him for life only to jump back up and bound forward. He was all energy, the embodiment of chaos. The red silk scarves around each limb flew behind him wildly as he prowled and jumped and collapsed and moved, like the bright coloring a venomous animal might wear to warn anything near it of its kiss of death.

The show continued on like this, Anubis never stopping to speak to the audience, never breaking character or showing any sign of humanity, fully becoming the black jackal mask he wore with nothing resembling a person beneath. At points he slowed down a bit, focusing on songs that throbbed with the rhythm of rough sex rather than the frantic craze before; Vittoria assumed that the pacing was because he could not continue on with such high energy for the entire duration of the show, not at his age, but he certainly never lost the power and ferocity, either. The sound echoed through Vittoria's body, her veins quivering beneath the reverberating noise as it pounded her, assaulting her senses, racking her body and overtaking her heartbeat with its own thumping pace.

Even during the slower moments, with Anubis standing upright, without the wild leaping from before, he had an air of something unearthly about him, and his hands clawed and gestured and grabbed desperately and ferociously at the air. Vittoria found herself standing up from where she sat on the stool, leaning closer to the stage, watching and wishing she could see his face from where she was in the back, wishing she knew what it looked like to see those soulless eyes lit up by the stage lights, those sharpened fangs biting the air as he growled through each song. She wished she could be in the crowd, which she could just barely see beneath the stage light had at some point broken out into a chaotic frenzy that matched the chaos of the music, spurred by the energy of the concert to match Anubis' animalism, ripping each other apart as if they were beasts in the Colosseum.

Each song came and went, and Anubis continued without fail or falter. At some point, from a pocket she had not noticed, he procured a sharp silver knife that shone and flickered in the light of the stage as he waved it about. He used it at first as something merely with which to gesticulate, to twirl and stab at the air, at the audience. He attached his microphone to a stand, freeing his hands. This song was sung in a lower, more gravelly voice, something between a threatening growl of a wild dog and the seductive groan of a passionate lover, and it was during this that he grabbed the knife's blade between his hands, squeezing it tight as if enraptured in prayer, until blood began to run from his palms and down his arms to the floor. He squeezed tighter, as if he was wringing out a bloody sponge, and Vittoria leaned forward, as far forward as she could without making herself visible to the audience, wondering if this was some sort of trick. Anubis' voice remained strong and certain, unphased by the injury.

He continued on still, finishing this trick and returning to gesturing with it, letting the blood that fell from his palms and soaked the blade drip and fall across the stage. Despite the injuries, which certainly seemed real, he continued on with twice the energy of before, as if he had been conserving his strength through the past songs and had been saving it for this very moment. He returned to the inhuman creature that he had embodied in the beginning, crawling and leaping, writhing, shrieking as the song shifted seamlessly into one sung as a mad and wild scream of agony. He collapsed onto the floor of the stage and reached out to the audience with bloody hands, screaming out lyrics from beneath his mask, and he lifted the knife up, up high above him. His words softened, as did the music, as the last song of the night came to the end of its life, the guitar whining at a high, squeaky pitch like a dying animal, the drums thudding at a gently slowing heartbeat tempo. Anubis lifted his microphone to his mouth, while the other still held the knife above him. The blood from his hands dripped down, staining the front of his robes.

In his distorted growl, he said, "*Night brings no gloom to the heart... with its welcome shade,*"

And it was to the beat of a final, deafening, echoing drum that Anubis plunged the knife directly into his own chest, and the shriek of agony that escaped him then sounded very, very real indeed.

The lights went dim, the music stopped, the show ended, and Anubis' body lay lifeless on the stage. The crowd went silent. There was no cheering, no screaming, no movement at all, other than the heavy panting of those who had been dancing with as much vigor as Anubis trying to catch their breath. Silence remained like a spirit of death over the audience, and the curtains were drawn to a close.

Immediately, from the other side of the stage, four men rushed to Anubis, carrying large bags that looked quite full and heavy. It was almost entirely dark, and although Vittoria could not see the auditorium from behind the curtain she could tell that the lights had gone out. She could see nothing but the dark figures bent over Anubis' body, talking in hushed voices and pulling out medical equipment, working tirelessly doing what she could not imagine. Vittoria stood up, wondering if she should go to him, heart still pounding with adrenaline.

And then, Vittoria realized, one of the figures in the shadows, sitting up in the center of the others, had long, pointed ears. Anubis was very much alive and fully conscious. In the complete silence of the great theater she could even hear the unmistakable coolness of his voice speaking in hushed tones to the other men, although from her distance she could not make out any words.

He stood, his back to her, facing the front of the stage, and gave a gesture with his hand. The curtains rose once more. Bright yellow light washed over the room, lighting him up in a warm glow that evoked splendor and glory. Vittoria was entirely blinded for a moment as her eyes worked to adjust, and as her vision returned she could see Anubis' tall figure, silhouetted by the golden light, as the audience erupted into a deafening cheer. It was just him, alone, on the stage now, for his bandmates had left during the chaos. It was a bookend to the journey, once more he was in the bright holy glow of Heaven after his descent into the depths of Hell. The wild applause continued without cease, and Anubis bowed once, then twice. In his hand he continued to hold the bloodied knife from before, and there was still a trickle of blood running from his palms down to the tip of the blade. He pulled off one of the long, silky red scarves from around his arm and tossed it into the audience, bowed once more, and, finally, walked to the back of the stage, and the curtain was drawn for a final time. The show was over.

Anubis did not say anything to his bandmates, who stood in the wings of the theater, but made a beeline immediately to where Vittoria stood, eyes wide in awe, speechless from fluster and shock, as the bloody, empty-eyed jackal approached her with a fanged smile. "I do hope you enjoyed the show, Vittoria, darling," he said to her.

Vittoria nodded eagerly. "I did!" she said, breathless. "Anubis, that was... that was amazing. Incredible. Unbelievable. I... How did you do that?" Any moment she had ever thought before that his stage stunts were only theatrics had been profoundly disproven by the closeness in which she had seen them transpire tonight.

Anubis' smile widened, the entire set of canine incisors visible as they protruded from his gums. "I mentioned to you earlier that I had undergone intensive surgery to transform my physical self. I will admit to you now that it is not just my exterior that has been modified," he said. He took her by the hand and pressed it to his left breast, where the knife had entered him during the show and where sat his heart. Or, at least, where it should have been. Vittoria, frozen still, could do nothing but breathe a little gasp as she realized that he had no heartbeat. She looked up at him and he brought her hand away from his chest and up to his mouth to kiss it, leaving red lipstick on the back of her hand and red blood on her fingertips.

Angel had, to Giovanni's surprise, made dinner while he was showering, and although it was hardly befitting of his personal standards, he could admit that it was impressive given the circumstances: Slices of cheese, a loaf of bread that had been toasted in the oven, soup, and thin slices of meat lay spread across the rickety kitchen table as a humble charcuterie board. Jarring downgrade from the luxurious gourmet that Giovanni had grown up with aside, after having barely eaten in the past twenty-four hours he could hardly complain.

Angel had set the soup into two bowls across from each other. It was a copper-colored tomato soup, and the sight of the steam rising from the top of it was enough to make Giovanni's mouth water after the icy cold shower and the lack of any sort of proper comfort in so long.

"It's not much," Angel said as he sat down, shifting uncomfortably in his chair, his wings twitching and stretching as he tried to get them to cooperate against the wooden backing. "Um... Most of what I have is, like, canned, or preserved. Stuff that'll last awhile."

"Do you have food out here?" Giovanni asked.

Angel gave a little nod and twiddled his thumbs. "There's a supermarket in town. I just... don't want to go out there much."

"Why not?"

Angel, who had been about to take a sip of the soup, dropped the spoon into the bowl at the question. "Well, um," he swallowed with enough force that it was as if he had taken a sip of the soup after all. "Well, we have... limited funds, you know."

Giovanni blinked, aware of the oddity of this response but unsure of what else to say. "And what about... clothing?" he asked, in reference to the plain white undershirts and boxers that Angel had seemingly miraculously procured for him to change into after his shower.

Angel was currently busy picking the now-dripping spoon up out of the bowl and wiping it off on a napkin in his lap. "Er, uh..." he fumbled with the spoon as if to distract himself a moment longer, then said, "I guess we've just been lucky out here." The response was terse, not at all thoughtful or dreamy or any sort of tone that Giovanni imagined one might use when expressing the practically cosmic luck that Angel seemed to possess to even be alive out here at all, with food, clothing, and a house with working amenities. Rather, his words served only the purpose of making it clear that he was not going to elaborate further.

Angel set the spoon down beside the bowl, as if giving up trying to use it for the time being, and reached to the center of the table to pick up a slice of bread and some cheese. Giovanni watched the motion, watching the delicacy with which Angel's hands, small and nimble, worked. He considered saying more, at least something to break the ice now that Angel had gone quiet, but was at a loss for how to continue, and so he settled with quietly taking a sip of soup and saying nothing else.

After a brief cleanup at the concert hall which mostly amounted to being treated for the cuts on his hands and chest by his on-site paramedics, collecting his belongings, and wishing his crew a job well done, Anubis left the majority of the mess and deep cleaning to the employees, and, still fully masked and costumed, led Vittoria out the back of the Pharaoh's Tomb to the building next door, the Golden Jackal Nightclub, for what he explained to her was the afterparty. Vittoria said very little, not wanting to humiliate herself by gushing about Anubis' performance to him, by acting like one of the crazed sea of faces in the crowd, a nameless worshiper without individual identity in the pit.

It was late into the night, and the sky above was starless, but the club was lit up and alive with music of similar genre to Anubis' blaring from within, audible even in the back parking lot, thumping like an industrial heartbeat through the city. The throb of the bass echoed through the streets and bright spotlights shot up into the heavens, illuminating the smoggy city clouds above and beckoning all inside, or else taunting outsiders that there was a party going on to which they had not been invited. Vittoria found her heart racing as she wondered what could possibly lie in store for her inside. She already felt like she was mentally juggling far too much to keep up with; the white lies she was telling Anubis, the electric awe she still felt over the show, how very overwhelmed she was by all of this as her mind raced, trying to anticipate what would happen next, trying to comprehend that all of this was truly happening at all, that Anubis' hand was in her own and that she was his guest to his own afterparty. The thought of crowds and alcohol caused everything to churn and shove upwards in her stomach, and the hand that was not in Anubis' clenched into a fist as she willed herself to stay calm.

They entered through a door around the back of the nightclub with a sign that was clearly marked "EXIT" in neon red, and instantaneously it was as if they had been transported to a new reality. The roar of the music, already proclaiming the power and volume of its sound as it tore through the silence of the night from outside, immediately shot at full blast through her ears with such force that she was surprised it did not physically blow her hair back. Neon lights lit up the interior of the building; Vittoria was bathed in iridescence as they walked through the back hallway, approaching the source of the noise, deeper into the belly of the beast.

Through a beaded curtain Anubis led Vittoria until finally they came upon what appeared to be only one of the club's rooms, this one bathed in a deep red light not unlike the light that Anubis himself had been drowned in on the stage, a darker color that subdued the room some and gave it a calmer atmosphere than the music would have one expecting—Across the way Vittoria could see another doorway, with flashing blue and green strobe lights and silhouetted figures flailing about wildly, and a sign on the wall that read **MORE RESTROOMS DOWNSTAIRS** indicated that this was a much, much larger space than she had realized. Not unlike the Embalmed building, concert posters littered the walls, alongside engravings and paintings of classical ancient Egyptian fashion; a large prop tomb (at least, Vittoria assumed there was no corpse inside) sat in the corner, and metallic golden scarabs decorated the wall and ceiling. There were couches and barstools made of black vinyl, and a long bar with a magnificent golden case of every form of alcohol she could imagine, as well as jars upon jars on the countertop of shimmering golden-wrapped Marcello candies.

There were a decent number of people around; couples sat speaking in hushed voices on the black vinyl, people talking at the bar, a few dancing in the spacious area at the center of the room, but it was a significantly smaller number than the audience had been comprised of, and Vittoria had a feeling that entering the Golden Jackal at all was not an easy—or cheap—feat. Still, as the partygoers became aware of Anubis' presence, they quickly began to congregate towards him. Eager faces, most of whom were decorated up themselves, in thick black eyeliner, drawings etched across cheeks, from Eyes of Horus to zodiac symbols, hair teased, jewelry flashy, every possible form of black fabric, came up to shake his hand, to compliment him on his work and thank him for the show, to pry eagerly with questions and ask to take photos or be blessed with an autograph on their records or skin. Anubis seemed to take it all in stride effortlessly, smiling brightly beneath his mask, shaking hands with each individual, thanking them for coming out, somehow having perfected the ability to speak over the music, just clear enough and loud enough that he could be heard without it sounding as if he were yelling. Vittoria stayed glued to his side.

At some point, Anubis' dreadlocked bandmate—Cosmo, Vittoria assumed, as she had put a face to Petyr earlier—came over with drinks, which he passed along to Anubis, Vittoria, and a handful of other partygoers with whom Anubis seemed on friendly enough terms that he did not send them straight away after bestowing upon them a moment of his time. Vittoria was handed a lime green thing that was unlike any alcoholic beverage she had seen before; it had what could only be described as a radioactive glow to it and a small sprinkle of unidentifiable black sparkles made it look truly toxic.

As Anubis continued to mingle with his fans and acquaintances, Vittoria felt a tap on the back and turned to see Cosmo, who gave her a wave once they made eye contact. "It's called cobra spit," he said, pointing to the drink.

"That was an amazing show," Vittoria said earnestly, somewhat starstruck before one of Anubis' bandmates after seeing the performance, despite Anubis' obvious attempts at keeping them relegated to the background.

Cosmo lit up at that, although the weakness and exhaustion perpetually etched into his features remained. "Glad you think so, Miss Marcello. I'm really trying to give it my all so Anubis doesn't kick my ass. He was real pissed when he heard I'd be fucking around with shit that could affect my performance." The tilt of Vittoria's eyebrow was enough to have him answer the unspoken question, although she had a feeling he would have continued on explaining himself either way. "I'm working with Himmel's Experimental Cosmetics division on a DNA splicing project. It's all kind of on the down-low right now, with the big transitions happening in the company... Well, I'm sure *you* know all about it."

"What are you doing?" Vittoria asked, interest piqued, but also eager to direct the conversation away from her brother's imminent promotion.

"Well, right now, I'm injecting myself with nonlethal doses of mamba venom. Once my body has enough of a tolerance we'll be splicing my DNA with a snake's. No idea what'll happen exactly, it's all pretty early research, but... well, I'm excited. I think it'll be the publicity I need to get my own project's name out there... In the meantime, I'm getting some preparatory work done." He grinned at her and stuck his tongue out. Or, rather, his *tongues*. It appeared as if it had been split down the middle, resulting in two separately moving chunks of flesh jutting from his mouth.

Vittoria stared in shock but did not have a chance to respond before Anubis suddenly wrapped an arm around her, drawing her close to him. He raised his glass to the entourage of fans and friends he had been fraternizing with. All eyes were on him, much like during the show. Loud enough that his voice rang clear over the pounding music, he said, "I dedicate this evening to my dear Vittoria," Vittoria felt her cheeks flush, as if she were a stranger to public attention. This was different, she supposed, as she thought again of the adoration she held for Anubis, the admiration and awe that his music, his performances, and his general demeanor brought to her. "Today was her first official day of training beneath my wing. Much like Virgil to Dante, I have taken great pleasure guiding her through Hell, from which I hope she will emerge beneath the stars of stage light."

There was a moment of polite clapping, before a voice in the crowd spoke up, "Vittoria... As in, the daughter of Vittorio Marcello?"

Vittoria's heart sank. Of course—there it was. She looked to Anubis anxiously, but with his mask on she could not read his expression, could not catch his reassuring glance beneath the blackness of his contacts, and she waited to see if he would do anything before making any statements herself, not wanting to shoot herself in the foot and make any claims, earnest or fabricated, about herself... not to mention her present relationship with her father and his company.

Thankfully, Anubis did speak up to answer the question first: "Indeed." There was a hushed murmur across the group. "Before our descent into the beyond today, she was a mere child of Vittorio Marcello, shadowed by the great Marcello empire. But when all is said and done, when I have passed on the many secrets I have kept to myself for far too long, when the Anubis you see before you is nothing but ash and the memory of the wonder and magic that I have instilled upon this earth, she will rise and embrace that wonder and will become Anubis reborn!"

Anubis' speech caused another, even more thunderous round of applause, his audience clearly delighted by these words. Vittoria, however, shrunk back, her heart remaining firmly sunken into the depths of her stomach, where it upset the bile and made her feel lightly nauseous.

There was much to take in about Anubis' words. Granted, there was still much to take in about all of this, but there was something in the way he spoke that unsettled her, and she wondered what Anubis' end goal for her truly was, what he envisioned the end result of this relationship would look like. Was she merely a daughter of Vittorio? Did the shadow of his company truly loom over her so greatly that she was swallowed up by it, and was Anubis her only path to illumination?

She gripped the bright green venom drink in her hand so tight that she half worried the glass would shatter, but she worried too that if she held it any looser it would slip from her hands, which had begun to grow sweaty. As Anubis continued to speak to the crowd and answer questions on her behalf, Vittoria threw her head back and swallowed the entire glass of neon green alcohol in one long, heavy gulp.

Angel's house, despite its less than impressive size, was home to two fully furnished bedrooms, one that Angel had made his own and one that was going entirely unused. It was somewhat dusty thanks to being left untouched for so long, but aside from that it was in perfectly good condition.

"Hollywood California does not stay with you?" Giovanni had asked at the initial revelation of the spare bedroom.

"No." Angel had answered. "She stays at Undercroft."

"Why? I thought you were friends."

"So nobody follows her back here." Angel said curtly.

Giovanni was surprised by the pleasant atmosphere of the room. The bed was rather small, but it was fully made up, with blue sheets and pillows and a surprisingly soft looking blanket over it. The room itself was decorated in a way that was reminiscent of a child's: The wallpaper, torn or riding up in some places, faded somewhat with age, was covered in what appeared to be smiling pink elephants, and the base of the lamp on the bedside table was shaped like a pig with little, fluffy wings jutting from its fat body. A blue teddy bear sat at the head of the bed, tucked in, looking out with dusty button eyes.

"I guess the, er, the people before had, um, a kid or something," Angel said as he stood in the doorway behind Giovanni.

Giovanni turned to Angel, brow furrowed. "The people before you... Who were they, Angel?"

Angel frowned and looked around uncomfortably. His wings shifted behind him, feathers standing up like a spooked cat's tail. Then he gave a weird little shrug that made his wings flop. "I- I dunno. Speculation." He breathed out, his eyes on his bare feet, and then mumbled, "Is the room, uh, okay for you?"

Giovanni was growing frustrated with Angel's constant refusal to give proper explanations for anything, but did not pry any further. He, too, had kept much from Angel, and the last thing he wanted was to make the playing field uneven again, to tell Angel too much or for Angel to say so much that he felt owed more on Giovanni's end. Not when he was still just trying to find some sense of stability after fearing for his life mere hours ago, not when shivers still ran down his spine and the fatigue was still noticeable, when all he wanted was a soft bed on which he could rest and recover without the sense that impending doom was creeping around every corner. He walked to the bed and sat down, where he was pleasantly surprised to find that he sunk down into it a bit, that he was not met with any spring or otherwise hard or painful material that would make attempting to sleep overly difficult. He pressed his hand into the mattress, testing its depth, and watched as the bed rose back up into its proper shape rather quickly. It was not the softest bed he had slept on, but it would do, he thought, much too exhausted and desperate to complain now. Giovanni then looked back up to find Angel staring at him silently with wide, studious eyes, as he seemed wont to do.

"Angel?" Giovanni asked, uneasy at the constant staring.

Angel twitched. "Mm?"

"Why allow me to stay with you?"

Angel's wings seemed to stiffen slightly. His expression did not change, eyes wide and mouth taut. Then he looked around, darting back and forth, and said in a vaguely stunted voice, tone indecipherable, "I guess I'm just a nice guy."

Giovanni blinked, staring at Angel and trying to figure out what to say to that, as it certainly did not sound like him, from what he knew of the boy thus far (which, he supposed, was very little). But Angel did not give him time to come up with a response before he walked over to Giovanni on the bed and sat down beside him, a movement that made Giovanni jump slightly, surprised by this even as he had watched Angel approach. The wings on his back were so close to him now, he could see each individual feather, the long, plastic-y rachis, the fluffy down feathers beneath the longer plumes, rustling gently even as the air was still. His thoughts slipping away as he grew distracted by the sight of the wings in all of their splendor, Giovanni was once more caught off guard enough to jump slightly when Angel reached to place a hand on his arm, lithe fingers gently brushing his shoulder, the sleeve of his undershirt, and then trailing down past the fabric to where his skin was bare, brushing downwards until he nearly reached his elbow with touch so light it threatened to give Giovanni goosebumps.

"Angel?" Giovanni said again, unsure of what question he was trying to ask even as he heard his own upwards inflection. Angel rested his hand on Giovanni's for a moment, before pulling it away to rest it in his own lap.

The touch of Angel's fingers on his skin seemed to leave ghostly traces of heat and he thought back to his own seduction techniques, the gentle touches and passionate whispers that made ladies swoon, although the confidence he had needed to instigate this felt as foreign to him now as Fresno City itself, miles and miles away. In the past, Giovanni had had an endless array of lovers, all of whom were consistently female. Between his father's servants, employees, and partygoers, there was an unending bounty of women to seduce, one of his favorite pastimes as he lounged about day after day in his splendorous room... now only a distant memory, most likely already repurposed by his father, his luxurious silky bed a thing of the past, replaced for the children's bed in the old room of this strange, decrepit house.

Angel's eyes had trailed away, scanning over a row of smiling elephants along the wall. Giovanni stared at the boy silently, trying to gleam some level of understanding from him. His features were soft and round, face heart shaped, like a doll, with plump cheeks and small lips. In the soft light he could see traces of light stubble on his chin, and the shadow of a faint Adam's apple, but the tank he wore did not conceal the curve of his breasts. Giovanni did not know what to make of him, finding himself unable to make heads or tails of Angel in any way whatsoever. And that was all without even mentioning...

"May I... see your wings?" Giovanni asked suddenly.

"Huh?" Angel looked up at him. "You can see them right now." He shrugged his shoulders, making the feathered appendages flop unceremoniously once more.

"I mean closer," Giovanni insisted, "I have never seen anything like them before,"

Angel gave another little shrug, and the magnificent white wings rose and fell on his shoulders again. "Yeah, you... you wouldn't have. They're the first of their kind." There was a hint of sarcasm there, speaking in a voice that was not his own, as if echoing something he had heard somebody else say once. Giovanni hesitated to continue speaking, not wanting to cause a problem. Angel broke the silence for him: "Gentle."

He turned now, arching away from Giovanni to reveal his back, where Giovanni noticed his wings jutted from around the thin straps of the shirt he wore; undoubtedly that was his reason for dressing in loose tank tops as he did, as any other sort of covering would certainly need some form of hole cut out of it in order for his wings to fit. But that was the last thing that Giovanni was worried about. He stared at the soft feathered appendages; he knew what birds' wings looked like, had seen countless of them in his life. He remembered his doves, fluttering about their pretty cage in the garden, white feathers glimmering like ripples of water in the sunlight, and as he stared at Angel the same awe and wonder befell him. These were a perfect replica of a dove's wing. Every feather was white and pristine, and they jutted from Angel's lower shoulders seamlessly, springing from bare flesh into downy white.

"They're real," Giovanni said, voice hardly above a whisper, "I mean... They are really a part of you."

From behind, Giovanni could see Angel give a little nod. "Er... yeah. I can't, um, fly with them or move them very well or anything, though, uh. Imagine if you had arms on the back of your... on your back, but they were, um, dead. Like you slept on them wrong. Like they were asleep all the time. That's sort of what it's like," As if to prove a point he unfurled them now and stretched them, batting them feebly; it was a weak gesture, an awkward little flapping motion that looked strained and somewhat stiff, but still, Giovanni was mesmerized. Despite the stiffness, the sight of the huge, snowy white wings attached to human flesh and moving as if they were trying to take off and soar upwards left him fully wonderstruck. He was only further delighted when Angel said after a moment, "You can touch them, if you like."

Giovanni did not hesitate. He reached out in an instant, running his fingertips over the pretty white feathers. He heard Angel make a noise, something between a sigh and a gasp, he was not exactly sure which, and felt his body twitch, causing the feathers themselves to jump slightly in his hands, once more serving a reminder that they were connected fully to Angel, alive and animate. Giovanni slipped fingers beneath the first layer of feather, feeling the soft coat of down protecting the flesh beneath. It was all unbelievably, unimaginably soft. The wings did not just appear to be perfect replicas visually, they felt just like a bird's wing as well, a sensation Giovanni was very familiar with, having held the lifeless bodies of his own pet birds after they had passed so many countless times.

Giovanni's hand moved lower, down to the tips of the wings where the longest feathers jutted out, and he brushed them curiously, then moved inwards to touch where the wings crept closer to the flesh of Angel's back. As he came closer to where the feather met bare skin, Angel shivered and tensed, and a small sound escaped him, somewhat reminiscent of a squeak. Quickly, he covered his mouth with both hands, and Giovanni felt his feathers bristle.

"Are you okay, Angel?" Giovanni asked, trying to lean around to look at Angel's face.

"That's sensitive," Angel mumbled through his fingers.

"Does it hurt?"

Angel turned back around to face Giovanni, his wings swiveling away with the rest of his body. "No, no, um... It's just sensitive. I dunno."

Giovanni looked at Angel's face again; his cheeks had turned a warm, rosy hue. His eyes traveled over the boy's body; he felt like a sea of contradictions, the softness and the delicacy of his features combined with the intensity of his wide-eyed stare, with the knife he had held to his neck, the roughness of his voice and harshness of the whole of the situation he was in, the glossy white of his feathers against his tan skin, the stuttering and the hesitation in every word he spoke amidst the intense intentionality behind each move he seemed to make.

Angel leaned in suddenly, coming closer to Giovanni's face. "Does it turn you on at all to feel out of control?"

The words were said in an almost breathless rush that did not feel remotely befitting of the content of the sentence. Giovanni blinked at Angel, whose big, dark eyes were very close to his own, dumbfounded and wondering if he was using a different definition of "turned on" than he. "Ou- Out of control?" Giovanni echoed pathetically, floundering as he tried to formulate a response aside from a plea for understanding.

Angel's words were spoken with a sort of eagerness, still in that hushed whisper of a tone: "So many people in Fresno don't have control over anything in their lives so they turn to anything they can get a hold of to feel some sort of control. They're all going crazy all the time, grasping for some sort of semblance of anything. But doesn't that excite you a little? Being at the mercy of the corporations? Ending up all the way out here because you couldn't get your next fix?" In the flurry of hushed words Angel's hand had traveled back to Giovanni's body, this time resting on his leg.

Giovanni had no idea what to say to this, but the touch shot electric sparks from Angel's fingertips through his body and he thought back again to the bountiful options, the endless women he had been able to sleep with prior, back in his father's mansion. It felt like a lifetime ago that he had last made love or felt the sense of intimacy and affection that sex promised. He felt a heat in his body that was markedly different from the feverishness he had been battling earlier, and with Angel's hand still on his leg and his face so very close, he made the quick second decision to lean in only a few inches closer and kiss him.

Angel replied with a soft "mmph" and Giovanni felt him twitch, but he did not pull back. Still, the awkwardness of the situation stifled Giovanni's prowess, and he remained somewhat reserved even in the kiss, mouths pressed against one another but making no move to bring their bodies closer, to touch Angel in any other way, to open his mouth or encourage Angel to open his.

Angel pulled away, staring at Giovanni with his lips parted. Giovanni stared back this time, wondering what in the world Angel would say to that, half fearing anger, half fearing encouragement.

"Himmel,"

"What?"

Angel looked left and right, as if checking to make sure they were not being watched. "I, uh, worked for Himmel Medicine. That's the company I modeled for."

Giovanni blinked. "O- Oh,"

"You told me you worked for Marcello Candies earlier. I worked for Himmel. Now we're even."

*Oh.* Giovanni stared, his own mouth slightly agape as he was once more left confounded by Angel. He knew very little about what went on within the walls of Himmel Medicine, aside from the current politics surrounding his brother's promotion and the pressure it had seemed to put on his family's business. Did that explain his wings? How could it? Giovanni had never seen anything like them, surely if Himmel had managed to produce something so magnificent there would be people walking about on every street corner with magnificent feathered wings.

Angel continued his pattern of unpredictability by suddenly climbing onto Giovanni's lap, facing him and straddling him. He held himself up over Giovanni on his knees in a position not unlike the one they had been in earlier today, when Giovanni had first arrived at his front door and was quickly overpowered despite the boy's stature being so very petite contrary to his own. Unease erupted in Giovanni, springing outwards from his chest, his heartbeat picking up in pace. He squirmed beneath Angel as if he were being threatened, as if Angel had suddenly pounced on him, as if he had a knife to his throat once again. From this position Giovanni was forced to strain his neck to look up at him, and he could feel Angel's breathing, his chest rising up and down against his throat.

"You called me beautiful," Angel said, "back when you thought I was a girl."

"Are you going to kill me, Angel?"

Angel snorted. "Only if you try to kill me first. I keep my knife in my back pocket."

"You are very beautiful,"

"Only if I'm a girl?"

Giovanni's heart raced as he began to develop a growing suspicion that all of those times he had slept with women he had been following a faulty script that could not begin to hold up against scrutiny such as whatever it was Angel was doing.

That was also, Giovanni realized, not the only thing that was beginning to grow. Angel stared down at him, waiting for an answer, wings tense on his shoulders, feathers rigid, eyes intense and hands slowly coming to rest on the back of Giovanni's head, fingers intertwining with his long, black hair. His fingernails delicately scraped along the nape of his neck.

"I don't know," Giovanni said finally, body hot and breathing labored as he struggled to catch his breath, as he felt his throat pulse against Angel's breasts and his eyes darted from those wide, dark eyes to the glimmer of soft white stitched lovingly to his back, magnificent and ethereal in the light of the child's bedroom.

Angel said nothing else, but promptly shifted his weight to drop down from the support his knees were giving him to sit on Giovanni's stiffening erection. And at that moment, Giovanni decided that he would allow his uncertainty to be a problem for later.

Vittoria walked through the door to Anubis' home, drunk and exhausted.

They had been late getting back—The party had gone on long into the night, and then, once that had ended, she had ridden with Anubis back to Embalmed Records, where he had left his beloved mask tucked safely back in its chest in the prop room. Vittoria had no idea how much Anubis had to drink, and she herself was too drunk to consider if he was safe behind the wheel; shortly after the first drink of the night she had lost count of her own alcohol consumption, and a decent amount of time between the party and now was strung together in blurry fragments in her memory. She had said nothing during the entirety of the drive back to Anubis' home: The driving made her nauseous, and her thoughts swam and sunk to the depths of her mind before floating back up to the top, drowned, unable to stay focused on one single thing and cycling through disconcerting fractures of uncertainties and anxieties.

"Vittoria, dear," Anubis called from the doorway as he followed her inside, voice a soft coo, "Is there something the matter? Did you not like the party?"

Vittoria looked about Anubis' personal gallery of oddities, too drunk to piece together a verbal response, feeling the gaze of each one staring down at her, each of his little figures and masks jeering at her from walls and countertop. She was confined, trapped, stuck in a world as foreign to her as if she had just gotten off a plane in another country. A canine skull on a shelf peered deep into her from empty eye sockets, and she turned away from it, around to face Anubis, his eyes still blackened by his contact lenses. He was smiling at her, and she was so distracted that she hardly noticed how tight her fists were, how deeply her nails dug into her own palms.

"You haven't spoken a word all night, love," Anubis continued, and he held out a hand to Vittoria. She noticed for the first time that he had long, fresh scars up and down his palms, jagged and red and swollen from the show, from the stunt with the knife on stage. "If something is the matter, you are always free to-"

"What are you going to do to me?" Vittoria asked abruptly, barely coherent enough to even think about how odd of a question it was.

Anubis stared at her for a moment, then shook his head. "Nothing, Vittoria. You've had quite a lot to drink, that's all-"

"The trick on stage," Vittoria interrupted again, slurring her words and taking a stumbling step towards him. "How did you do that?"

Anubis walked to her, meeting her where she stood. "Did I frighten you, Vittoria?" he asked. Vittoria said nothing but glared up at him helplessly. He wore a plain shirt, a black tank top that he had put on beneath his stage costume, which exposed all of his thin, bony arms.

He proceeded to lift the shirt, pulling it up and over his head, over his dark curls that had become slightly unkempt and matted beneath the full head covering he had worn all evening. Vittoria's eyes went wide.

Anubis had a fresh wound directly where his heart should have been, visibly stapled and stitched up only hours before. The skin was a bright, inflamed pink, swollen around where it had been sewn like fabric, a deep red line severing the flesh in half. Vittoria felt sick. Anubis smiled a deep red smile.

"It was real?" Vittoria asked, although she had already known it to be true.

"In a way," Anubis answered. He gingerly touched around the cut with his long nails, tracing just before where the skin swelled. "In the early days of my career I would have actually killed myself," he chuckled and looked back up at Vittoria. "Technology is a wonderful thing, and we live in a time when it can work miracles. It wasn't long ago that an expecting mother had to fight her deepest natures in order to distance herself from emotional attachment to an unborn child in light of staggering infant mortality rates. Now, with access to the right equipment, with the right amount of money in our pockets, we no longer need to fear death at all. I have done it all, Vittoria. I've hanged myself, stabbed myself, electrocuted myself, slit my wrists and my neck. I have likely been legally dead more than any other human being who has ever lived. No other musician, no other mortal being, can say that they have managed to evade death as I have." He reached to take Vittoria's hand in his own. It was not until her fingers went slack in Anubis' that she was aware of the red sting in her flesh from her clenching.

Anubis continued: "But as I have grown older, I have grown also more aware that not even the greatest doctor can stop the aging process. Not yet. With each year my body grew frail, each death setting me closer to my actual, *final* death, each recovery harder than the last on my decaying physical being. I needed to find a new alternative to keep my career alive while also keeping myself alive. By then, of course, I had a great deal of money to my name, more than enough to pay a state-of-the-art surgeon to perform an experimental surgery that had as good a chance of killing me as it did of saving my career. Ah, the lovely Himmel." He gently traced his nail across the freshly stitched wound. Then, after staring down at it for a moment, took the hand that held Vittoria's and pressed her knuckles to the side of his stomach, near where his appendix would be. Vittoria's breath caught in her throat when she felt a heartbeat pulse against her fingers. "You see, Vittoria, dear, stabbing myself in the chest is entirely safe, so long as I am properly sewn up once the show ends. My heart is simply tucked away elsewhere. As I told you tonight, it is not only my exterior that has been modified."

"You want me to do the same," Vittoria said, her mind swimming in alcohol, returning to his statements about her earlier in the night, her last painfully sober memory of the evening, about becoming Anubis reborn.

Anubis squeezed Vittoria's hand. "You will be able to follow in my footsteps and defy death itself. Doesn't that just sound marvelous, Vittoria?"

Did it sound marvelous? Vittoria was having trouble forming coherent thoughts. She blinked at Anubis, stared at his hand, long and delicate, clasping her own, stared up at his empty black eyes and the incisors that jutted from his mouth when he smiled. "It scares me," she said finally, hesitant, feeling childish, weak, and helpless the moment the words left her lips. She looked away, at the floor, until she felt Anubis reach out to take hold of her chin, gently stroking her cheek with his nail, causing her to shiver and look back up at him with a frown.

"Vittoria, dear. Don't you want to be something fantastic? Don't you want to be *art*?"

The words made Vittoria shiver even more than his touch, and all at once she pulled away from him. She stared at the man before her, her mind racing yet her thoughts sluggish, her brain acting in such discordance it made her feel seasick, or perhaps it was still just the alcohol. She felt like she was in a dream, her vision blurring, Anubis and all of his collections staring down at her and waiting for her response, to see who it was she was going to allow herself to be, who it was she would allow herself to become. Anubis was so tall, and from her own height she was in the perfect position to stare at that fresh, angry scar, pulsing, taunting her, threatening to bleed. Her panic rose slowly, sludgy like hot magma threatening to burst forth from the ground and swallow up everything in a devastating heat. Vittoria pushed past Anubis then and rushed to the front door, which she opened, stumbling down the front steps and onto the sidewalk. There she stood, the door ajar behind her and the world before her dark and still in the late, late evening. Cars sat lifeless by the pavement and every window in every home was dark; all was silent save for the faint echoes of the city some distance away, beyond the suburbia.

She could hear, barely, as Anubis stepped nimbly down the stairs and came to stand behind her. She could see his shadow on the pavement, cast by the yellow glow of a nearby streetlamp, but she did not need it to know that he was there; she could sense his presence beside her, the empty gaze of his blackened eyes, feel his breath on her neck. She tensed, raising her head, but not turning to Anubis, keeping her eyes on the road before her and the houses across the way.

"Vittoria, lover, please," Anubis said, speaking softly, voice barely above a whisper of warm nighttime breeze, "Do you not want more to life than being your father's daughter? Do you not see the potential you have to surpass the confines of the Marcello name? You know very well that as you are now the world will see you as nothing but the child of the city's resident candyman for the rest of history. You will live, and you will die, and for but a moment the front of the papers will proclaim that Vittoria Marcello, daughter of the much greater Vittorio Marcello, after whom she was named, has expired at last. And you will be forgotten."

Vittoria listened to Anubis' words and a chill unbefitting of the Fresno heat ran down her spine. How did he know what to say? she wondered. How did he know what fears she had lived with, what terror she felt in every moment of her waking life, sources of dread far more existential, far more horrific than any nightmare she could possibly conjure, or anything Anubis could possibly act out on his stage? At that moment her mind drunkenly grasped onto the memory of earlier in the night, of the admiration she had felt then, the awe and wonder Anubis had instilled in her as she had watched him on the stage, and even prior to that, she thought to his records, his music, the countless times he had been the soundtrack of her despair, her joys, her hopes, her fears. She breathed out, a breath she had not even realized she had been holding, and for a moment the only sound in the universe was her breathing and his breathing, alone together in the darkness of the city, and Vittoria wondered if she would ever see her father again.

"I'll do it," she said after a moment.

Anubis placed his long, thin hands, with their fresh cuts and sharp claws, on Vittoria's shoulders. She stiffened and drew another breath. Anubis brushed her hair away to kiss the back of her neck. "Marvelous," he said. "I will arrange a date with my finest surgeons. You are making the right choice, Vittoria, I assure you. You entered my domain a barren chamber, and you will leave it an altar."

# Act III

As Vittoria turned around to walk with Anubis back into his home, she wondered: *To whom?*

# ACT IV

A Note on Fresno Fashion: Teeth

Truly, is there anything worse than imperfect teeth? Yellowed like rot, caked in plaque, worn down flat or chipped and ragged and jutting crooked from gums. And that's to say nothing of the discomfort! Ranging from toothaches that throb with no end in sight to the nightmarish fear of losing a tooth altogether, there is no doubt in our minds that teeth provide far greater risk than reward. Unfortunately, as the Marcello Candy Company's popularity began to grow, there was a moment in Fresno history, dark and rotten as untreated teeth, that tooth decay became increasingly commonplace.

Thankfully, Himmel Medicine has long since found a way to eradicate such fears and unpleasantries among those capable of affording it, and we're sure that Marcello Candies can thank them for it, as it undoubtedly correlated to their even more rapid success from that point onwards. A worthy preventative treatment to save for indeed: That is, a full tooth transplant plan, which involves the simple procedure of removing each tooth individually and replacing it with a sturdier artificial one, virtually unable to rot or damage... And, of course, there are insurance plans and warranties one may opt in for an additional fee as well, should they desire it. With the lifetime warranty and posthumous identification guarantee, Himmel has boldly made the claim that should a body undergo damage so horrific that it leaves the unfortunate victim mangled beyond the point of standard means of identification, the teeth would remain intact, pristine as ever, with an ID number carefully engraved in the furthest back molar. An end to missing persons, unidentifiable corpses, and toothaches, all in one!

Of course, as the wheels of progress spin faster and faster down the Fresno freeways, novel economic disparities evolve alongside it. In recent years, imperfect teeth have developed into something of a symbol of the lower class. Various activist groups, including the ever-controversial anti-Marcello group Fresno Smiles, helmed by Dr. Sofia Cruz, have worked over the past few years to bring toothbrushes, toothpaste, and affordable dental care to the impoverished areas of Fresno, hoping to give those coming from less opportunity at least a fighting chance of accessing job opportunities for which they would otherwise be overlooked. When asked about accessibility, a representative from Himmel stated that there may be a chance that the company will down the line offer the opportunity to take part in individual tooth transplants, so that a person of lower income may be able to pay to replace only the most visible teeth, or prioritize only the ones in the most dire need of replacement.

Any citizen of Fresno will undoubtedly be unable to discuss such matters without thinking of the resident rogue of tooth transplants, Embalmed Records' CEO and legendary musician and performance artist, Anubis, who underwent a surgery that pushed past the boundaries of Himmel's standard transplant procedure. The teeth that replaced his natural ones were structured after a canine's—According to an anonymous source from within the walls of Embalmed Records, the skeleton of a jackal sits in one of the backrooms of the site downtown, and it was this beast's feral maw that was used as the mold for what now rest nestled underneath the Rock God of Death's iconic mask.

Giovanni had four older brothers. The one closest in age to himself was Dante, whom he only met once, when he was eighteen years old, Dante twenty-one. It had been a truly bizarre encounter: Dante, being a half sibling and the bastard child of an affair, had been disinherited since birth, and thus had not grown up within the walls of the Marcello mansion, instead living in what their father described as a "shack" downtown with his mother. He had not been permitted to be near the Marcello family or estate, including Giovanni himself, until Giovanni was legally of age to make the decision for himself.

Giovanni would not have pursued the relationship, but he remembered vividly the moment only a week after his eighteenth birthday when he had received a handwritten envelope in the mail, which he presumed to be a late birthday card (he had refused a party, too swept up in postpubescent awareness of mortality and aging and overcome with an insecurity so crippling it left him unable to imagine socializing with a crowd as the center of attention, the performance of appreciation he would have to put on as each guest, undoubtedly his father's friends, as he had none of his own, scrutinized and judged him, expected exemplary etiquette, a shining pillar of his father's superb parenting even as he fought the hardships of a single father trying to support his family alone).

To his surprise, it was an invitation from his elder half-brother, a complete stranger to him at the time. The letter requested to meet with him at a coffee shop downtown, in the lower fashion district, a semi-safe middle class area of Fresno proper that he had never braved alone. Giovanni had, for reasons he could not explain, decided not to tell his father anything about this letter, as if he was some sort of refugee, a convict or a prisoner of war attempting to break free of his confinement, choosing to sneak out of the house on the day of the meeting just as the sun was coming up, tiptoeing down hallways so as not to wake his sister before school and calling a taxi as he could not drive. He arrived when the sky was still an early morning gray and the sidewalks empty save for the bundled bodies of people nestled beneath shuttered doorways and atop bus stop benches. Pigeons and mourning doves hopped about, and Giovanni felt naked and exposed, very aware that his adulthood was just as fresh and new as the day.

Arriving at the storefront of the coffee shop, Giovanni was surprised to see it already open, the neon sign proclaiming it such dimly lit and faded in the morning light but still visibly shining out for all those who passed by. Beneath the sign was an old, handwritten list of hours, stating that the shop opened at five, the perfect time for many early morning workers to stop by before their shifts. Would his brother already be in? Giovanni wondered, feeling an awkwardness creep up on him at the thought of sitting or standing around the shop alone. He didn't even know what Dante looked like, let alone how they would greet each other, what they would say to each other. He looked around the city street once more. Cars drove past in sporadic clusters as the unending blink of traffic lights herded them onward, splashing oily water that smelled like rot, the corpse-like bodies of the homeless lay about, litter sat piled on the ground, garbage overflowed from the trashcans. The world felt very foreign, and Giovanni felt very helpless and alone.

Despite the warmth of early summer Giovanni had worn a jacket in order to cover himself up and shield himself from outsiders, and between the heat and the discomfort he felt as he looked about the city street, he decided to go ahead and enter the coffee shop.

"Giovanni!" The call of his name as he entered was immediate.

Giovanni turned to see the owner of the voice and came to stare at the man at the counter in shock: They were very obviously brothers, Giovanni a spitting image of the man save for a few key features. Rather than Giovanni's pale blue eyes, this man's were a dark brown. Giovanni had put on a decent amount of weight as a teenager, between a relatively static homeschooling lifestyle and puberty, while this man looked almost emaciated, cheeks hollow and eyes sunken, body stick thin. Still, they had the same nose, the same long, thick, dark hair, the same rounded jawline that Giovanni so detested.

As it turned out, Dante was one of the managers of the shop, an assistant and close friend to the owner. He offered Giovanni a lavender white mocha, on the house, a delicately crafted coffee that tasted fresh and bright like his father's garden, with Marcello candy sugar sprinkled across the top which helped ease his nerves about the meeting. As the shop was empty and there was one other employee on the clock, Dante sat down with Giovanni by the window, where paper fliers for local events and missing persons posters were taped over the ghostly traces of scrubbed graffiti.

"I didn't expect you to be here so early," Dante said. He had no accent, speaking in a very standard California English.

Giovanni stuttered over himself. Why *had* he arrived so early? He had known the anticipation through the rest of the day would have killed him. He looked down at his feet awkwardly, unsure of what to say, realizing that there was nothing *to* say, that this man was a stranger regardless of the blood they shared.

"I mean... to be honest, I'm glad you came at all. It's nice to finally meet you," Dante continued kindly.

Giovanni remained silent, feeling Dante's eyes on him like daggers as he imagined what his brother must have been seeing, this awkward boy, shifting uncomfortably in his own body, smothering himself in his jacket in the heat of Central Valley summer. He was new to makeup then, and was still dealing with the last of teenage grease, his skin constantly erupting into breakouts; haphazardly, poorly blended spots of concealer dotted his skin and made him look diseased, obvious patches of paint that stuck out on his face. He had shakily applied an attempt at makeup, something he had only begun experimenting with recently, which amounted to uneven black lines around his eyes, a smudge of red on his cheeks, lipstick that he had smudged around the edges of his mouth. Giovanni felt like a clown, and the Marcello candy that dusted his drink could hardly counteract the rapid heartbeat caused by caffeine and nerves now that Dante watched him and waited, aggravatingly patiently, for a response.

In the end, Giovanni remembered the humiliation he had felt during the meeting more than anything else about it; the conversation had been largely uneventful, stilted and awkward as it had begun, with Dante asking vague, safe questions that were answered with nervous murmurs, Giovanni feeling like an interrogation subject even as Dante asked things as simple as "what do you like to do for fun?" and "do you have any girlfriends? Boyfriends?"

Giovanni, in turn, had ultimately asked Dante nothing, initiated nothing. He most certainly had questions, but he hardly knew how to ask them. He had never met this man before, he was as much a stranger as any of the random bodies that littered the Fresno sidewalks, and yet they were connected, so much so that Dante had felt the urge to meet with him like this. And Giovanni had accepted the offer—Why had he done that? Perhaps because he hoped to learn something more about himself, and yet here he was, and neither said anything of value.

For Dante, too, seemed to be saying less than he was thinking, his words careful and cautious. At times he would pause, and there would be a long, heavy silence between the two of them, and Giovanni would wonder if Dante was thinking about saying more, asking more. Giovanni had almost hoped he would, if anything so that he would be forced to confront... something. He wished Dante would look him in the eye and tell him about something terrible and tragic that would haunt him through the rest of his life. But he didn't. Instead, the conversation went on, awkward, questions that meant nothing, pregnant pauses and aborted sentences, with Giovanni trembling and exposed even beneath his jacket and his makeup until finally Dante stood.

"I should get back to work," He stretched, fingers clasping together as he raised his arms over his head with a small grunt. Then he looked at Giovanni and said, "This was nice,"

Giovanni did not see or hear from Dante again. He did not tell his father of their meeting, or anybody, for that matter. He had gone home and slept, and Vittorio quipped later in the evening that it was uncharacteristic of him to sleep in, that he was used to seeing him up and about, disturbing the hired help in the early hours and rummaging through the pantry for food when all good people should be asleep, but he had not questioned anything. The next time he would hear about his brother would be in passing at a family dinner, one consisting of only the children Vittorio had conceived in wedlock: himself, Vittoria, his elder half siblings from Vittorio's previous marriage. Giorgio had been there, drunk and delighted, and it had been he who gleefully announced in the lascivious salesman hiss in which he spoke that Dante had allegedly taken his own life, *"not that they had to worry about splitting inheritance with him to begin with."* Giovanni never sought to confirm this claim.

Giovanni awoke in the child's bedroom. He sat up, confused at first as he tried to remember where he was, a splitting headache disorienting him even more, his eyes and mouth dry and his thoughts sluggish. He faintly remembered falling asleep with Angel in his arms, but the boy was nowhere to be seen. He sat, alone and aching, wondering what was in store for him out here. Pale morning light poured in through the single window in the room, beyond which were vast, dry fields, sprawling onwards for what seemed like eternity, Fresno city a distant, dreamlike memory now.

When Vittoria awoke she was still nursing the dregs of a nasty hangover. She also learned quickly enough that she had slept well into the later hours of the afternoon, with only the faintest traces of memories of the restless night prior: occasionally awakening to a splitting headache and nausea, Anubis bringing her glasses of water and rubbing her shoulders, before passing out again, desperate to sleep off the pain that wracked her body, tossing and turning, in and out of half-delirious drunken unconsciousness.

The night was a blur of color and sound, red and noise. Her head throbbed in a rhythm not unlike the banging and pounding of the drum on the stage, of the booming bass in Anubis' club. She rubbed at her temples as she sat up slowly, groaning, stretching, feeling her limbs ache and tremble as they continued to fight through the alcohol as it cleared from her system. She wondered what Anubis was up to, as he was nowhere to be found in the bedroom.

Fighting back the dizziness that came with each step, Vittoria trudged out of the bedroom and descended down the staircases. The single comfort she had today was that, because she had gone shopping the day before in order to begin slowly restoring her wardrobe, she now had actual pajamas to wear, a soft black nightgown made of cheap, itchy velvet. She was still on a tight enough budget that she had not wanted to risk buying anything more expensive, although she had a sneaking suspicion that Anubis would be able to recognize the quality in an instant and wonder why in the world someone as supposedly wealthy as herself would not choose to buy finer material.

It was as she was formulating a series of viable excuses (currently, she was pondering over the idea of claiming an allergy to finer textiles), intermingled with the sneaking guilt of her continued, much larger lie to Anubis regarding her familial circumstance, that she made it to the bottom of the staircase, where she found her host in the living room, lounging in one of his chairs, surrounded by the many figures he owned gazing down at him in a way reminiscent of the thralls of people that had gazed up at him from his audience last night, an image burned well into Vittoria's memory.

"Anubis?" Vittoria called, because he was occupied by a book.

He looked up at that and smiled when he saw Vittoria standing at the foot of the stairway. He was no longer the horrible creature he had allowed to possess him the night before. Here he was fully himself again, the cool, collected man who had been so generous as to allow her to stay with him—in reading glasses, no less. "Vittoria, love!" he greeted, setting his book down, dog-earing it to mark his spot. "You slept late. How are you feeling?"

Vittoria gave a feeble shrug. "I have a headache," she grumbled, walking over to sit down on the couch across from him. "Do you have any aspirin or something?"

Anubis nodded, set his glasses down beside the book, and stood. "Oh, of course! One moment, please," He made his way briskly towards the kitchen. Vittoria watched him exit, and once he was gone from the room she rested her head back against the couch and sighed, shutting her eyes. It was in just a few slow, deep breaths that Anubis returned with a call of, "Here, darling!" He walked to her and handed her a glass of water and two small, white pills, which Vittoria accepted gratefully.

It was while downing the first pill that she saw Anubis sit back down where he had been before, and with the second that she heard him say, "While you were resting I took it upon myself to set up an appointment for you tomorrow afternoon"

The water in Vittoria's throat seemed to come to a halt. She choked, coughed, sputtered, clenched the glass tightly in her hands to keep from dropping it in fingers that suddenly felt quite shaky. "What?"

Anubis was smiling. "I figured there's no reason to dawdle. Ideally, I would like you to be ready come my next show." He spoke in a thoughtful purr laced with seduction. "I spoke to one of my most trusted surgeons. He's quite familiar with the whole process by now, he's done it plenty of times on me, with many individual organs. He's starting only with your heart this time. It will be smooth and painless, Vittoria."

Vittoria could not bring herself to believe that the surgical relocation of her heart would be anything remotely close to "painless." She also could not bring herself to say a word, her mind revolving quite quickly around multiple risks and options, tentatively seeking a way out even as another part of her sought to convince her that this was right, as her heartbeat picked up at the thrill of imagining herself up on the stage beside Anubis, their blood intermingling from open wounds, the eyes gazing up at her and him, together, creating and becoming art. The pills felt as if they had caught in her throat, burning a hole in her esophagus. She took another sip of water.

Giovanni spent a disappointing portion of the day bedridden with a headache that followed him out of his restless dreams into reality, the sharp sting of awareness that he was horribly dehydrated. His body felt feverish and weak, reminiscent of a hangover that he knew he did not have. He suspected the actual source to be the lingering withdrawal from his beloved candies, combined with whatever unimaginable harm the last few days had done to his delicate physical and mental wellbeing. He was starving and dizzy, his limbs felt both weighed down by lead and floating above themselves. He was almost certain that he could sink down into the bed and dissolve into it, like a corpse decaying until it was overtaken by dirt and weeds.

When Giovanni finally stood it was out of desperation, as although the pain in his head was no easier to bear, nausea began to persistently tug at his throat and the only thing he could tolerate less than the current realm of discomfort he was trapped in was the idea of puking on himself while in it. He was met with static behind his eyes that briefly blinded him, turning his vision hazy and worsening his dizziness tenfold, and he stumbled about in the direction of the bathroom, still feeling very much only half alive at most.

After choking up a few measly chunks of phlegmy saliva Giovanni was left only slightly satiated, his stomach still writhing and his throat now burning, his head still aching as if his brain was swollen and throbbing against the sides of his skull, but at least the immediate urgency was alleviated for the time being. He staggered then towards the kitchen, and in that moment he felt very animalistic, driven purely by primal directives, trying desperately to satiate need after need—Or perhaps something akin to covering up cracks in a pitcher with tape, one by one, to try to keep the water from spurting out.

Giovanni's mind was swimming with odd metaphors when he saw his host for the first time that day, sat, nonchalant, in one of the living room chairs, legs crossed and hands clutching a book that looked very old and worn.

He looked up at Giovanni. "Finally up?"

"I feel just awful, Angel," Giovanni moaned, rubbing his temples.

"Hopefully nothing contagious," Angel replied with a little sound reminiscent of a snicker. "You probably just need water,"

"What are you reading?"

Angel shrugged and held the book up, it was a dark green with gold text across it, titled: *Everyday Uses for Exotic Vegetables.* Giovanni stared quizzically, and Angel answered the unspoken question right away with, "I don't, uhm, actually give a shit about vegetable cultivation. It's just something to do." He nodded towards an old bookshelf, where dusty old books sat in rows, many of which, from what Giovanni could make out from where he stood, seemingly about agriculture, farming, cooking: basic household skills and tricks. It all sounded dreadfully boring to him, and it was also, he thought, nothing he had ever even thought much about before, having had servants happy to do the dirty work that was household chores throughout his life. It seemed easy enough, he thought, and he could not understand why someone would desire such a massive collection of written word on the subject.

"What does one... do all day out here, Angel?" Giovanni asked, uneasy as he thought about having to throw himself into the study of arranging a table or growing an herb garden.

Angel shrugged again. "I dunno. Read books? Jerk off? Pray? Whatever passes the time." He stood, setting the book down on the chair and stretching. His wings unfurled too, expanding out so the tips jutted from each side, feathers ruffling and trembling with the intensity of the stretch, very much alive before Giovanni's eyes. So fixated on the magnificent wings was he that he had to blink himself out of a trance when Angel asked, "Are you hungry?"

"Starved."

Giovanni had a feeling he should have been grateful for the food situation—he certainly had been the day before, when he had been greeted to a warm meal after what had felt like endless strife, fear, and discomfort—but he struggled to find himself particularly thrilled by the options before him today. He was finally beginning to feel like his old self, and his old self had much higher standards. As Angel had warned, the cupboard was made up largely of preservatives: Canned ingredients of which Giovanni could practically taste the metallic brine just by looking at them, sacks of rice, nuts and dried fruit making up the options for snacks which felt far from worthy of being snacked on. The few exciting ingredients—a quarter round of some nameless hard cheese, part of a loaf of fresh-ish bread, a half tube of dried meat—still left much to be desired and seemed to be in limited quantities. Giovanni's stomach already churned with discomfort from the morning, and he fumbled through the cabinet and small, near-empty refrigerator with uncertainty.

"Well?" Angel asked after a moment of staring, watching Giovanni rummage.

"I don't think my stomach is suited to this food," Giovanni mumbled.

"Well, what's it suited to?"

Giovanni froze at the question, realizing he perhaps had said too much. He fumbled out a series of noises that landed nowhere near coherent words, feigned a cough to clear his throat, and grabbed a can of chicken noodle soup. Angel watched for a moment, and Giovanni felt very aware of his eyes on him, as if he was judging each one of his movements, evaluating how naturally he was able to maneuver the can opener, how convincingly he could peer down at the murky, gooey brown substance, unrecognizable bits of things, once vegetables and noodles and, god forbid, meat, sloshing around in it, and appear to find it scrumptious.

After a moment of Giovanni struggling through this pathetic display, Angel said, "Could you go into town sometime and pick up more food? Er, when you're up for it."

Giovanni looked at Angel. "I thought money was a problem..." he said, distinctly remembering Angel's "limited funds" comment from yesterday. Why else would he be living off preservatives and canned goods, scraping by with stale bread and dry meat?

"I have money." Angel said abruptly. Giovanni went quiet, staring in surprise. Angel looked up at the ceiling, expressionless, and the two of them remained silent, as if both were trying to figure out the next step in this elaborate game of half-answers. Then Angel finally made the next move. Speaking again, he said, "Look, there are some people out there who wouldn't take kindly to these," He nodded towards his wings, flopping one up a bit the way one would shrug a single shoulder to further emphasize his point. "This place is ruthless, I don't... I don't know what would happen if- if certain people were to... get any ideas. But you... you're indiscriminate enough."

Giovanni had never, in the entirety of his life, been called "indiscriminate," but he supposed, glancing down at his own body for a moment, right now he more or less was. Cleaned up and without makeup, his face was plain, if not still slightly bruised and swollen from the events of the day before. He was devoid of his jewelry, his skincare products, his perfumes, the lovely clothing, all that he had defined himself by, worn like armor against the outside world. He could see his soft stomach protrude slightly from the undershirt he wore, was sure that by now stubble was breaking through the surface of his clean-shaven skin, and he felt very plain indeed. He walked to the stovetop with his soup can, preparing to heat it up.

"I will go," Giovanni agreed, as the awful substance fell into the pot with a sickening *plop* and a splatter of semi-solid brown chunks.

Vittoria did not touch her dinner that night, unable to bring herself to have an appetite even if it felt a bit rude to leave the food that Anubis had lovingly prepared to grow cold. When Anubis suggested dessert she did not have the heart to tell him that even attempting to make her eat something with sugar in it would be a lost cause, which meant shortly after wasting a plate of food she now sat before a slice of German chocolate cake that was doomed to the garbage bin as well. She felt akin to a prisoner eating her last meal on death row, pushing some frosting around her plate in a halfhearted attempt to appear as if she were working it over.

"Maybe some tea, Vittoria?" Anubis offered after watching Vittoria sit and stare at the cake in silence for a while longer. "I have chamomile and mint, or perhaps something Eastern-"

"I'm just... not hungry, Anubis," Vittoria interrupted, not wanting to have anything else placed in front of her. She looked down at her hands, noticing the way that the black polish on her nails had begun to chip and wondering if she could afford to buy more to repaint them.

"Vittoria, darling, I understand pre-surgery nerves, I certainly had them the first few times as well," Anubis said, casually stretching out a long, thin arm, to reach across the table and push her plate closer to her. Vittoria kept her eyes down because she was certain she would be sick if she looked at the cake any longer. "But this will be your last meal prior to the operation, you really do need your strength."

Vittoria had given up trying to argue and instead opted to remain silent, a rather stubborn move that Anubis seemed to take note of, for he responded with a long sigh before continuing to speak, tone gentle and alarmingly patient given her attitude: "Perhaps it would do us both good if I were to show you something. I figure that with the extremity of what you will be undergoing tomorrow, how willing you have been to go so far in such a short period of time for art, the least I could do is show you some of my secrets." He stood up and walked to the front of the dining room, towards the front of the house, the living room and the staircase to the second floor. Vittoria simply stared at him, unsure of what he was about to do. "Unless you have a miraculous change of heart and decide that you would like to partake in dessert after all, why don't you come with me?"

Eager to escape the cake, Vittoria accepted.

Anubis led her down through the living room and to the stairs, which they ascended together. Immediately by the staircase was the bedroom that she and Anubis shared, and on the other side was a bathroom, as well as a third room that Vittoria had not given any thought to. In fact, Anubis himself had referred to it as a supply closet, and mentioned that it was not of any importance whatsoever, and in the stress of the past few days there had not been a moment in which Vittoria had mustered the time or energy to even begin to question this, let alone defy Anubis' word and investigate it herself.

Now, he led her to it, and as they reached the door Anubis placed his hand on the doorknob but did not move to open it yet. Instead, he turned to Vittoria and smiled. "You are a very special girl, Vittoria Marcello, for you are the first person beside myself to enter this room," He opened the door then and held it for Vittoria. "After you, dearest,"

Vittoria entered and for a moment could not process what exactly she was supposed to be looking at. The room was certainly not a supply closet, and was around the size of a bedroom—In fact, given its size and position in the house, it may have initially been intended to be the master bedroom. It was also probably the brightest room in the house; Anubis kept his lights dim, but the overhead lights of this room shone blinding white, giving the surroundings an almost sterile, medical atmosphere. This atmosphere was furthered by the display cases that sat throughout the room, glass cubes full of an array of objects not unlike one might find at a museum, many of them medical as well: syringes, scalpels, scissors... Hung up on the walls were numerous posters and photos reminiscent of the ones Anubis hung up in the Embalmed Records building but of names and faces that she did not recognize. They looked old, faded around the edges with graphic design on logos that very much would have read as quaintly vintage now.

Anubis' silence as Vittoria looked around led her to believe that perhaps he wanted her to continue to explore, perhaps he was waiting for her to say something first. She walked slowly up to the center of the room, where a lone display case sat, a single light shining down directly onto it. Its insides protected by the glass covering, it all but glowed, crystalline in the bright light.

What lay in the case was the strangest display of items that Vittoria had ever seen. A pair of golden, circular glasses, a little pile of various jewelry of all shapes and sizes, mostly comprised of piercings and rings, and a skull, which looked very much like a human's, and looked very, very real, which sat in the center on a little red velvet cushion with gold trim along the outside of it. Vittoria stared at it, then turned back to Anubis and asked, "What- *Who* is this?"

Anubis was smiling at Vittoria and watching her the way one might watch a pet explore its surroundings after being introduced to its new home, studying the behavior with delight. "My dear, lovely Sugar," Anubis answered, walking to the case and gingerly touching the top of the glass, "He may very well have been my first love, and he taught me what true art really is." He gazed down at the skull with a warm smile, and delicately traced an outline of a heart over it on the glass with his long nails.

"What... What happened to him?" Vittoria asked, breath catching in her throat as she attempted to make sense of what she was being shown. "I mean... Did... you..."

"Did I what, Vittoria?" Anubis asked, turning to look at her now with eyebrows raised. There was an edge to his tone, an accusatory sharpness that made her even more tense. "He left his skull to me. I played no part in his death, and I acquired it perfectly legally. Sugar took his own life. But, if you want me to be honest with you, I will admit that I do not regret his death, nor do I have any regrets that I did not stop it from happening." He walked then to one of the posters on the wall, this one a full-body image of a person. He may have been quite pretty, with a few features that Vittoria could recognize right away as attractive, a cute round face and small nose, a rather pixie-like, almost childish demeanor despite being, Vittoria guessed, somewhere around forty; shoulder length hair dyed black and white, a body that appeared both small and soft but still sturdy. But that was really the most of his features that she could make out, for the rest of him was covered in blood. He was entirely naked, and he lay as if he were a pin-up model in a bed of what appeared to be wilting rose petals. What distracted her even more from properly evaluating the man was the needles, which pierced through his flesh all over. Up his bare arms and legs, through the most sensitive flesh of his inner elbows and thighs, through his nipples, his flaccid penis, his testicles, through his tongue, which stuck out and dripped with red saliva down his chin.

"One of his favorite performances. Before the show he asked the audience where they wanted him to begin. At the time nobody realized that he meant it," Anubis mused. Vittoria could imagine—they were long, thick metal rods akin to nails, she could hardly conceptualize willingly puncturing her own skin with even one, let alone so many, and in such locations. "When people began shouting out suggestions, he followed them. Soon enough they weren't suggesting anything anymore, but Sugar persisted on his own accord. He called it the Gradual Release of Responsibility." He let out a wistful half-laugh half-hum, a sort of tender nostalgia in his voice that Vittoria had not heard before.

"He took me under his wing when I was still a young and aimless musician, directionless, in dead-end bands going nowhere with dreams stuck at the far end of the dullest of suburban cul-de-sacs. He showed me the truth that I had been missing, ignited the spark that had evaded me for so many years, that despite my countless years as a student of philosophy no class had ever been brave enough to teach." Anubis turned back around to Vittoria. "For his final art piece Sugar chose to take his own life, and it was marvelous. Hung up in lace and ribbon like a sacrificial lamb birthday cake. I was the one who found his body."

Vittoria was stunned to silence for a long while, staring at the poster, then to Anubis, then back to the wall again. Most of the other posters featured Sugar as well, each equally macabre, with pins and needles, knives and syringes, candle wax and matches, an eroticism delicately interwoven into each display of automasochism. These were the weapons in the cases, she realized; they were all artifacts from Sugar's performances. When she finally found her words, her voice was very soft: "Why are you showing me all this?"

"Sugar's death taught me more than his life ever did," Anubis said, and there was an intensity mounting in his voice, a sort of excitement as if he were about to read his manifesto to a crowd of cultists, "I spent years, Vittoria, *years*, pondering the reason for it, what he had meant by it. My very core, any belief I had held about death and the afterlife and what may or may not lie beyond the barbed wire edges of our reality crumbled to nothing. And then I understood."

"What did you understand?" Vittoria asked with bated breath.

"The Nirvana of human existence is to become art."

Vittoria felt very overwhelmed. There was an adrenaline rush building in her much like the intensity of Anubis' words as she stared at the images around her, thought back to Anubis' own show, imagined the prick of needle and burn of fire to her skin, her flesh being stripped away like lingerie to reveal something horrific and red and indisputably human beneath. She looked around the room another time, and this time her eyes caught another figure in one of the posters, a young man with tan skin and curly hair, eyes so dark that in the old camera quality the iris faded into the pupils, a wide smile that revealed a normal set of *Homo sapien* teeth, his arm around Sugar. This photo was tender and warm, despite the blood that ran from Sugar's mouth and the black eyes he sported; both were smiling. This must have been Anubis himself, Vittoria realized, but he looked very, very different, and this must have been decades before she herself was even alive. She was reminded briefly of her own paintings back in her old home, the dozens of unique portraits she had spent years collecting only to lose in an instant when her father had forced her out. She remembered the way each one stared down at her, watching over her with eyes given their own separate soul by each artist who created them, lives lost to her disownment.

"So you see, Vittoria," Anubis said gently, when Vittoria remained quiet, "I am trying to help you. I am giving you access to secrets that very few people in this world will ever truly unlock, but with my help you have had the key dropped neatly into your lap. All you must do now is put it in the lock and turn it." He took her hand then and made a very gentle turning gesture. "And I can help you. You do not need to fear anything."

Vittoria nodded slowly and wet her lips. She did not know what to make of it all, but that surge of exhilaration continued to rush through her veins, straight to her heart. She thought back to the years where music was her closest, if not sole, companion, where she immersed herself in the guttural cries and screaming, the electric distortion and machinescape throb of music that reverberated through the darkest depths of her black heart and pulled at something hidden very, very deep within, a caged self that gripped cold bars and listened to that music as if it were her only lifeline, her only measly connection to something much more, to the world beyond the bars.

When she spoke, the words tumbled from her mouth with little thought. "When I was younger I went to college for an art degree,"

"Oh?" Anubis asked, his tone as cool and relaxed as ever despite the jarring change of topic.

Vittoria's eyes remained transfixed on the poster of Anubis and Sugar. "I wanted to study art, but, um..." She faltered. "I ended up dropping out a semester in so that I could open a fashion line instead, since, uh," She hesitated again, unsure of what to say. Truthfully, she had been hit with the crippling terror that there simply was no chance at success, let alone survival, with an art degree; not as her father was pushing for product, for something tangible to show for herself, not when she was attached to a name that demanded profitable perfection. "...I wanted to do something a little more practical. People were really into the idea of Marcello-brand clothing." Sort of. The project had more or less failed, the tie-in too forced and obfuscating (or *ambitious*, as the news outlets had kindly reported after a friendly sum of money), and with the designers her father had paid to do the heavy lifting for her, she had felt no attachment to anything she was representing. The entire division of the company was dissolved shortly after, and Marcello-brand clothes became relegated to nothing but a rare collector's item, or a mildly interesting thrift store find.

Anubis gave Vittoria's hands a gentle squeeze before taking her by the arms to pull her close to him. He rubbed her back. The portraits of Sugar stared down at them. "As I have said already, you are more than your father's daughter, Vittoria. You will be so much more."

Giovanni lay in the child's bed, feeling dazed and weak, head spinning and body going through a series of shivering aches that seemed to erupt from his core and spread out into each limb like a terrible shockwave. He had managed to keep food down, at least, and with access to water he was continuing to gradually feel better. It was a pathetic display, he thought, but he was finally optimistic about his own survival, something that had felt significantly more tenuous only a day ago.

"Hey," a voice called, and Giovanni tensed slightly, turning to look towards the doorway to see Angel standing there. Giovanni stared at the boy; he had not even heard the door open, had not heard the soft sound of footsteps on the creaky floor. Angel's ability to drift as if he were a ghost through the house, to sneak up on him with such ease, never ceased to surprise him.

"You startled me," Giovanni admitted, sitting up slightly as Angel walked towards his bed.

"Always gotta be on your toes out here," Angel said. He approached the bed now, and as Giovanni was just sitting up fully Angel swung a leg around to straddle him again, sitting down on his lap and facing him, so close that their noses were nearly touching.

Giovanni tensed and arched away from Angel, face feeling hot. "Wh-What are you doing?" he asked.

"Better way to pass the time than jerk off or pray," Angel grabbed the rim of Giovanni's shirt and gave it a tug upwards.

"Wait!"

Giovanni placed a hand on Angel's sternum, forcefully enough that it kept him at bay. Angel looked at Giovanni with his brow furrowed, tilting his head like a confused animal being scolded for an action to which it had never personally ascribed moral. "What? Do you have, like, an issue with sex, or something?"

Giovanni stared at Angel, trying to find the words as the warmth in his body distracted him and made his thoughts feel sluggish, as if the heat were melting them away. Never in his life had he considered himself "having an issue" with sex. Sex had been, up until quite recently, a near-daily occurrence, and something he had actively sought quite vivaciously, and enjoyed with equal enthusiasm. It had been a go-to activity of a caliber beneath only candy and makeup. But the memories of previous sexual encounters felt as distant as a half-forgotten dream, and they felt so disconnected from who he was and where he was now that he could hardly believe it had really been him experiencing all of it, that it had been himself, his current consciousness in its current form, existing in those soft, silken sheets, in the beloved bedroom filled with delightful decorations, regal and pristine, naked body pressed to naked body, touch and taste and all senses alight.

Very early Giovanni had learned that the women who worked for his father rarely rejected his sexual advances. He had taken full advantage of this, and he had felt very clever in the way he had cheated his way through the social ladder of relationships and sex that most others spent years climbing rung by rung. His father employed women he assumed to be very beautiful, as he knew his father had an eye for beauty, and he had felt very good then, knowing that those he slept with were of high enough quality to be deserving not only of his father's employment, but of employment in his family's home. He knew how much his father cared about family. And it had felt good, then, to feel that there was always an option, always somebody around to offer up to him something so intimate, something that promised closeness, connectedness, the warmth of contact, even if only for a moment.

But Angel stared at him with those wide, inquisitive eyes of his, waiting to hear what Giovanni's reservations about sex—sex, of all things!—could possibly be about, and Giovanni wondered suddenly if he had ever *desired* any of these women, beyond their touch, beyond the feeling of their skin against his, beyond the way the sex made his head spin in a way not particularly dissimilar to the candies. Did he desire Angel? Did Angel desire *him*?

"N- No," Giovanni said, not wholly confident, "I have just been through a lot in these past few days, Angel. I am trying to figure out what it is I am doing out here. What... what's next," Surely he could not just stay out here like this forever, with this boy he hardly knew, in the middle of nowhere.

Angel sighed and got off of Giovanni, instead opting to sit beside him on the small bed, so close that their shoulders touched. "This isn't the end of the line for me," he said. "I'm just... waiting for someone."

"Waiting for someone?"

"California, she's... she's on the lookout right now."

"For... a... mechanic?" Giovanni asked, remembering faintly one of the first things Angel ever asked him.

Angel seemed to have forgotten. His wings twitched, unfurling slightly as the feathers puffed like an angry bird, and he went silent, eyes a little wider than usual, indicating to Giovanni that he had forgotten that he had said such a thing. Giovanni almost considered commenting on this, a half-joke on how this did not seem to be information that he had been expected to live to remember, but remembering Angel kept his weapons even closer than his secrets, he decided against it.

"Yeah," Angel said briskly. "Once he's here, we'll be able to go on."

"Go on?"

"Beyond the Valley,"

"Oh," Giovanni had never pictured what exactly lay beyond the Central Valley, very rarely had he even left with his family—he had hardly even left *Fresno*. By the time he and his sister had been born the allure of family vacation had long since faded; his older siblings traveled, his father for business, once even Vittoria for a class trip, but nothing of excitement had come up in their stories upon returning. Everywhere else had sounded about the same to Giovanni, who found the idea of travel to be more difficult than it was worth, anyway. He remembered the time that his family had gone on a vacation to the sea and stayed at a lovely beach house, decorated with shells and sea stars and framed paintings of boats and seagulls on the water, where the sky was cherry colored at sunset and the water sparkled cotton candy pink, but primarily he remembered the sunburns, the sand nestled uncomfortably between his toes, the way the water had irritated his skin, the sweat, the way his elder siblings had ridiculed him for packing too much, the way he had cried when his favorite nail polish spilled out onto the off-white carpet like a pool of violet blood and the way he had been reprimanded by his father for making a mess.

"You can wait with me, if you like," Angel said, freeing Giovanni from his memories.

Giovanni thought about this for a moment. What other choice did he have, really? Refuse this offer and go where—On foot into the wasteland beyond the outskirts, into the dry dirt region that had once been countless acres of farmland now reduced to dead fields, cooking beneath sweltering heat? Or back to the city, where he risked violence in the face of enemies he had never known he had? Take up work like California in the back of a bar? Here he had company and shelter, food, a bed... and Angel, who he was beginning to get the sneaking suspicion he liked, in some strange way. Even beyond the fascination he had for the boy, beyond the awe he had for the wondrous white wings on his back, he was beginning to feel some sort of draw to him that made him keen on remaining in his presence. Or perhaps he was just succumbing to a new vice, now that the candies were slowly leaving his system and clearing his head for the first time in many years; perhaps he was just drawn to Angel's desire.

And yet... What else was there to do?

*Does it turn you on at all to feel out of control?* Angel's words from the night before echoed in Giovanni's mind and he leaned over, cupping Angel's cheek in his hand and bringing him in for a kiss on the mouth which Angel did not reject.

Anubis allowed Vittoria to sleep through the morning, but at eleven he came to wake her, and after she had showered and dressed (she was denied coffee, as Anubis insisted that a procedure such as this must be done on an empty stomach, and reassured her with a snarky grin that "the painkillers she would be given could handle much, much more than a caffeine headache"), she was led out to his car. Vittoria walked to it like she imagined a misbehaving dog might walk to its owner, hesitant with fear of punishment but unable to resist the loyalty ingrained deep within it at the call of its name. She felt odd, tingly all over, a strange discomfort that seeped out of her skin and made her clothes feel unpleasant against her body. She said very little to Anubis, who, in contrast to her, seemed even more lively than usual, jovial and full of playful quips that she could hardly process in her zombified state.

"There will be no complications," Anubis said, although Vittoria had not even been thinking about that.

"I know," Vittoria said, and she took an embarrassingly long time trying to buckle her seatbelt, her hand trembling against her will. But now she *was* thinking about complications, and anesthetic, and the full intensiveness of surgery, something she was only marginally familiar with through experience she had with a minor cosmetic procedure years ago. She thought now about the fact that she would be recovering from a major alteration to her body in a house still foreign to her, with a man who was nearly a stranger... If she had told her younger self that Anubis himself would be tending to her after a surgery, would she have even been able to begin imagining such a thing? It was an absurd scenario, something that felt out of place within the normal timeline of any individual's life. She turned to Anubis as he drove. "Anubis?" She said his name as if hoping that vocalizing it would remind her that it was really him.

Anubis glanced to her. "Yes?"

"You said you've legally died more times than anyone. Did you... see anything? While you were dead?" She had heard stories of people who had died during surgery and were revived, only to recount incredible out of body experiences, visions of afterlives both hellish and heavenly, deceased loved ones awaiting them in the beyond, telling them to turn back, that they still had more life to live before it would be their time to rest.

Anubis was silent for a very long time. He turned off of the street he lived on, down a perpendicular road that would lead towards the freeway into the city. "No," he said finally, "I just awoke as if no time had passed at all. Consciousness is a funny thing." There was a strangeness to Anubis' tone, perhaps not anger, but a sort of irritation that Vittoria could not figure the direction of. She decided it was better not to ask anything else, not wanting to make the situation even more tense than it already was.

When Anubis spoke again his voice took the brighter, more conversational tone from before: "These are exciting times for you, my dear! Have you been in contact with your family at all? I was wondering if you had mentioned your current endeavors to any of them."

"No," Vittoria said, echoing Anubis' response only moments prior. Anubis swerved quite suddenly to avoid hitting a squirrel that had run into the street and she felt her stomach lurch.

After a few more days of rest, Giovanni's health had improved significantly. No longer did he get sudden onslaughts of chills and nausea, and his headaches had become much more sporadic. He certainly had other ailments to attend to, though, kept up at night with thoughts that rushed through his head much faster than he could catch them, the creeping awareness of the knives in Angel's pockets, the way the boy tiptoed about, secretive, knowing far more than he, leaving him at a disadvantage as he lay alone in the child's bedroom, the dizzying fatigue that came with a diet much more meager than anything he had ever lived on before...

His diet. That was truly something he loathed about living out here. Try as he might, and despite possessing a will to live that at this point had even surprised himself, so tired was he of snacking exclusively on dried fruits, canned vegetables, and box spaghetti that he was beginning to sense the impressive recovery he had undergone was being slowly reversed by the fact that there were some days where he would choose starving over the options presented to him.

Keeping true to his promise to brave exiting Angel's home and make the great expedition back into town, Giovanni, feeling desperate, took up Angel's request to see if the legendary supermarket he had mentioned was a reality. Angel did not hesitate to rush off to his room, returning with a wadded handful of twenty-dollar bills and very brief directions on how to find his way through the town. Giovanni wondered, then, how much money Angel had on him, for he had now received mixed answers about the full scope of his affluence. He supposed California could be contributing some financial aid, but he did not have numbers on that, either, nor had he seen California since their auspicious introduction, so how, when, and if that exchange happened was lost on him.

But he supposed that these answers would come—or not—with time, and until then, he wanted to prioritize making his living arrangement as marginally comfortable as he possibly could. And so, pulling on a pair of ugly denim pants that Angel had dug up from a closet (they were visibly too tight on him, constricting his stomach in a way that made it just bit harder to breathe, faded with wear and age, much too rough against his legs) and the cleanest plain white undershirt he could find, he set out on his journey.

The walk back to the town was still terrible, exhausting and hot and desolate, surrounded by the dry wasteland of the outskirts of Fresno and the derelict shacks that had most likely once been some sort of stunted proto-suburbia. There had once been, he imagined, a time when there had been some sort of hope nestled within these quaint homes, of people who had left Fresno, or who had perhaps never even seen it in the first place, who were eager to begin their lives out here, perhaps envisioning that it would someday be the sprawling suburbs of Fresno itself, not unlike the streets on which he had grown up, ornamented with green lawns and playing children. But now, there was nothing but dirt and brown grass, nothing but the overbearing sun overhead which had instantly sucked up the days of rehydration that he had needed to regain his strength to begin with. His throat felt dry and his head spun, but he carried on.

Beyond the worst of the crumbling rural suburbs the buildings took on larger forms, becoming the skeleton of a small town, although it hardly look better for wear than the smaller homes in the direction from which he had come: barren as ever, the streets paved with nothing but dirt, roofs caved in and doors falling from hinges and windows boarded or shattered, leaving fragments of glass glistening in the hot sun. Giovanni found his way back to Undercroft, because Angel had used it as a landmark in his directions, as he had known Giovanni would be able to recognize it. From there he was to turn a direction he had not before traveled, taking a road perpendicular from the bar and deeper into the town than he had gone prior. Through these streets, Giovanni began to see signs of life that he had not been privy to before. The occasional person, often visibly sunburnt or sporting a dark tan, in old, worn clothing, stepping in and out of buildings that often looked as if a single breeze would cause them to collapse (not that there was any risk of a breeze out here). Some glanced to him as he walked past, but there was less judgment in their weary eyes than in the cold glances of the bargoers when he had first arrived. His face was bare now, not smeared in the smudgy remains of the makeup he had been wearing, no longer caked with dried blood. He had the shadow of stubble which he hated but did not have the means to shave off, his clothing reduced to clothing for necessity's sake rather than anything that could begin to bring him any form of joy or be the conducer of self-expression. Beads of sweat ran from his forehead. No longer did people stare at him with indignation, but, still, as he walked through the hot, dry dirt roads of the crumbling town, he felt a great deal out of place, like a puzzle piece that did not quite fit into the rest of the set, although it had been painted as if it were meant to.

Giovanni looked to a woman in a dirt-caked apron who sat, eyes closed, on an old wooden porch with an unlabeled glass bottle in her hands. The building behind her had a sign that appeared to have once lit up, reading the words "Barbershop," but now looked like it had been burnt out for many years, with a thick layer of dust coating each letter. He wondered if this was indeed a barbershop still, or if it had been converted into a home of some sort. Why anyone would choose to live out here was beyond him, although he supposed he had no room to talk. He remembered California's "strength in numbers" attitude, as if this was some sort of odd, ragtag resistance. But what was anybody out here trying to resist?

Finally, Giovanni came upon the fabled store, a little building that was unlabeled but clearly open to the public and kept in a state of surprising quality compared to some of the other buildings in the town. It even had sliding glass doors, although a crack ran along the glass on the right side. Even in the brightness of day Giovanni could see the cool light shining from inside, beckoning all to enter, invitingly enticing passersby with the implicit promise of air conditioning.

Giovanni approached the storefront nervously, mentally preparing himself for any potential social interaction that was about to take place within the confines of this new realm, and flinched when the glass doors opened, sliding apart with surprisingly clean ease but letting out a long, shrill creak as they did. As he stepped inside he was pleasantly surprised to find what appeared before him: Although not particularly large, probably just bigger than a gas station convenience store, the place looked well-kept and clean, almost even sterile, with its dim blue lighting and gray floors, shelves lined with colorful products of various types, cool and fresh in comparison to the suffocatingly dry heat of the outdoors.

Forced to be conservative with money now that he was on a tangible budget, Giovanni began to wander through the aisles, and found that things were absolutely not cheap out here. He looked around aimlessly, searching for anything that looked appealing, that he could afford, that could be prepared with Angel's limited resources at home. Oh, how he envied his father's servants now, being given clear instructions before any outing, knowing that back home there were endless chefs and more cookware than many could ever imagine laying waiting, that the options were limitless yet the expectations clear enough to not leave them floundering.

Giovanni turned a corner, trying to decide still on what to grab, when he caught sight of a shimmer of gold near the front of the store. His heart seemed to momentarily stop as his eyes locked to his target, recognizing the metallic shine in an instant. Sitting in a small box by the cashier, round and nestled together and wrapped in pretty gold foil like some sort of cherished egg or gemstone, sat a very limited supply of Marcello-brand candy.

As if hypnotized like a bug to light, Giovanni all but stumbled towards the front of the store. Surely this was one of those fantastical desert mirages, he thought, heart racing, practically salivating at the thought of his tongue once again making itself acquainted with the sweet, sugary bliss as it was melted and absorbed into the delicate and wet permeable inner flesh of his mouth.

In his stupor, he nearly ran directly into a man standing in the aisle. Giovanni, heart pounding, jumped back with a timid "Oh!," but, just as he was about to apologize and move along, he got a proper look at the stranger and fell silent.

He was a very, very tall man, easily towering around a foot over Giovanni, in dark clothing and a dark wide-brimmed hat and a scarf that covered his face up to his nose. But these were far from the most interesting features this man possessed. Much more notable was the fact that beneath the hat, on either side of the man's head, jutted a pair of long, sharp, metal bull horns.

The man stared down at Giovanni, who was not used to having to tilt his head to meet another man's eyes.

"You from these parts, sir?" the man asked beneath his scarf, voice gruff.

Giovanni hesitated and then gave a nod, at a loss for words. Giovanni knew that this man was not from here, that they were equally outsiders. In part, this was due to the fact that the man's clothing, unlike every other citizen of this place, was not aged, decrepit, and caked in any layer of dirt, but instead looked expensive and fine, specially tailored for his enormous size, with straps and buckles and steel toe boots made of shiny metal.

The man nodded back and looked around for a moment, then leaned in close, crouching just a bit to reach Giovanni's level. He looked into Giovanni's eyes with intense, dark eyes of his own, and Giovanni quickly broke the gaze and looked away. "I'm gonna ask you somethin' crazy, and you gotta believe that I'm not outta my mind," he said, voice hushed, "An' if you have an answer for me, I'll pay you a hefty sum, but I ain't got time for liars so it'd only be after whatever the hell you say proves valuable. Understand?"

Giovanni gave another tense, little nod.

"Alright. I'm out here looking for someone. He's caused a lotta trouble for some important people and I'm just looking to make sure that everything is resolved." The man chuckled quietly in his deep rasp of a voice. "Now this might sound crazy, but try to bear with me here. Have you ever seen a human being with wings?"

Giovanni felt his heart rise to his throat, where it pounded so aggressively it instantly made him feel sick. Angel? This man was out here looking for *Angel?* He gave a weak laugh, his voice an octave higher than normal, most definitely unusually loud for the quiet calm of the market. "That's insane," he said. "I have never- ever seen a human with wings before,"

The man sighed and straightened himself up, once more reminding Giovanni of his great, imposing height. "Carry on with yer day, then," he said curtly, obvious disappointment in his voice. Giovanni, feeling quite proud of his ability to retain composure and believing that he had successfully duped the stranger, eager to get as far away as fast as possible, quickly turned to walk back the way he had come when the man called out to him again, this time saying, "Say, stranger, how the hell do ya get cash out here, anyway?"

Giovanni froze, relieved that his back was turned so that this time he did not have to fight as hard to keep the visible panic from his face. "Ah- We find work," he said awkwardly, his voice still weak. Feeling that this vague answer was entirely unconvincing, his mind ran to the first profession he had seen out here. California's glittery outfit burned into the back of his mind, and he said at once, "Er, it is not always the most respectable of jobs, you see. Certainly not anything one would want to discuss in a public store. So if you'll excuse me-"

"Well, I've been tryin' to get a better feel for the area, and a local might be o'some use to me. I could buy you a drink and we could have a proper talk,"

Giovanni's heart had skipped far too many beats, surely he would soon have a heart attack. He remained frozen, weighing the offer. He certainly did not trust this stranger, and he had already run his mouth enough as it was, stuttering over crucial information and humiliating himself with each attempt to lie, feeling the overbearing force of the man, the damage he could easily do; his nose still ached occasionally from the last time he had been punched, he could hardly imagine what a man of this strength could do to him, and he was pretty sure he had seen metal lining the knuckles of the dark gloves he wore. Part of him wanted to escape, to run back to the small home he had made his safehouse, where the chaos and ruins of the outskirts were less apparent, and he was amongst those he... trusted...?

*Did* he trust Angel? A part of him, Giovanni realized, was deeply curious to know just what in the world this man wanted with Angel. Were his bull horns, so jarring, so intensely inhuman against his otherwise perfectly human head, in any way connected to Angel's wings? These odd, animalistic features that these strange, secretive men wore; while Angel's were stitched to his flesh, these looked like they protruded almost violently, as if they had been jammed into his skull with hammers and nails, their cold, metallic sheen unlike the organic softness of Angel's wings. What exactly had he gotten himself into?

"Alright," Giovanni said nervously, "Er... Let me buy some groceries first, though."

If attempting to come up with groceries for the household had been difficult before, trying to do so while being watched by the massive, shadowy man proved nearly impossible for poor Giovanni, who spent the new few minutes comically stumbling about the aisles, rushing to pick up cans, inspect them only briefly, fumble with bags of frozen vegetables, grab refrigerated perishables at random—Hummus, moments before realizing he had no bread or crackers or anything to put it on, butter without any consideration as to what it would be used for, multiple types of dry pastas when he really felt they hardly even needed one, a bottle of cheap wine, all while the man stood by the doorway, watching and waiting.

"I did not get your name," Giovanni said, after the two had exited the shop.

The man stopped walking and paused to look at Giovanni, and from his cold, intense stare, expression hidden otherwise beneath the scarf, just his dark eyes to pierce through him and once more calculate him from head to toe, Giovanni felt that he had made a grave mistake. He clutched the bag of groceries and swallowed.

"Tell me, stranger: If I were to ask you your name, would you willingly give it 'round these parts?"

Giovanni shook his head. The man nodded. They stood there outside of the store in the sweltering heat in a sort of tense, silent agreement.

Then, after a moment, the man said, "You know where to find the nearest bar? I hear that of all the things ya'll are lackin', alcohol ain't one of 'em."

Giovanni was not sure if that was true, and he certainly had not had the chance to explore the town much, but, knowing he had to seem as unsuspicious as possible, he immediately gave the most confident nod that he could possibly muster. "*Si, si,* follow me!" He gestured towards the direction of Undercroft, and quite frankly he had no idea if that was the closest bar, but it was certainly the only one he was familiar with. They began to walk with Giovanni taking a marginal lead, acutely aware of the man's hulking presence behind him like a dark, overcast cloud, and he hoped that the man would say nothing else to him for the walk, that he would allow him to navigate in peace—But, alas, after another moment he struck up conversation once more.

"Yuh know, my family was from around here, back in the day. A good while before I was born," he said, and Giovanni turned to glance over his shoulder at him. In dark clothes that covered nearly every inch of his body, Giovanni wondered if he was hot out here as the sun bore down. He seemed perfectly fine, wholly unaware of the heat, even. Giovanni tried to picture the man's flesh beneath the clothes; was he hairy, like a bull? Or made of steel, like those metallic horns that shone so bright in the sun they were nearly blinding? "Back before the city dried up the water, when farming was still a viable way t'make an honest living. My family valued the old traditions, I learned to hunt, we'd come out this way every so often, 'till the animals seemed to disappear along with every other sign o' life..."

Giovanni listened, unsure of what to say. "M- My family came from... Italy," he mumbled, wondering as soon as the words had left his mouth if he should have lied about that. *Is your accent real?* was a question he had heard numerous times, back in Fresno, and perhaps he could have used this to his advantage. Being undercover was still very new to him. "My- My father immigrated with his parents,"

"And y'all went from Italy to this shithole?"

"N- No," Giovanni shook his head, "I- I came out here... alone." He had a feeling that this sounded suspicious as well and he sucked in a breath, his mind racing, but did not have the time to come up with a decent addition to strengthen his story, for at that moment they reached the dusty front door of Undercroft. "We're here!" he said, desperation to change the subject palpable in his voice.

They walked into the bar together, and it looked as it had before— Perhaps even emptier, which Giovanni was relieved to see. A woman sat alone at a table, a man at the bar, the same bartender from before was cleaning a spill on the counter and tilted his head only vaguely upwards as a brief acknowledgment of their entrance. Giovanni walked to the bar stiffly and waved at the bartender, an awkward, forced gesture of politeness that he hoped would make it appear as if he was a regular here, someone who came in often and was on good terms with the staff, rather than someone who had one, single, embarrassing altercation while practically on the brink of death before never showing his face again. The bartender looked up at the motion, expression unchanged, and said, "Can I get you two anything?"

The bull-horned man ordered a beer for himself, and Giovanni in a panic said he would have the same, although beer was far from his favorite alcoholic beverage; he had always felt it was not sweet nor alcoholic enough to be worth the time. They were handed their drinks in dark glass bottles before Giovanni steered them into a booth in the far corner of the room, out of sight from most others and far enough away from the bartender that he would not have to pretend to make conversation with him. They sat down across from each other, Giovanni shifting uncomfortably as he sunk into the stiff vinyl, setting his groceries to his side. He realized with a sinking sense of dread that in this position he could do nothing but stare directly at the man, feeling cornered like a prey animal and getting the creeping suspicion that he should have been regretting his decision to come here at all. He held the beer bottle between his legs, too tense to think to set it down on the table, let alone drink it.

"So, you- you mentioned a boy with wings...?" Giovanni asked finally alongside a hopefully inconspicuous gulp, his nails tapping against the metal bottle cap that jutted from his thighs. The bartender had opened the bottles, so the cap sat only precariously at the top of the bottleneck, rocking a little as he fidgeted with it.

The man was silent for a long time, long enough that Giovanni grew afraid that he had said something gravely wrong. He stared at Giovanni from beneath his hat, from under his scarf, only those dark eyes of his visible to gaze at him, and then, slowly, he gave a nod. "He's wanted," he said, "Took something from some very important people and I've been asked t'bring him back so as that justice can rightfully be served. If ya know anything, I'd be happy to, ah, reimburse you for your efforts once he's caught."

"Who... who is he?" Giovanni asked, and this question was totally sincere.

"You said you came out here from Fresno, didn't'cha?"

"Mm-hm," Giovanni felt a renewed tinge of discomfort at the realization that the man was keeping track of his stories.

"It's Himmel Medicine."

Giovanni did remember Angel mentioning he had worked for Himmel. He had modeled for the company, he had said. But what had happened? What had led to his departure, his alleged theft, his arriving out here in the middle of nowhere, hiding out in the rundown makeshift safehouse? He thought back to Angel's behavior, his tendency to stutter over his own words, his hesitation to finish sentences, the way he seemed to reconsider thoughts even as he said them, constantly mentally editing his own sentences, the briskness in his answers, the lightness of his footstep, the sense that he was always looking over his shoulder. Was this what he was hiding? What *was* "this"? Did he fear that Giovanni himself may have been out to get him, or that if he had known the truth he would have turned on him?

For the first time, the man pulled the scarf down, just below his lower lip, to reveal a silver ring hanging from the center of his nose and dark stubble around his mouth. He took a swig of beer and then pulled the scarf back up.

Giovanni was unsure of how much time had passed when he finally answered delicately, "As... as I said before, I do not know anything about that. And I'm sure that if a boy with wings *were* out here word would spread rather fast, so you- you may need to turn your search elsewhere."

"This a talkative place, is it?" the man asked. He looked around at the other people in the bar, their blank, wall-eyed stares, the exhaustion that lay heavy in their brows and the dark bags beneath their eyes, the silence aside from the clinking of glassware that seemed to permeate thickly through the room.

Giovanni swallowed hard and gave the neck of his bottle a squeeze. "Well, not much excitement ever comes through here," he tried to reason, "So- So if something like that *were* to... show up... I am sure that it would be quite the spectacle. But, as I said, I have seen nothing." He forced an awkward smile, and he wondered suddenly, as his heart pounded and his mouth turned dry, why he was bothering to cover for Angel at all. It was not as if he knew Angel particularly well, or that he had any reason to trust him, really. He supposed, if anything, he had a vague sense of loyalty that he owed him, after all he had done over the past few days. After all, if not for Angel, he would likely be dead by now.

And, besides, Giovanni thought, the intrigue that he felt towards Angel, the loyalty and gratitude he held for him, had begun to intermingle with something else, a deeper sense of fascination and awe that made his head spin and his heart flutter, that made him crave to know him better, to uncover his secrets, not to see him dragged away by this intimidating, likely quite dangerous stranger. He thought of the way Angel touched him, the intensity in his eyes as he gazed at Giovanni, the way his wings shone pure white in the soft bedroom light, the ethereal, almost otherworldly aura he seemed to carry as he flitted through the hallways. He supposed he could even say that he *liked* Angel.

"Himmel hasn't had much luck anywhere closer," the man said, pulling Giovanni from his thoughts, "Higher-ups are worried he may have died out here, but I doubt it. The outskirts are rough, but if you have the balls to run away the way he did I can't imagine getting this far and giving up. He's a resilient fucker." He shook his head, then continued darkly, "But, even if he is dead, I imagine his body would be damn recognizable, and I'm sure the bossman would be happy enough with a corpse if it came down to it."

Giovanni's hand moved unsteadily and he accidentally knocked the loose bottlecap to the floor, where it landed with a little clinking noise. He twitched, although the sound was very soft and certainly not obtrusive enough to be deserving of such a reaction.

"I'll... keep my eyes open,"

"'Course you will," the man said, after taking another drink. "Everyone out here needs the money. Only a fool would pass up the offer to make cash so easily. There ain't anyone well off in the outskirts... Well, other than him."

Giovanni nodded. "Right,"

Silence settled over them. The man kept his eyes on Giovanni, and Giovanni, realizing he had not touched his drink, finally removed his beer from his thighs and brought it to his mouth to take a little sip of it. He had missed alcohol, even if beer was not particularly his preference, and he took a bigger sip a moment after. With this brought a small amount of relief from his tenseness, but hardly. The silence remained, uncomfortably heavy, and there was nothing to break it, no one else in the bar willing to make a sound save for the occasional ambiance of the bartender, the clink of a glass or the whoosh of a faucet, a cough, a foot tapping on the floor.

"Can I ask you something?" the man asked suddenly, and Giovanni's shoulders tensed a bit but he gave a nod, setting his drink down on the table before him. "Your profession... you said you're a prostitute," Despite his words, it was not a question at all, but rather a very direct statement indeed.

Giovanni winced and looked around, as if worried that the other handful of patrons would overhear and react. He felt that he had certainly been vaguer in his words than the stranger's rephrasing, but he could not think fast enough to explain anything else, to correct his own story or clarify anything when everything he had said had stemmed from falsities to begin with. "That's right," he said at last, "Things are difficult out here..." Then, in what he felt was a stroke of genius, he added, "But you do get to know people! In such a... profession... so- so that would be... that would be how I would know if the- the winged boy turns up." He sucked in a breath and waited, feeling as if he was offering bait to an animal and seeing if it would take.

"Where do you normally work? From your home?"

Fuck. Giovanni shook his head. "No, ah, various bars have back rooms that work quite well for that. It's... it's a great deal, er, I mean, you can split the money with the bars for the space, you see." This was entirely guesswork, or perhaps lying, at this point, based only on the vaguest idea that he had from his and Hollywood California's briefest of interactions.

"So is this where you work, then?" the man asked.

Giovanni, panicking, gave another nod. "Y- Yes...?" It was a lie that hopefully could be defended if needed; California knew him, he could explain the situation and hopefully she would back him up, if absolutely necessary. She seemed kind and she had helped him before, after all. "Why do you-"

"Well? Care to show me the back room?" the man asked, and his tone has a sort of sarcastic edge as if there was an implicit "duh" in his words. Then he took another drink and chuckled a bit, his grin appearing for only a fraction of a second before being covered by his scarf. "I reckon these back rooms would be a fine place to hide if you had wings on your back. Might be good to take a look around, get acquainted."

Giovanni was not wholly convinced of the man's reasoning, and was growing increasingly concerned with the web of lies he was becoming entangled in. He tried to envision what exactly would happen to him if things began to ravel, what the man would do to him if he were caught, what he would do to *Angel*, and abruptly stood, hoping to distract the man from his increasingly rapid heartbeat and the beads of sweat along his brow by fulfilling his request. "Of course," he said stiffly, leaving the beer he had hardly touched on the table, picking up his groceries, and stumbling to the back room with the man following close behind.

He had not given thought to the neon "GIRLS!" sign that hung from the door. He hoped the man behind him would not, either.

Giovanni tried to open the door and found it locked. Trying not to panic, he knocked instead, and was greeted with a lazy call of, "Oi, I don't have any appointments today, talk to Bobby about walk-in upcharges or bugger off."

The voice was unmistakable. Giovanni was unsure of if he was relieved or even more distressed to hear that California was currently residing within. "Hollywood!" Giovanni hissed, voice erupting with much more urgency than he realized it should have, with the looming shadow of the bull man behind him. He cleared his throat and attempted a calmer approach, "Are you- Can I... Can I come in?"

There was a momentary silence, an excruciatingly long pause as the horned man continued to breathe down Giovanni's neck, before, finally, a quiet click came from the other side of the door and it creaked open, very slowly, to reveal one of California's fiery eyes, decorated up in glittering silver and gold makeup.

"Need something, love?" she asked, voice suspicious despite the pleasantries of her words. Her eyes flashed to the silhouette that towered over Giovanni.

Giovanni was relatively certain that he had never had to think so fast in his entire life. It was too late to go back on his lie, he reasoned. And California— She was understanding, right? She had been the one to help him before, she certainly would see the dire situation he was in. He would be able to explain himself to her and she would understand... After the bull man had left, after he had cleared his name and convinced this man that he was a dead end, that Angel must be sought after elsewhere. If anything, with California's association with Angel, he was doing this for her, as well, right? This was altruism, really.

"I am here to relieve you of your- your duties," Words that felt clunky and clinical, but they were the best Giovanni could come up with, given the situation. California stared at him blankly, clearly not understanding. Why would she? He did his best not to panic. "I—we— need the room,"

California blinked again, the gears in her head clearly turning. Expression unchanging, she gave a nod and opened the door the rest of the way, revealing herself in all of her faded silver glory, luxurious gray curls sprawling around her shoulders, hands encased in her long gloves, jewelry hanging from her neck. She looked much more presentable than him, and he felt somewhat guilty for judging the frayed edges of her dress before.

"Right, sorry about that," California said, tone turning friendlier, holding the door open for the two of them to enter. Giovanni noticed the long look she gave the man, but her expression did not change, eyes simply lingering on him without any other acknowledgement. "I'll leave you two to it!"

She slammed the door shut and left without another word, leaving Giovanni alone with the bull man, any brightness or warmth that had radiated from her presence, the brief comfort in the fact that Giovanni was not alone and had some sort of ally on his side, dissipating instantly.

"Who was that?" the man asked, nodding towards the door.

"Coworker," Giovanni said instinctively, "I do not know her well." When the man said nothing else, Giovanni scrambled to fill the silence with, "It's not much. I think it would be hard for a- a fugitive like you are seeking to hide somewhere like this,"

"Maybe so," the man said, after looking around for a moment longer, surveying every inch of the room with those dark eyes, expression still hidden, horns bobbing up and down on the top of his head as he tilted his head up to the roof, then down to the carpeted floor. Then he turned back to Giovanni and grabbed him by the collar of his shirt. Giovanni was instantly in a panic, all of his earlier fears of being caught in his lies returning full throttle, every grueling attempt he had made to hold himself together spilling over now as he swore his heart all but stopped.

"What are you-"

The man pulled Giovanni into a rough kiss; his scarf had been pulled down with such adept ease that Giovanni had not even noticed the moment his mouth had been freed. Their teeth clattered, his stubble rubbed like sandpaper against Giovanni's skin, leaving goosebumps that trailed all of the way down his spine. Giovanni whimpered and went still, like an animal playing dead, squirming only when the man dragged his teeth across his lower lip before biting down hard enough that it would surely swell.

Then the man pulled away, freeing Giovanni's mouth but still gripping tightly to his shirt. "This is your job, ain't it?" he asked, voice as rough as the kiss. He spoke so close to Giovanni's face that he could feel the breath of each word as he snarled them out, "I figured you may want a taste of the amount of cash I'd be willing to part with, if you can get me my information,"

Giovanni stared into the dark eyes of the stranger—and strange he was, with the jewelry that hung from his nose, the black he wore from his scarf to the leather straps around his waist to his steel-toed boots, the flash of silver that Giovanni could see even now that jutted from the top of his head, looming over the both of them. And when the stranger shoved Giovanni to his knees, he did not resist.

Giovanni returned to Angel, groceries in hand, later than he had intended.

Late enough, in fact, that when he arrived he found Angel on the front porch, sitting cross-legged, chin in his hands. The setting sun gave a warmth to his snowy white wings, making them look almost as if they had an orange sherbet hue to them. As he saw Giovanni approaching he perked up, lifting his head, wings unfurling outward, but in the dimming light of early sunset Giovanni could see an intensity in his eyes. His dagger sat beside him, and Giovanni suddenly had the grave feeling that Angel was very upset.

"What happened?!" Angel called, standing up with the knife in his hand. It wasn't really a question, but an order; the implicit threat was palpable in his voice, face, and the blade that glinted like embers from the darkening sky above.

How much did Angel know? Giovanni wondered. He opened his mouth to speak and then closed it, unsure of what to say, where to start, the entirety of the day already a hazy whirlwind of sensation, blurry memories, decisions made so quickly he could hardly process them.

"Has the prodigal fag returned?" a voice called from inside, no doubt alerted by Angel's greeting. California appeared through the front door, still dolled up in her silver dress and makeup. She had probably come right over after their meeting in the bar.

Giovanni felt as though he were in a daze. Blinking, looking between Angel and California, he tried again to find the words to explain the day: "He... he was looking for you." He stared right at Angel as he spoke, at his face, then at his wings.

Angel stiffened a bit. An expression Giovanni could not read replaced the anger for only a moment before he did the best he could to return his features to the scowl that had been there a moment before. "Well? What did you say?"

"I said that I do not know anything."

Angel's demeanor changed in an instant, as if a candle had been blown out—his shoulders went slack, his lips parted, his wings lowered from where they had been poised tensely—but the smoky remains of anxiety remained. "Oh," he said. He exchanged a glance with California, who shrugged. "Well, then. Good."

Was that it? Giovanni breathed out with frustration. "Who was he, Angel?" he asked. He could not get answers from the bull man, he could not get them from Angel. What was going on? He felt his head would surely explode if he continued to play these mind games, continued to try to make the right moves, carefully tiptoe step after step in complete darkness, mystery and danger and shadowy half-human creations lurking around each corner. "He said that he was being paid to find you, he told me that you stole something from- from Himmel Medicine. He had... horns. Like a cow."

California nodded, corroborating the story with, "He was bloody massive, Steele, and all done up in fetishwear." Then she turned to

Giovanni, "Was his cock as big as the rest of him, loverboy?" Giovanni did not answer this question.

Angel snorted. "Giorgio's newest creation, it sounds like,"

"Giorgio?" Giovanni repeated the name.

California and Angel seemed to ignore Giovanni entirely. "You think he's building his own personal army just to hunt you down? That's very romantic, if you ignore the crimes against humanity," California said, leaning against the doorway.

Angel seemed to find this sentiment less funny than California. He grunted and rolled his eyes. "Can you shut the fuck up? I'm trying to come up with a plan,"

Giovanni blinked. Angel's demeanor around California was strikingly different from what he had displayed when it was just the two of them; he was harsher, more direct, the obfuscation and the secrecy melted away to reveal something significantly less delicate. Angel paced back and forth for a moment.

"I can whisper sweet nothings and red herrings if he stops by Undercroft again," California offered, but Angel did not respond, instead staring at his own feet as he continued to pace. Giovanni watched helplessly, still standing in the dirt before the house, the groceries he had somehow managed to retain through the duration of the day hanging from plastic bags at his side.

The dying sunlight was streaking the sky with deep, fiery oranges and rich, crimson reds above them; in the east darkness was already stretching across the earth. Where was the bull man now? Giovanni wondered. Did he have some sort of lodging? Did he even require sleep at all, or would he stay up, tirelessly searching the outskirts of Fresno, leaving no stone unturned until he found Angel? And what would become of either of them, then? The whole situation left a bitter taste in his mouth, and he wondered vaguely if he had made the right choice, covering for Angel. What if he had instead agreed to partner with the bull man, to lead him to Angel's safehouse and collect whatever portion of the allegedly impressive reward he was promised, returned to Fresno prosperous, made his father proud as he began a new life for himself with newfound riches? His heart pounded as he watched Angel, watched his shadow grow long against the porch in the sunset to reveal the silhouette of something uncanny and alien, wings stretched and jutting from his shadow self like the polymelian aberrations that they were.

"Please!" Giovanni cried out, voice piercing the night so suddenly that both Angel and California turned quick to look at him, "What is going on? Who was that man, Angel? *Who are you?*"

Angel and California exchanged a look.

"How much have you told him?" California asked.

"Nothing," Angel said. Giovanni was relieved to hear that in that regard they were on the same page.

"I have just spent the day scared for my life to protect you," Giovanni insisted, "And I do not even know why it is you need protecting!" He raised the groceries up. "And I am *quite* tired of carrying these around!"

Angel sighed and rubbed his temples. "Let's go in," he said, nodding to the door. California, who stood closest to the entrance, opened the door and held it as Angel, and then Giovanni, entered. They walked to the kitchen in defeated silence, where Giovanni set the groceries down on the dining room table. California rummaged through the cabinets.

"Do you still have tea?" she asked.

"Probably. You know I don't drink that shit, it's wherever you put it."

California eventually found a small metal tin full of teabags. She walked over to Giovanni. "It's mint. Do you want any?" she asked. Right as Giovanni was about to answer, she pulled off her wig and set it unceremoniously on the table beside the groceries. Giovanni was stunned into silence. California's natural hair was very short and very dark, a striking contrast from the long, silver curls she wore normally, but, more notably, to the side of her head, just above her ear, was a distinct hairless patch of what should have been bare scalp. Rather than flesh, however, there was a flat, gray disk covering the side of the skull, perhaps even replacing the skull, like metal patchwork. "I told you before: it's rude to stare, darling," she said kindly, although the twitch in the smile that played over her lips betrayed the vaguest of annoyances at his bewilderment.

Giovanni decided it best not to ask, and instead said weakly, "I will have some tea; *sí.*"

Angel was standing against a cabinet, arms folded, brow furrowed and eyes at his feet, deep in thought. California made her way to the stovetop to boil water in a small pot by lighting a match over the burner. Giovanni stared between the two, at the way the warm kitchen light reflected bright yellow off of the metal in California's skull, the way the feathers of Angel's wings shuttered as the large white appendages rose up and down with each breath, and he felt very alone, a stranger in a foreign land.

"Will somebody please tell me what is going on now?"

Angel lifted his head. For a split second their eyes met, before he promptly rolled his and huffed. "Use your fucking head, you know the pieces already, right? We worked for Himmel, we fled, Himmel's pissed. What else do you need explained, exactly?"

"Your wings? The bull man? G- Giorgio?"

Angel sighed loudly again. "Giovanni, I will tell you things, but you must know that if you betray me I will kill you. Do you understand that?"

The statement was said so matter-of-factly that Giovanni could hardly grasp the reality of the words. Death, as close as Giovanni had felt to it throughout the recent past, felt very intangible, and the threat of it from someone like Angel even more so. But then again, all of this, the whole of the day, the whole situation, felt very dreamlike, and this was no different.

"I do," he said.

Angel nodded. California glanced up only for a moment before returning to her tea. "I was a runner for medicine raids," Angel said.

"*You* partook in raids?" Giovani's mind flashed back to images he had seen on the overhead screens across Downtown Fresno of overturned trucks, smoke rising, debris and blood scattered across the road, the newscasters reading out the death toll as bodies were carted off.

"It's the second easiest job. All I had to do was wait outside the medicine cars. I was never close enough to the scene to be targeted by the Birds of Prey and I was fast and small and, uh, innocuous looking enough. I'd hide out nearby, someone would bring the medicine to me, and I'd make a run for it, simple as. We'd take it to a third party who would hide it in a safe location. That was the first easiest job. Then we'd all get a cut of the money we made selling it."

"So... how did you end up..."

"Well, it had to happen eventually, right? I got caught." he shrugged, and Giovanni blinked in confusion. The nonchalant demeanor Angel spoke in was unfathomable to him. He had not thought before now that anybody caught by Himmel's Birds of Prey would live to tell of it, much less so casually. "I wasn't actively participating in a raid at the time, mind you. They found one of our hideouts, executed a bunch of the other guys and took me in for questioning."

"Ooh, don't leave out my favorite part, Steele," California piped up as she walked over, "He was spared because he told the guys he would tell them everything they wanted to know about the larger crime ring." She winked at Giovanni and held out a mug with steam twirling up from it in the warm light.

Angel made no acknowledgment of California's words. "They took me in and questioned me and I was told that I could have my own criminal record expunged if I signed away my rights to Himmel in exchange."

"How is that an exchange?" Giovanni asked.

"My criminal record was far and away enough to get me executed. Giving my life to Himmel meant it was still no longer my own, but at least I could retain my consciousness. Neat, right? And, uh, Himmel was really big into this whole redemption idea. Like, changing the lives of these horrible criminals and making them upstanding contributors to the evolution of the sciences. So everyone wins. Kind of. And the rest is history, I guess." Angel tapped his fingers on the table in thought, as if trying to figure out what else to say, gave a shrug that made his wings flop up and down, and let his eyes linger on California. After another moment of pause, he added, "I met Hollywood because we were assigned to the same room in Himmel's dormitories."

"Their own private prison, really," California added with a nod, "Himmel had all these big, bright ideas about criminal reformation in the press when they first bought out the police department. Very progressive. What they're really doing is funneling irredeemable lowlifes like ourselves off of the street and into the operating room for their batshit experiments."

"Giorgio's batshit experiments, mostly,"

Giovanni did not have to ask. And yet, still, he did: "Giorgio?"

To which Angel replied: "Giorgio Marcello...? Hello? Only Fresno's premier mad scientist and celebrity human rights violator?"

Giovanni had known the moment the name was first uttered that it would be his elder brother whom Angel and California were speaking of, but the direct admittance of it now made his blood run cold. He thought back to his father's final rebuking, to the altercation that had landed him his bloody nose and to the old woman in the small apartment who had told him so severely to keep his identity to himself. *You and your family are not seen kindly out here. They are a symbol of the powerful evil that permeates our world, and their reach stretches further across this city every day.* It was good, he thought, that he had told Angel nothing of his past, for he could not even begin to imagine what would have happened to him had the winged boy known of his connection to the man who was responsible for all of this.

"Giorgio Marcello did this to you?"

Angel nodded. "Hollywood had a different general surgeon, someone working in neurology. But I was carted off to Experimental Cosmetics while it was all still in its infancy. They called it the Icarus Project." He flopped his right wing up and down gracelessly. "Just a test-run on the grafting of artificial cosmetic limbs. Semi-successful."

Angel had said so much, but there were still so many questions. If anything, Giovanni felt that he had even more questions than before, and he could not begin to parse where to start. California had referred to Angel as "Steele" multiple times. Another name, perhaps? Or was it "Steel," like metal—had Angel, too, had his bioflesh spliced with metal, not unlike the threatening silver of the horns attached to the bull man and the plate in California's skull? And for that matter, what *had* happened to California? What was her backstory? She seemed relatively unscathed, compared to the wings jutting from Angel's back and the horns that sprung from the bull man's head, but the thought of the dent in her head, combined with her being involved in unspecified brain experiments, made him shiver. He wanted to know more about his brother, what he was doing behind Himmel's closed doors, how deep the corruption of the Birds of Prey went, what Angel had seen, felt, experienced during those days, subjugated by his brother and the Experimental Cosmetics department that had caused such a fuss in the media. But perhaps, most importantly...

"So how did you end up out here, Angel?" Giovanni's voice was just above a whisper, so lost in thought was he.

Angel and California exchanged a quick glance with each other, and then Angel shrugged. "I couldn't just leave, obviously. Contractually, I belonged to Himmel, and the wings cemented that fact. They were Himmel's property, and so was I. So I took what I needed to survive and did what I've always been best at."

"And that is...?"

"Run."

Vittoria was bedridden for nearly a week.

The first day or two—she was unsure of the exact timeline—passed her by without any coherency at all. She was heavily drugged, her memory flitting in and out alongside her consciousness. In her most acutely cognizant moments her limbs felt floaty and her senses dreamlike, experiencing the world through a haze of television static. She was vaguely aware of Anubis' presence; she remembered his tall frame, the cool, gentle tone of his voice, his touch feeling wispy as the breeze from a fan on her skin, but that was it, and the rest of the twenty-four, thirty-six, forty-eight hours that passed in this state were nothing but dreamless sleep and the occasional dull pain, no worse than a minor cramp, that was quickly subdued by more drugs that only worked to push her down further into nonexistence.

Gradually, her consciousness began to right itself, a more structured sense of the passage of time reforming. She could remember being awake, she could remember the long, boring hours, too sedated to do anything, to feel anything, but smell the rather nauseatingly sweet incense that Anubis burned and listen to him as he spoke to her about a variety of topics: music, philosophy, religion, art. He read poetry to her, sometimes his own. Her ability to focus flitted in and out, her brain exercising its ability to remain aware and engaged after the muscle for such things had fallen out of use, and at her most uncomfortable, when her back felt stiff and she felt simultaneously restless and as if her limbs were filled with lead, she would get the feeling that he was using her in a way, getting his thoughts out to another living person, who was unable to reply but awake enough to listen. And at times she may have replied, but she was still too out of it to fully remember what it was she was saying, to follow her half-formed thoughts to a confident conclusion. But Anubis handled it with tact and grace, his chivalry never wavering, so that she had no way of knowing how offensive her drugged-out, semi-conscious ramblings truly were.

The following days were only marginally better than the ones prior in terms of coherency, but now she could stumble into the bathroom without Anubis all but dragging her like dead weight, although she still clung to him until she was safely back in bed, and she was able to hold conversations with Anubis for some period of time. These conversations, like the ones before, were also about music, philosophy, religion, and art. By far the most memorable aspect of this phase of recovery was near the very end of it, when Anubis explained gently before bed that she would be weaned off of the post-surgery drugs which he had been feeding her in favor of something that would make her be more functional, an appealing thought initially but one with downsides that quickly made themselves known to her when she was woken from sleep with a searing pain up her torso from her stomach to her breast. There was a terrible throbbing in her chest that seemed to spread rapidly through the rest of her body and she was blinded by a pain that left her screaming and seeing white and she was certain, absolutely certain, that she was dying.

Anubis came rushing to her side and administered more drugs as he spoke in a rushed hush, apologizing profusely as he explained that she was late to take her medicine, that the changeover had caused some discrepancy, that she was perfectly fine and would feel right as rain very soon. But the pain never again returned to the manageable dull cramp from before, instead remaining a throb deep within her chest, a hollow ache unlike anything she had ever experienced.

The rest of Vittoria's night was restless, full of aborted attempts at sleep that were torn through with sharp, sudden pains like a knife tearing through a canvas. Anubis remained beside her, a calm presence in the midst of it all, administering more drugs as needed, speaking to her in a gentle voice, touching her with ginger fingertips.

The next morning, Anubis encouraged Vittoria to try to get up and walk around a bit. She did, slowly, with his help and encouragement. She clung to him still, stumbling and gripping his thin and bony arm like a child, her movements stiff like a reanimated corpse. Soon enough, however, she was walking around independently on trembling legs, and Anubis suggested that she change into something clean, as it may help her feel more comfortable. What she really wanted, she thought, feeling the way her sweat had built up a layer of oily grime across her skin and her hair clung stickily to her neck, was a shower, but Anubis told her that she was still a ways away from such luxuries—not with her scar still healing.

This was, incidentally, when Vittoria first saw the scar.

She saw it in the bedroom mirror as she was changing. It ran down her chest, between her breasts to her stomach, red and swollen, her entire abdomen stitched together as if she were a plush doll. She shivered some as she imagined the surgeon slicing deep into her, slicing her open in a perfect line that left everything inside of her opened and exposed to his hands and his tools.

Feeling queasy, she looked away, and behind her she heard a soft, amused chuckle. Vittoria turned to see Anubis sitting on the bed, eyes on her and a smile on his lips. Although she had known he was there, something about his gaze made her freeze; he, sitting in his room, decorated so that all senses were assaulted by his presence, his incense, his paintings, the silk pillows and dark wallpaper and dim lighting from his ornate, golden lamp, reminded her of the sensation one might experience upon stumbling face to face with a wild animal in its natural habitat, all of the exhilaration and fear of gazing into the eyes of a grinning hyena, and she felt very exposed, very aware of her nakedness, of the scar that tore her open and the angry pinkness of it that teased at the red meats held beneath.

"It will heal," Anubis said, as if reading her mind.

"Yours didn't," Vittoria retorted, a quiver in her voice.

Anubis shook his head and made a soft "tsk" noise with his tongue against his teeth. "Vittoria, if my scars did not eventually heal, I would have no skin left at all. What you saw were only my freshest wounds. Trust the process, my love."

"Do you expect me to do that too?" Vittoria asked, swallowing despite the dryness that burned her throat, forcing herself to grab hold of the tremble in her voice and keep it still. "To slice myself up so much that I have a hundred stitches in me at any given time?" She slipped into a maroon nightgown made of silk—very Anubis. He must have bought it for her at some point, because it certainly was not hers. She ran a hand through greasy hair, pushing it out of her face and looked down at her chest again. It was largely covered by the dress, and yet the very topmost part of it, pink and irritated, still stuck out the top.

But her eyes were drawn to Anubis again as he stood and walked to her. As if she had forgotten his massive height, as if she in that moment became an animal of instinct and could see a creature so much larger than herself as nothing but a threat, her foot jerked to take a step back as he approached, but she stopped herself, holding her ground and planting both feet firmly on the carpet just as his hands found her shoulders to give them a light squeeze.

"One step at a time, Vittoria," Anubis promised, and he leaned in to kiss her forehead. Vittoria did not move. "The body is a primitive thing. It cannot differentiate forms of pain particularly well. You have undergone a great deal of physical trauma and it believes itself to be fighting to keep you alive, like our ancestors in the wild did long before. Unbeknownst to it, you have nothing to worry about, even as your silly little body sends desperate signals for panic to your brain." The hand on her left shoulder slid down to her hand, which Anubis squeezed lovingly, and then tugged gently towards the bed. "Why don't you get some rest?"

Anubis tugged on her hand again, and Vittoria was not sure if he had tugged significantly harder or if physical exhaustion was simply getting the best of her, for this time she lurched forward quite suddenly, legs giving out as she lost balance, and Anubis had to catch her in his arms.

"You see?" Anubis said, voice soft. With their proximity to each other Vittoria could feel the reverberation of his voice in his chest, deep and gentle and alluring, throbbing like the bassline of one of his songs. One of his hands moved to run long fingers with sharp nails through her hair. "You're still weak, Vittoria. You must sleep."

Vittoria did indeed feel very weak. She gave a small gesture with her head, half a nod but half an attempt at shaking his hand away as she felt goosebumps prickle across her sensitive skin. Anubis helped her to bed, where she sat up for a moment, dazed and feverish, looking around Anubis' bedroom and taking in the increasingly familiar characteristics of it as if she were in a familiar dream. Dizzy, she lay down, and Anubis brought her more medicine to assist her in falling back into uneasy sleep.

For some time, Anubis took charge of Vittoria's schedule, waking her to feed her, to clean her, to help her walk around the house, deciding when she had had enough and when it was time to lay down and rest once more. Vittoria, still drugged and weak and recovering, did not object.

Time seemed to lose meaning as she allowed Anubis to take control of her schedule, waking when he wanted, sleeping as he suggested, eating when he said it was time for another meal, but, slowly, she could feel her strength returning to her, could feel the drugs leaving her system as she was weaned from them to gentler medications that left her initially physically weaker but in the long term with a clearer head and more mental and physical autonomy. The pain subsided each day and she could walk with a confidence that had been lost since the surgery. She could shower comfortably, dress herself, eat without any hesitation aside from the regular dislike of consumption which she had already possessed, and the spinning of her head coming to a gradual halt. Still, all the while, Anubis' eyes remained on her, her sole caretaker and friend through this trying time.

And then, one day, Vittoria woke up on her own, and Anubis was nowhere to be seen.

She sat up, slowly, looked around for a sign of him, but the bed was very empty and the room quiet. So used to being awoken by him, or otherwise waking to his presence, as constant and reliable as her shadow, that alone the bedroom took an almost surreal quality, feeling too spacious and too silent, the gold-embroidered curtains too still, the bed too large and seemingly bursting with textures and patterns, the furs, the silks, the velvety pillows, and her own body too small nestled beneath it all it like the yolk at the center of an egg. The remnants of the flowery incense Anubis burned left a certain haze in the air and the dim light that flitted through the slivers of the curtain suggested either dawn or dusk, but Vittoria could not tell which.

Vittoria stood cautiously and paced a bit on feet that had regained significant strength. There was a dull pain in her chest, always, but it was minimal now, and she was not sure if she had drugs or the miracle of the self-healing machine that was the human body to thank for it. She walked to the door of the bedroom, opened it, and stood in the doorway, looking around upstairs for Anubis and finding that still he was nowhere to be found. Her eyes glanced only briefly towards the door within which Sugar rested, but she quickly looked away, and her eyes landed next on the staircase.

She had not yet attempted the stairs, and she was unsure of if it was wise to try without Anubis' guidance, but with a surge of determination she clenched her fists and walked out of the bedroom.

Standing at the top of the staircase, Vittoria could hear the faint sound of voices from below, presumably wafting up from the living room not unlike the incense. Anubis must have guests over, she thought, although such a possibility only increased the vague uneasiness of the whole situation, as she had never before even heard Anubis so much as contemplate the idea of hosting guests, nor could she imagine who he would desire to host. Intrigued, Vittoria became even more set on managing the staircase, which she was becoming increasingly confident in her ability to do, for the interest she had in what was going on below had easily managed to conquer any remaining post-surgery weakness.

The physical act of stepping down the stairs was as easy as it would have been prior to the surgery, Vittoria found. Like riding a bicycle, her legs had no trouble with the extremely familiar motion and they carried her with ease. Still, there was a slight discomfort to it as her limbs worked just a bit harder than they had once needed, making her heart beat with a bit more force—within, from what she could tell, her stomach.

It was not painful, but it was remarkably uncomfortable; it was as if her intestines had come alive and squirmed like earthworms to escape the confines of her gut. She stopped only a few steps down, clutching her abdomen, the dizziness she had been fighting off successfully returning with a vengeance as she felt the rhythmic thumping of her heartbeat reverberate from beneath her bellybutton.

Vittoria's hand rushed to her chest, pressing down hard and firm to where her heart should have been, would have been a few days—weeks?

She had lost track of time—ago, and a cold shiver ran down her spine at the emptiness there, the hollow cavity that remained still beneath her breast. She stood, stuck like that for a while, the worms in her stomach writhing about and her hand trembling against her chest, only inches away from the long, thin scar.

She forced a weak breath, shoving air through her nostrils and down her throat in spite of the way that her head spun and the horrible slithering discomfort that wracked her internal organ system. This should have been a dream, she thought. It should have been the punchline to a terrible nightmare, the product of a stomachache that had transformed itself in her subconscious to the thumping she currently felt in her guts, one where she would have woken up and clutched her chest and laughed as she felt her heart beat where it belonged, comfortably nestled between her breasts, laughed at the absurdity of such a thing even as the cold sweat along her brow trickled from the fear that had woken her from her slumber to begin with.

But she did not wake up. Vittoria took another step down the stairs.

Her stomach churned and her misplaced heart pounded in her belly, but she was determined to continue onwards, down the stairs one step at a time. When she reached the end, her feat finding solid ground, she stood still for a moment, willing her body to relax, panting very softly, struggling to catch her breath as if the descent had been remarkably strenuous, although she did not feel particularly overexerted. At least not physically.

As she relaxed at the foot of the stairs, she became increasingly aware of what was going on outside of her body. There was a distinctly new smell in the air down here, something sweeter than any of the incense Anubis had burned before, and smokier, too. She could hear his voice echoing from the living room in front of her, sultry and eloquent, speaking with a boisterous passion that was reminiscent of the way he spoke to the crowd at the Golden Jackal. She heard murmurs of other voices, quieter than his, and she recognized them, but in the state she was in she could not place them with confidence. However, by the time she had walked into the living room, she was able to say before even surveying her surroundings, "Your band is over?"

Indeed, both band members whom she had gotten the chance to meet prior, Petyr and Cosmo, sat on the couch. They looked up, clearly surprised, when they saw her, Petyr appearing to nearly spill the drink in his hand while Cosmo, who sat near the fireplace, with its dying orange embers and weak flickering flames as the last of a log that had been placed sometime prior burnt to ash, twitched and tensed slightly, recoiling not unlike a disturbed reptile. However, after the momentary surprise had worn off a smile broke on Cosmo's face as he greeted, "Miss Marcello! We didn't wake you, did we?" He hiccupped.

Before Vittoria could formulate a response to this, she noticed Anubis, who sat across from them in his regal chair like the great king he was, watching her coolly with a smile on his painted lips. He wore his mask, everything from his nose upward hidden beneath the hungry stare of the ebony jackal, and she could see the flash of his very real fangs as he said, "Vittoria, dear, whatever are you doing awake? It's nearly six in the morning, you know." He was holding a long chord with a pipe at the end that was attached to a beautiful device which sat in the center of the room, golden and jewel-encrusted with rubies and emeralds adorning it and a serpent coiled around the base, scales intricately carved in detail. Three coal cubes sat atop it. Anubis lifted the pipe to his lips and inhaled, then let out a long breath which caused smoke to pour from his mouth like a dragon.

Vittoria blinked. So it was sunrise. Why were Cosmo and Petyr here? She looked between the two men, then at Anubis' masked self, then stammered out an uncertain, "What are you-"

"I didn't expect you to wake without me, love. Especially at an hour such as this. My deepest apologies, I assume that must have been very... disconcerting." Anubis spoke with a warm gentleness to his tone, much like the dying flames that lit up his bandmate's dreadlocks, but there was something strangely stiff in his movements. Perhaps the mask was hindering him some, blocking his vision, Vittoria reasoned. He had not gotten up, had not moved from where he sat, had not shown her the jovial affection that she had come to expect from him, and his words were spoken with overt and intentional calculation, as if she could hear the cogs of his brain turn as he decided on each one before speaking. His eyes were fully obscured by black contacts, but he remained transfixed in her direction, staring with empty sclera directly at her. Somewhat unnerved by this, Vittoria made her way around the room to sit on the couch beside Cosmo and Petyr, across from Anubis, whose mask followed her trajectory like a haunted painting.

Her unease was interrupted when she felt something against her shoulder and turned to see Petyr, who sat closest to her, had placed his hand on her. "Miss Vittoria! Very good to see you again. How have you been?" His words were somewhat slurred.

Vittoria forced a polite smile as her stomach squirmed, although at this point she could hardly tell if it was from the physical shift in her internal arrangement or simply the discomfort with the whole scenario. Perhaps a bit of both. "Er, I'm fine, Petyr," she said, "I mean, it was rough for a few days, but-"

"I invited Mister Vassili and Mister Halloway over to discuss future plans for upcoming performances, Vittoria," Anubis explained, surprising Vittoria by the suddenness of his interruption. "Big changes are on the horizon, dear."

Vittoria said nothing, looking between the three men in silence. Perhaps it was due to the drugs still waning from her system, or the lack of social interaction she had had for days, or the fact that Anubis, the one she knew the best among the three, had donned his death god identity and was practically a stranger to her now, but she felt very much like a foreigner in this room, just as she did in her own body, presently. She wet her lips, thinking over Anubis' words, and then looked to the wine bottle that sat on the small table beside him.

"Why don't'cha come join us?" Cosmo said, seemingly following her gaze. "Anubis, poor the lady a glass!"

What was visible of Anubis' expression twitched a bit. "Mm, I doubt that would be a good idea. What with... everything."

Vittoria furrowed her brow. "Everything?"

Anubis managed to recapture the composure that had only briefly tried to slip from his grasp. "Things have been quite hectic around here and I know you have quite a bit on your plate at the moment, love, what with all of the preparation. Personally, in times of great stress, I tend to prefer sobriety, even if my more animalistic senses may disagree and demand indulgence." His expression remained unchanged as he stared at her, and Vittoria struggled to make out what it was he was trying to say. There was much being left unsaid; she knew Anubis, knew his speaking mannerisms well enough by now to detect when he was being remarkably reserved, even secretive. Anubis was talkative and emphatic, his words flowed like poetry when he wanted them to, and there was an intentionality in his brevity now.

He was, it dawned on Vittoria slowly, intentionally not disclosing that she had just undergone surgery.

"Anubis was talking about- about how you have all these big sexy projects you're workin' on," Cosmo spoke up. She turned to him and he grinned, looking as sickly as ever, eyelids heavy, with a slight waver to his movement that may have been from alcohol but came across as if his head was too heavy for his shoulders. "Secret stuff that'll blow people's mindsss. I was saying: 'Man, she really has become your prodigy, eh, Anubis?' Wasn't I saying that, Pete?" He nudged his bandmate, causing him to nearly fall over on the couch.

"You were," Petyr agreed with a chuckle as he set himself upright again, his own voice trailing off in drunken distraction as he spoke, "We were trying to pry more, but, well, Anubis is always secretive about these things."

"But you're his bandmates," Vittoria said, shifting uncomfortably as her stomach churned.

"Well, he calls the shots," Petyr answered. Both he and Cosmo went silent and Anubis said nothing. Vittoria was very aware of the tension in the room. There was an obvious strain between the three men, things left unsaid, things not allowed to be said, and a stiff acceptance of that from all parties. She was reminded of the way that Anubis' bandmates dressed compared to him on the stage, their outfits modest and subdued, their beings hidden in shadow, mere spectral presences in comparison to the godly Anubis, the king of the dead, the Rock God of Death Himself, who now sat in his throne before them all now, lit by the flame in the fireplace and haloed by hookah smoke, sipping red wine as the sun rose over Fresno. For a moment, just briefly, Vittoria had half a mind to challenge his authority and blurt out, right then and there, what he was refusing to disclose and make his kingdom crumble under the earthquake that would undoubtedly ensue. She tried to imagine how he would react, cool and charming as he was, so clever and quick, if his plans were shattered before his eyes. Would he be able to pick up the pieces? Rebuild the empire? Would he be able to use all of that charm and allure when the situation was dire?

Anubis stood and stretched, his narrow frame elongating and his long, talon-like fingers clawing outwards to the ceiling for a moment. All eyes turned to look upon him. "Well, I think we're quite finished here. I would like very much for the four of us to meet up at some other time to eat and drink and make merry and wrap up all of the pretty ribbons of ideas into one magnificent bow, but now, I'm afraid that it is very late, or very early, if you prefer to look at it as such, and the discussion would be one hindered by inebriation and exhaustion." He sighed and looked between his two bandmates. "I suggest you take your leave now. I will have your checks in the mail by tomorrow morning."

Cosmo and Petyr slowly stood, Cosmo stumbling slightly as he got to his feet, Petyr gripping the couch for a moment in order to unceremoniously shove himself up, and Vittoria frowned at how drunk they both seemed. "Er, see you later," she said, knowing the tone of her words did nothing to help the stiffness in the room. She watched in silence, unmoving from where she sat, as Anubis walked them to the front of the house and bid them farewell, and when he opened the front door the pale morning sunlight poured in, making Vittoria wince at the brightness. The three men, but mostly Anubis, spoke in hushed voices for a moment longer, and then he shut the door on his bandmates, leaving her and him alone in artificial lighting once more. There was silence between the two of them, Anubis' back to Vittoria, the candy-scented smoke rising from the hookah pipe in the center of the room and the crackling fire providing the only source of noise to break the quiet, before she said, "Are they safe to drive?"

"No matter," Anubis said. He turned to Vittoria and walked to her, pulling off his mask as he approached and allowing the long curls of black and silver hair that had been flattened and hidden by the hood to cascade down around his shoulders. "You caused me a spot of trouble there, Vittoria. I did not expect you down the stairs."

Vittoria was taken aback by these words. She blinked, still staring at him from where she sat on the couch, trying to wrap her brain around the entirety of what she had just witnessed, still feeling just vaguely like she would wake up in Anubis' bed, perhaps even her bedroom in her father's house, somewhere other than here, to find that all of this had been some very strange, disconcerting dream. After running her teeth along her lower lip in thought, she finally said, "Why didn't you tell them?"

Anubis did not answer as he walked back to his chair. He placed the mask delicately down on the living room table, where its lifeless gaze and canine snout pointed upwards, and then, as he sat back down, he picked up the bottle and poured himself another glass of wine. "Because it is, as they say, none of their business. They no longer work for me."

"What?!"

"I fired them."

"But they seemed so... happy."

"Psychoactive substances have a lovely way of manipulating one's emotions, don't they? They're doing clinical trials on it, you know, the therapeutic effects of various drugs when given bad news. Prognoses, diagnoses, those sorts of things. Bad news is all about endings, isn't it? Funny, that." Anubis sighed thoughtfully and picked up the chord of the hookah pipe again. "Do not fret, Vittoria. They are being given an *enviable* retirement package and it is truly nothing personal. They've served me well, but I am simply in the planning stages of a new chapter and I do not foresee there being room for them on the page... Once the outline is finished I will move forward into the first draft, and I'm sure everything will be much more enlightening once you've flipped through the pages."

Vittoria pursed her lips. Was he drunk? Or high? She was unsure. He certainly seemed more sober, or at least more coherent, than his (former) colleagues, but she could hardly follow what he was talking about, and he seemed less collected than his usual self. Or was it her, in her own recovering state? Had she lost the ability to comprehend, had something in her brain managed to come apart, through all the drugs, the isolation, the physical trauma, the hours upon hours drifting in and out of reality? She watched him silently, waiting to see if he would continue without her having to attempt a response, and, sure enough, he spoke up once more, saying,

"So, hm, you braved the stairs all on your own?"

"I did,"

Anubis nodded and tapped the tip of the mouthpiece of the hookah hose thoughtfully. "I'm proud of you, dear. Taking initiative like that. You truly have been recovering beautifully." He turned to look at her, his eyes blackened by his contacts still, and Vittoria struggled to meet his gaze. "You are a very special woman, Vittoria. I have high hopes for our future. I imagine very few would have the strength to do what you have done. You should be very proud, indeed."

Vittoria felt her stomach twist where her heart pumped in its recently relocated home and she wet her lips, unsure of how to react. "Th- Thank you," she finally managed out, a weakness in her tone betraying and denying the praise of strength which she had just been given. She cleared her throat but did not speak again.

"I did mean what I said before about the time, however. It is quite early, and I think plenty of rest is still of the essence. Do you need my accompaniment getting back up the stairs, or would you prefer to make the journey on your own?"

"Are you not coming to bed?" Vittoria asked.

Anubis shook his head. "No, no, I apologize if my presence is missed, but I have much to do, and with less time to do it than I previously thought, I'm afraid." He rubbed his hands together, and Vittoria stared at his long nails, which he had painted a deep, blood red.

Vittoria did not understand what Anubis could possibly be up to at this time of day, but she could also tell that he was not necessarily interested in answering questions, at least not in a way that was comprehensible to her. There was, still, a part of her that considered arguing, demanding more, undermining his authority, but she hesitated as the reality of the situation settled deeper into her mind and her heart settled into its newfound spot in her gut. She was more dependent on Anubis now than ever, weak and still working to adjust to the way that her body had been reshaped from the inside out, recovering and without anywhere else to go.

Anubis walked to her and took her hand. She looked up at him as he brought it to his mouth and kissed it with maroon lips. "Do you need anything at all, dear? I have sleeping pills, if it would help,"

Vittoria shook her head and stood. "No, I'm fine," she said. She glanced to the staircase, and her heart skipped a beat in the depths of her stomach, and she drew in a deep breath. "I think I'd prefer to stay sober."

After finishing her tea, California bid Giovanni and Angel goodnight and returned back to Undercroft with the promise that should the bull man return she would do her best to continue to mislead him, hopefully sending him somewhere far, far away from the outskirts entirely. Giovanni felt a bit bad allowing her to go, worrying for her safety as she disappeared into the darkness of the wasteland, but Angel was adamant she take her leave, insisting that it was better for all of them that they remain separated.

Giovanni and Angel fucked that night. Giovanni had never particularly liked the word, preferring *making love* or even the more straightforward *having sex*, but he felt that he had been doing quite a bit of *fucking* recently, and this in particular most certainly could be described as such, dirty and aggressive as the harsh consonants that the word was comprised of. Little was spoken between the two through the duration of their intercourse, the tension of the previous conversation hanging over the both of them the same way Angel's deceptively small frame hung over Giovanni's.

When they had finished, Giovanni wished he had a smoke, or some candy, or a bottle of wine, or anything, really, to alleviate the awkwardness that returned the moment Angel's back was facing him, his wings tightly folded to his back in a manner that evoked arms folded across the chest.

"Why did you cover for me?" Angel asked, piercing the silence like the knife he always held close.

"Maybe I am just a nice guy,"

"Shut up," said Angel, clearly unamused by the referential non-answer, "Stop trying to be clever and answer the question."

"Did you only allow me to stay with you because you were attracted to me?"

"Answer the fucking question, Giovanni."

Giovanni was still not used to the harshness that Angel's tone had taken on since earlier in the evening, so discordant it felt from the fluffy white wings and distinctly soft features the boy carried, so alien from the wide-eyed, nervous stutter he had spoken with initially. He stared at the back of his neck, his eyes traveled down to the massive appendages that jutted from his shoulders, and figured that he would never get used to them no matter how many times he stared at them, and he would never not be filled with the sort of reverent awe that they had brought the very first time he had laid his eyes upon them, delirious in the sweltering heat.

His mind traveling backwards, he remembered what it was California had said when he had first asked why she had agreed to help him in the first place. It felt very long ago now. "I told you what Hollywood said, *si*? That- that we are stronger if we stand together," he did not remember the exact wording anymore, he realized, but it was something to that extent.

Angel turned to glance at Giovanni over his shoulder and let out a soft huff that resembled laughter. "Cal actually believes that shit, I think. I think she's been alone long enough that she's started to fantasize, have these rose-tinted glasses about what it would be like to have friends. Isn't that sad?" He snorted.

"If I had not covered for you that man would have found you," Giovanni said.

"If you hadn't been out there in the first place he never would have questioned you to begin with," Angel countered.

"You asked me to bring groceries!"

"I never asked you to be here to *begin with*, Giovanni. I *let* you stay."

Giovanni went silent, surprised by how much these words stung. Angel seemed to like him, he desired him in a way that he had never felt before, and Giovanni liked that. And yet, he still could not grasp Angel entirely. Even as the boy opened up to him, even as he shared details from his past that should have demystified at least some of his very foggy trove of secrets, Giovanni was at an utter loss. He stirred uncomfortably where he sat and felt very naked even as Angel turned to look away from him once again. His body felt too exposed, all of the flesh that spread out over muscle and fat and bone looking misshapen and deformed in his eyes, too much of it, too saggy, too lumpy. He stood suddenly to gather his clothing from the floor and finally spoke again to end the silence: "What is your history with Hollywood, Angel?"

Angel shrugged. "I told you, we met in Himmel's dorms," Giovanni pulled up his boxers. "She claims she was framed for a murder she didn't commit. She wouldn't share the details. Giorgio didn't really know them, either. Neurology isn't his field. But, uh, it was something about theorizing that one could be, um, made to be more inclined to follow the law. That crime is a neurological problem, or something."

"What did they do to her...?"

"I dunno. She mostly just complained about headaches."

Giovanni said nothing as he pulled his pants up.

"We used to fuck."

"Oh," Giovanni was not sure if anything would surprise him at this point.

"And she was a real bitch when she realized I was trying to get out of there and leave her behind. She told me if I didn't let her come then she would report me to Himmel. So much for all that lovey-dovey solidarity shit, right?"

Giovanni sat back down on the bed, unsure of what to do with any of this. He stared at the baby pink elephants that covered the wall, smiling bright, human smiles, their trunks pointed upwards as if they were ringing out like trumpets, marching in straight lines across the room. He wondered how many times the child who had lived here before him had stared at their frozen parade each night as he tossed and turned and tried to sleep, how many nightmares he had woken from to gaze up at them; he wondered if they had brought some sort of childish comfort, if he had tried to count them like sheep, and Giovanni wondered too how long he would be here before he would start doing similar, how many times he would awaken in the small room, with Angel and his knife one room over, with the army of elephants peering down at him.

"What is your plan, Angel? You cannot expect to live out here forever, surely?"

Angel let out a long sigh and stood. "Follow me," he said, and he walked to the door. Giovanni did as told, eager to uncover even the slightest bit more of Angel's secrets, and followed him through the doorway, down the hall, to a door that led from the living room to the outdoors, behind the house. It occurred to Giovanni that he had never been to the back of the house, in the time he had lived here he spent the majority of it recovering, feeling terribly weak with illness and spending his days nearly bedridden. Even Angel's bedroom he had not yet seen, let alone the outer parts of the property, which had hardly even been a point of interest amongst all of the excitement he had been dealing with, and would have required exploration into the outdoors, exposed to the elements of Central California.

It was very dark now, but the light from the living room flooded out into the night and illuminated what appeared to be the silhouette of a small truck sitting in the back of the property. Angel stepped out, keeping the door open, no doubt for light, and slipped on a pair of sandals that sat out by the door. Giovanni looked down to see two other pairs; reminded much of old fairy tales, Angel had put on the middle-sized pair, leaving a larger pair and a pair that looked so small they would only fit a child. Giovanni put on the larger pair, which fit just right, and followed Angel outside and towards the truck.

The air was warm, but not nearly as hot as the oppressive heat of daytime. The truck sat where just the furthest rays of the warm living room light could reach, and Giovanni could see the shine of orange rust, the shadows dipping into crevices of dented metal, oil and mud caking it. It was a rather pathetic thing, he thought, and he had a hard time making out what color the truck truly was beneath it all, out in the dark. Perhaps some sort of gray or pale blue?

Angel climbed up onto the hood and sat down on it, and when Giovanni placed a hand on it he recoiled, for it was so covered in dirt that his hand was practically coated with it in an instant. He stared at Angel in the dark, waiting for an explanation.

"We tried everything, but it won't run," Angel said, patting the car, seemingly unbothered by the way it dirtied his hands. "I've got the key to it, but it won't start. I don't know shit about cars so I can't do anything to fix it. I made a deal with California when we first ended up out here that if she stayed in town and kept an eye out for anyone who might be able to get it running, then I'd let her come with me and we could get outta here together."

"Where will you go?" Giovanni asked.

Angel shrugged. "Somewhere far. Way beyond the scope of where Himmel would be willing to search for us. I've heard things aren't like they are in Fresno in other parts of the world. So we'd just... keep driving until we found somewhere better." His voice had an enraptured sigh to it that Giovanni was unused to, rarely did Angel speak with such candid reverence.

Giovanni tried to picture what "somewhere better" than Fresno would look like but found himself drawing a blank. He had quite liked Fresno until very recently, he thought. He had never dreamed of leaving it. The most comfortable place in the world had been his own big bed, safe and cozy in the confines of his bedroom, beneath blankets of the softest material and surrounded by things that were so clearly *his*. His clothes, his makeup, his satchels of candy and bottles of his favorite wines, his pet birds, the garden out back, the kitchens full of any food he could possibly desire, from platters of rare, delicate meats to the daintiest, fluffiest of desserts. What, he thought, could possibly be better than that?

"We'll travel the whole world if we have to," Angel said, continuing to speak even as Giovanni remained lost in thought. "It won't even matter how long it takes, because we'll be so far gone from Fresno that no one will ever be able to find us. Not Himmel, not California."

"California?" Giovanni looked to Angel quizzically at that.

Angel reached out to take Giovanni's hands in his own. Angel's hands always seemed very small to Giovanni, so very delicate and lithe, but they squeezed Giovanni's hands tight now. In the dark he could see the warm glow of the interior light reflecting in Angel's eyes, but very little else. "I don't want California to come with us," he said evenly. "I just want to leave this place with you."

"What? Why?"

Angel shrugged; the outline of those massive, white wings flopped alongside the motion, visible in the shadows. Giovanni thought the gorgeous white tips must be filthy with dirt from where they rested on the hood of the truck. "You've done right by me. More than she has. And you just seem... special."

"Special?" Giovanni echoed the word like it was made of gold.

"Yeah. I can picture it already. We drop the dead weight and it's just the two of us. Like- like it has been. It's been nice, right? Once Cal finds a mechanic, we can just take off driving and find somewhere to start our lives together, where we can have sex whenever we want and eat anything we want and have a great big home, like those ones out in the rich neighborhoods around Fresno, where the parks are green all the time."

Giovanni felt Angel's small hands against his own and felt his heart flutter in his chest not unlike the feathers on Angel's back. In all of his years, throughout his many, many sexual encounters, throughout the modeling opportunities, the interviews, the polite conversations with his father's work acquaintances, the conversations with his father himself, he was not sure he had ever been told he was special before. He thought of the way that Angel grabbed at him when they made love, so confidently and so certainly, the way he felt almost out of control in the boy's presence sometimes. He felt drunk on Angel's desire for him whenever they touched, on the thought that the bearer of such ethereal form could crave him as he craved the beautiful women in his father's mansion.

He was chosen by Angel over even California, he thought in a sort of bewildered awe. Angel, with all his secrets, enigmatic and ethereal, wanted *him*. He pictured the boy now, with him in his father's home, in his soft, lavish bed, Angel's soft skin against the soft silks and floral embroidery, looking down at him, the warm light of the chandelier haloing his soft, doll-like features as his wings cast great shadows over the both of them.

"You want me to go with you? To this... this somewhere, beyond Fresno? Just us?" Giovanni stood in place before Angel; from where he stood Angel was taller than him for once, looking down at him from the roof of the truck.

As the stars bore down much brighter in air much clearer than in Fresno and Angel's eyes reflected the glow of the house like a cat's, peering down at him, Giovanni was struck all at once with an incredible, all-encompassing, crushing guilt at the thought that still, even now, he continued to keep his family name hidden from the boy. He thought of Giorgio, the man behind Angel's current circumstance, he thought of Angel, an unwilling pawn, his own body no longer his own, at the mercy of his elder brother's whim, and he shuddered to think what would happen if Angel knew.

Angel nodded again, seeming not to notice the iciness that had just seeped into Giovanni, causing sweat to break out along his brow and his skin to feel cold and clammy in the shadows. "Just the two of us, without a care in the world," he said. He leaned back against the front window of the car and looked up at a sky littered with stars. "Where we can both stop running."

Giovanni did not know what to say. He thought back to the way in which Angel had told him about working for Himmel when they had first met. *We're even*, Angel had said. Were they uneven now, with how much Giovanni knew, in comparison to Angel knowing his truth? Could this wonderful future Angel was spinning, the two of them together, far beyond the outskirts of Fresno, flourish with this unbalance, or were they doomed?

He thought of his father, his brother, of his bloody nose, of Beatrice's warning, of the long, lonely bus ride out of Fresno into the hot, dry unknown, everything up to and including his own name taken from him, and he thought again of Angel over him, of Angel desiring him, of Angel's touch and Angel's promise of a life beyond everything that had ever hurt either of them, where they would be together and they would care for each other. He wanted it, he thought. He had no idea what *it* truly was, but he was enthralled by Angel just as Angel was enthralled with this unknown utopia in the far-off distance, further than the buses would drive, further than his family's name could reach.

It was clear to Giovanni, then, when he looked at it altogether, that there was no world where he could have Angel as a Marcello, and he resolved that he could not tell Angel about who he was. Or, at least, whom he had once been.

"I would like that future very much, Angel," Giovanni said quietly.

"Sit up here with me?" Angel shifted a bit, making the truck creak slightly beneath him.

Giovanni winced and rubbed his fingers against the palm of his hand where he had touched the truck earlier, remembering the way it had immediately covered it in dirt. But Angel continued to stare down at him, expectedly, and despite the boy's otherworldly beauty he seemed to have no concern whatsoever about the filth. So Giovanni, resigning himself once and for all, clamored up.

The moment he had gotten somewhat comfortable—as comfortable as he could be, given the stiffness of the rusted metal beneath him and the hard, curved windshield behind him, not fit at all for a human to sit, let alone two of them—Angel leaned over to rest his head against Giovanni's shoulder. Giovanni stared at the boy and said nothing. It was such a tender gesture, something so small and yet so intimate, a world apart from the rough sex of before and the even rougher language he had taken on since earlier this evening, and yet it caused goosebumps to erupt from where Angel's hair brushed his skin accompanied by a chill that made his heart seem to skip a beat.

They sat together like that, saying very little, until the pale and sickly hues of early sunrise outshone the stars.

It had been a quiet morning; Vittoria was making herself coffee, something she had taken to doing so as to avoid Anubis over-sweetening it or adding strange flavors. Right then she heard footsteps, pace brisk, behind her, and she turned just in time to see Anubis enter and begin to speak:

"Vittoria, my darling, I have it all worked out!" He took her by the hands and clasped them tight, a gesture so quick and urgent that she hardly had the chance to set down her coffee mug beforehand.

"...Yes?"

"The performance, Vittoria! I have all of the details worked out, all the pieces have *finally* come into place, and we may now proceed to the next step!"

Vittoria stared at Anubis, bewildered. He looked delighted in a way that she had not seen before. He was grinning wildly at her, the sharp canine fangs barred in full, teeth that would only have been seen on their previous owner in a snarl. Anubis tended to remain cool, stylish yet reserved in everything he did, but now there was a joy in his eyes and the way that his hands pressed into her own, gripping her as if attempting to transfer some of that joy from his veins and into hers. Vittoria supposed it was working somewhat, because she smiled in return, in part a sort of bemused confusion and in part sincerity, an earnest, excited curiosity for whatever it was he had planned.

"There is still much to do, though, do not think for a moment that we are nearing the end!" Anubis suddenly let go of her and walked to the refrigerator. He stepped hurriedly, nimble still on his long legs but his usual graceful intentionality disrupted by his excitement. "-No, no! We are just reaching the starting line-" He rummaged through the fridge until he found a cup of strawberry yogurt. "The future is sweeter than you can imagine, my love!" Vittoria had all but forgotten about the coffee, transfixed watching Anubis in this new state of being, the delight that left him more frazzled than she had ever seen him before as he dug almost clumsily for a spoon in his silverware drawer, his long, wine-colored nails clamoring about like a bird pecking at ants.

"So... what's next?" Vittoria asked as Anubis pried open the top of the yogurt cup and offered her some, to which she shook her head.

"Next? Next!" Anubis sounded more excited than ever at the question, his voice raising an octave as he gestured with his spoon with boisterous dramatics, "Next, we begin the preparations for the show, my darling Vittoria!" As if unable to contain himself to a single spot, he began to pace now, walking back and forth across the kitchen. Vittoria watched him, her coffee still untouched, until he said, "You will begin rehearsal with me immediately. Er, no- Not immediately, forgive me. Tomorrow. Tomorrow morning. The dress is still being made, but no matter. You will not need it until the night of the show."

At Anubis' words, Vittoria's bemusement soured some and was replaced with the early workings of a nervous knot in her stomach.

"Rehearsal?" she repeated. Her heart sank deeper into where it nestled in her guts, a sensation that in turn made her feel somewhat nauseous.

"You and I will be performing together at the Pharaoh's Tomb, Vittoria!" Anubis declared, tone triumphant as if he were imparting upon her the most important piece of information she had ever been told. He rushed to her again and grabbed her arms, making her jump in surprise by the suddenness of his touch. "This will be your awakening, your birth, your- your baptism, your debut as- as whoever you want to be. The beginning of the rest of your life!" Anubis was all but panting, his breathing heavy, the pleasure he took from this leaving him struggling to remain composed, and he grinned at her with those sharp canine teeth glistening in his mouth.

Vittoria could feel the nervousness and excitement fighting a vicious game of tug-of-war with the knot in her belly. She tried, as Anubis continued to cling to her arms, to imagine herself in his position, up on the stage, a bloody mass of rage, conjuring fear and shrieking like a dying animal. And yet, another part of her chided herself for her concern, because she thought too of the intensity of it, the reverence in which she had felt for him, the awe of the enraptured audience, the power he held that was nothing short of holy as he embodied pure *rock and roll* on the stage. She thought of the admiration she held deeply for him, and how much he had done for her, and the way in which he believed in her, and how much she had done for *him...* far too much to back out now. They felt linked almost cosmically at this point, her body his and his future and legacy dependent on her.

"Vittoria? Is something the matter?" Anubis said, and Vittoria imagined guiltily that he was likely disappointed that her reaction had not been as explosive with delight and excitement as his own.

Vittoria shook herself free of his grip, which had loosened somewhat. She turned away, embarrassed that she had quenched his flame, to focus on the coffee she had been preparing. "You have so many years of experience up there. I haven't... I mean... What if I- What if I just open for you...?"

"I don't do openers." Anubis said tersely, and Vittoria could hear the edge to his voice and continued refusing to look at him for fear she had crossed a line. But when he touched her again it was gentle, reaching out to place his long fingers on her shoulder as she poured her coffee. She turned hesitantly to him again to see him smiling a more subdued smile. "Vittoria, darling, to be entirely frank, at the age which I am at now I would not take risks for somebody else. My career has been built on taking my own risks, risking my very life for my art, but I am aware that I am aging and I am aware that even the Rock God of Death cannot escape the inevitability of his body's decay, and I have far too much to lose if I were to be altruistically optimistic. That is to say: I would not have you up on that stage if I did not believe in your capability." He squeezed her shoulder gently and then reached to her chin and took it in his hand. "The empire does not have to die with the king. I have built a legacy, a name not only for myself but for everything I have founded through my long and prolific career, and through you it will continue to thrive. Oh, I have everything planned, everything down to the peskiest of details. I have the setlist, the costumes, the sponsors, all lined up-"

"But what if I can't do it?" Vittoria asked, finally deciding to cut to the point.

Anubis' smile widened. "It is quite normal to be nervous, my love. In fact, I would call it a sign of great humility. But I have studied you carefully, and you have proven yourself to me in ways that I imagine even you cannot fully grasp. You and your youth, your naivete... I promise you, Vittoria, my lovely muse, that I will make sure that what happens on that stage is nothing short of true art."

He leaned in and kissed her then, and, for just a moment, Vittoria hesitated before kissing back in full.

The warmth of the day crept up from behind the sun, as the barren fields of the outskirts were illuminated so too came the oppressive heat, and with the sky still pale Giovanni and Angel headed back into the house to sleep. Giovanni thought there was perhaps some poeticism to the fact that the day could be so very long and yet, still, the next one did not wait for him to rest, instead moving forward into the next whether he slept or not.

"Do you, uh... want to sleep in my room?" Angel offered, as the two reached the fork in the hallway that led to their separate beds. "I mean, if we're going to be doing this whole, er, partners in crime thing together... might as well have each other's backs at our most vulnerable, eh?" He gave a little smile.

"*Si!* I would most enjoy that, Angel,"

The master bedroom, if one could even call it that, was hardly larger than the child's room Giovanni had been staying in, but the maturity in the decor was immediately apparent. It had a homely, rustic feel to it, with wooden accents on the furniture, wallpaper that had most likely once been a plain but inviting off-white but had faded with time to something more yellowish, and copper-red bed sheets with an elegant damask printed in maroon. The bed itself was significantly larger than his measly twin, this one a California King that could easily fit a couple.

"There's a Bible in the drawer next to the bed," Angel said as he walked inside, casually plopping himself down onto the edge of the bed.

"Isn't that funny? I swear it felt like a... like a hotel or something, when I first got here." He crawled up to the head of the bed now and collapsed on his stomach into the pillows. Wings as big and stiff as they were, Giovanni figured it was probably difficult to sleep in many other positions. Still, although he imagined there was no intentional fanfare to the movement, he found himself, as always, drawn to the sight of the appendages, in awe of the way that each feather fluttered in the breeze created by his sudden downwards motion. He was living art, Giovanni thought.

"Um... Did you want to come to bed?" Angel asked awkwardly after Giovanni remained lost in wonder. "It's almost seven in the morning, I'm fucking exhausted."

Giovanni blinked himself free of his mesmer. "*Si, si,* s- sorry," He clambered onto the bed and crawled up beside Angel, amazed by the spaciousness compared to his recent living quarters. It almost, just for a moment, made him think of his old bed, massive and luxurious, and the countless time he had spent buried deep within its soft, inviting folds.

It occurred to him at once that this was the first time that he had been invited into somebody *else's* bed, and again Giovanni felt his heart seem to skip a beat, a sort of electric excitement course through him at the thought of Angel's desire for him, of the budding relationship blossoming forth between them, of his incredible luck that he had managed to discover the boy out here in the first place, that such a lovely creature could have been living out here on his own, looking for a new partner to replace one that had become dysfunctional.

He thought of fate, of Giorgio, of the guilt that still weighed, but he thought too of his own disownment. Giorgio had been the culprit in that situation as well, he thought. Without Giorgio's upcoming success as the straw that broke the camel's back, perhaps he would still be in his father's house, in his grand bed, buzzed and horny. But would that have been better? Could he admit to himself that he was grateful, in a way, for his removal from his father's home and lineage, to instead find himself out here with the beautiful winged boy who seemed to adore him so, in a way in which he had never been adored before? Both of their lives intertwined through his brother. It felt like fate, Giovanni thought, just like the Bible in the bedside table signifying to Angel that this home was a place of lodging. It was meant to be.

Giovanni cuddled up next to Angel, an awkward position in order to avoid his wings but nonetheless worth it as he desired nothing more than closeness to the boy at present.

"Angel?"

"Mm?" Angel opened his eyes and tilted his head slightly in order to glance to Giovanni.

"Would you do the same for me?"

"What?"

"With... with the bull man today, when I covered for you. You would do that? For me?"

"Huh...?" Angel paused for a moment. Giovanni waited with bated breath. "Yeah, yeah, of course," he said after another second of delay, speaking through a yawn. "I told you a second ago, we're- we're partners in crime, remember?" He closed his eyes once more. "Now, uh, can we go to sleep?"

"*Sì.*" Giovanni breathed out a contented sigh. Although he was protected from the heat of the day by the bedroom they now shared, he felt very warm indeed, cozy and safe as he nestled into Angel, feeling the soft rise and fall of his breaths and the soft feathers of his wings brush gently against his skin. With his head spinning with thoughts of fate and destiny and the inevitable passage of time into uncertain futures, of hopes and dreams and a world where everything happened for a reason, Giovanni fell into much-needed sleep.

When Vittoria and Anubis arrived at the Pharaoh's Tomb the following morning things were just as they had been the first time around, except this time, without Cosmo or Petyr around, the stage felt noticeably emptier. It was just the two of them, and Vittoria felt very small indeed in the inconceivably monumental theater, the ceiling far above her head and the heavy curtain before her hiding what she knew was an equally massive—and equally empty—auditorium space. She felt a sort of dizzying nervousness that she tried her best to quell by instead focusing on Anubis, masked just as before, presently opening a coffin-shaped case to reveal from within it a beautiful electric guitar, sleek and black with gold accents, stylish and elegant and simple.

"My dear, old friend," Anubis said, half to Vittoria and half to the guitar itself, running his long nails over the chords lovingly. "The show is still a while off, my dear, but I admit my desire to begin rehearsing early is not only to ensure your own comfort... I, too, may be somewhat rusty."

"You'll be playing?" Vittoria asked. In all her years as a fan of his work, she had never seen Anubis with an instrument. He had backing musicians for that... backing musicians which he had fired quite recently, and, judging by the oppressive emptiness of the theater, had not sought to replace.

Anubis nodded. "It was my musical conception, the guitar. A small part of my senescent heart will always be held only for it alone, and it is the only instrument which must be played live for my music. Everything else is... extra. Unnecessary for my vision. In solitude man has a sanity and revelations which in his passage into new worlds he may carry with him. Drum machines and synthesizers are easy to program and better ensure perfection... and they avoid attention being drawn from the main attraction." He stepped to Vittoria, the heeled boots he wore echoing, *click, click, click,* across the smooth floor in the emptiness. "You."

Vittoria felt her heart thump in her stomach, a sensation that never failed to send her body spiraling down into other abdominal ailments, leaving her nauseous and sore. She felt stuck at the edge of a sea which she was hardly prepared to even dip her toes into, rapids filled with swaths of Anubis' expectant fans, of technology she hardly understood, of music industry jargon that could have practically been written in foreign language, of Anubis' grand expectations...

"Well now, shall we get started?"

Anubis walked away, leaving Vittoria in a daze, and a moment later, with a dramatic whoosh and a long, high creaking sound, the curtain opened, revealing the empty concert hall before them. It was, just as Vittoria had imagined, vast and empty, an ocean wide and deep and far too easy to drown in. She stood there, peering out into the empty depths, dazed by the prospect of the crowd that would fill the hall when the time came.

"What if I disappoint you?" Vittoria said as Anubis walked back over—She had not taken her eyes from the vast space of the auditorium, but she heard his approach as his heels continued to click across the floor, saw his tall figure from the corner of her eye.

And then she felt his hand rest on her shoulder. "You will not," he said. She turned to him. "Vittoria, dear, you are... what, in your mid-twenties?" Late twenties, Vittoria thought, but she did not correct him. "I have found myself on the stage for much longer than you have been alive, my darling, and I promise that as you descend into the Underworld I will remain by your side." He took her hand and brought it to his mouth, beneath the jaws of the jackal mask, and kissed it. "I assure you that the next steps you take shall bring you closer than you have ever been to freedom, to escaping your bondage and becoming the creator of your own world. I will guide you, you may cling to me as you need, but you must take the steps yourself." Vittoria said nothing, in part because she did not know what to say, and in part because she knew Anubis well enough to know that he was not yet finished. He squeezed her hand again and then gestured with his other hand to the empty caverns of the auditorium. "Look out into the audience, Vittoria, and be silent so that we may hear the whisper of the gods."

Vittoria did as told, looking out into the vastness, the endless space meant for crowds upon crowds of people, the eager masses which would fill it up seamlessly in spite of the unimaginable spaciousness, and in doing so become the faceless congregate, the crazed throng of screams and cheers, sweat and skin, all in reverence for Anubis' art, for the mysticism he harnessed and the chaos he channeled on the stage.

"You remember the audience the night that you watched me perform, Vittoria?" Anubis said, as if reading her mind, yet another mystical power of his.

"I do." Vittoria nodded. Anubis reached to gently brush some hair from her face. The goosebumps that sprung from his touch made her heart quiver in her belly.

"If you do as I say, they will be yours, and they will see your power and your might, and you will be art to them. And as you give yourself to them, they in turn will give everything to you, and you will be the most powerful woman alive, Vittoria. You will be my Queen of Hell. Are you willing?"

Vittoria looked away from the imaginary audience, breaking her trance and instead turning to look into Anubis' eyes. Although they could not be seen from beneath the contacts he wore, she could see the shadows of the deep wrinkles that outlined them. Gazing into the empty blackness, she nodded.

"I am," she said, and with her head spinning with thoughts of fate and destiny and the inevitable passage of time into uncertain futures, of hopes and dreams and a world where everything happened for a reason, Vittoria turned to face the audience again.

# ACT V

A Note on Fresno History: The Marcello Candy Company

The history of Marcello Candies is truly that of the underdog. A family-owned, family-centered company from the very start, Marcello Candies' humble origins begin in Italy, when the original Mister and Misses Marcello would journey across the ocean to the United States and set up a small, rickety chocolate shop in the immigrant ghetto of the east coast. With persistence and the intrigue of a secret recipe, Marcello Chocolates would slowly expand, finding a small bit of financial success as the company was passed down through generations. However, it was not until the handing of the company to a certain Vittorio Marcello, our city's most beloved candyman, that the company would be moved across the country to reside in Fresno, California. An astute businessman since the beginning, this change in location was made just as the population was spiking and the economy flourishing, the overpopulation from Northern and Southern California causing a sonic boom to erupt in the very heart of the state and transforming the once-humble town of Fresno into the thriving metropolis we know and love today.

Following this move, as reported by shocked and schadenfreudian tabloids, Vittorio would make the daring—although some, at the time, called it utterly foolish—decision to put the majority of the company's profits into funding dozens of the most successful and innovative chemists in order to patent a unique drug with which to infuse his candies. Soon, the tabloids were eating their words (and the candies!). More successful than ever imagined, Marcello Candies quickly rose to the top of the markets. Not only were the candies delicious, they could provide short-term relief from various aches and pains, be they physical or emotional. As Himmel, who recently bought out the pharmaceutical companies and has been tasked with the arduous challenge of making over-the-counter medicines more readily accessible, deals with its own constant fight for accessible healthcare for all, Marcello Candies have been a godsend short-term replacement for the unfortunate among us unable to meet Himmel's prices.

It will further ensure buyers of the sincerity of Marcello Candies to know that Vittorio Marcello himself is, as the roots of the company would lead one to hope, a family man through and through. Dedicated first and foremost to his eight children, Vittorio has fought tooth and nail to provide for them as a single parent while running one of the most powerful companies in the world entirely alone. Many of his children have come to be powerful members of the community themselves, such as leading Himmel Medicine's various medical departments, owning high-end fashion or makeup lines, or overseeing chapters of the Birds of Prey.

"I am by no means a perfect man," Mister Marcello himself tells us in a candid and earnest interview, "Nobody is. But my family will always be my number one priority. Everything I do, I do for my children."

Vittoria was silent save for the softest panting as her nails dug deep into Anubis' flesh and his hair fell down in dark curls against her face. He smelled of the incense that he kept in his home as if it had seeped into the scars that painted his skin, intermingled with the smokey scent of the candle that leapt and flickered on the bedside table beside them.

"Tomorrow night," Anubis said breathily, just enough above a whisper that the smooth, deep coolness of his voice melted and dripped from his mouth like wax. Vittoria buried her face into the crook of his neck. "I will be- the God of Hell and you- you-" His words were stifled through panting, seeming to lose their rhythm just as experimental music rejected it; flesh against flesh echoed through the quiet with each pause for breath. "-You will be the Goddess, the Queen of Hell, *my* Queen-"

His nails clawed at her and pierced her skin, scratching much harder than she had, and she gripped to him in silence, pressing herself against him as she clung to his neck, and in that moment she was very aware of two things: The adoration she had long since held for him, the many long years prior to their meeting that had led to this moment, the hours upon hours adoring his music, adoring him, the way he had pervaded her imagination like no other, how surreal it continued to feel each time he touched her, spoke to her in such ways, entered her. And, secondly, the sensation of her heart beating against his where their bare stomachs touched.

"Just you and I," Anubis murmured quietly as he kissed her shoulder. "Holding dominion over the damned, together," He kissed her again and Vittoria slowly let go of him, allowing herself to fall back against the pillows beneath them, where she looked up at him and saw his eyes on her, shining faintly in the candlelight, staring over her face, her body, watching her with a gaze that felt predatory and consuming like the carnivore he masqueraded as on the stage. "You will be perfect."

"I will be."

"You will." Anubis kissed her mouth, missing the center and pressing his lips to the side of hers, then down to her jaw and finally to her pale neck, where she felt his canine teeth, sharp enough that they could rip her open right there, leave her to bleed out, glistening with sweat and gushing blood as the faintest glimmer of Fresno city night seeped through the closed curtains.

When Vittoria awoke she was alone in the bedroom, and the clock on the bedside table told her that it was just after six in the morning, and she cursed herself for having grown accustomed to Anubis' schedule. He was always up at daybreak, and over the course of the past few weeks he had begun to force her up too, gradually getting her out of bed earlier as he insisted that there was much to be done, much he wanted to prepare for and much that he needed her help with, as his future partner on the stage. And now, here she was, an unwilling victim to his circadian rhythm.

Vittoria stood, stretching to wake herself up fully, and she could sense a strange weight in her stomach—not the heart, which she was still doing her best to grow accustomed to, but the impending sense of the day that lay before her, the culmination of whatever it was that Anubis had spent so long planning. There was a strange surrealness to it, like the very opposite of a dream: Rather than waking and remembering only the faintest trace of half-conscious memory of the night before, here she was, fully awake and only half capable of comprehending the events that lay immediately in store for her. She tried then, standing there alone in the bedroom, to picture what could possibly transpire later this evening, tried to picture the concert hall full with an eager mass of audience, tried to picture herself, dressed up, microphone in hand, standing before all of them, Anubis beside her with the guitar and the music swallowing them both even as they conceived it together. But it was all still a distant dream, and in the quiet of the early Fresno morning, standing alone in her nightgown, it was not yet fathomable to her.

Vittoria made her way to the door and descended the staircase, a much easier feat than it had been when she had first attempted them post-surgery, her body growing better acclimated to the rearrangement of her organs each day. The soft thump of her bare feet on the wooden stairs, the cool smoothness of the rail in her hand, the smoky warmth and dim light of Anubis' home and the collection of statuesque creatures that sat, tranquil and calm, on shelves and tables as she reached the bottom, all felt very normal, very comfortably in their place, the world at perfect peace with itself, and it was only her, and only the deep pit in her stomach, the awareness of her impending fate, that was out of place among it all.

She reached the living room and walked through it into the kitchen, where she found Anubis with his back turned. Hearing her as she centered, his head perked up not unlike a hunting dog's at the sound of a bird snapping a twig as it landed, and he turned from where he stood to look at her with a wide smile on his face. "Vittoria, dearest!" he called, rushing to her and taking one of her hands in his own, his long, thin fingers stroking the top of her hand. "Good morning! I've made coffee already."

Vittoria's heart sank even deeper than it already was; undoubtedly, he'd already sweetened it. Sure enough, he went to the fridge and pulled from it a glass of iced coffee that he had already taken upon himself to prepare, pale and milky. She watched helplessly as Anubis stirred it, the metal spoon he used hitting the glass in a little rhythmic tinkling sound, and then reluctantly accepted it, knowing that she needed the caffeine and deciding it was not worth the effort or time to remake it on her own— perhaps even, for once, willing to accept whatever tranquilizing, analgesic effect the sugar possessed. It was overbearingly sweet, and she winced at the saccharine coldness against her teeth, but Anubis' smile did not falter, and after a moment of watching her, he said,

"Big day today, hm?"

"Yeah," Vittoria replied quietly, forcing down another sip of the coffee.

Anubis chuckled and turned back around; Vittoria noticed that he was making omelets. He whisked at a bowl full of egg mix as he said, "No need to be nervous, my love, I will make sure-"

"I'm not nervous." Vittoria said quickly. She had swallowed the coffee in her mouth quickly so as to get the words out before Anubis could finish speaking and she shivered as the cold, sweet drink ran down her throat, almost choking but managing to stifle it with a huff. "Shut up or you'll make me nervous. Right now it just feels... Normal."

"Normal?" Anubis questioned, glancing to her before turning to pour the omelet mix into a pan. He laughed a little. "Why, you truly are adapting to the life of a performer quickly, hmm? Just willing to accept it all that fast?"

Vittoria shrugged, although Anubis' eyes were not on her to see, and said, "I guess it just doesn't feel real yet."

Anubis flipped the omelet-to-be in a show of expertise that impressed Vittoria quite a bit, and then turned to her with the smile still on his lips. "Just wait until tonight, dear, it will be the most *real* thing you have ever done, I assure you." He turned back around to devote more attention to his cooking. "You will be more alive, more aware, more free than you can even imagine now. You must only be willing to, ah-" He laughed suddenly, as he carefully slid the omelet onto a plate. "-break a few eggs, is all." It was almost a giggle, amused at his own joke.

Vittoria took another sip of the cold, sweet coffee, and gave an uncertain nod. "Well, I'm... I..." she faltered, a weak smile tugging on the corners of her mouth, "I'm egg...xcited. About tonight."

Anubis, who had just turned back to the cooking station, whipped around at that, so quickly that the curls of his hair bounced with the momentum of the motion, and his eyes lit up. He laughed again, a delighted show of appreciation for Vittoria's joke that made the wrinkles around his eyes deepen and stretch to his grinning lips and revealed the glisten of his canine fangs, and Vittoria thought that in that moment he looked quite handsome.

As the morning wore on, and early morning turned into slightly later morning, still the reality of the evening had not fully sunk in, although when Anubis suggested they get ready to go down to the Pharaoh's Tomb and prepare, the first real wave of nerves washed over Vittoria like the iced coffee she had forced down earlier. Still, as she got into the passenger seat, she tried to fall back again into the comfort of routine that the drive to the theater had become for her. It had become like clockwork, this trip: They had spent almost every day practicing and rehearsing, Anubis teaching Vittoria the music that he wanted her to sing and how he wanted her to sing it.

Quickly, however, this sense of normalcy was dashed as Vittoria became aware of Anubis deviating from the standard route to the venue.

"Where are we going?" she asked.

"Embalmed Records. We'll be picking up the new props and costumes on the way to the theater," Anubis explained. A sly smile curled at the corner of his plum-colored lips. "And you will receive your first viewing of the dress I had custom-made for you."

They drove the rest of the way in silence, Anubis' eyes on the road, although Vittoria noticed how he glanced her way occasionally, and the small smile that never left his lips. She said nothing and watched out the window as pigeons pecked at a fallen crepe that sat rotting in the Fresno heat.

It was a Saturday, and the Fresno streets were very alive, roads packed with cars and people bustling down the sidewalk, in and out of the expensive stores in the upper level of the city, where designer fashion was rolled out and only those with money most found inconceivable—even her, nowadays—could have the first look at it, could be the first to touch whatever the newest synthetic fabric trend was and feel it against their bare bodies.

Finally, the car came to the imposing black building that was Embalmed Records, and Vittoria noticed the massive screen was once more lit up with a countdown clock. This time, beneath it, in a blood red font that looked like long slash wounds, as if a knife had been viciously dragged down bare flesh, were the words SPECIAL BROADCAST.

"You'll be broadcasting the show?" Vittoria asked, looking to Anubis.

Anubis nodded but kept his eyes ahead. "I will indeed," he said. "What better way to reveal the crowning of the Queen than by way of a public coronation? This will be the modern-day equivalent of a parade through the streets. Except, I hope, with a much lower risk of assassination by dissidents. You do not have any political opponents to worry about, I hope?" He laughed at that. Vittoria did not.

The vast size of the building struck Vittoria as odd for the first time as they entered, although nothing had changed since last time. Perhaps she had grown so accustomed to the smaller scales of Anubis' home that the grandness of the downtown skyscrapers had turned foreign, she pondered, as her eyes scanned over the golden hieroglyphics that decorated the walls. Anubis led her through the sleek hallway, through the front office and finally to the elevator, pausing only as he once more revealed his card to the receptionist who had no idea of his true identity. For what purpose did Anubis need with such a big building? Vittoria wondered, as they clambered into the elevator. What inhabited the countless floors above them? She pictured the endless hallways of recording studios, storage facilities, conference rooms, all looking out over the city, and felt very small.

As Anubis inputted the desired floor, she decided to ask.

"Forgive me, if I were a proper host I would have given you a tour," Anubis answered as the elevator rode up to the fourteenth floor. "I suppose it's not too late, although we're much too busy today for it. Tomorrow, perhaps, or the day after... We'll have all the time in the world for things such as that. And someday, well... this will be yours, I imagine, and you can grow as familiar with it as your lovely heart desires."

"What?" Vittoria asked. The doors opened with a mechanical whoosh.

Anubis stepped out; Vittoria followed. "Mm-hm, I cannot see anyone more fitting of owning the company once I have claimed my place in the afterlife save for my protégé." He spoke with an air of casualty, as if simply sharing a passing thought of mild interest, even as Vittoria's head spun. "I have no children, no blood relatives. I most certainly have no coworkers who I have ever trusted. These are hard times, Vittoria, love. We must learn to trust ourselves to trust others worthy of trusting, and I would, I believe, entrust Embalmed Records to you, assuming all goes smoothly tonight." They reached the prop room. Anubis opened the door and held it for Vittoria. "And I trust that it will."

As they entered the prop room Anubis grabbed Vittoria's hand, making her turn to look at him. He was beaming at her, and he said, "Come and see, Vittoria," He led her, tugging gently, towards a rack of outfits, where shirts and robes and capes hung, and where one piece of clothing stood out, for it was covered in a plastic casing like a translucent body bag. From here, Vittoria could not make out the details, but as Anubis unhooked the hanger she could see it shine in the bright artificial light of the prop room.

It was a dress, Vittoria realized as Anubis freed it from its plastic confinements, and a very regal one at that, colored like pure gold, glittering and sparkling every time it shifted even the slightest bit in Anubis' hands. It was almost comical in its luxury, a long and flowing Rococo ball gown with lace and ribbon decorating the skirt that would undoubtedly drag along the ground like a long cape behind her. She furrowed her brow and looked at Anubis, confused. "It's... It's a little much, isn't it?" she asked, thinking back to the outfits she had seen Anubis wear, which included plenty of capes and scarves but still had an edge, a darkness to them, not to mention more mobility than this.

Anubis continued to smile at that, which Vittoria supposed was better than him growing angry with her for her lack of excitement, but she was no less baffled. "This is what you will start in," he explained. "But the real you will be pried open, revealed beneath the veneer. Think of it like... a candy wrapper," He turned the dress around, revealing the zipper in the back. He unzipped it and revealed black latex beneath, that glimmered like sunlight reflecting off an oil spill. "Of course, on the stage, you won't be using the zipper."

Anubis handed Vittoria the dress and she was shocked to find how heavy it was, how much weight was in the elaborate, multilayered skirt. She looked at it closely and saw the flecks of gold that painted it like starlight, twirled the dress slightly where it hung from the hanger in her hands and watched, mesmerized, as it glistened gold in the light, and she wondered what it would look like from the stage, illuminated for all to see, or from the great screen out in the streets, shining over all of Fresno city.

But she did not get to think about it for very much longer, because suddenly there was a knife in front of her, and Vittoria jumped back in surprise, which made Anubis, who held the knife, laugh.

"Apologies, dear, I didn't mean to frighten you. You will have to get more accustomed to a blade before the show tonight, though," Anubis said, as Vittoria's momentary surprise settled and she realized that he had simply been trying to hand it to her. With the hand not holding the dress she reached out and took hold of the knife from the hilt and looked at it, admiring the unique metallic silver shine of it. "The dress was put together with care so that it would tear in all the right places as you cut into it," Anubis explained. "When the time is right, you will rip through it. It will already have been damaged by the wear of the rest of the show, so the audience will know that there is more beneath it and will be waiting with baited breath for the entirety of it to be revealed, but you will have to do the rest of the work yourself. It will be magnificent, I can assure you."

Vittoria looked between the knife in one hand and the dress in the other, uncertain still, trying to imagine the heavy, frilly thing on her body. She moved it up and down, feeling its weight where it hung from the hanger and watching the gold sparkle and glitter jovially, and then looked up at Anubis again. "If you say so,"

"I *know* so, Vittoria."

She supposed she was not in a position to fight with him on this— He knew what to do, she did not. He had experience, she did not. His vision had served to propel him to success beyond her wildest dreams. Everything from here on out was in his hands, and she could do little but follow and trust that he would not let her fail. She supposed that what he had said before was true: He had too much to lose, taking a chance on her that he himself did not believe in. They would be sharing the stage, and the show would be broadcasted live—truly live, not the lie that her father had told her. If she failed, Anubis, too, would be humiliated, the empire built for himself tarnished. He absolutely would not allow himself that humiliation, if nothing else. She sighed and nodded, resigning herself to believe in the golden weight that hung from her hand.

"Well, I believe it's time we gather up our belongings and head to the theater!" Anubis said.

"Already?"

"We are striving for perfection, Vittoria, love. The clock is ticking! From here on out there is no such thing as too much preparation. And besides, I would like adequate time to do your makeup as well." Anubis explained to her as he began to rummage through the hanging racks again for his own costume.

"You'll be doing my makeup?"

"Yes, not that I have any doubt in your own ability. Forgive me for being a bit of a 'control freak,' as they say, but I cannot express to you enough the vividness of the image in my head for this night, down to the most minute of detail!"

Anubis turned away from the closet and walked to Vittoria, his expression softening from the lively grin to something softer, more tender. He took her hands in his own and pressed a kiss to her forehead. "Although you will have yourself to thank as much as I once we are finished. You have been my muse through the duration of this, Vittoria, and to paint your face will be not unlike a monastic painting the Saints, blurring the lines between reverence and idolatry." He kissed her again, on the mouth this time, and Vittoria kissed back, knife still in one hand and dress in the other.

Vittoria felt like a princess, which was not something she had ever necessarily wanted to feel like.

At her father's home she had been "Mistress," because it sounded powerful, mature, and dominant; it set her apart as the only woman still living within the walls of the Marcello mansion who was not a pitiful servant. It set her apart from her elder half-sister, the proud "Misses Francesca Marcello-Baer," who, despite marrying into prestige of her own via one of the most successful newscasters in the city, had been so proud to air to the world her Marcello lineage that she not only kept the surname even after marriage, she had actually added it—as a bastard child, Marcello had never been her legal last name to begin with. Vittoria remembered the many nights she had spent baffled by this decision upon learning it, and upon learning that her father, thrilled to find himself the opportunity to be connected directly to a newscaster of such prestige, had given her his blessing to do so.

Vittoria looked at herself in the dressing room mirror, expressionless save for her brow furrowed slightly, quizzically. The dress was as heavy as it had felt in her hand and as overbearingly regal as well, the skirt trailing behind her and the bows covered in glittering gold shimmering and sparkling at each little motion, even the slightest rise and fall of her chest. Her mobility was limited, but not drastically; she could still *move*, but she had to take steps carefully so as not to drag the skirt on the floor or trip over it. Although she still did not quite understand Anubis' vision in its entirety, she was more excited than ever to break free of it when the time came, feeling the oppressive weight of it quite literally; perhaps that had been his intention all along. Under the dress she wore what had been beneath it on the hanger, what she had caught the briefest glimpse of before, a tight, sleek latex bodysuit that glimmered similarly to the knife despite it being stark, raven black. It was much more comfortable, not necessarily against her skin (which it clung to like a boa constrictor, quite frankly), but most certainly in terms of how she wanted to be perceived on the stage. But she would have to wait to reveal that—*Like a candy wrapper*, Anubis had said.

After one more long, uncertain glance in the mirror, Vittoria exited the dressing room and found herself exposed to the back hallways of the Pharaoh's Tomb, where Anubis had left her a few moments prior to get into costume. She began to stumble towards the stage, clumsily at first, trying not to trip on the rippling golden waves of fabric that surrounded her, feeling like a spectacle as she clamored unsteadily through the dark, empty halls, past closed doors, some with signs and some lacking any indication to what they were entirely, and was starkly aware of the fact that Anubis' world felt much like a maze to her yet, and she still glaringly out of place within it, more so now than ever as she glittered, illustrious in the gray light.

Upon returning to the stage, and after much praise and flattery from Anubis, in part towards her but in part too towards the ingeniousness of his own design, Vittoria was led to a second dressing room—how many did this place hold? she thought dizzyingly. Here was where Anubis kept his makeup, he explained, in a dressing room meant only for that one, sole purpose. It had fantastic lighting, as well as brilliant, clear mirrors of various shapes and sizes that captured the essence of the soul and projected back only its perfections. Or at least, that was how Anubis described it as they entered.

The mirrors were indeed flattering, and given the scale of everything that existed within the domain of Embalmed Records, Vittoria supposed she could hardly pretend to be surprised by the array of colorful products that surrounded them: Scattered across the room was an assortment of makeups and products the likes of which she could hardly even begin to fathom, and she had been wearing makeup for the majority of her life, had even worked briefly in cosmetics and sold a line of her own, for a short moment in time. Bottles and vials and little containers of products lined the desk, organized carefully and neatly in a way that made it look like a window display in a high-end boutique. Shelves upon shelves and racks upon racks of lipsticks, brushes, sponges, powders, long, delicate sticks of various colors. She looked to Anubis.

"You can't wear all of this- Your mask-"

"Of course, for my shows my face tends to need very little from the nose up, but I do enjoy the options, and the thrill of collecting interesting makeup that I see of all varieties." She supposed he did often have makeup on, even just around the house, when there was nobody but her to see it. "I rather like having the ability to create art at my disposal at all times, and makeup possesses the wonderful quality that the canvas it requires will remain with you, inevitably, until you depart from this realm." Anubis walked to a container of liquid hues that sat beneath a large vanity mirror lined with bright bulbs and picked up a vial of a navy-blue substance, holding it up to the bright light of the dressing room so that Vittoria could see little silver flecks in it. He set that down and picked up a sleek black container, which he opened to reveal a sparkling black powder inside. Then he placed his hand on the back of the chair that sat in front of the mirror. "Come here, Vittoria. Why don't we get started?"

Vittoria had had makeup applied for her before. She had once insisted on her father's servants doing her makeup, and although it had been her idea, an optimistic belief that it would save her time and stress overthinking about her appearance if it was done for her, she remembered that brief moment with nothing but disdain and annoyance, because she had found none of her father's servants brave enough to do anything remotely interesting. They had directly ignored her requests to do something stark or daring, had powdered her cheeks with warm red blush that made her look as if she was in a constant state of embarrassment, had painted her lips so subtly that the only noticeable makeup on them was the irritating slime of lip gloss. She had made sure to see them fired, of course, and she had tried again with a number of other servants, until her father complained about the amount of staff he was losing, and told her she would not be requesting makeup help any longer if it would continue to cost him employees. Vittoria, sick to death of seeing herself with sunny cheeks and cherry lips anyway, had happily accepted this order. For once she and her father had agreed on something.

She had also had her makeup done for a number of interviews and photoshoots and other various public appearances, by professionals paid a great sum of money by her father, which was equally grueling. She had little say in the matter, forced to let a stranger at her father's direction decide what would make her look most presentable to the public, while also dolling her up, exaggerating her smile, her eyes, as they rambled on in obnoxious voices about how she really should speak in her natural accent, it's quite lovely, quite exotic, and how she would be very beautiful if she only wore the proper outfit, and how even if her last business venture, and the one before that, and the one before that too, even, had fallen through, this new project was surely to be a success, and she would certainly make her family name proud this time. She remembered being complimented for her nose, calling it very authentically Marcello, as layers of foundation and powder and concealer were applied to it, and she had been very aware that everything they told her were placating works of fiction, as she had gotten her nose done to escape that very compliment years prior—An added nuisance to think that even that was overlooked by the fast-talking artist that treated her more a billboard than a person.

Anubis did not present the bumbling cowardice that the servants had possessed with each uncertain puff of red blush, nor was there the artificiality of the professional artists hired by her father present in his craftmanship. He began by tying her hair up, in pigtails rather than a ponytail as she had expected, which felt very juvenile, but she did not complain. His fingers in her hair made her shiver and his nails dragged carefully against her scalp as he gently sculpted the dark strands, and this demeanor remained throughout the course of the makeup application. His motions and touches were calm and delicate, performed with the grace and fluid coolness that seemed to come so naturally to all of his mannerisms. His eyes, a deep brown that held the black centers of his pupils in a shadow almost as dark, studied her face intently, never left her features. He squinted through the many wrinkles that gathered at the corners of his eyes and he touched her with a gentle, reverent purposefulness.

Creams and foundations glided over her skin and powder was applied like it was made of gold, like *she* was made of gold, and she shivered at the light touch of small brushes against her cheeks, against her eyelids. Even when she shut her eyes she could feel Anubis' gaze, the way his deep eyes fixated on every detail of her, studied her like she was fine art. She could feel his breath, warm against her skin, and through the smells of the assortment of makeups she caught the faintest scent of the incense that seemed to linger in his black and silver curls. It was a hypnotic sensation, the whole of it, and as his brushes ran gently over her face she felt the anxiety of the impending evening settle from the roaring storm in the depths of her stomach to a tranquil ripple.

"There!" Anubis' voice broke through the silence and Vittoria jumped a little, as if he had dropped a rock into the slowly calming waters of her gut. Her eyes opened and the brightness of the room left Anubis' presence over her a jarring mass of dark for a moment, and then she blinked and saw he was smiling down at her, makeup brush in hand. "All done. What do you think, dear?"

Anubis nodded towards the mirror before which Vittoria sat, and she blinked eyes that were heavy with makeup; her lashes sticky with mascara, glitter framing the edge of her vision. She looked to the mirror to see herself, although it was a self she hardly recognized—from the neck down in her sparkling golden mass of dress that weighed on her shoulders, that rubbed against the latex that suffocated her flesh beneath, and the sight from the neck up was no less jarring. Her hair was pulled back to keep it out of her face, exposing much more than she was used to seeing, her own eyes foreign to her. Anubis had applied the makeup thick, as per usual with stage makeup, she supposed. Her lips were navy blue, so dark that for a moment they appeared black until she processed the depth of the color, thick and glistening. Golden pens that turned up at the edge of her eyes like wings posed a stark contrast to the darkness that surrounded them, and silver flecks adorned her eyelashes and cheeks. She stared at herself longer still, silent, surveying the golds and blacks and silvers and blues, the glistening and glittering of the various products, her cheeks higher and sharper, her eyes narrowed by eyeliner to artificially match the natural curve of Anubis', and she thought to herself that the pale blue eyes that pierced through the dark makeup and gazed back out at her from the reflection of the pristine vanity mirror were her brother's.

Anubis and Vittoria left the dressing room and returned to the back of the theater, where the curtain was still drawn and the silence of the grand concert hall that lay beyond was deafening, and they shared a glass of red wine, which Anubis toasted: "To the past, the present, and the future."

Anubis brought Vittoria to the other side of the theater then, and showed her the workings of the sound system in a small back room, explaining cords and cables as he set up, and she stood silently, face sticky with makeup and dress heavy on her latex-clad shoulders, her entire being a mass of sparkles, and she found herself able to listen with only vague interest as her mind wandered to the thick curtain at the front of the stage and the inevitable parting of it that was soon to come, the reveal of the crowd. She imagined herself over them, and as Anubis was in the process of explaining what he was doing as he twisted a knob, Vittoria asked suddenly, "When are doors?"

"Mm... Soon, but don't let it worry you, dear." Anubis replied absentmindedly, seemingly unphased by her interruption. "But I do recommend not looking out into the audience prior to the show starting. It certainly won't help your nerves. Stay safe within the maternal womb of the curtains until the time is right for you to be born."

Vittoria frowned but said nothing else. Anubis flipped a switch he shouldn't have and the shriek of feedback pierced the air, the sound puncturing Vittoria's ear like a knife slicing its way down a chalkboard, and she and Anubis both grimaced. Then the banshee cries stopped and as the ringing in her ears slowly subsided the sound was replaced by Anubis' soft laughter. "So sorry," he said, his smile of shocked amusement audible.

After the work in the sound room was complete, Anubis insisted they return once more to the dressing room, for he had yet to get ready himself. Vittoria sat, her bottom awkwardly pillowed by the thick, sparkling gown of her dress. She crossed her legs and watched in silence as Anubis did his own makeup, applying glitter and eyeliner that was dark and sharp around his eyes, maroon lipstick to his lips, the shadow of contour across already high cheekbones. He put in his black sclera contacts. He got into his costume, a black outfit made of what appeared to be crushed velvet, although it was tattered and frayed in places and covered in off-white scarves that hung off of his body and made him look a bit like a mummified pharaoh, and a magnificent black cape with shimmering golden embroidery that matched the glitter of Vittoria's dress. Last was his Anubis mask, which had its own unique glimmer in the bright dressing room light, and once he had fit it snugly over his head and buried his curls beneath the hood, disguising his face behind the obsidian beast, immediately the man that Vittoria had spent so much time with was replaced by the Rock God of Death himself, and although she had seen the transformation before her very eyes she was left with a sort of quiet awe at his presence before her.

They returned to the back of the stage and continued preparations. As the time wore on they spoke little to each other, Vittoria becoming increasingly distracted by her impending fate, Anubis distracted by the technical side of things that were far beyond her skillset. They shared another cup of wine; Anubis asked Vittoria to make a toast this time. She fumbled with the cup, almost spilling it when Anubis handed it to her, watching her from behind empty, black eyes. She toasted—"To the unknown." Anubis was delighted.

After this short break, Anubis stood from where they had both been sitting in the engineering room, stretching, and the contortion of his body in this motion made Vittoria have to tilt her neck to look up at him, and she was reminded once more of his great size over her, how tall he was, how powerful he appeared in the mask of death he wore. He looked down at her with his darkened eyes and said, "Well, dear, the doors will open soon enough, I suggest we head out. I would like to check that all is well at the front of the house, if you don't mind my brief absence." He held out a hand to her and Vittoria took it and stood on feet that were briefly unbalanced due to the heaviness of her dress skirt. She gripped his hand tighter for a moment as she collected herself. Anubis pulled her to him, and she felt the nose of his jackal mask tap gently, smooth and cold, against her forehead.

They walked out to the stage once more and Anubis squeezed Vittoria's hand before walking to the far side. Vittoria did not follow, but watched, silently, until he turned back around and said, "I will return momentarily, I only must make sure that the live recording system is set up properly and all is well in the land of the living. Venue staff should be in place by now."

Vittoria felt the need to ask, "Didn't you say you were doing this all alone?"

Anubis laughed a big laugh that left his fangs glistening beneath the mask, and then said, "Yes, Vittoria, I certainly did, and I certainly am. It has been you and I alone all day, has it not? But I cannot run a kingdom as grand as this without relegating some of the menial tasks to those better suited to handle such busywork while I take care of what truly matters: You." He smiled at her, and then he was gone, and Vittoria was left alone.

Vittoria looked down at the glittering dress she wore, trying to figure out what to do while she waited for Anubis' return, for the show to begin, but her brain felt numb, overwhelmed, unable or unwilling to fully comprehend what the future had in store for her. She had been on stages before, she thought, reminding herself, self-soothing as she felt the bubbling of nerves, She had been on television, she had done interviews, she had modeled, she had even had a brief interest in acting and her face could be found in a collection of films that would hardly be remembered a year or two after their release. Her most recent preparation prior to this to appear in the public sphere had been the day before her father had kicked her out, she remembered faintly, the memory feeling as distant to her now as her heart from its natal placement in her chest. She pressed the palm of her hand to her breast, feeling for the beating that she knew would not come.

Had she grown? She wondered. She heard what sounded like the opening of a door and the soft pattering of footsteps beginning to echo through the showroom. She reached down to her stomach. If she looked at the woman she had been the night she had been removed from her father's home, would they be the same, would they understand each other? Would she understand herself then—Did she understand herself now?

The soft tapping of footsteps turned more erratic and more frequent until it began to sound like heavy rainfall, a torrential downpour of shoes on the hard ground of the theater as the audience filed in for the performance. Vittoria pressed down against the side of her torso, feeling through the layers of fabric she wore to find the soft beating of her heart nestled in her abdomen, a reminder of life persisting in spite of it all. Anubis was still not back. She looked to the curtain, and could see the sliver of bright light where it parted grow dim. She could hear voices, the deluge of people becoming the wild sea that Anubis had used before to drown himself in worship.

Anubis had told her not to look past the curtain. Why not? Vittoria tried to remember. Stage fright, she thought. He had been worried that the sight of the crowd would make her nerves worse. But, standing backstage on her own, although there had been the gradual rise of anxiety through the day and a distinct nervousness casting a shadow, dark and inescapable, over her, she felt numb to such concerns. She wet her lips and tasted lipstick and hoped she had not rubbed any off.

Suddenly, her attention was caught by a scent in the air, something faint and sweet, sweeter than Anubis' incense, which had been her first thought upon detecting it. This was richer, milkier, warmer. She looked up urgently, sniffing the air like an animal, for she realized with a faint lurching of her stomach that it was incredibly familiar. It was coming from the front of the house, behind the curtain.

And then all at once it hit her, and she felt quite stupid for having taken as long a time to recognize the scent as she had, but she supposed, it had just felt so incredibly out of place, an asynchronicity, an oxymoron of the senses.

It was the smell of chocolate. Her father's chocolates. Vittoria remembered the smell of them in the hotel room that night, overwhelmingly sweet, unpleasant in the aroma that teased almost at being liquor but too creamy and too sugary and too close to her brother, to her father, to the life she had spent decades confined within. She walked closer to the curtain and the smell grew stronger still. Why chocolate? She didn't remember it smelling like that before, the first time she had watched Anubis perform. She certainly would have remembered.

As she reached the curtain she could hear the sea of people speaking, although she could not make out any individual voices. It was a cacophony of sound, voices reverberating off the walls of the grand palace, everyone speaking amongst each other and against each other. The crowd must have been enormous—Of course it was, this was an Anubis show, after all. Everyone who could possibly afford to come had come. If they did not enjoy the music, if they had no interest in the performance, then they would go if for no other reason than to be able to say that they had witnessed the mystery of Anubis' miracles in the flesh. In another lifetime she herself undoubtedly would have been on the other side of the curtain, a starry-eyed believer waiting eagerly for the service to begin.

Before she had even realized what she was doing she was clutching the curtain, the material so thick that even as she clasped it tight it hardly bunched in her hands, heavier even than her dress. She rubbed the soft material, staring at it, feeling it in her hands and struggling to comprehend that, as thick as it was, it was all that stood between herself and the audience. She hesitated for a moment, but as the smell of the chocolate overwhelmed her, nauseated her, left her head spinning with a disgust that she had not missed, she continued onwards in her investigation.

She pulled the curtain apart just the tiniest bit, just enough that she could peer through with a single eye, and felt like she could hurl.

The elaborate, ornate, golden, calligraphic symbol that was the Marcello-brand *M* shone bright and clear even in the dim light of the theater, fluttering from a massive banner above the crowd, hanging over them, size incomprehensible in the cavernous room. Looking into the audience she could see that everyone there had shiny candy bags that glistened like pyrite.

Vittoria was tugged back into the stage, so unexpectedly and with such force that she lost her balance and fell backwards, into the chest of Anubis, who looked down at her with empty, black eyes, his grip tight on her arms.

Vittoria stammered, unable to form the words she wanted as she struggled to free herself from Anubis' grip and regain her balance. "Anubis- Why-"

"Vittoria, my dear, what did I tell you about looking out into the crowd?" Anubis asked, an annoyance in his voice that made Vittoria's skin crawl. She felt dizzy from the scent of chocolate. Anubis clicked his tongue and shook his head so that the jackal's muzzle bobbed from side to side.

"What is that out there, Anubis?"

"Why, your crowd, love."

Vittoria shook her head and took a step back, backing up closer to the curtain again and away from Anubis. "No- No, I'm not stupid, that's not- I mean- The candy, Anubis."

Anubis reached out to Vittoria and she stepped back again, rejecting his touch outright and nearly hitting the curtain. He sighed. "Vittoria, relax, pet. You're all worked up from pre-concert nerves, is all."

"I'm not." Vittoria insisted. Her hands bunched into fists. "What haven't you told me?"

Anubis reached out again and again Vittoria tried to escape his touch, but she hit the back of the curtain, causing it to ripple and shudder threateningly, and Anubis took the chance to lunge then, and grab hold of her wrists and tug her close to him with enough force that it made her wince in pain. She tried and failed to pull away from his grip. She could smell his incense, floral spice clashing with the chocolates. "Vittoria, I implore you to trust me." He spoke in an abrasive, impatient hiss, but his voice quickly softened as he regained composure, seemingly realizing that such a tone would do little to help de-escalate the situation. "I have been preparing a surprise for you, that's all," He let go of her, and Vittoria took a single step back, putting enough distance between her and him that she could look at him fully, eye him up and down. "I am giving you the opportunity of a lifetime. I am helping you free yourself. Please, do not think now, after all I have done, that I would do anything that is not with your best interest at heart, sugar."

"What opportunity?" Vittoria asked, rubbing her nails against the palms of her hands.

Anubis nodded to the curtain. "I have worked tirelessly these past few weeks to secure a sponsorship with Marcello Candies. I rarely collaborate with anyone, you know, and I certainly have never before allied with your family's company aside from selling candies at my venue alongside the typical snacks and alcohol. But this is a very special occasion." He smiled his wide, carnivorous smile.

"You said... You said I would be more than a Marcello forever." Vittoria said, drawing in a breath that trembled as she pushed it up and out of her empty chest. "Why- Why would you bring my father into this?"

"You must confront your past to escape it, Vittoria. I have not promised any loyalty to your father, only that I would give out his samples, that I would raise his banner, that I would state his name somewhere, somehow, within tonight's performance, and that we shall—Or, rather, *you* shall: When the curtains raise, you will appear in your golden splendor, and then you will denounce your past, your family, your name, and you will free yourself from the bondage in which you have been trapped, and you will die to yourself and be reborn as my Queen of Hell." As he spoke Anubis walked forward, slowly, approaching Vittoria as if she were an injured, scared animal, and Vittoria did not move away this time as he took his hands in her own and squeezed them gently, brought one up to kiss the back of it, but she did nothing to reciprocate, only indifferently allowing his administrations.

"How." Vittoria said at last.

Anubis let go of one of her hands and reached out, and she willed herself not to flinch as his hand touched her chest, where her heart had been until she had consented to its displacement. Despite the many layers of fabric and latex between Anubis' nails and her flesh, despite the fact that the scar that ran up it had served to desensitize the flesh, she felt goosebumps erupt on her skin as he touched her.

"You have seen my trick, Vittoria. Tonight, you will do the same." He reached into a pocket of his costume and procured from it the dagger he had possessed earlier that day. He reached out to give it to her. Vittoria did not accept. "Take it, Vittoria. Feel it in your hands and let it become an extension of yourself, a symbol of your power as you-"

"Why didn't you tell me about this?" Vittoria demanded, finding herself tired of the poetics. The goosebumps Anubis had conjured had not left, but rather had turned into a ceaseless shiver down her spine and she drew in breaths clouded with the haze of milk chocolate as she tried to steady herself.

Anubis sighed, the coolness in his demeanor slipping with frustration, a visible frown twitching at the corner of his painted lips. "It would be insincere if you practiced it, Vittoria, and I knew there would be hesitation, and worry, and fear. In order to become art you must be willing to let all of that go and to die to yourself, to die to who you are now and become something much greater."

"I don't want to die."

"Well, what *do* you want then, Vittoria? To live as Vittorio Marcello's brat for the rest of your life?"

A sudden, glacial coldness, anger like shards of ice, kept Vittoria frozen in place, and she stared at the man before her, hidden behind the mask of a monster. "My father kicked me out weeks ago, you fucking idiot," she snapped, "You think you know so fucking much about me, but you don't even know that he wants nothing to do with me. You think he'd give a shit about me cutting myself up on your stage tonight? You think there's a single fucking thing I could say to him that he doesn't feel twice as strong towards me?"

Anubis was visibly surprised, and Vittoria felt a sense of pride that she had, somehow, all this time, kept that information hidden. She had always known, amidst all of his wisdom, his agedness, his seemingly unshakeable confidence, at least one thing that he had not, and now he stood, having to recalculate before her very eyes, rebuild the facade she had managed to finally poke a substantial hole in. He cleared his throat.

"And yet you hold his identity to your own so closely that you bear even his name? *Vittoria Marcello?*" He tried to hand her the knife again, jabbing it out at her and making her flinch. His tone had turned quite animated. "None of that matters, Vittoria. This is not about *him*. It's about *you*. It's about you becoming art, being born again as something so much greater than what you are now and what you have ever been. Is that not what you want?"

Vittoria did not answer. Anubis groaned loudly in frustration.

"I have given you everything, Vittoria, everything you could possibly need," There was a desperation in his voice that Vittoria had not heard before, creeping through the cracks as the coolness and composure and waxing poetics began to crumble. "I have built your throne with my own hands. I have given you the opportunity to become a living art piece, to ascend the confines of humanity, of death itself. How dare you hesitate now? Are you giving up on me, after all I have done, just as you always have? Am I nothing to you but another failed business endeavor, or will you believe in something for once? Will you prove yourself to be more than the specters of failure that haunt you, or will you send yet another dream of greatness to its early grave? Tell me, Vittoria, where does your heart truly lie?"

Vittoria took a step away from Anubis, away from the curtain, from the knife, from the chocolate, towards the exit.

What happened next happened very quickly, and for a moment there was nothing but the blur of Anubis lunging at her for a second time, grabbing her, and then she thought that he had hit her with force much mightier than she had ever imagined he could possess in his age, so intense and so sharp that she felt the air knocked from her lungs and her body seize. It was as if a shock of electricity was surging through her, and then the electricity seeped into her blood and her chest felt hotter than all of Hell's flames, and Anubis' incense seeped into every pore, bled into her mouth and nose and eyes as he kept himself against her, kept his fist against her chest, and the roaring of the flames in her ears and the thick aroma of incense and chocolate muffled his voice and she barely heard him when he said, "You see, Vittoria. You need not be afraid. You will not die."

The flames amassed within the depths of Vittoria's body into a wildfire that sought nothing but to scorch everything in its path. Vittoria looked at Anubis, his hand wrapped around the hilt of the dagger, against her chest, where her heart should have been beating, would have beaten no more had it been where it belonged. She grabbed him, grabbed his hand, grabbed his fingers, clawed and writhed like her body was aflame and she was bent on burning him up with her, and when her fingers found the blade, cool and metallic but wet with the sweat of Anubis' palms, she pulled it from its flesh case. She raised the blade with such speed that her own blood fell back onto her face, into her hair, onto the pretty sparkling dress that was rapidly dampening, reddening.

She drove the blade, shining silver beneath droplets of her own blood, deep into Anubis' side, deep into his abdomen, and she could not imagine what his insides must have looked like after the years upon years he had spent reorganizing them, but she knew, she remembered, exactly where his heart was safely nestled, protected from all except those who knew where to find it, those who had felt it pressed to them in moments of passion not fully unlike this one. The dagger plunged deeper, Vittoria shoved it in with as much force as she could possibly muster, summoning the rest of the energy that was quickly draining from her limbs like the blood that poured from her breast. It penetrated cleanly, sliced through skin with ease in its sharpened splendor, and Anubis stumbled back, but Vittoria did not let go, causing him to pull himself off of it and subsequently open a wound that instantly began gushing dark blood.

Vittoria dropped the knife. It hit the ground and sat in a puddle of her and Anubis' blood intertwined. She watched him, and her breathing was weak and ragged, and she trembled with such force that the world around her seemed to tremble too. She was dizzy, and she watched as Anubis stumbled, as blood soaked through his clothing and poured onto the floor. He looked like he had pissed himself, she thought, and she thought that he looked like a pathetic old man, grasping helplessly at the wound, clutching at it as if he thought through his will alone he could close it. But he had never been the God of Life.

Vittoria expected him to say something. He always had something to say, always found the perfect words for every occasion. He made every passing thought seem stylish and intentional. He could speak in such a manner that his words always seemed to matter. He was never tongue tied, never stuck in a situation in which he could not make use of his eloquence, his coolness, his knowledge of art or philosophy or life itself.

But he said nothing, and Vittoria watched as he looked up at her from where he had crumpled, doubled over, his eyes empty behind black contacts, his expression hidden behind his precious mask save for his mouth hanging open, drool running from his lips, oily with the makeup he had applied. And then, silently, he collapsed in his own scarlet waste.

And then, just as sudden as Anubis' fall, came the pain. Her body seemingly relinquishing itself of the survival instinct that it had thrown itself into in order to fight, a searing, burning, agonizing pain erupted through Vittoria, deep in her hollow chest. Every nerve screamed at her, alarms seemed to blare in her head, her vision blurred as tears welled in her makeup-clad eyes. She clutched at the open wound. It bled less than Anubis'. There had been nothing vital there, but she felt the burn deep in her and she saw blood run down her hand. She stumbled on legs that could barely carry her, using muscles that were hardly responsive as her brain overrode all functionality to shriek pain. She shoved her way through the curtains, caught up in heavy velvet briefly, fighting her way through the darkness, until she emerged before the crowd of people holding their pretty bag of chocolates, talking amongst themselves as they waited cheerfully for the show. In an instant every eye in the theater was on her.

She stood there, heaving, bleeding out on Anubis' grand stage, trembling before her audience, her heart pounding rapidly in her guts as it fought to pump less and less blood through her weakening body. She looked into the front row and her eyes locked with Cosmo's. He must have come to see the show. Relief at a familiar face washed over her.

"Get me a doctor!" she gasped out, at Cosmo, at the audience, at the golden *M* that towered over them all. "There's- there's been an accident."

"How does anyone survive out here, Angel?"

"They usually don't."

Giovanni moaned as he ran fingers through his long, black hair— Black, *mostly*, but with gray strands flecking the perfect raven darkness, ruining it, staining it like mold or maggots or some other distasteful product of waste and desecration that he could not exterminate.

"I curse my genetics," Giovanni gave a wiry gray hair a tug and groaned again as he inspected himself in the bathroom mirror. "Do you know when I found my first gray hair, Angel? I was twenty-nine. Less than three decades on this earth and already my body had begun the process of decay!" He had dyed his hair continuously to perfection from that day forward. The bitter chemical smell of hair dye was one of comfort and protection to him, and with all of this time out in the outskirts, showering without his precious shampoos and conditioners, it had begun, tragically, to fade and grow out.

Angel sat on the toilet seat, his legs crossed and his chin in his hands. "You look okay to me. I mean... You looked like shit when you first showed up out here. I thought you were gonna die on my couch or something. If I thought you were worth saving then, you must look like a million bucks now, huh?"

Giovanni hardly acknowledged this attempt at comfort. "The lack of makeup has been hard enough, but I have managed," he said, continuing on with the inspection of his own features from the neck up. "I have even been able to confront my face, blemished and wrinkled, aged as it is." He shook his head sullenly and leaned into the mirror to peer at a notch on his upper cheek. "I got that when I was fifteen, and I was so horrified by the idea of acne that I thought it was wise to steal a knife and cut any pimples I found right off. I only did one before I realized what a grave mistake I had made, but when my father inspected it he told me it was not deep enough to need treatment and I would let it heal on its own and suffer the consequences of the scar, or pay for the surgery to cover it from my own pocket. Can you believe that?"

Angel stared at Giovanni for another moment, and then said, "When I was fifteen I killed the guy I had been staying with- He'd, er, he said he'd let me stay if I fucked him, and gave him half the earnings I made from running. When I refused one night he tried to kill me, so I killed him first."

"Refused to sleep with him, or refused to give him the money?"

"It doesn't matter."

Giovanni sighed and finally looked away from the mirror to Angel, watching with a curious awe at the way that even in the bathroom of all places, the brightness that seeped in from the small window and the pale light above the mirror that cast a white shine over the porcelain made him glow radiantly, like a seraphic Renaissance painting. "I suppose all of this complaining sounds rather pathetic to you, doesn't it?".

Angel shook his head. "It doesn't," he said. "I was just talking." There was a moment of silence between the two of them. Giovanni looked back to himself in the mirror and rubbed at the uneven stubble that grew around his chin, that he did not have the resources to shave smooth any longer, feeling the scratchiness on his fingertips. Angel continued to speak: "Hey. Wh- Wherever we go once we escape this place—I bet they'll have nicer beauty supplies than anywhere else in the world. Better than you could even imagine. It'll be a whole city of beautiful people, and not... not fake beautiful, like Himmel pulling people apart and sewing them back together and sticking things into them to try to make them prettier..." He let out a sharp snort of a laugh and added, "Or California's dumbass wig."

Giovanni turned to look at Angel, who smiled up at him from where he sat. His warm brown eyes lit up in the glow of light from the midday sun through the bathroom window, and Giovanni felt butterflies in his stomach. Eager to engage with Angel's fantasy, hoping very much for it to be true, he added, "Once we have found this oasis of pleasures and delights, I could do your makeup sometime. It would be an honor to paint a pretty face like yours." That was, in some ways, the ultimate compliment Giovanni could imagine giving another person. Makeup had for a very long time been his lifeline, the source of so much of his joy and identity, his primary source of artistic drive and creative inspiration. To offer an act so intimate to Angel was in some felt as significant as offering up his virginity. "I was quite good at it. I could give you cherry red lips and strawberry cheeks and pretty scarlet dust around your eyes that look like a spring bouquet, or a sunset on a warm summer evening."

Angel was quiet. He chuckled a little and pulled a wing around from his back to run his fingers through the feathers. "You associate red with a lot of really nice things," he said.

"Well, what do you associate red with, little Angel?"

Angel laughed quietly for a second time. "Mostly blood."

Life in the outskirts was stagnant.

Giovanni had long grown bored of it, and the dull biding of time that each passing day consisted of, even as Angel swore that a plan was being made, that progress was happening quietly beneath the surface, if they could only hang on a bit longer. But if nothing else, Giovanni had come to adore Angel, and it was Angel's company that made the long, slow, hot days in the small house worthwhile enough to stand. Giovanni spent many hours listening intently to Angel's strange and riveting stories of his life before Himmel, before those majestic, fantastic wings of his had been sewn to his back; Giovanni remained ever-hypnotized by them, and one of the incentives of listening to Angel's stories was the way the boy curled up against him as he talked, at an angle which allowed him to run his fingers through the soft wings as he listened.

Giovanni, too, tried to tell stories of his own, but was often stunted by the amount which he had to withhold from Angel. Angel could not know that he was a Marcello... and what then? Giovanni realized quickly, to some embarrassment, that he had very little to share beyond the confines of his father's mansion. While Angel divulged stories of heroism and antiheroism, of escaping the Birds of Prey time and time again, of the characters he met in the lowest rings of the city where Giovanni himself never dared step foot (and, when he had, he had wound up with a nearly broken nose and his earrings plucked directly out of the holes they had rested in), he stumbled through stories about his birds, stories about the garden, stories about the endless, uncomfortable dinner parties he had attended throughout his life, all of which were told with a marked, nervous brevity, stumbling over his own words to check repeatedly that he had said nothing to give away his father's identity, and his own, by proxy.

"I can see why Marcello would want you as a model," Angel said one night while over Giovanni, beads of sweat dripping from his forehead down to Giovanni's face, lips parted, cheeks flushed, violently tugging Giovanni from the moment, leaving him utterly unable to appreciate the feeling of Angel atop him with the awareness of the lies he had told seeping from Angel not unlike the sweat that rolled off of him, lies and obfuscations that weighed on him much heavier than Angel's small, naked body being brought to the forefront, Giovanni desperately trying to stay erect.

At another time, over dinner, Angel asked, "How rich *is* your family?", causing Giovanni to nearly choke on his pasta. "You talk so much about dinner parties and big green gardens when you were younger. What do they do?"

"My father is... m- moderately well off," Certainly not how one would typically describe one of the most successful businessmen in all of Fresno, if not the world. Giovanni dabbed his mouth with a napkin as he attempted to gather his composure and come up with a quickly thought-out lie. "He was a chef. He- He worked in catering, for higher end events. That was... that was how I was able to find connections to Marcello Candies. G- Get my foot in the door that way."

"You never met Giorgio Marcello, did you?"

"No," Giovanni could feel his dinner working its way upwards.

Giovanni wondered, sometimes, what would have happened had he told Angel everything. Would Angel have killed him? Would he have understood, absolved him of his brother's sins and welcomed him, reborn again free of his family's misdeeds? Would they be even closer now than they currently were, able to speak of their lives without the stilted half-answers that permeated their conversations? He wondered too at points if Angel already knew everything, if he had made the connection that he was indeed the son of Vittorio Marcello, but he had not said anything because he did not have the heart to reveal to Giovanni how bad of a liar he was, or perhaps because he loved him so much that he did not want to have his suspicions confirmed, and thus pretended it not to be true.

And so the days passed full of stunted conversations. Some days were spent wandering around in the dust until the sun bore down so hot and oppressive that Giovanni's skin burned and itched and he could bear it no more, on others he went into town to pick up groceries for the two of them, and never again did he run into the bull man he had encountered upon his first outing, nor did he meet with Hollywood California for fear that he would not be able to face her, to look into her bright eyes knowing the betrayal that Angel planned when she was left behind as the two of them made their romantic escape into the future. Giovanni scoured the pages of the books in the sitting room, reading about flora and fauna, about gardening that could not be done, about caring for animals that they did not have, preparing meals with ingredients to which they had no access. There was nothing on fixing cars, however, nor was there anything about what could possibly lie beyond the outskirts, and Giovanni liked to imagine that this meant the possibilities were limitless.

Giovanni grew used to sleeping in, which had previously been quite unusual for him. Not because he had enjoyed waking early, nor had he typically had anything to do or anywhere to be, but because he had never been able to sleep very well to begin with. He had always been a light sleeper, his dreams, when he had them, impacted by anything happening around him in the physical world, easily disturbed. A single footstep in the hallway became the clap of earth-shattering thunder and the sound of a car honking down the street becoming a lion, freeing itself from its cage and lunging at him, throwing him into consciousness with a jolt. On other nights he was prone to terrible insomnia, his mind racing and his body growing restless against the bed, aware of the way his nostrils plugged and unplugged, aware of the way his limbs prickled if he lay at the wrong angle, aware of every quiet sound through the night, until pale sunlight poured through the curtains and he was faced with the reality that he had not slept at all. Candy helped, but often only served to soothe his mind, not shut it off completely. At least it made the insomnia less painful.

But nowadays, living in the old farm home, this was no longer the case for reasons he could not fully comprehend. Perhaps it was because Angel liked warmth, and despite the mounting heat outside as the days passed and the spring edged into the deadly Californian summer, he kept the air conditioning low, and Giovanni fell asleep each night and woke up each morning surrounded by the warmth of the midyear Valley air, with the heat of Angel's body pressed tight to his own and the heavy comfort of the blankets over them both, feeling much like he imagined a baby slept nestled in the womb. Perhaps Angel's big, soft bed was just that comfortable, perhaps his plush wings were evocative of the stuffed animals of his youth. One thing that was for certain was that Giovanni found himself increasingly capable of sleeping for long periods of time with Angel pressed up against him and waking up to slow and lazy mornings.

It was for that reason that Giovanni was so startled when he was awoken early one morning by a pounding on the front door. Too tired to comprehend what was going on, his brain hazy with the deep sleep it had adjusted to receiving, he blinked heavy eyes and slowly began to prop himself up. Angel, however, sprang up without a moment of recovery from this sudden awakening, jumping to his feet and going entirely still, head tilting towards the door to listen with his breath all but held. Giovanni, tired, leaned back in bed lazily, looked at Angel with significantly less concern than his companion's poised, ready-to-strike posture suggested.

"Relax, little Angel," Giovanni said through a yawn. The boy was topless, as he was most nights, for it was difficult to comfortably wear anything over his wings, and Giovanni sleepily thought he looked quite cute. "I am sure it-"

"*Sh.*" Angel's tone was sharp and urgent enough that despite the quietness of the sound Giovanni instantly shut up, but he made no change in his posture save for his brow furrowing slightly. Surely it was just California, coming to visit early in the morning with news—good news, even. News of a mechanic. His eyelids grew heavier, weighing down over his eyes in a stubborn refusal to allow him vision as sleep crept over him, and just as he was nodding off again a second knocking, louder and more abrasive than the last, echoed through the house. Giovanni jumped, eyes opening wide once more.

Angel reached for the bedside table and slowly, with painstaking care so as to avoid making a single sound, stopping even the wood from scraping the slightest bit against the side of the table, pulled the drawer open and revealed his trusted knife where it sat atop the old Bible.

Angel picked the knife up. Right as his delicate fingers had curled carefully around the handle, the sound of the front door swinging open with such force that it slammed into the wall like a gunshot echoed down the hall, and Angel wasted no time in hissing, "We need to hide *now.*"

As Angel grabbed him by the wrist the reality of the situation sank deep into Giovanni's squirming guts. Someone was in the house—his tired brain still felt vaguely numb, unable to comprehend it, and yet a shock of fear burned through him as Angel, knife in one hand and Giovanni's wrist in the other, made a dash for the closet in the corner of the room. Despite the swiftness in which he moved Angel was careful to open the closet door carefully, to avoid any noise above the softest inevitable click of the door as he turned the handle, and then he pulled Giovanni inside. Giovanni, in a panicked daze, could do nothing but follow Angel, and the moment he had entered Angel hissed, "*Shut the door,*" with such urgency that Giovanni jumped again.

Try as he might to be as gracefully silent as Angel had been in his swiftness, Giovanni pulled the door shut with just enough force that the thud of it shutting could be heard distinctly through the room, and he winced and held his breath, stifling a whimper. They sat there in the darkness, and Angel sat so still beside Giovanni that his silhouette looked more like something inanimate, a mannequin or a doll, than any living creature. And yet, in the utter silence of the room, Giovanni could hear Angel's breathing softly, could feel the warmth that radiated from one living being to another against him in the close confines of the closet, could feel him brush ever so slightly against him, the soft feathers resting against Giovanni's shoulder.

Giovanni wanted to speak, wanted to tell Angel that they had certainly waited long enough, and if there was any risk of danger it certainly would have revealed itself to them by now, but in reality he had no idea how long it had been, and he had no idea if this was true. The situation felt surreal to Giovanni, much like how he had felt upon his initial arrival, dehydrated and in the throes of withdrawal, uncertain of if he would survive but fully unable to imagine death, let alone how very on the brink of it he may have been. Here, too, he could not fully comprehend it, could not come to terms with the reality that there may have been danger lurking in the house, that his whole life could be upheaved again—or ended.

The silence remained as the two sat together, side by side; it was an eternity in limbo, Giovanni thought, the risk of impending doom coupled with the slow ease of his anxiety as he became increasingly hopeful in weak desperation that perhaps they had misinterpreted what they had heard, somehow, and that they were safe and alone together after all.

Rustling from another room caused Angel to tense beside him in unison with Giovanni's own heart skipping a beat. He had to stifle a squeak of surprise, and he twitched again when he felt Angel suddenly clasp his wrist in the darkness, and in that same darkness Giovanni could not read Angel's expression, could not tell what had prompted him to take hold of him as he had. Fear, perhaps? Giovanni found himself wishing he could whisper some sort of comfort to Angel, for himself as much as if not more than the winged boy. He could not remember a time that he had ever seen Angel afraid, and he wanted to believe that he was misinterpreting the gesture. Perhaps it had been an animal, or perhaps California was playing a cruel trick, Giovanni continued to try to rationalize, or perhaps pray to the universe to manifest it so. Perhaps they had imagined the entire thing in a state of sleep-induced delirium. Perhaps they were both dreaming now, and the goosebumps prickling down his spine were misplaced, mistranslated, and were in reality merely the result of Angel, cuddled up close to him still, hogging the blankets and leaving him exposed to the open air—

The bedroom door flew open and slammed with such force that the walls around them shook.

Giovanni sucked in a breath so quickly that he nearly choked on air, and Angel's grip tightened so much and so fast that Giovanni's wrist throbbed, his fingers numb. The shirts that hung on the hangers above them in the closet swayed slightly from the sudden violence of the entry of their mystery guest.

The thud of heavy footsteps echoed from the bedroom. Stealth was clearly not the intruder's goal. Giovanni looked to Angel in the darkness, looked down to where his hand still gripped his wrist, and wished he could ask what his plan was, but he dared not speak.

"Well, if yer hidin' out in here, ya ain't got anywhere to run," a man's voice called from beyond the shut closet doors.

Giovanni knew that voice.

He looked to Angel again. His silhouette remained frozen still; he could not even hear his breathing. It occurred to Giovanni how very obvious the closet door was. One would have to be an utter fool not to open it should they be looking for someone hiding. And he knew the man on the other side of the door was no fool. When he breathed again his throat trembled, his breath entering his lungs in weak gasps for air, and he almost wished that he would suffocate in the small closet, that his heart would give out from fear prematurely, and die peacefully by Angel's side rather than face whatever awaited him.

Light.

The light of the bedroom burst into the closet like a bomb and Giovanni was blinded by it for a split moment, unable to process the dark shape of the figure who stood above him as his eyes struggled to adjust to the sudden assault.

"Well, well. Looks like I finally found y-"

But Angel had been waiting, and no sooner had Giovanni's eyes begun to adjust and the being who stood before him had begun to speak than Angel had leaped up and forward, crying out a warning as he lunged with knife in hand. And Giovanni, who Angel still clung to tightly, was thrown forward with him, for although he was stronger and larger than Angel he was caught entirely unaware, and in the disoriented panic that pulsed through him he was easily tugged along.

Angel let go of Giovanni as his small body met the much larger figure of the bull man, and Giovanni nearly fell backwards as he was released. Before him he witnessed Angel, a flurry of feathers and limbs as he grappled with the horned man. Giovanni was frozen still, in awe and fear. The glisten of Angel's silver knife; a choking whimper as a metal-clad fist slammed into flesh; Angel flapping his wings with such violent force that he looked like he was truly trying to pick himself up off the ground and fly away, but instead this caused only a sort of chaotic confusion as his soft white feathers scattered in the air like a down pillow had been ripped apart by a wild animal.

"Run, Giovanni!"

"But-"

"Run!"

Giovanni nearly tripped over his own feet; he could hardly feel them, could hardly feel anything, his body seeming to move on an autopilot he hardly realized he possessed as he rushed from where he stood to the open doorway on legs that felt like jelly. Out of the bedroom and through the house, down the hallway to the living room. As he turned the corner towards the coveted front door he heard the rush of feet down the hallway and Angel came tearing through, his pace much faster than Giovanni's own legs had carried him, his body clearly adapted to making fast sprints to safety.

"This way!" he cried, and Giovanni followed behind as they rushed to the front door, which hung open where the bull man had left it, out into the bright heat of the early summer morning.

The duo made their way past the front porch, and then Angel took charge and led Giovanni to the right, rather than forward towards town. They ran—Giovanni still hardly able to keep up with Angel but following loyally, driven forward purely by instinct and by the hope and trust that Angel knew more than he and would lead them to safety. His chest ached and his head spun, and as they continued onwards his breathing grew labored and heavy, sweat gathered and then rolled like wax down his forehead, and his feet burned as they hit the hot dirt and they stung as they were punctured by dried goat's heads buried in the chaparral.

Giovanni's eyes swam as he scanned the endless horizon of barren, dead field. As they traveled further still, and an all-too-familiar hoarse burn filled his lungs and chest with each ragged, gasping breath, the adrenaline of panic began to wear off and he felt himself slowly slipping. His shirt clung to his flesh, his sides ached with a stitch that deepened each time he moved, his head spun and the vast, dry unknown before him seemed to span outwards forever into oblivion. Finally he slowed to a stop, keeling over and heaving.

"Angel-" Giovanni gasped. "I- I'm going to collapse-"

Angel stopped and turned to Giovanni, and when they locked eyes Giovanni could tell the boy showed none of the signs of exhaustion that he did, save for the red in his face and the sweat that coated his body, making it gleam in the heat of the day. For a moment he wondered how the boy could possibly possess so much stamina when he was lugging so much extra weight on his back, but after a moment his eyes focused better and his attention was diverted to a much more pressing matter, as he processed the state that Angel was in with a muted horror—he wore a deep red, rapidly swelling welt across his bare stomach. He had been punched, and badly, by the looks of it, by the bull man's metal gloves.

"How are you able to run with that?" Giovanni asked. As they settled slightly, no longer running, Giovanni dug his stinging feet into the dirt, attempting to dig beneath the burning top layer into something cooler, although he found only moderate reprieve.

"Practice," Angel replied, looking down to brush his fingers gingerly over the wound. He then looked back up at Giovanni. "And it's not too bad. The bitch had a gun on him, I can't- I can't believe he didn't use it."

"Did you kill him?"

Angel laughed breathily. "If I thought I did, we wouldn't have run."

"Then why does he not chase after us?"

Angel shrugged. "I stabbed him. But, I mean, did you *see* him? I don't think that'll keep him down for long. Himmel's probably pumped him full of shit to keep him going."

Angel looked over Giovanni's shoulder, and Giovanni followed his gaze to the house back in the distance, hardly as far as the long run from it had felt. Giovanni swallowed a hard lump in his throat, his body feeling cold even as sweat poured from every orifice. They seemed horribly exposed out here, with even the tallest trees comprised only of rickety, charred branches with little to no foliage, no obvious hiding places and nothing but flat earth until the mountains in the farthest distance, the edges of the valley, that would take weeks to travel on foot and promised little sign of life along the way.

"We can't stay here," Giovanni said, sick from the realization he was suddenly stricken with of how truly helpless they were, surrounded on all sides by death. "We- We should go into town. California... California can help us, right?"

"No."

"N- No?"

"We have to go back to the house."

"What? You are mad!" Giovanni cried, feeling a rush of energy return to him at the mere thought of such a thing, as if such an incredulous, preposterous suggestion was enough to reawaken that which within him was slowly collapsing. "The- The horned man, he will-"

"Everything that matters to me is in that house, Giovanni." Angel looked at Giovanni, his gaze intense, brow furrowed and expression taut, clearly unshakably certain in his decision. He walked to him and took his hands in his own, and Giovanni clung to them immediately, grabbing at them for comfort and wishing more than anything they were still in bed together, holding each other lazily into the morning. "The- the key to my future. The key to *our* future."

"The- The key to the truck? Surely we can manage without that. There will be other keys, other trucks-" Giovanni pleaded. But with a shake of his head, Angel cut him off:

"No, no, it's- it's not- I can't." He shook his head again and then let go of Giovanni to bring his hands to his face, pressing his palms to his eyes, grabbing the front of his hair, and let out a long groan. "Fuck me." he said, voice muffled by his hands. "Fuck us both."

Giovanni's heart was slamming against his chest as if he were still running. He stared at Angel incredulously. "You- You can go back, and I will go to California and- and get help-"

Angel shook his head immediately. "No," he lowered his hands and stared at Giovanni again, "Come back with me."

"Have you lost your mind, Angel?!"

"We're partners, right? I- I don't want to do this alone. I need you."

Despite the oppressive heat bearing down on them, Giovanni froze. To be needed—it was a feeling totally foreign to him. When had he ever been *needed* before? Most certainly not by his father, his sister, any of the women whom he had just managed to capture the attention of for a meager few hours, by the newscasters who used him as a stand-in for his father, much more eager to talk to him but settling for the less in-demand second option. How unreal it felt to imagine being desired as Angel desired him.

As Giovanni pondered these words, Angel raised his knife up in the air, making Giovanni wince as it caught the sun's light and flashed so brightly that it threatened to blind him for a moment, and said, "You don't have to go if you don't want to. But I really believed in a future for us both..." He glanced back to Giovanni for only a second, only allowing the briefest hint of hot copper irises to meet Giovanni's cold blue before he had turned once more to the house. "But I'm going back whether you come or not. I can't let him take everything from me. I've worked too hard to get here."

So he had; Giovanni could hardly comprehend Angel's life, his history, the events that had led him from the bloody streets, evading the Birds of Prey and narrowly escaping certain death, up to his encounter with his brother, when the massive appendages were sewn into his back and he had functionally become Himmel's slave. Giovanni thought of the many times he had been called stupid, or a variation of it—mostly by his father, at times by his sister or another family member. He felt very stupid sometimes, a truth he disliked admitting even to himself. Especially in the recent past, he had felt significantly less capable, more over his head, than he ever had before. Angel, on the other hand, seemed so worldly, so confident, and Giovanni felt more enthralled by the affection the winged boy showed him than by any amount of candy.

"If I go with you... we will have the future you speak of? The two of us?"

"Uh-huh," Angel grunted, and without giving Giovanni another glance turned back towards the house, a motion that immediately made Giovanni's stomach drop as the gravity of the decision he was making set in. He nervously followed, his hands balled into fists. "We need to hurry."

Giovanni refused to allow himself to believe that there was a chance—a big chance, which grew larger and larger with each step towards the little house that he had slowly learned to call home—that his death was very near. He tried to imagine it, only briefly, to imagine what death might feel like, after fighting so hard to evade it, and although he felt faint and dizzy from this attempt his brain refused to come to anything solid. He had been taught of Heaven and Hell, but had not been raised to believe in either particularly strongly, and the idea of an afterlife felt far beyond anything he could bring himself to comprehend as a reality. But then again, it had been very recently that he had been forced to assimilate winged humans, horned humans, humans with metal plates lodged in their skull, into his understanding of the world, and, as he continued his death march back towards the house, he tried with little success to comfort himself with the thought of the fantastic being realer than he had ever imagined.

Giovanni kept his eyes low, scanning the ground in a futile attempt to avoid the goat's heads that lay like vipers in the dirt, waiting to strike and puncture the soles of his bare feet, and in spite of his dread he found himself walking fast in order to avoid them burning against the hot ground. From the corner of his eye he could see Angel's pretty white feathers swaying as he walked ahead of him.

Angel stopped walking. Giovanni wished he hadn't, because his feet began to burn and the rising anxiety in the pit of his stomach began to boil over now that it was left to sit still. He looked back at Giovanni, watching him over his shoulder with an expression that Giovanni could not read. "Thank you," he said quietly, and then he began to walk again, and Giovanni followed, towards the little farmhouse nestled in the sprawling wasteland and the beastman that waited within.

As Giovanni approached the house he could hardly believe that there was supposedly somebody inside, let alone the massive, monstrous man that had attacked them earlier. It sat there silent and empty in the field, still as always, the home Giovanni had come to rely on for shelter from the blistering heat of the outskirts, a safe haven, refuge from the pain and fear he had felt upon his arrival, within which his love for Angel had sprung forth and blossomed. Nothing looked any different, except for the door remaining ajar as they had left it upon running out earlier. From the outside it appeared perfectly normal, and Giovanni desperately wished that it was, could hardly believe that it was not, his brain dizzy with a numb disbelief.

"Should we-" Giovanni began to speak, only to be cut off by Angel giving a sharp, quiet, *"Shh!"* Giovanni swallowed and nodded, trying again under his breath with, "Should we not go around the back?"

Angel shook his head. Voice even quieter than Giovanni's, he whispered, barely audibly: "That's what he'd expect."

Giovanni felt a heavy weight drop in his stomach at yet another realization that he was completely unprepared for whatever it was he was getting himself into. Angel knew more than he did, was more familiar with the world of knives and bruises and sneaking and running. All Giovanni could do was defer to him.

Angel stepped, very quietly, up onto the porch and into the house. When he was not instantly shot dead, Giovanni followed.

Inside, the damage was more apparent, although still the scene of the crime was calmer than he had expected (not that he had any idea what to expect whatsoever, not that he had wanted to give worse alternatives a particularly large amount of thought). Furniture was upturned, chairs sat on their side, the couch lay on its back. Books lay scattered across the floor, the table in the dining room sat upside down so that its legs pointed upwards into the air like a bug stuck on its back.

"In the bedroom." Angel said quietly with a nod of his head towards the hallway, voice so soft that Giovanni would not have been able to rely on hearing alone and had to partly read his lips to understand. He watched the way Angel walked, watched the way his eyes darted when he turned his head, quick but not frantic, an intentionality to every momentary glance. The hand with the knife was raised slightly, his grip tight, and his wings were folded compactly to his back. Giovanni almost expected him to duck down to all fours, to prowl through the scene like some sort of carnivorous animal seeking prey, actions driven by instinct above all else.

They walked down the hallway single file, Angel leading the way. The door to the master bedroom, too, was open, partly off its hinge, crooked in the doorway, another sign of the physical trauma the space had undergone, despite the source nowhere to be seen. Angel, eyes darting about carefully with each step, walked in. The closet door was still open, coat hangers and the clothing they had held scattered across the ground like blood at a crime scene.

Giovanni stood in the doorway watching, waiting apprehensively, before Angel snapped in a whisper: "Come in!"

Giovanni rushed inside, whipping around so quickly for fear of there being something behind him that he nearly tripped, stumbling a few feet backwards. "I don't like this, Angel," he said with a gulp, feeling the way each new movement caused panic to set into his limbs and guts, even as they had yet to encounter anything to fear.

Angel did not reply, but rather walked to the dresser in the back of the room. "Watch my back," he said as he turned to it fully and knelt down, exposing his back and the wings which jutted from it to the open bedroom doorway. Giovanni had never had to "watch someone's back" before and was not quite sure what he was supposed to watch for, nor what he was to do if there came a need for him to react. As such, he stood and glanced aimlessly back and forth between Angel, who pulled the bottom drawer of the dresser open very, very slowly, and the still-empty doorway.

Just as Angel began to rummage through the drawer—for what, Giovanni could not imagine—the hulking figure of a shadow blocked the doorway before them.

The silver of a gun jutted from the black of his gloves, leading the way as he stepped into the room. He ducked a bit so that his horns could avoid the doorway, and then he stood there, and Giovanni stared in shock for a moment, feeling his mouth twitch open as he attempted to verbalize a warning to Angel but feeling stricken to silence, as if in a nightmare where his most important bodily functions shut down as he needed them most. He certainly felt as though he were in a nightmare, the presence of the bull man feeling as surreal as ever even as his heart felt it would all but explode.

"Angel—!" Giovanni finally managed out in a choked gasp.

A clap of sound so loud it made every hair on Giovanni's body stand on end thundered through the room. Giovanni leaped, his ears ringing, his vision feeling blurry from pure fear as he struggled to catch a breath. He half expected to die. But no pain came. Angel reacted as lightning-fast as ever, flipping around and back to his feet with knife in hand. He, too, seemed unscathed. The man had fired the gun, but not towards either of them. Giovanni tried to wrap his head around why: A demand for attention? A display of power? In truth, he could not fathom any of this, nor could he fathom that he had interacted with this man before, in circumstances much less dire. He had told him about his past, had shared a drink... And now he stood, and with the gun still smoking in his hand it was clear that he intended to shoot again, and that his bullets would find more resistance between the end of the barrel and the bedroom wall the next time.

"Welcome home!" the man said, his voice slightly muffled by the ringing of Giovanni's ears only instilling further a dreamlike aura to his presence. His eyes darted between Angel and Giovanni with the same precision as Angel's own measured glances, revealing quickly to Giovanni his prowess in this profession that he and Angel seemed to share. He thrust the gun out at Angel, who, in spite of managing to stand still without so much as flinching otherwise, betrayed a momentary surprise when his wings twitched against his back, feathers sticking up like goosebumps. The man laughed at that. "You know, the city declared you a terrorist and listed you as an 'extreme threat' when word of your getaway was first announced. I saw your pictures, I knew you were just a li'l guy, so I assumed you had to have balls of fucking steel and some serious tricks up your sleeve." He took another step further into the room. Giovanni stepped back. Angel did not.

"Any Bird of Prey worth his shit would have shot me by now," Angel retorted.

"I ain't your regular Hawk or Falcon," the man grunted, "Doctor Marcello is cooking up something new. Genetically modified huntsmen to do Himmel's dirty work. What you see before you is the very first of a new breed!" He gave a sarcastic little bow, gesturing cartoonishly with the gun. "What d'you think we should be called? Fuckin' pterodactyls?" He laughed as he stepped forward again, gradually closing the space between himself and Angel.

"Freak of fucking nature," Angel hissed. Giovanni wondered if insults were the best idea in their current position.

The man snorted and pointed the gun at Angel's head. "Listen, bitch, I'm prepared to make you a deal. I'm under the impression that upon your resignation from Himmel, you brought with you a, erm, *generous* sum of money—far more than anyone is willing to say. Got close with the boss and swindled him from right under his nose, clever boy."

"What's it to you?"

"Doctor Marcello prefers you alive, which I think you and I both know would be a fate much worse than a quick and easy death. You tell me where your money is now, and I'm prepared to mercifully offer you a painless death at my hands, rather than the reconstructing of every tissue in yer body from the inside out at his."

Angel blinked, and Giovanni watched his expression change, although for why he was not sure.

"It's easier for us both this way. I can go off to live my life free of Himmel poking and prodding me any longer," The bull man stepped forward again, close enough finally that, if he reached out, the gun would press to Angel's bare chest long before his arm was fully extended, "And you can finally stop running."

Giovanni watched the encounter before him, frozen, unable to break free of the shock that held him, paralyzed, in its clutches. His most selfish thoughts wondered if he would be spared, as this interaction appeared to be personal between the bull man and Angel, so built on a foundation he could hardly follow. What of this money the man spoke of? What of

Giorgio and his experiments and what incomprehensible horrors took place within Himmel's operating rooms? He imagined for a moment telling the man that he, too, was a Marcello, but would that spare him, or only serve to have his death be made more painful?

And even then, the thought disgusted Giovanni, as he remembered in an instant the commitment he had made to himself, to Angel, to remove himself of his past, of his family, and be something new, something better, a future where he was born again and he and Angel could be happy far from here.

God, how he wished they were both so very far from here.

"Hey!" Giovanni found his voice. "Why- Why don't you pick on somebody your own size!" The words sounded silly even as they left his lips, and his voice trembled and cracked as he spoke, but it did the job: The man turned in an instant, gun pointed directly to Giovanni's chest. Truth be told, Giovanni himself was hardly his "own size" at all, and the man easily towered above him.

"Think your fat boytoy is going to protect you?" the man asked with a sneer as he looked back towards Angel. Then he turned his attention fully to Giovanni. "You're a bad fuck and a bad liar." He pushed the cold metal of the gun to Giovanni's chest, then shoved it into him with such force that he collapsed backwards, hitting the ground and looking up at the man in a position not particularly unfamiliar. The man pointed the gun to Giovanni's head where he lay. Giovanni's breathing was fast and erratic. "Himmel doesn't give a shit about you. No one does."

A blur of white feathers in the corner of his eye lunged from behind the man. This was the distraction that Angel had needed to regain an upper hand. Giovanni remained where he had fallen, staring with wide, horrified eyes, helpless to do anything but watch as Angel and the bull man wrestled, Angel managing to pin the man for a moment through sheer surprise but quickly being thrown off, but the man now at an angle awkward enough that Angel was able to rush him again. Black leather and white wings swam and intermingled in Giovanni's vision, the deadly silver of gun and knife glistened hazily in the light. Angel lunged with his knife out, missed, and flew forward to the ground by the open closet with a nauseating sound of flesh slamming against flesh.

A gunshot resounded, a second deafening echo through the room that made Giovanni jump and wince, eyes shutting. When he opened them he saw that Angel had avoided it by rolling sideways and had sprung up with his knife again.

"Don't let me fuck ya up too bad, now. Don'tcha want to look pretty when I present you to Doctor Marcello?"

"I don't give a shit about how pretty he thinks I am anymore." Angel replied, trying and failing to stab at the bull man again. The man grabbed at Angel but he evaded him, his advantage clearly being the nimbleness of his movement when opposed to a man nearly double his size, slipping away but once more closing the space between them with a jab of his knife, his movements quick to avoid ever allowing himself to be an easy target for a bullet.

Then a third gunshot went off, and this time Angel let out a shrill cry. Giovanni sat up urgently.

The man's back faced Giovanni from where he watched on the floor. Angel was obscured entirely save for the tips of his wings. Neither moved. There was stillness in the room save for the heaving of faint, ragged breaths, and when a feather dropped to the floor Giovanni was almost surprised that he could not hear it.

The bull man dropped to his knees and collapsed backwards.

Angel was bleeding where he stood and he moved like a ragdoll, jerking as if forcing all of the strength in his body into each limb, physically dragging them into their correct motions. He all but fell atop the bull man, but rather than collapse he remained instead on all fours, and with the rest of his strength he jabbed the knife deep through the dark man's chin, upwards into his skull, making the head snap and jerk lifelessly as blood gushed from the neck. He pulled the knife back out with an equally aggressive jerking motion, stood back upright on limbs that swayed, and looked around, his eyes lacking the focused alertness of before and instead swimming with dazed uncertainty.

"Angel!" Giovanni forced himself up, feeling for a moment a pain in his chest where he had been shoved and an ache in his back where he had hit the floor but hardly paying attention to either, instead rushing to help the boy. Angel looked up at Giovanni, staring at him as if he were a stranger for a moment, and then collapsed.

Giovanni gasped and fell to his knees. He repeated Angel's name for a second time, then pulled him up onto his lap, noticing the bullet hole that punctured his shoulder. "Angel?" Giovanni said again, having now repeated his name as many times as the gun—which sat at the lifeless bull man's side—had been fired.

After a moment Angel opened his eyes and sat up just a little, raising his head. He was conscious, and Giovanni breathed a relieved sigh at that.

"Gi- Giovanni." Angel said his name as if it were a statement, an acknowledgement of his own self-awareness. He blinked a few times, and then, as if his own comprehension of the world was returning slowly, grimaced and said, "Fuck, I knew I'd- knew I'd have to take a blow to get him." His knife fell from the other hand with a clatter as it hit the floor; Giovanni had not even noticed he was still holding onto it. Then he reached to gingerly touch the blood-soaked skin around the wound. "Jeez, the bitch really- fucked me up. I've never been shot before." He laughed a little, a sound that relieved Giovanni some, but when he tried to shift his position a bit, perhaps in an attempt to sit up further, he seemed to be struck with a sudden, jolting pain and he gasped out and collapsed again.

Giovanni continued to hold Angel in his arms, watching him slowly begin to attempt to recover, as the awareness of the bull man's timely end began to sink in and he came to realize that they were free of him, that life would continue onwards, that normalcy could return, if Angel would only regain his strength.

"Why did you do that?" Angel asked.

"Do what?"

"Distract him like that. He could've killed you."

Giovanni blinked. Even he had hardly considered the answer to that question; he had been acting on instinct, desperate first and foremost to make sure that he had not had to watch Angel die while he did nothing to stop it. "We're- We're a team. Partners in crime. I promised you I would, I- You said you would do the same for me." He tried to wipe some of the blood from around the wound but more poured in its place, running over his pale fingertips and painting Angel's tan skin red.

"Goddamn, Giovanni," Angel said, voice still weak, "You really are better than California."

"What?"

Angel tried again to sit up, and for a moment it seemed he had been successful, as he managed to raise himself up slightly, but suddenly he cried out, a cry of agonizing pain so loud that it seemed to nearly shatter Giovanni's raw ears, already damaged no doubt from the multiple gunshots that had gone off in such close quarters. He collapsed back onto Giovanni's lap and groaned out, blood leaking from the wound. He was a mess, his stomach protruding in a mass of swollen flesh where he had received multiple beatings, blood, both his and the bull man's, on his arms, his face, his chest, dirtying his pretty wings. His breathing was labored, and Giovanni could feel the small convulsions as he heaved in and out against him.

"Giovanni." Angel said weakly, looking up at him with those big, wide eyes of his, "I need you to do something for me if- if I- if I don't recover from this. My money is under the driver's seat. The key is in the bottom drawer. Get it and burn it all for me, okay?"

"B- Burn it? Why?"

"Because I don't want anybody else getting to it?" He stated this as if it was so painfully obvious it was a waste of his limited energy to even say aloud.

Giovanni wondered if he was going a bit insane for feeling somewhat hurt that Angel had not suggested it go to *him*. In fact, Angel had not once even mentioned the amount of money he had hidden, that such an amount existed to begin with, and he wondered if it was selfish to feel a bit miffed by the realization of the potential sum that Angel had been obfuscating. "What about... me...?" he risked asking.

"This isn't about you, Giovanni."

"What about *us*?" he persisted, "As a- as a team?"

"What do you want me to tell you, Giovanni? That I love you?" Angel laughed a harsh laugh that sounded half like a cough, and then winced when the motion made more blood ooze from the wound and his breath came to a shuddering halt for a moment as another bout of pain seemed to wrack his body.

Giovanni stared at Angel, trying to make heads and tails of the situation, of Angel's words and what they implied, of what the future held for him, for them both, for the ways that Angel made him feel as no one else ever had. Desired. Adored. *Needed.* He had never had that before, and he had believed it when Angel had said it, when he had touched him and kissed him and told tales of a future where they were together and their lives were forever intertwined.

"I love you, Angel."

Giovanni put his hand to Angel's face. The skin felt very cold.

"That's crazy."

Giovanni stared down at Angel's limp body. He touched one of his wings, feeling the soft feathers. Angel shivered a little, his breathing ragged. His deep brown eyes were caught by the light in the room in a strange way that made them look like they had become trapped behind glass, his gaze hazy and unfocused. There were tears in Angel's eyes, Giovanni realized, perhaps from the pain he was in. He must have been in a great deal of pain.

Giovanni's hand left the soft feathers and he reached and found the handle of Angel's knife, smooth and cool in his bloodstained fingers. He looked down at Angel's face again. He had shut his eyes.

Giovanni lifted the knife and silently sliced Angel's throat.

Angel's body was left in the back seat of the truck. It looked somewhat grotesque, laying unevenly over the seats, crumpled a bit to fit horizontally, covered in the culmination of dust and cobweb that had collected on the old upholstery, but Giovanni felt it was where he would most want to be.

Just as Angel had promised, under the front seat was a sum of money that could last any individual well beyond a lifetime. It was initially difficult to discern what Giovanni was looking at upon finding it, for it was kept in a velvety red, heart-shaped box with a familiar golden M insignia embroidered onto it. This was part of the Valentine's Day collection, and when he opened it to find the money inside the interior still smelled like sugar. Written on the bottom of the box was: *To my dearest Angel: You have my 'heart!' Yours, Giorgio.*

Giovanni took enough to pay for bus fare and to help him get by for a little while. After showering and changing into clean clothes, he walked to Undercroft, where he left the box for Hollywood California in the back room. He then walked to the bus stop, which was hardly a bus stop at all, but a worn sign by the side of the long, empty road. There, he waited.

# FINAL BOW

It was summer in California but the park was lush and green.

Even as the world browned and wilted and shriveled into dust in the heat, the water companies of Fresno made sure that the parks in the upper ring of the city remained pristine as ever, flourishing with plant and animal life of all kinds. After all, what was the point of owning all of the water if Fresno's most important citizens were not able to appreciate it, to have the luxury of the world's natural beauty amidst the smog and skyscrapers that grayed the horizon? It certainly did good for the housing market.

The park appeared to be devoid of human presence today, courtesy of the heat, no doubt, and, shaded by the trees, Giovanni felt very alone indeed, away from the bustling people who walked from store to store on hot pavement or waited in thick traffic for a chance to exit the freeway. He had not been here since he was a child.

Giovanni watched a duck waddle by the pondside, and when he came near its pace picked up a little, clearly attempting to distance itself from the approaching stranger, webbed feet slapping against the muddy ground, until it slid with ease into the water, away from him. He watched as it swam away, and then he returned to the trail he had been following, where he noticed the dark figure of a person ahead of him. He walked to it, following it as he had the duck.

Vittoria was watching two squirrels chase one another in a tree when she heard someone approach her, and she turned.

Giovanni and Vittoria stood, staring at each other. The pale blue they shared met for the first time in a very long while. Then, silently, they looked each other up and down, studying each other's clothes, bodies, the way they stood, the expressions on their faces. Giovanni wore a plain undershirt and jeans, the simple clothing he had grown accustomed to through a sheer lack of possessing anything else but the meager providings of the outskirts. His face was shaved haphazardly and bare of makeup, blemishes and imperfections hidden only by the shadows cast by the branches looming overhead; his hair had grown longer and it fell freely down his back and shoulders, stained blood dried copper on his sweat-soaked clothing. Vittoria wore fine clothing, jewelry around her neck and wrists and hanging from her ears that glistened in the light as sun flecked through the leaves, a low-cut blouse, a leather skirt, dark makeup with gold accents. Giovanni noticed the outline of a scar that began just above her breasts and disappeared into the top of her blouse.

"Giovanni." Vittoria was the first to speak. She took a step forward. "You, um..." She faltered, bit her lip, ran her fingers across her palms at her sides, and then said, "So you lived."

Giovanni smiled a little. "I suppose I did. As did you. And... dare I say, perhaps a bit more successfully than I."

Vittoria looked down at her own clothes, then to Giovanni again. "I... I don't know if it's comparable. I mean... You're either alive or not."

They were silent for a moment. The world around them was very quiet as well. A pigeon pecked at a beetle on the ground. Giovanni and Vittoria both watched it, distracted momentarily by it, or perhaps just eager for a reason to prolong the silence. Finally, without looking up, Vittoria said, "But you do actually look terrible. Where are you living right now?"

Giovanni's face flushed. "Ah... I have not decided just yet. I have only just returned from a trip, you see."

Finally Vittoria looked up, perhaps curious by the statement. "Well, I have a place. Would you, er... want to come back and stay? Just for a couple of days, um... while you get back on your feet."

Giovanni laughed a little. "What I would much prefer is a place to sit and rest awhile. I have been on my feet for far too long, I think."

"I'm trying to be nice, smart ass."

"And I was only kidding, sister." Giovanni smiled. "I would appreciate it deeply."

"Come on, then," Vittoria turned the way she had come, the way Giovanni had already been walking, and motioned for him to follow her. "You can't be stupid, though. I'm really fucking busy. I have a record company to run."

"I am trying very hard to be less stupid," Giovanni said seriously. "But a record company! How fancy!"

"It was, um, for my boyfriend, mostly. I was just gonna sell the thing, but he saw an in to get his first real record deal if I stuck with it, so..."

"I imagine nepotism is lovely when you are on the other side of it?"

"Hah, I guess."

They walked, then, in silence for a while, through the park, until the space between the trees began to widen, revealing the city roads and streetlights and the tall buildings in the distance at the heart of Fresno and the bright summer sun burning overhead. Finally, Giovanni turned to Vittoria, watching her for a moment, and said, "Oh, Vittoria, I believe I forgot to ask: How are you?"

Char Luerlock is a Los Angeles-based, Arab-American author of queer genre fiction. He graduated from UCLA in 2020 with a Bachelor's in English with a focus on 19th and 20th century American Literature.

In his free time, he can be found in the many dark and dingy clubs and bars of his local dark alternative music community, dancing to industrial music with his partner and closest friends late into the night, which serves as the primary inspiration for his next novel.

Stay up to date at www.charluerlock.net.

*Waxed and Feathered* is the culmination of 7 years of work. I extend a warm and humble thank you to all who have supported my endeavors through the near-decade I've spent working on it, and all who read it.

Syrette Press, 2024.

www.ingramcontent.com/pod-product-compliance
Lightning Source LLC
Chambersburg PA
CBHW032151190626
46814CB00005BA/1941